We

...From this day forward!

Wedlocked

MAIL-ORDER BRIDEGROOM
by
Day Leclaire

A FAULKNER POSSESSION
by
Margaret Way

THE ALEXAKIS BRIDE
by
Anne McAllister

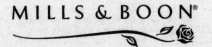

MILLS & BOON®

*MILLS & BOON and MILLS & BOON with the Rose Device
are registered trademarks of the publisher.
Harlequin Mills & Boon Limited,
Eton House, 18-24 Paradise Road, Richmond, Surrey, TW9 1SR*

WEDLOCKED
© by Harlequin Enterprises II B.V., 1999

Mail-Order Bridegroom, A Faulkner Possession and *The Alexakis Bride*
were first published in Great Britain by Mills & Boon Limited
in separate, single volumes.

Mail-Order Bridegroom © Day Totton Smith 1995
A Faulkner Possession © Margaret Way 1996
The Alexakis Bride © Barbara Schenck 1994

ISBN 0 263 81541 2

05-9909

*Printed and bound in Great Britain
by Caledonian International Book Manufacturing Ltd, Glasgow*

Day Leclaire is a much-loved romance author who has written more than twenty books for Mills & Boon®. She and her family live in the midst of a maritime forest on a small island off the coast of North Carolina. Despite the yearly storms that batter them and the frequent power outages, they find the beautiful climate, superb fishing and unbeatable seascape more than adequate compensation. One of their first acquisitions upon moving to Hatteras Island was a cat named Fuzzy. He has recently discovered that laps are wonderful places to curl up and nap—and that Day's son really was kidding when he named the hamster Cat Food.

MAIL-ORDER BRIDEGROOM

by

DAY LECLAIRE

My special thanks to Kevin Jackson for explaining which is the serious end of a rifle. And my special, special thanks to Sandra Marton...just for being there. Thank you.

PROLOGUE

Husband Wanted!

Woman rancher in immediate and desperate need of a man! Interested applicants should:

1. Be 25-45 years of age and looking for a permanent relationship—a kind and gentle personality is a plus!
2. Have extensive ranching background—be able to sit a horse, deal fairly with employees, herd cattle, etc.
3. Have solid business know-how—particularly the type necessary to please a bullheaded banker.

I am a twenty-six-year-old woman and can offer you a comfortable home, three square meals and some of the most beautiful scenery in Texas Hill Country. (Details of a more personal nature are open to negotiation.) Interested parties should send a letter of introduction, a resumé and references to 'Miss Bluebonnet', Box 42, Crossroads, Texas.

HUNTER PRYDE picked up the newspaper ad and reread it, a remorseless smile edging his mouth. So Leah was in 'desperate need' of a husband. How interesting. How very, very interesting...

CHAPTER ONE

'THIS will be a real marriage, right?' the applicant interrupted. 'I cain't take over the place 'lessen it's a real marriage.'

Leah glanced up from the resumé of one Titus T. Culpepper and regarded the man in question with a cool gaze. 'Could you by any chance be referring to your conjugal rights, Mr Culpepper?'

'If that means us sleepin' together, then that's what I'm referring to. Hell, yes, I mean conjugal rights.' He rocked his chair back on to two legs, her grandmother's precious Chippendale groaning beneath his bulky frame. 'You're a fine-looking woman, Miz Hampton. Always was partial to blue-eyed blondes.'

She stiffened, struggling to hide her distaste. 'I'm… flattered, but—'

'Like a bit of sweet-talk, do you?' He offered a toothy grin. 'So long as it'll get me what I want, I don't mind. Because as far as I'm concerned there's not much point in gettin' hitched if we ain't gonna share a bed.'

'I think any discussion about rights—conjugal or otherwise—is a trifle premature at this point,' she informed him shortly. Especially when she intended to find a nice, tame husband, willing to agree to a safe, platonic relationship. One brief, youthful brush with the more volatile type of emotions had been quite sufficient. 'About your resumé, Mr Culpepper—'

'Titus T.'

'Pardon me?'

'Most folks call me Titus T. If'n we're to be wed, you might as well get used to calling me by my proper name.' He winked.

'I see.' Leah glanced at the papers before her with a jaundiced eye. This interview was definitely not turning out as she'd hoped. Unfortunately she'd already eliminated all the other applicants, except Titus T. and one other—H.P. Smith, her final interview of the day. She didn't have any choice but to give Mr Culpepper a fair and thorough hearing. 'It says here that you have extensive ranching experience.'

'Fact is, it was a farm I ran. But ranch...farm.' He shrugged. 'Same difference. So long's I can tell which end of a cow to stick the bucket under it don't matter, right?'

She stared, appalled. 'Actually, it does.'

'Not to my way of thinking.' Before she had a chance to argue the point he leaned forward, studying her intently. 'Your ad also says you need a businessman. Why's that?'

He'd hit on the main reason for her ad. While she could run a ranch with no problem, she needed a husband well-skilled in business to handle her financial obligations. Leah hesitated, reluctant to explain the precariousness of her monetary situation, but knowing she didn't have much choice.

'The ranch is experiencing financial difficulties,' she admitted. 'In all honesty, we face bankruptcy if I can't obtain a loan. Our banker suggested that if I were married to an experienced rancher who had a strong business background they'd be willing to make that loan. That's why I placed the ad.'

Titus T. nodded, a thoughtful frown creasing his brow. 'I can understand a sweet thing like you having trouble with ciphering, so I'd be more than happy to keep track of the money for you.' An expansive smile slid across his face. 'Matter of fact, it might be a good idea to put all the accounts and such in my name for safekeeping. Then I'll talk the bank into giving us a nice fat loan. Don't you worry your head none about that.'

Leah fought to conceal her horror. There wasn't any point in continuing the interview. She knew a con-man when she met one. How had she managed to get herself into this predicament? She should have found some excuse the minute he opened his mouth. If she hadn't been so desperate, she would have. Determined to tread warily, she inclined her head, as though she found his every word to be perfectly acceptable.

'Of course. I don't see any problem with that,' she lied without a qualm, and stood, brushing her waist-length braid back over her shoulder. 'But I'm afraid our time is up. My next appointment is due any minute.' She could only pray that the final applicant would prove more suitable. The alternatives were unthinkable.

'Now, Miz Hampton...'

'I appreciate your coming,' she said, not giving him an opportunity to debate the issue. Loath as she was to come out from behind the protection of her father's huge oak desk, she wanted Titus T. Culpepper out of her study and on his way. Heading for the door, she kept a wary eye on him, hoping it wouldn't be necessary to call for Patrick, her foreman. 'I'll be making my decision in the next few days and will let you know.'

A trifle reluctantly he gained his feet and approached. 'You best think about one more thing afore you make that decision.'

She never saw it coming. Moving with amazing speed

for a man of his size, he closed the distance separating them and snatched her into his arms. She turned her head just in time, his clumsy attempt at a kiss landing on her cheek instead of her mouth.

'Come on, sweetpea,' he growled, tightening his hold. 'How're you gonna know what sort of husband I'd be without a smooch or two?'

'Let go of me!'

Thoroughly disgusted and more than a little frightened, she fought his hold with a desperation that must have taken him by surprise, for his grip slackened just enough for her to wriggle out of his embrace. Taking instant advantage, Leah bolted across the room to the gun-rack. Snatching free her rifle, she rammed several slugs into the magazine and confronted Titus T.

'Time to leave, Mr Culpepper. And I do mean now,' she announced in a furious voice, giving him a brisk poke in the gut with the barrel of the rifle.

To her relief, he didn't require any further encouragement. His hands shot into the air and he took a hasty step backward. 'Now, Miz Hampton,' he protested. 'No need to get yourself in an uproar. It were jez a kiss. If we're to be wed—'

'I think you can forget that idea,' she cut in with conviction. Wisps of silver-blonde hair drifted into her eyes, but she didn't dare release her grip on the rifle long enough to push them back.

He glared in outrage. 'You sayin' no because of a little bitty kiss? Unless you marry a mouse, any man worthy of the name's gonna want a hell of a lot more from you than that.'

She refused to debate the point…especially when she'd lose the argument. It was the one detail in this whole crazy scheme that she preferred not to dwell on. 'It's not your problem, Mr Culpepper, since you won't be that man.'

'Damned tootin'.' He reached out and snatched a battered hat from off the rack by the study door. 'Don't know why you put an ad in the paper, if'n you didn't want a real husband. False advertising, that's what I call it.'

He stomped from the room and Leah followed, still carrying the rifle. No point in taking unnecessary risks. If nothing else, it would give Titus T. pause should he decide to turn amorous again. She needn't have worried. Without another word, he marched across the front porch and down the steps. Climbing into his battered flatbed truck, he slammed the rusty door closed. A minute later he disappeared down the drive.

Watching him leave, Leah's shoulders sagged. 'I must have been crazy to believe this would work,' she muttered, rubbing a weary hand across her brow. 'What am I doing?'

But she knew the answer to that. She was doing exactly what her father would have wanted her to do when faced with a buy-out attempt from one of the largest and most ruthless companies in the state: protecting the ranch and her grandmother by marrying. While every last ranch in the area had caved in to Lyon Enterprises' ruthless tactics and sold their property, Hampton Homestead remained firm. Even completely surrounded by the 'enemy', they refused to sell, no matter what.

Of course, there had been no other choice but to defy Lyon. For, as much as the ranch meant to Leah, it meant even more to Grandmother Rose. And Leah would do anything for her grandmother. Anything. Even stand up to a huge, ruthless company against overwhelming odds. Even offer herself in marriage in order to get the money necessary to win their fight.

'We're not selling the place; I don't care what dirty tricks they pull,' the elderly woman had announced just that morning, after the latest offer from Lyon Enterprises had arrived. 'The only way they'll get me out of here is in a pine box! My grandfather died fighting for this land. So did my father. And so will I, if that's what it comes to.'

Then she'd crossed her skinny arms across her non-existent bosom, stuck her chin in the air and squeezed her eyes closed, as though waiting for the undertaker to arrive.

But Leah had believed her. If the ranch went bankrupt and they were forced off the land, it would kill her grandmother. It was that simple. Keeping the ranch in the family was essential, which meant finding a solution to their current predicament. The problem was, unless she found a way to pry some money from the local bank, losing the ranch would soon be inevitable.

It had taken three long years of arguing to realize that the bank wouldn't loan money to a single woman in her mid-twenties. They'd proven especially reluctant when they'd discovered that she alone shouldered the financial burden of an elderly grandmother and a ranch full of human and animal 'lame ducks'. Learning of this year's running battle to prevent a take-over bid from one of the most powerful companies in the state gave them the best excuse of all to refuse any aid.

On the other hand, she'd recently been told that lending money to a family whose male head consisted in equal parts of a businessman and a rancher was a different proposition altogether. And, though she didn't fully understand why that should matter, it provided the loophole for which she'd been so desperately searching.

She took instant advantage. She immediately set out to find herself just such a husband, even if it meant putting an ad in the paper and offering herself to the highest bidder. She frowned, thinking of Titus T. Unfortunately, she wouldn't be offering herself to any of the applicants she'd interviewed to date.

What she really needed was a knight in shining armor to come riding up her drive, ready and able to slay all her dragons. A foolish wish, she knew. But still... Some silly, romantic part of her couldn't help dreaming for the impossible.

Leah glanced at her watch. Her final interview should arrive any time. She could only hope that he'd prove more acceptable than the others—docile enough to agree to all her demands and yet skilled in business matters to satisfy the bank. As though in response to her silent wish, a solitary rider appeared over a low ridge, shadowed black against the burnt-orange glow of a low-hanging sun. She shaded her eyes and studied him with keen curiosity. Could this be H.P. Smith, her final applicant?

He rode easily, at home in the saddle, swaying with a natural, effortless rhythm. Even from a distance she could tell that his horse was a beauty—the pale tan coat without a blemish, the ebony mane and tail gleaming beneath the golden rays of a setting sun. The animal was also a handful. But a handful he mastered without difficulty.

She frowned, something about him bothering her. If only she could figure out what. Then it hit her. She knew the man. On some basic, intuitive level she recognized the way he sat his horse, the simple, decisive manner with which he controlled the animal, the square, authoritative set of his shoulders. Even the angle of his hat was faintly familiar.

But who the hell was he?

She waited and watched, intent on the stranger's every movement. He rode into the yard as though he owned the place…as though he were lord here and her purpose in life was to cater to his every pleasure. From beneath the brim of his hat Leah caught a glimpse of jet-black hair and deep-set, watchful eyes, his shadowed features taut and angled, as though hewn from granite. Then he dismounted, tying his buckskin to the hitching post. Not giving the vaguest acknowledgement, he turned to cross the yard toward her.

He stripped his gloves from his hands as he came, tucking them into his belt, and she found herself staring at those hands, at the strength and power conveyed by his loosely held fists. She knew those hands… But where? A flash of memory hit her—the gentle sweep of callused fingers against her breasts, tender and yet forceful, pain mixed with ecstasy—and she gasped.

And that was when he looked up.

Full sunlight cast the shadow from his face and revealed to her the threat—and the promise—in his cold black eyes. In that instant she realized who he was, and why he'd come.

'This just isn't my day,' she muttered and, acting on blind instinct, shouldered her rifle and fired.

The first blast cratered the ground a foot in front of him. He didn't flinch. He didn't even break stride. He came at her, his steady gaze fixed firmly on her face. She jacked out the shell and pumped another into the chamber. The second blast landed square between his boots, showering the black leather with dirt and debris. Still he kept coming, faster now, hard-packed muscle moving with cat-like speed. She wasn't given the opportunity to get off another round.

He hit the porch steps two at a time. Not hesitating a moment, he grabbed the barrel of the rifle and yanked it from her grasp, tossing it aside. His hands landed heavily on her shoulder, catapulting her straight into his arms. With a muffled shriek, she grabbed a fistful of shirt to keep from falling.

'You never were much of a shot,' he said, his voice low and rough. And then he kissed her.

His kiss was everything she remembered and more. He'd always combined strength with tenderness, but now there was also a ruthless demand to his kiss, a fierce assault on both mind and body that held her stunned and unmoving. His mouth shifted over hers, subduing any hint of resistance, taking with a relentless thirst, but also giving a wealth of passion in return. One hand settled low on her back, arching her into the tight cradle of his thighs. His other hand slid up her spine, beneath the heavy fall of her braid, his fingers thrusting through the silken strands of her hair and cupping her head.

Unable to help herself, she felt her arms tighten around him, discovering again the breadth of his shoulders and the lean, compact muscles sculpting his ribs and chest. With trembling fingers she searched out the tiny mole that hid in the hollow at the base of his throat, knowing that she should fight him, that she should end this farce. But somehow she couldn't. He'd been her first lover...her only lover. There was a connection between them that could never be severed, much as she might wish it otherwise.

He deepened the kiss between them, his thumb sliding along her jaw to the corner of her mouth and teasing the sensitive spot until her lips parted beneath his. To her shame, she kissed him back, kissed him with eight lonely years' worth of pent-up yearning. She needed this moment out of time, and part of her rejoiced in the exquisite memories his touch resurrected. She came alive in his arms, became the woman she'd once been. But another part of her, the part that had suffered at his hands, knew the danger, knew the price she'd pay for allowing him to sweep away the barriers she'd fought so hard to build. She couldn't afford to feel again. She'd almost been destroyed once by this man; she wouldn't offer him the opportunity to complete the job.

He kissed her at length, the conqueror staking his claim, and a small growl of satisfaction rumbled deep in his chest. It was that tiny sound which finally brought her to her senses. She fought her way free of his embrace and retreated several steps across the porch. Raising trembling fingers to her mouth, she stared at him...stared in stunned disbelief at Hunter Pryde—the one man she'd hoped never to see again.

He returned her look, his expression one of cool amusement. 'Hello, Leah,' he said. 'It's been a long time.'

His careless words brought a world of hurt. She struggled to conceal her devastation, to hide the pain his kiss had resurrected. After all that had gone before, after all they had once meant to each other, how could he be so casual, so heartless? Hadn't he caused enough anguish by walking out on her without...this?

'It hasn't been long enough, as far as I'm concerned. Why are you here, Hunter?' she demanded in a raw voice. 'What do you want?'

He smiled briefly, a flash of white teeth in a bronzed face. 'You know what I want. The same thing I've always wanted.'

She shook her head in desperation. 'No. Not the ranch.'

'The ranch? Try again, Leah.' He reached into his shirt pocket and retrieved a newspaper clipping. 'I've come in response to your ad.'

A small gasp escaped. 'You can't be serious,' she protested.

'I'm very serious.'

His voice held an implicit warning and she took another unthinking step away from him. 'You…you can't do this. You don't even have an appointment!' She used the first ridiculous excuse that occurred to her, but she was grasping at straws and they both knew it.

'Would you have given me one?' he asked, seemingly content to play the game her way. For now.

'Not a chance.'

'No. I didn't think so. Which is why I answered your ad under the name H.P. Smith.'

Briefly, she shut her eyes. After her experience with Titus T. Culpepper, she'd pinned ridiculously high hopes on the unknown H.P. Smith. So much for dreaming of a knight in shining armor. Hunter Pryde was no knight—a former lover, a one-time wrangler on her father's ranch, and a thief who'd stolen her heart before vanishing like the morning mist—but no knight. More likely he'd prove to be one more battle she'd have to fight…and win.

He tucked her ad back into his shirt pocket and cupped her elbow. 'Inside, Leah. We have a lot to discuss.'

'No!' she protested, yanking free of his grasp. 'I have nothing to discuss with you.'

He bent down, picked up her rifle and emptied the chamber of shells. He stared first at the slugs in his hand, then at her. 'I suggest you reconsider,' he told her.

It took every ounce of self-possession not to apologize for shooting at him. She faced him, hands planted on her hips. 'You're not wanted here.' She gestured toward the rifle, adding drily, 'You should have taken the hint.'

'Last chance, Leah. You don't want to fight me on this.'

The words were arctic-cold, the threat inexorable. He gazed down at her, and the expression in his eyes almost stopped her breath. Why did he look at her like that—as though all the sins in the world could be laid at her doorstep and he'd come to exact retribution? She'd done nothing to him, except love him. And he'd repaid that love with desertion. His fierce gaze continued to hold her, and with a sudden, gut-wrenching certainty she realized that somehow she'd wronged him and he'd come to even the score. She fought a mind-numbing panic. If she succumbed to panic she didn't stand a chance against him.

Instinct urged her to throw him off her property and be done with it. But she didn't have that luxury. Knowing him, he wouldn't go until he'd had his say. Instead, she'd handle this in a calm, intelligent manner. She'd hear him out—not that she had much choice in the matter. Then she'd throw him off her property.

'Leah,' Hunter prompted in a surprisingly gentle voice.

She didn't allow his mildness to mislead her. The softer he spoke, the more dangerous he became. Right now, he was deadly serious. 'All right, Hunter.' She forced out the words. 'We'll play it your way…for the time being.'

He rattled the rifle-slugs fisted in his hand, the sound more sinister than any made by a diamond-back snake. Settling his hat more firmly on his head, he snagged her elbow, his grip firm and purposeful. 'Let's go.'

She didn't flinch. Instead, she allowed herself to be drawn into the house. Peeking up at his rigid features, she released a silent sigh. With no rescue in sight, it looked as if she'd fight this battle alone. And she could, too.

So long as he didn't touch her again.

Once inside the study, Hunter closed the door and crossed to the far wall, where the family photos hung. He paused, assessing them, one in particular seeming to capture his attention. It had been taken around the time he'd known her; she'd been just eighteen.

In the picture she sat on a fence-rail, faded jeans clinging to her coltish legs, a sleeveless checked shirt revealing slim, sun-browned arms. She stared off into the distance, a half-smile curving her mouth, her gaze unfocused as though her thoughts were far, far away. Just as the picture had been snapped she'd raised a hand to her cheek, brushing a stray curl from her face.

'I expected your hair to have darkened.' He glanced from the photo to Leah. 'It hasn't. It's still almost silver. As I recall, it used to flow through my fingers like silk. I wonder if it still would.'

'Stop it, Hunter,' she ordered tightly.

He glanced back at the photo. 'It doesn't do you justice, you know.'

'What, the picture?' She shrugged uneasily. 'If you say so. I think it looks just like I used to.'

'Not quite.' His mouth curled to one side. 'It doesn't show the passion...nor the ruthlessness. Even at that age you had a surplus of both.' He turned to study her. 'Do you still?'

Her mouth tightened. 'I've changed a lot since then. You figure out how.'

Turning away, she took a stance behind the huge oak desk, hoping it would put her in a stronger, more authoritative position. She hoped in vain. Hunter removed his hat, dropped it in the middle of the desk and edged his hip on to the corner nearest her.

'You knew the ad in the paper was mine, didn't you?' she began, determined to get their confrontation over as quickly as possible. 'How?'

'The nickname you used. Miss Bluebonnet.'

She nodded in acknowledgement. 'Dad used to call me that because of my eyes.' Then, with a sigh, she asked, 'Why are you really here, Hunter? Because I don't believe for one minute that it's in response to that ad.'

'You know why I'm here,' he said.

'I can guess.' Pierced by eyes that were panther-black and jungle-watchful, she'd never felt so intimidated in her life. And it took every ounce of resolve not to let it show.

Hunter Pryde had changed, attained a sophistication she'd never have believed possible. Eight years ago he'd been in his mid-twenties and wild, both in appearance and in attitude. In those days his black hair had brushed his shoulders, held back by a leather thong, his eyes reflecting a savage determination to succeed in a world just as determined to see him fail. But what had attracted her most had been his face—the high, sculpted cheekbones, the hawk-like nose, and the tough, bronzed features that reflected an unmistakable strength and vitality.

His long-limbed arms and legs, his broad chest and lean, sinewy build spoke of a mix of conquistadors and native American Indian, of a proud and noble heritage. When he'd taken her into his arms she'd sensed that no one else would ever make her come alive the way she did with him, that she'd never love anyone quite as much.

And she'd been right.

'You've come to see the Hamptons broken, is that it?' Leah asked with a directness she knew he'd appreciate.

A cynical smile touched his mouth. 'Swayed, never broken. Wasn't that your father's motto? No. I've come to discover why, if things are so bad, you haven't sold out. Are you really so destitute that you need to resort to this?' Removing the ad once more from his shirt pocket, he balled it in his fist and flicked the crumpled newspaper toward the trash can. It arched over the rim and hit the bottom with a faint metallic thud.

He couldn't have made his disapproval any clearer. She found it mortifying that he, of all people, had happened across that ad. But she wasn't a shy, easily coerced teenager any more. And she wouldn't be bullied. Not by anyone. Certainly not by Hunter.

'This isn't any of your business,' she informed him. 'I don't owe you a thing, least of all an explanation for my actions.'

'I'm making it my business,' he corrected in a hard, resolute voice. 'And, one way or another, I will have an explanation.'

She struggled to curb her anger. It wasn't easy. He had an uncanny knack for driving her into an uncontrollable fury. 'Are you really interested,' she snapped, 'or have you come to gloat?'

He folded his arms across his chest. 'I wouldn't be here if I wasn't interested.'

'Fine.' She'd try taking him at his word and see where it led. Though she suspected she wouldn't like it when they got there. 'I didn't have any choice but to place that ad.'

He dismissed her excuse with a contemptuous gesture. 'Don't give me that. We always have choices. You just have a knack for picking the wrong ones.'

'You may not agree with my decisions, but that doesn't make them wrong,' she retorted, stung. 'The last few years haven't been easy. Dad...Dad died a year after you left.' Hunter's leaving at a time she needed him most still hurt, even after all these years. Until he'd ridden up today, she hadn't realized how much of that pain lingered.

'Yes, I know.'

She flinched. 'You knew?' Knew and never bothered to

return? Never bothered to see how she was, see if she required any help or support? She straightened her shoulders. No, not support. She'd support herself. And her grandmother. And the ranch. And all those she'd gathered beneath her wing. No matter what it cost.

'I read his obit in the papers.' He leaned closer, and she caught her breath, drawing in the rich, spicy scent of his aftershave. 'I understand the ranch has gone downhill ever since. You may be just as ruthless and single-minded as your old man, but you're sure as hell not the rancher he was.'

She jerked as though slapped, and for a moment the defiant, protective mask she'd kept rigidly in place slipped, leaving her vulnerable and exposed. How could she ever have been seduced by this man? Even at eighteen she should have had the sense to see the cold, heartless soul that ruled his keen intellect, no matter how attractive the outer packing.

'I won't defend myself to you. Why should I? Nor will I be judged by your yardstick,' she insisted fiercely. 'So spit out what you came to say and get the hell off my land.'

She saw the familiar spark of anger flicker to life in his eyes and wondered if she'd pushed him too far. Not that she cared. With her back against the wall, both literally and figuratively, she'd fight free any way she could and damn the consequences.

With an abrupt sweep of his arm he snagged her waist, and forced her between his legs. 'Don't you know why I'm here?' He cupped her shoulders to curb her instinctive opposition, rough amusement edging his words.

As much as she wanted to tell him to go to hell, she knew he wouldn't release her until she'd answered. Glaring at him, she said, 'You came in response to the ad.'

'More than that, Leah. Much, much more,' he corrected, a bitter smile twisting his mouth. 'I came for the ranch.' His eyes grew black and pitiless, searing her with a burning determination. 'And…I came for you.'

CHAPTER TWO

SHOCK held Leah immobile for a split-second. Recovering swiftly, she lifted her chin. 'That's a real shame, Hunter,' she retorted, continuing to fight his hold. 'Because you aren't getting either one.'

His grip tightened. 'We'll see.'

She stopped struggling. Resistance was fruitless. Instead, she used the only other weapon she possessed. Words. 'Did you really believe that after all these years you could just come strolling back up my drive? Your arrogance is incredible. After what you did to me, I wouldn't give you so much as the time of day!'

'A little melodramatic, don't you think?'

Fury ripped through her and she gave in to it, needing the satisfaction losing her temper would provide. 'Melodramatic? Not by a long shot. You stole my innocence, you bastard. And you did it solely to get your hands on this ranch.' Bitterness spilled over, pouring out after years of suppression. Her pain, her agony, stripped of any protective cover, lay bare for him to see. 'I was eighteen and crazy in love. And you used me. *You used me!*'

'The hell I did. I just took what you offered.'

His cruelty cut her to the quick and it required all her willpower not to hit him. But she remembered his lightning-fast speed of old. Her blow would never land and his retaliation would be swift and unpleasant. She looked him straight in the eye. 'You can't get out of your responsibilities that easily. You took exactly what you wanted, no matter who suffered in the process.'

His mouth settled into a grim line. 'You never knew what I wanted. You still don't.'

'Oh, no?' Did he really consider her so blind, so ignorant of man's baser motivations? Perhaps eight years ago she'd been guilty of such an oversight, but no longer. He'd cured her of that. 'It's the same then as now. You want my land. Well, get in line.'

'There is no line,' he bit out. 'Nor will there be. You'd better face that fact right here and now.'

He tugged her closer, as though to obstruct any chance of flight. Slowly, relentlessly, he gathered her in, trapping her in a grasp as binding and inescapable as a mist-net around a struggling sparrow. She pressed her hands against his chest, striving to keep some small distance between them. But instead she found that touching him only resurrected long-forgotten emotions, reminding her of all that had gone before. Tears threatened, but she ruthlessly forced them back. Tears wouldn't accomplish a thing. Not with this man.

'Why are you doing this?' she asked. 'Why now, after all this time?'

'Because it will give me what I want most.'

She laughed quietly, the sound one of pain and disillusionment rather than amusement. 'When you said that eight years ago, I foolishly thought you meant me. But now I realize you meant the ranch.'

His expression closed over. 'Did I?'

'Yes! Is that why you bedded me? Because it would give you your dream? It didn't work out that way, did it?'

'Bedded you? A rather quaint description for what we did together. Something a bit more elemental and a lot cruder would be closer to the truth. And, as I recall, we never did get around to using a bed.'

She refused to feel shame for an act that had been the most beautiful experience of her life. 'No, we didn't. Because you left before we ever had the chance. Of course, you didn't hit the road until Dad threatened to disinherit me. He offered me a choice. You or the ranch.'

'And we both know which you chose.'

She caught his shirt in her fists. 'How would you know that?' she demanded passionately, her distress breaking free of her control. 'You didn't stick around long enough to find out. But I can guarantee choosing you was a mistake I've lived to regret. It never occurred to me that, without the ranch, I wasn't much of a bargain.' Her pride had suffered from that knowledge. But her pride had handled the battering. Her heart hadn't been nearly so sturdy. 'So you took what you could and walked.'

A hard smile tilted his mouth to one side and his hands closed over hers, prying them free of his shirt. 'Let's be accurate. I didn't walk. I was dragged.'

'Don't give me that. I waited in the line-shack for hours. Does that amuse you?' Her breathing grew shallow and rapid, the dark recollections ones she rarely dredged from her memory. 'The afternoon was sweltering, but I waited inside the cabin for you anyway. I was so afraid one of the wranglers would stop by…that there'd be some unexpected strays to round up or fence to string and he'd decide to spend the night out there and I'd get caught. But I didn't leave. I kept telling myself you'd come. The hours became an eternity, as though the world had moved on and I'd somehow been left behind. Even after the sun set, I found excuse after excuse to explain your absence.'

'Stop it, Leah.'

But she couldn't. Once started, the memories continued to unravel, like a wind-up music-box grinding out its song until the music played down. 'It was a full moon that night. I sat on the floor and watched as it drifted from window to window, inching a path across the sky.'

He stared at her, impassive and remote. 'It rained.'

Surfacing from the remembered nightmare, she focused on his face. 'Not until two that morning,' she corrected, her voice dull and lifeless. 'The storm rolled in from the south and blotted out the stars as though an angry hand had wiped them from the sky. The roof leaked like a sieve but, fool that I was, I stayed.' She bowed her head, her emotions nearly spent. 'I stayed and stayed and stayed.'

'Why? Why did you stay?' he asked insistently. 'Look at me, Leah. Look me in the eye and tell me the rest of your lies. Because that's all they are.'

'How could you possibly know what's fact and what's fiction,' she whispered, 'when you weren't there to see?'

'Tell me!'

Forced by the relentless command, she lifted her head. He swept a wisp of ash-blonde hair from her face, and though he touched her with a tender hand his expression was anything but.

'I stayed because I was waiting for you to ride up and take me away like you promised,' she admitted, her voice breaking. 'At daybreak I finally realized you weren't coming. And I vowed that I'd never trust a man again. I'd never give him that sort of power over me or leave myself open and vulnerable to that much misery. So tell me, Hunter. Tell me the truth. What happened? What was so vital that it *dragged* you away and you couldn't be bothered to come back?'

'Sheriff Lomax happened.'

It took a long minute for his words to sink in. 'What do you mean?' she asked, dread balling in her stomach.

He laughed, the jarring sound slicing across her nerves like a finely honed blade. 'Cut the bull, Leah. All that nonsense about waiting for me at the line-shack and sweltering in the heat and watching the moon. It didn't happen. I know it. And you know it. Though I did enjoy the part about the roof leaking. Very pathetic.'

'What's the sheriff got to do with this?' she demanded, more urgently.

'I went to the line-shack, as agreed. You weren't there.' He paused significantly. 'The sheriff was. Along with a few of his men.'

'No. I don't believe you.'

'It took six of them to pull me out of there. You forgot to mention, in your heartbreaking tale of woe, about the smashed furniture or the broken window. Or the unhinged door. They might have taken me, but I didn't go easy.'

'I don't know…' She struggled to remember. Had the window and furniture been broken? 'Things were a bit of a mess, but—'

He didn't give her a chance to finish. 'I guess you were so busy staring at the stars you didn't notice.' Catching hold of her long, silver braid, he wound it around his hand, pulling her close. His mouth hovered a hair's-breadth above hers. 'Or maybe you didn't notice because every word you've uttered is a lie. Admit it. You were never at that line-shack.'

'I was there!'

'Not a chance. Only two people knew about our meeting. You…and me. I didn't tell a soul. But, since the sheriff came in your place, there's only one explanation. You changed your mind. And, afraid of how I'd react, you spilled your guts to Daddy and begged him to get you out of a sticky situation.'

'No! It didn't happen that way.'

'Didn't it? Tell me this. If we had met that afternoon, would you have come away with me? Well…?' He pinned her with a hard, savage gaze. 'Would you?'

She'd never lied to him in the past and she wouldn't start now. No matter how it might look to him, no matter how he might react, she'd tell him the truth. 'No. I wouldn't have gone with you.'

For an instant his grip tightened and she waited for him to master his anger, unafraid, knowing with an absolute certainty that he'd never physically harm her. 'I didn't think so,' he said. He released her and stood, and she sensed that he'd set himself apart, distancing himself from her.

Her explanation wouldn't change anything, but she had to try. For the first time she deliberately touched him, placing a hand on his upper arm, feeling the rock-like muscles clench in reaction. 'There's a reason I wouldn't have gone away with you—'

'Enough, Leah.' He turned flat, cold eyes in her direction. 'I've heard enough. It's water under the bridge. And, to be honest, your excuses don't interest me.'

There was no point in trying to force him to listen. Not now. Maybe not ever. 'Then why are you here?' she asked. 'Why cause more grief—grief neither of us needs?'

'Because what's important is today. Here and now. Your ranch and that ad.'

'I won't let you get your hands on this ranch…or on me,' she informed him fiercely. 'You might as well give up and move on, because I won't marry you.'

He laughed, the sound harsh and mocking. 'I don't recall asking, sweetheart.'

A tide of color washed into her face at his biting response. 'I assumed that was why you'd come. You had the ad and you implied—'

He lifted an eyebrow. 'Implied what?'

'That you were interested in marrying me,' she maintained stubbornly. 'You came in response to my notice, didn't you?'

'Not to offer marriage, that's for damned sure. I came because you wouldn't have placed that ad if you weren't desperate, which makes it a powerful bargaining chip. So let's bargain. I want the ranch, Leah, and I mean to get it.'

They stared at each other for an endless moment. Before she could respond, a car horn sounded out front, and Hunter glanced towards the windows. 'Someone's here. Another applicant, perhaps?'

Slipping past him, Leah crossed to the window, recognizing the pick-up parked in front. The occupant leaned on the horn again and her mouth tightened in response. 'It would appear this is my day for surprises,' she murmured. 'Unpleasant surprises, that is.' She crossed to the picture wall where Hunter had left her rifle and snatched it up.

'What's going on, Leah?' Hunter demanded, picking up his hat. 'Who's your company?'

Intent on reloading, she spared him a brief glance. 'His name is Bull Jones. He's the foreman of the Circle P.'

Hunter's eyes narrowed. 'The Circle P?'

'A new outfit. Actually, they're now the *only* outfit in these parts, except for us. They're owned by a big conglomerate, Lyon Enterprises, and they're not particularly friendly. So do me a favor and stay out of this, okay? It doesn't concern you.'

He looked as if he might debate the issue. Then, with an abrupt nod, he followed her out to the porch. Propping his shoulder against a pillar, he tipped his hat low on his brow, his face thrown into shadow. Satisfied by Hunter's apparent compliance, Leah turned her attention to the more immediate and far more menacing problem confronting her.

Bull Jones leaned negligently against the door of his pick-up—a pick-up parked directly in the middle of the tiny strip of flowerbed Grandmother Rose had painstakingly labored over these past three weeks. 'Afternoon, Miz Hampton,' he said, grinning around the stub of a thick cigar.

She ignored his greeting, taking a stand at the top of the porch steps. 'Get off my property, you thieving rattlesnake,' she ordered coldly, 'before I call the sheriff.'

'In one of your feisty moods, are you?' She didn't bother responding and he sighed. 'Call the sheriff if it'll make you feel any better. But you know and I know he won't be coming. He's tired of all your phone-calls.'

She couldn't argue with the truth. Instead, she brought the rifle to her shoulder and aimed the hurting end exactly six inches below Bull's massive silver belt buckle. 'Spit out why you came and get the hell off my land before I send you home with a few vital parts missing,' she said.

He didn't seem the least intimidated. In fact he laughed in genuine amusement. 'You do have a way with words.' He jerked his head toward Hunter. 'This *hombre* one of your prospective suitors? Doesn't have much to say for himself.'

Hunter smiled without amusement. 'Give it time, friend.'

Leah couldn't conceal her surprise. If Bull considered Hunter a potential suitor, then he knew about her advertisement. But how had he found out? Before the two men could exchange further words, she hastened to ask, 'Is that it, Jones? That's what you came about? My ad?'

'One of the reasons,' Bull acknowledged. 'I even considered offering myself up as a possible candidate. But I didn't think you'd go for it.'

'You thought right.'

'As to the other matter....' He paused to savor his cigar, puffing contentedly for a long minute. She knew it was a deliberate maneuver on his part—an attempt to drive her crazy. Unfortunately it was working.

'Out with it, Jones.'

'My, my. You are in a hurry.' He shrugged, a quick grin sliding across his face. 'You want it straight? Okay. I'll give it to you straight. I came to offer a friendly little warning.'

'*Friendly*?'

'I'm a friendly sort of guy.' He took a step in her direction. 'You give me half the chance, you'd find just how friendly I can be.'

She didn't know whether it was the sound of her pumping home the shell in her rifle or the fact that Hunter suddenly straightened from his lounging position that stopped Bull in his tracks. Whichever it was, he froze. Then she glanced at Hunter and knew what had checked the foreman's movements.

She'd always found Hunter's eyes fascinating. One minute the blackness appeared, cold and remote, the next minute glittering with fire and passion. For the first time she saw his eyes burn with an implacable threat and for the first time she realized how intimidating it could be.

He leveled that look on Bull. 'If you have something more to say,' he informed the foreman softly, 'I suggest you say it. Fast.'

Bull Jones shot Hunter a look of fury, but Leah noticed he obeyed. 'Seems Lyon Enterprises is getting tired of playing games over this place.' His gaze shifted to Leah. 'Thought you should know they've decided to call in the big guns.'

'I'm shaking in my boots,' she said.

He removed his cigar from between his teeth and threw it to the ground. It landed amongst a clump of crushed pink begonias, wisps of smoke drifting up from the smoldering tip. 'You will be. From what I hear, this new guy's tough. You don't stand a chance.'

His words terrified her. But she refused to crack. She wouldn't allow her fear to show. Not to this bastard. 'You've been saying that for a full year now,' she said calmly enough. 'And I've managed just fine.'

'That was kid-glove treatment.'

Anger stirred. The temptation to pull the trigger and be done with it was all too inviting. 'You call fouling wells and cutting fence-line and stampeding my herd kid-glove treatment?'

He shrugged. 'We were having a little fun, is all. But now the gloves are off. Don't say I didn't warn you.'

With that, he stomped through what remained of Grandmother Rose's flowerbed and climbed into his pick-up. The engine started with a noisy roar and he gunned it, a rooster-tail of dirt and grass spraying up from beneath his rear wheels. They watched in silence as he disappeared down the dirt drive. A minute later all that remained of Bull's passing was a tiny whirlwind of dust, spinning lazily in the distance. Leah eyed it with a thoughtful frown.

Hunter slipped the rifle from her grasp and leaned it against the porch rail. 'Something you forgot to tell me?' he murmured sardonically.

She lifted her chin. 'There might be one or two minor

details we didn't get around to discussing. Not that it's any concern of yours.'

'I don't agree. I suggest we go back inside and discuss those minor details.'

'No!' She rounded on him. First Titus T., then Bull and now Hunter. This definitely wasn't her day. 'You know full well that there's nothing left to talk over. You want the ranch and I won't let you have it. Even if you were interested in responding to my ad—interested in marriage—I won't choose you for the position. How could you think I would?'

He raised an eyebrow. 'Position? I thought you wanted a husband.'

'That's right, I do. But since you aren't interested…' Fighting to keep the distress from her voice, she said, 'You've had your fun. So why don't you leave?'

He shook his head. 'We're not through with our conversation, and I'm not leaving until we are. If that means applying for your…position, then consider me applied.'

'Forget it. You don't qualify,' she insisted. 'That ends the conversation as far as I'm concerned.'

'I qualify, all right. On every point.'

She didn't want to continue with this charade but, aside from picking up her rifle and trying to force him off her property at gunpoint, she didn't see any other option available to her. Especially considering how far she'd gotten the last time she'd turned her rifle on him. 'Fine. You think you qualify? Then prove it,' she demanded.

'A challenge? Not a wise move, Leah, because once I've proven myself we'll finish that discussion.' He tilted his head to one side, his brow furrowed in thought. 'Let's see if I can get this right… Number one. You want a man between the ages of twenty-five and forty-five. No problem there.'

'You should have read the ad more carefully, Hunter! It says a *kind and gentle* man. You are neither kind nor gentle.'

His gaze, black and merciless, met hers. 'You'd do well to remember that.'

Tempted as she was, she didn't back down. 'I haven't forgotten. The ad also says applicants should be looking for a permanent type of relationship.' She shot him a skeptical glance. 'Don't tell me you're finally ready to settle down?'

'That isn't my first choice, no. But I'd consider it if the right offer came along. Number two. As I recall that concerns ranching experience.' He folded his arms across his chest. 'You planning to debate my qualifications there?'

She shook her head. After all, there was nothing to debate. 'I'll concede your ranching abilities,' she agreed.

A grim smile touched his mouth. 'You'll concede a hell of a lot more before we're finished. Number three. He should also have solid business skills—particularly those skills necessary to please a bullheaded banker.' He settled his hat lower on his forehead. 'You've tipped your hand with that one.'

'Have I?' Something about his attitude worried her. He acted as though this were all a game, as though she'd already lost the match but didn't yet know it. What she couldn't figure was…how? How could she lose a game that she wasn't even playing?

His smile turned predatory. 'You're having financial difficulties and the bank won't help without a man backing you. Close enough?'

She gritted her teeth. 'Close enough,' she forced herself to confess. 'But you aren't that man. End of discussion.'

'Far from it. There isn't a bank in the world who wouldn't back me.'

That gave her pause. 'Since when?'

He closed the distance between them, crowding her against the porch rail. 'It's been eight years since our last meeting. A lot has happened in that time. I'm not the poor ranch-hand you once knew. You need me, Leah. And soon—very soon—I'm going to prove it to you.'

'I don't need you!' she denied passionately. 'I'll *never* need you.'

'Yes, you will.' His voice dropped, the timbre soft and caressing, but his words were as hard and chipped as stone. 'Because you won't get any cooperation from the bank without me. I guarantee it. And by tomorrow you'll know it, too.'

She caught her breath. 'You can prove that?'

'I'll give you all the proof you need. Count on it.' He lowered his head, his mouth inches from hers. 'Seems I've qualified after all.'

She glared, slipping from between him and the rail. 'I disagree. You've already admitted that you aren't kind or gentle. And since that *is* one of the qualifications...' She shrugged. ''Fraid I'll have to pass.'

'And I'm afraid I'll have to insist. In the business world all negotiations are subject to compromise. You'll have to compromise on "kind and gentle".'

'And what will you compromise about?' she shot back.

'If I can get away with it...nothing.' He edged his hip on to the rail and glanced at her. 'Tell me something, Leah. Why haven't you sold the ranch?'

She shifted impatiently. 'I think you can guess. Hampton Homestead has been in our family for—'

'Generations. Yes, your father made that point quite clear. Along with the point that he wouldn't allow his ranch or his daughter to fall into the hands of some penniless mongrel whose bloodlines couldn't be traced past the orphanage where he'd been dumped.'

She stared at him, genuinely shocked. 'He said that to you?'

'He said it. But that's not the point. You're out of options, Leah. Soon you won't have any other alternative. My sources tell me that either you sell or you go bankrupt. At least if you sell you'll walk away with enough money to live in comfort.'

She lifted her chin. 'There is another alternative.'

His mouth twisted. 'The ad.'

'Don't look at me like that! It's not as foolish a decision as you might think. The banks will loan me the money I need to stay afloat if I have a husband who's both a businessman and a rancher.'

He stilled. 'They've guaranteed you the money?'

She shook her head. 'Not in writing, if that's what you mean. But Conrad Michaels is the senior loan officer and an old family friend. And, though he hasn't been in a position to help us in the past, he feels our business reversals are correctable, with some work. He's a bit…old-fashioned. It was his idea that I find an appropriate husband. He hasn't been able to get the loan committee to approve financing so far, but he's positive he can if I marry.'

She'd never seen Hunter look so furious. 'Are you telling me that this Michaels instructed you to advertise in the paper for a husband and you went along with his harebrained notion?'

'It's not a hare-brained notion,' she protested. 'It's very practical. Conrad simply suggested I find a husband with the necessary qualifications as quickly as possible. Once I'd done that, he'd get the loan package put through.'

'He suggested that, did he? In his position as your banker?' Hunter didn't bother to conceal his contempt. 'Did it ever occur to you he could have trouble living up to that promise? He has a board of directors to answer to who might not agree with him any more now than before. And then where would you be? Bankrupt and married to some cowpoke who'll take whatever he can lay hands on and toss you over when the going gets tough.'

'You should know,' she shot back. 'You're a past master of that fine art.'

'Don't start something you can't finish, Leah,' he warned softly. 'I'm telling you—marry the next man who responds to your ad and you'll sacrifice everything and receive nothing but trouble.'

'You're wrong,' she said with absolute confidence. 'I have faith in Conrad. He'll put the loan through.'

She could tell Hunter didn't agree, but he kept his opinion to himself. 'What about the ad?' he asked.

'The ad was my idea. I needed results and I needed them fast.' She folded her arms across her chest in perfect imitation of his stance. 'And I got them.'

He laughed without amusement. 'If you got "kind and gentle" I'm less than impressed.'

'It's not you who has to be impressed,' she retorted defensively. 'It's Conrad whose approval I need.'

'I don't doubt your banker friend will make sure your prospective husband is qualified as a rancher and a businessman,' he stated with marked disapproval. 'But what about as a husband and lover? Who's going to make sure he qualifies in that area?' Hunter's voice dropped, the sound rough and seductive. '"Kind and gentle" couldn't satisfy you in bed in a million years.'

She silently cursed the color surging into her cheeks. 'That's the least of my concerns.'

'You're right. It will be.' He regarded her with derision. 'Is that how you see married life? A sterile partnership with a husband who hasn't a clue how to please his wife?'

Images leapt to her mind, images of the two of them entwined beneath an endless blue sky, their clothes scattered haphazardly around them, their nudity cloaked by thick, knee-high grass. She resisted the seductive pull of the memory. She couldn't afford to remember those times, couldn't afford to risk her emotions on something so fleeting and uncertain...nor so painful. Not if she intended to save the ranch.

'That's not important,' she stated coldly. 'Conrad has promised that if I marry someone the bank considers a sound businessman and rancher, I'll get my loan. And that's what I intend to do. Period. End of discussion. I'm keeping this ranch even if it means accepting the first qualified man who walks through my door. And nothing you say or do will change that.'

'I've got news for you. I *am* the first qualified man to walk through your door. The first and the last.' He reached into his pocket and retrieved a business card. 'Perhaps you'd better know who you're up against.'

'No, let me tell you who *you're* up against,' she retorted, almost at the end of her rope. 'That huge company I mentioned—Lyon Enterprises—is after this ranch. And they'll use any means necessary to acquire it. You've met Bull Jones. He's encouraged almost all my workers to leave with exorbitant bribes. Nor was I kidding when I accused him of cutting my fences and stampeding my herd and fouling the wells. The man I marry will have to contend with that.' She planted her hands on her hips. 'Well, Hunter? Maybe now that you have all the facts in your possession you'll decide to get out of my life. Just be sure that when you do, you make it for good.'

His eyes narrowed and, in a move so swift she didn't see it coming, he caught her by the elbows and swung her into his arms. She slammed into him, the breath knocked from her lungs. 'Don't threaten me, Leah. You won't like the results,' he warned curtly. 'Give it to me straight. Are you really being harassed, or is this another of your imaginative little fantasies?'

This time she didn't even try to fight his hold. She'd learned the hard way how pointless it would be. 'It's no fantasy! You saw a prime example today. Or ask my fore-man. Patrick will tell you. He's one of the few they haven't managed to run off.'

His eyes glittered with barely suppressed wrath and a frown slashed deep furrows across his brow. Without re-leasing her, he tucked his business card back into his pocket. 'You're serious, aren't you?'

She nodded. 'Dead serious.'

'You're also serious about marrying, even if it means losing the ranch?'

'I am.'

'In that case you're down to one option.'

She sighed, weary of their argument. 'I told you. I'm not selling.'

'No, you're not. You're going to marry me.'

If he hadn't been holding her, she would have fallen. 'What?' she whispered, unable to hide her shock.

'You heard me. We'll marry and I'll see to it that you get your loan.'

She stared at him in bewilderment, the fierce determination she read there filling her with a sense of unease. 'You said... I thought you didn't want to marry me.'

'It wasn't my first choice, no,' he agreed. 'But the more I consider the idea, the greater the appeal.'

She caught her breath. 'That's the most insulting offer I've ever heard.'

'Count on it,' he said with a grim smile. 'I can get much more insulting than that.'

'I wouldn't advise it,' she snapped back. 'Not if you'd like me to accept.'

He inclined his head, but whether in acknowledgement or concurrence she wasn't quite clear. An endless moment stretched between them, a moment where they fought a silent battle of wills. It wasn't an even match. Slowly, Leah lowered her eyes. 'You agree,' Hunter stated in satisfaction.

'I didn't say that.' She stalled for time—not that it would help. Exhaustion dogged her heels, making it impossible to think straight. She needed time alone, time to consider, time to put all he'd told her into perspective. But she strongly suspected she wouldn't be given that time. 'What about the bank? Can you guarantee I'll get the loan?'

His expression hardened. 'I have some small influence. I'm not the poor, mixed-breed cur I was eight years ago.'

'I never saw you that way,' she reacted instantly, despising the crude comparison. 'And if my father did, he was wrong.'

He shrugged off her rejoinder. 'What's your decision, Leah?'

This time she did try and free herself. Not that she succeeded. 'What's your rush?' she asked. His touch grew gentle, soothing rather than restraining, at striking odds with his clipped tone. Had he decided an illusion of tenderness might better influence her? If so, he'd soon discover his mistake.

'I don't want anyone else coming along messing up my deal. You have twenty-four hours to make up your mind. Sell the ranch to me or marry me; I don't give a damn which. Because I know it all, Leah,' he informed her tautly. 'I've had your financial situation investigated. You're broke. Without a loan you'll go bankrupt. And without me you won't get that loan.'

She caught her breath in disbelief. 'I don't believe you!'

'You will. You will when the banks tell you that I'm your only choice other than bankruptcy.'

She shook her head, desperate to deny his words. 'How can you possibly do that?'

'You'd be surprised at what I can do.'

'What's happened to you?' she whispered. 'Mercy used to be a part of your nature.'

He gazed at her impassively. 'Not any more. You saw to that. It's your decision. And to help you decide…'

She knew what he intended; she recognized the passion in his expression, saw the resolve in his eyes. To her eternal disgust she lifted her face to meet his kiss. Curiosity, that was all it was, she told herself. But she lied. Her curiosity had been appeased earlier. She knew from that first kiss that her reaction to his touch hadn't changed, not even after eight years.

No, she returned his kiss because she wanted to experience the wonder of it again. To come alive beneath his mouth and hands. To relive, if only for a moment, the mind-splintering rapture only he could arouse. He took his time, drinking his fill, sharing the passion that blazed with such incredible urgency.

But it was all an illusion. She knew that. He wanted the ranch and would use any means available to get it. Even seducing her. Even marrying her. And she'd be a fool to forget that.

Lifting his head, he gazed down at her. 'What we once had isn't finished, Leah,' he informed her in a rough, husky voice. 'There's still something between us. Something that needs to be settled, once and for all.'

She eased back. 'And you think our marriage will settle it?'

'One way or another,' he confirmed.

'You don't leave me much choice.'

'I've left you one choice. And I'm it.'

He set her from him, his expression once more cool and distant. In that instant she hated him. Hated him for making her want again. Hated him for resurrecting all that she'd struggled so hard to forget. But she especially hated him for being able to turn off his emotions with so little effort. Because she knew her emotions weren't as easily mastered.

'Twenty-four hours, Leah. After that, you're history.' And, without another word, he left her.

Long after he'd ridden away she stood on the front porch, unable to move, unable to think. Finally, with a muffled sob, she buried her head in her hands and allowed the tears to come.

CHAPTER THREE

HUNTER walked into his office and set his briefcase on his desk. A brief knock sounded on the door behind him and his assistant, Kevin Anderson, poked his head in the door.

'Oh, you're back. How did it go? Did she agree to sell the ranch?'

Opening his briefcase, Hunter removed a bulky file and tossed it to one side. 'Not yet. But I'll have it soon…one way or another.' He turned and faced his assistant, allowing his displeasure to show. 'Why didn't you tell me about Bull Jones and what he's been up to?'

'The foreman?' Kevin hesitated, then shrugged. 'I didn't think it was important.'

Anger made Hunter speak more sharply than he would have otherwise. 'Well, it damned well is important. You don't make those decisions. I do.'

'Sorry, boss. It won't happen again,' came Kevin's swift apology. Then he asked cautiously, 'I assume you've made the foreman's acquaintance?'

'In a manner of speaking.'

'Did he recognize you?'

Hunter didn't answer immediately. Instead, he crossed to the window and stared out at the Houston skyline. The intense humidity from the Gulf of Mexico rippled the air on the far side of the thick, tinted glass, signaling the start of another South Texas heatwave. 'No,' he finally said. 'He didn't recognize me. But then I didn't go out of my way to introduce myself.'

'That's probably smart. What do you want done about him?'

'Nothing for now.' Hunter turned back and faced his assistant. 'But I may need to take action in the future.'

'Whatever you say. You're the boss.'

Hunter inclined his head. 'One last thing before you go.'

'Sure. Anything.'

'You keep me informed from now on. No matter how minor or insignificant. I won't be caught off-guard again.'

'Yes, sir. Sorry, sir,' Kevin agreed. Then he quietly excused himself and slipped from the room.

After a brief hesitation Hunter crossed to his desk and flipped open the file marked 'Hampton Homestead.' A white tide of letters, legal documents and several photos spilled across the gleaming ebony surface. Reaching out, he selected two photos of Leah—one identical to the picture he'd studied in the Hampton study, the other a snapshot only a month old.

Examining the more recent of the two, a savage desire clawed through him, unexpected and intense. He still wanted her...wanted to rip her hair free of her braid, feel her silken limbs clinging to him, feel again her softness beneath him.

He dropped the photo to his desk. Soon, he promised himself. Very, very soon.

'We have to talk,' Grandmother Rose announced the next morning, slamming a thick porcelain mug in front of Leah.

Leah closed her eyes, stifling a groan. She hadn't slept a wink last night and could barely face the unrelenting morning sun, let alone a more unrelenting grandmother. 'If this is about Hunter, I don't want to discuss it.'

'It's about Hunter.'

'I don't want to discuss it.'

'Tough toenails. I have a confession to make and you're going to listen to every last word, even if I have to wrestle you to the floor and sit on you.'

The picture of her ninety-pound grandmother putting her in a headlock and forcing her to the tile floor brought a reluctant smile to Leah's mouth. 'Can we at least talk about the weather for five minutes while I drink my coffee?'

'It's sunny and eighty-five in the shade. Hope you swallowed fast. Now. About Hunter.'

Deep purplish-blue eyes held Leah's in a direct, steady gaze. The eye color and a relentless determination were only two of the qualities Leah shared with her grandmother. Unfortunately, Rose's determination included a stubbornness even beyond Leah's. She gave up. She'd never won an argument with her grandmother, a circumstance unlikely to change any time in the near future. 'What about him?' she asked with a sigh.

'What he said yesterday about the sheriff was true,' Rose announced. 'Every word.'

Leah straightened in her chair. 'You heard? You were listening?'

'I did and I was, and I'm not one bit ashamed to admit it. What I *am* ashamed to admit is that I betrayed your confidence to your father eight years ago.' She twisted her thick gold wedding-band around a knobby finger, the only external sign of her agitation.

'You warned Dad that I planned to run away with Hunter.' It wasn't a question. Leah had already figured out what must have happened. The only person she'd confessed to about that long-ago meeting sat across the table from her. Not that she'd ever expose her grandmother's involvement to Hunter.

'Yes, I told your father,' Rose confirmed. 'I told Ben because, selfishly, I didn't want you to leave.'

'But I promised you I wouldn't go!'

Leah shoved back her chair and stood. Struggling to conceal her distress, she made a production of pouring herself another cup of coffee. She'd told Rose about her meeting for one simple reason: she couldn't leave the woman who'd loved and raised her without a single word of farewell. What she hadn't anticipated was her grandmother's revelation that Leah's father was dying of cancer. Once in possession of the grim news she hadn't had any alternative. She couldn't abandon her father in his time of need, no matter how desperately she yearned to be with Hunter. It just wasn't in her nature.

Leah turned and faced her grandmother. 'I told you I'd meet Hunter and explain about Dad's illness. I planned to ask him to wait…to return after…after…'

Rose shrugged. 'Perhaps he'd have agreed. But I couldn't count on that—on his going away and letting you stay.' She sighed. 'Listen, girl, the reason I'm telling you all this is because I've decided. I want you to marry Hunter.'

Leah stared in shock. 'Come again?'

'What are you, deaf? I said, I want you to marry Hunter.'

'But…why?'

'Because…' Rose lifted her chin and confessed. 'Because I had a call from Conrad Michaels this morning.'

'What did he want?'

'Officially…to announce his retirement. Unofficially…to withdraw his offer of help. No bank loan in any circumstances was the message I got.'

'Hunter!' Leah released his name with a soft sigh.

'That thought occurred to me, too.' Her grandmother's

eyes narrowed. 'You suppose his pull is strong enough to force Connie's retirement?'

'Possibly. Though if Hunter is as ruthless as you suspect, I'm surprised you're so anxious to marry me off to him.'

'Ruthless isn't bad…if it's working on your side. And, right now, we could use a whole lot of ruthless on our side.'

'Could we?' Leah questioned. 'I'm not so sure.'

Rose stared into her coffee-cup as though the answers to all their problems lay written in the dregs. Finally she glanced up, her expression as hard and set as Leah had ever seen it. 'You have two choices. You can sell or you can fight to win against Lyon Enterprises. If you want to sell, say the word, and we'll give up and clear out. But if you want to win, Hunter's the man for the job. It took you years to get over him. Fact is, I don't believe you ever did. Marry him or don't. It's your decision. But my vote is to snatch him up fast. Men like that only come along once in a lifetime. You've gotten a lucky break. He's come through your door twice.'

Lucky? Leah had her doubts. He'd loved her with a passion that she'd never forgotten and she'd let him down. He wouldn't give her the chance to hurt him like that again. She simply couldn't read too much into his return. If anything, he'd come back to wreak revenge. And, if that was the case, by placing that ad she had indeed exposed her vulnerability and given him the perfect opportunity to even an old score.

And he'd been swift to take advantage.

One by one he'd cut off every avenue of escape until she faced two tough alternatives. Unfortunately, learning that any possibility of a bank loan had been circumvented left her with no alternatives…if she intended to save the ranch.

Leah returned her mug to the counter, the coffee having gone stone-cold. She looked at her grandmother and saw the hint of desperation lurking in Rose's otherwise impassive expression. No matter what she'd said, losing the ranch would be the death of her. And to be responsible for her demise, when Leah had it within her power to prevent it, just couldn't be borne.

'I'll call Hunter,' she announced quietly.

For the first time in her life, Leah saw tears glitter in her grandmother's eyes. 'Don't accept his first offer, girl,' she advised gruffly. 'Bargain for position and you can still come out of this on top.'

'I'm not your granddaughter for nothing,' Leah said with a teasing smile. 'He won't have it all his own way.'

And he wouldn't. Very soon she'd find out just how badly he wanted the ranch—and just how much ground he'd give up in order to get it.

Not until Leah had completed her list of requests for Hunter—she hesitated to call them demands—did she realize that he hadn't left her a number where he could be reached. Not that it truly presented a problem. Precisely twenty-four hours after their original meeting, Hunter phoned.

'What's your answer?' he asked, dispensing with the preliminaries.

'I want to meet with you and discuss the situation,' Leah temporized.

'You mean discuss terms of surrender?'

'Yes.' She practically choked getting the word out. He must have known, darn him, for a low, intimate laugh sounded in her ear.

'You did that very well,' he approved. 'See? Giving in isn't so bad.'

'Yes, it is,' she assured him. 'You try it some time and you'll know what I mean.'

'No, you handle it much better than I would. All you need is a little more practice.'

Married to him, she didn't doubt she'd get it, either. 'Where are you staying?' she asked, deliberately changing the subject. She knew when to give up on a losing hand. 'Should I meet you there?'

'I'm in Houston. And no, I don't expect you to drive that far. We'll meet tomorrow. Noon. The line-shack.'

She caught her breath in disbelief. 'That's not funny, Hunter!'

'It wasn't meant to be.' All trace of amusement vanished from his voice, his tone acquiring a sharp, cutting edge. 'I'm dead serious. Tomorrow meet me at the line-shack at noon. Just like before. See that you make it this time. There won't be any second chances.'

'There weren't eight years ago. Why should this occasion be any different?'

'It will be different,' he promised. 'You'd be smart to realize that right from the start.'

'Fine. You've made your point and I realize it. Things will be different.'

'Very good, Leah. There's hope for you yet.'

She clamped down on her temper, determined not to be provoked. 'So, let's meet at the ranch-house instead. Okay? Hunter?' But she spoke into a dead phone. So much for not being provoked. She was thoroughly provoked.

Slowly she hung up. This did not bode well for their future together. Not well at all. She reached for her list. She wouldn't have that disaster at the line-shack held over her head like the sword of Damocles for the rest of her life. She'd done all the explaining she intended to do, but apparently he had more to say. Well, this meeting would end it once and for all. She wouldn't spend the rest of her life paying for something that, though her ultimate responsibility, wasn't her fault.

Early the next morning she headed for the south pasture to pay a visit to Dreamseeker, the stallion she'd recently acquired. At the fence she whistled, low and piercing, waiting for the familiar whickered response. From the concealing stand of cottonwoods he came, a coal-black stallion, racing across the grass. He danced to a stop ten yards from the fence, pawing at the ground and shaking his mane.

'You don't fool me,' she called to him. 'You want it. I know you do. All you have to do is come and take it.' She held out her hand so he could see the lumps of sugar she'd brought him.

Without further hesitation he charged the fence, but she didn't flinch. Her hand remained rock-steady. Skidding to a halt beside her, the horse ducked his head into her hand and snatched the sugar from her palm. Then he nipped her fingers—not hard, just enough to establish dominance. With a snort, he spun around and galloped across the pasture.

She cradled her palm, refusing to show her hurt. She wouldn't let herself be hurt. It was an indulgence that she couldn't afford. She'd made her decision—a decision that would protect the stallion, protect her ranch, and protect all the wounded creatures she'd gathered safely beneath her wing.

She also understood why Dreamseeker had bitten her. He'd done it to prove that he was still free—free to choose, free to approach or flee. It saddened her, because she knew he lived a lie. They had that in common. For, no matter how hard they tried, neither was truly free.

Not any more.

Leaving the fence, she saddled a horse and rode to the line-shack. The spring weather had taken a turn for the worse, becoming every bit as hot and humid as that fateful day eight years ago. A sullen mugginess weighted the air, filled it with the threat of a thunderstorm. Leah shuddered. The similarities between then and now were more than she cared to contemplate.

At the line-shack she ground-hitched her gelding. Hunter hadn't arrived yet and she stood outside, reluctant to enter the cabin…reluctant to face any more memories. She'd avoided this place for eight long years. Thanks to Hunter she couldn't avoid it any longer. Setting her chin, she crossed to the door and thrust it open.

She stepped cautiously inside, looking around in disbelief. Everything was spotless. A table, two chairs, a bed—everything in its place. A thin layer of dust was the only visible sign of neglect. Someone had gone to great pains to restore the shack. But who? And why?

'Reliving old memories?'

Leah whirled around. 'Hunter! You startled me.'

He filled the threshold, a blackened silhouette that blocked the sun and caused the walls to close in around them. 'You shouldn't be so easily startled.'

Searching for something to say, she gestured to indicate the cabin. 'It's changed. For some reason I thought the place would have fallen down by now.'

He shrugged. 'You can't run a ranch this size without working line-shacks. The men need someplace to hole up when they're working this far out. Allowing it to fall into ruin would be counterproductive.'

She could feel the tension building between them, despite his air of casual indifference. She wouldn't be able to handle this confrontation for long. Best to get it over with—and fast. She turned and faced him. Unfortunately that only served to heighten her awareness. 'Why did you want to meet here?' she asked, taking the offensive.

'To annoy you.'

Her mouth tightened. 'You succeeded. Was that your only reason?'

'No. I could have had you drive to Houston and negotiate on my turf. But, considering our history...' He shrugged, relaxing against the doorjamb.

He tucked his thumbs into his belt-loops, his jeans hugging his lean hips and clinging to the powerful muscles of his thighs and buttocks. She shouldn't stare, shouldn't remember the times he'd shed his jeans and shirt, exposing his coppery skin to her gaze. But it proved next to impossible to resist the old memories.

He'd had a magnificent physique, something that clearly hadn't changed with time. If anything, his shoulders had broadened, his features had sharpened, becoming more tautly defined. How she wished their circumstances were different, that she didn't fear he'd use her attraction to achieve his goal...to gain his revenge.

Desperately, she forced her attention back to the issue at hand. 'Negotiating here is just as much to your advantage. Dredging up the old memories, playing on my guilt, is supposed to give you added leverage, is that it?'

'Yes. I play to win. You'd be wise to learn that now.'

She ground her teeth in frustration. 'And if I don't?'

He smiled. 'You will. We've come full circle, you and I. We're back where we left off. But nothing's the same as it was. You've changed. I've changed.' He added significantly, 'And our situation has changed.'

'How has it changed?' she asked with sudden curiosity.

'How have you changed? What did you do after you left here?'

He hesitated, and for a minute she thought he wouldn't answer. Then he said, 'I finished my education, for a start. Then I worked twenty-four hours a day building my... fortune.'

'You succeeded, I assume?' she pressed.

'You could say that.'

'That's it? That's all you have to say—you got an education and made your fortune?'

He shrugged. 'That's it.'

She stared at him suspiciously, wondering what he was concealing. Because she didn't doubt for a minute that he hadn't told her everything. What had he left out? And, more importantly, *why*? 'Why so mysterious?' she demanded, voicing her concerns. 'What are you hiding?'

He straightened. 'Still trying to call the shots, Leah? You better get past that, pronto.'

'It's my ranch,' she protested. 'Of course I'm still calling the shots.'

He shook his head. 'It may be your ranch, but I'm the one who'll be in charge. Are we clear on that?'

'No, we're not clear on that!' she asserted vehemently. 'In fact, we're not clear on anything. For one thing, I won't have our past thrown in my face day after day. I won't spend the rest of my life apologizing for what happened.'

'I have no intention of bringing it up again. But I wanted to make it plain, so there's no doubt in your mind. I won't have you claiming later that I didn't warn you.'

She eyed him warily. 'Warn me about what?'

'You've been managing this ranch for over seven years and you've almost run it into the ground. Now I'm supposed to come in and save it. And I will. But you're going to have to understand and accept that I'm in charge. What I say goes. I won't have you questioning me in front of the hired help or second-guessing my decisions. You're going to have to trust me. Implicitly. Without question. And that's going to start here and now.'

'You've been gone a lot of years. It isn't reasonable—'

He grabbed his shirtsleeve and ripped it with one brutal yank, the harsh sound of rending cotton stemming her flow of words. 'You see that scar?' A long, ragged silver line streaked up his forearm.

She swallowed, feeling the blood drain from her face. 'I see it.'

'I got it when the sheriff helped me through that window.' He jerked his head toward the south wall. 'I have another on my inner thigh. One of Lomax's deputies tried to make a point with his spur. He almost succeeded. I broke my collarbone and a couple of ribs on the door here.' He shoved at the casing and it wobbled. 'Still isn't square. Seems I did leave my mark, after all.'

She felt sick. How could her father and Sheriff Lomax have been so cruel? Had Hunter really been such a threat to them? 'Are you doing this for revenge?' she asked in a low voice. 'Trying to get control of the ranch because of how Dad treated you and because I wouldn't go away with you?'

'Believe what you want, but understand this…' He leaned closer, his words cold and harsh. 'I got dragged off this land once. It won't happen again. If you can't accept that, sell out. But if you marry me, don't expect a partnership. I don't work by committee.'

'Those are your conditions? What you say goes? That's it?'

He inclined his head. 'That just about covers it.'

'It doesn't come close to covering it,' she protested. 'I have a few conditions of my own.'

'I didn't doubt it for a minute.'

She pulled the list she'd compiled from her pocket and, ignoring his quiet laugh, asked, 'What about my employees? They've been with me for a long time. What sort of guarantee are you offering that changes won't be made?'

'I'm not making any guarantees. If they can pull their weight, they stay. It's as simple as that.'

She stared in alarm. Pull their weight? Every last one of them pulled his or her own weight…to the best of their ability. But that might not be good enough to suit Hunter's high standards. Patrick had a bad leg and wasn't as fast or strong as another foreman might be.

And what about the Arroyas? Mateo and his wife Inez would have starved if she hadn't taken them in. Inez, as competent a housekeeper as she was, had six children to care for. Leah had always insisted that the children's needs come first, even at the expense of routine chores. Would Hunter feel the same way? And Mateo was a wonder with horses but, having lost his arm in a car accident, certain jobs were difficult for him—tasks she performed in his stead.

'But—'

'Are you already questioning my judgement?' he asked softly.

She stirred uneasily. 'No, not exactly. I'd just appreciate some sort of guarantee that these people won't be fired.' She saw his expression close over. 'I'm responsible for them,' she forced herself to explain. 'They couldn't find work anywhere else. At least, not easily.'

'I'm not an unfair or unreasonable man,' he said in a

clipped voice. 'They won't be terminated without due cause.'

It was the best she'd get from him. 'And Grandmother Rose?'

A tiny flicker of anger burned in his eyes. 'Do you think I don't know how much Hampton Homestead means to her? Believe me, I'm well aware of the extent she'd go to to keep the ranch.'

Her fingers tightened on the list. 'You don't expect her to move?'

She could tell from his expression that she'd offended him, and she suspected that it was a slight he wouldn't soon forgive. 'As much as the idea appeals, it isn't my intention to turn her from her home,' he said curtly. 'What's next on your list?'

Taking him at his word, she plunged on. 'I want a pre-nuptial agreement that states that in the event of a divorce I get to keep the ranch.'

'There won't be a divorce.'

She lifted her chin. 'Then you won't object to the agreement, will you?'

He ran a hand across the back of his neck, clearly impatient with her requests. 'We'll let our lawyers hammer out the finer details. I refuse to start our marriage discussing an imaginary divorce.'

She wouldn't get any more of a concession than that. 'Agreed.'

'Next?'

She took a deep breath. This final item would be the trickiest of all. 'I won't sleep with you.'

His smile was derisive. 'That's an unrealistic request and you damned well know it.'

'It's not. I—'

He cut her off without hesitation. 'This is going to be a real marriage—in every sense of the word. We sleep together, drink, eat and make love together.'

'Not a chance,' she protested, her voice taking on an edge of desperation even she couldn't mistake. 'You wanted control of the ranch and you're getting that. I won't be part of the bargain. I won't barter myself.'

Sardonic amusement touched his expression. 'You will and you'll like it,' he informed her softly. 'I know you too well not to make it good for you.'

'You knew an inexperienced eighteen-year-old girl,' she declared passionately. 'You know nothing about the person I've become. You know nothing of my hopes or dreams or desires. And you never will.'

'Another challenge?' He moved closer. 'Shall we settle that here and now? The bed's a little narrow, but it'll do. I guarantee you won't be disappointed.'

She took a hasty step back, knowing there was nowhere to escape should he decide to put action to words. 'You bastard,' she whispered. 'I won't be forced.'

'I don't use force. I don't have to.' For a horrifying second she thought he'd prove it, that he'd sweep her up without regard and carry her to the bed. That he'd scatter her resistance like so much chaff before the breeze. Then he relaxed, though his gaze remained guarded and watchful. 'What about children?' he asked unexpectedly. 'Or are they off your list, too?'

Events had proceeded so swiftly that she hadn't given the possibility any thought at all. 'Do you want children?' she asked uncertainly.

He cocked his head to one side, eyeing her with an uncomfortable intensity. 'Do you? Or, should I say, do you want *my* children?'

'Once, that was all I dreamed about,' she confessed in a low voice.

'And now?'

She looked at him, fighting her nervousness. 'Yes, I want children.'

'You won't get them if I agree to your condition. Cross it off your list, Leah. It's not a negotiable point.'

She didn't want to concede defeat, didn't want to agree to give herself to him without love, without commitment. But he'd left her without choice. 'Hunter, please…'

He closed the distance between them. Cupping her head, he tilted her face up to his. 'We'll make love, you and I, and we'll have children. Plenty of them. Though chances are they won't be blue-eyed blondes. Can you live with that?'

'I'm not my father. I know you don't believe it, but it's true. Do you really think I could love my child less because he's dark…' she dared to feather her fingers through his hair '…instead of fair?'

He caught her hand and drew it to his scarred arm, her pale skin standing out starkly against his sun-bronzed tan. 'It matters to some.'

'Not to me. It never mattered to me.'

He nodded, apparently accepting her words at face value. 'Any more conditions?' he asked, flicking her list with a finger.

'No,' she admitted. 'But you'd better know up-front—I can't promise I won't argue with you. I love this ranch. And I'll do all I can to protect the people on it.'

He shook his head. 'That's my job now.'

'That doesn't mean I won't worry.'

'Worrying is also my job,' he informed her gravely.

She nodded. That left only one last decision to be made. 'About the wedding…'

'I want to marry by the end of the week. Tell me where and when and I'll be there. Just make sure it's no later than Saturday.'

'So soon?' she asked in dismay. 'That's less than a week.'

'Are you having second thoughts?'

'Constantly. But it won't change anything. I won't sell and I can't save the ranch unless I marry you. But a wedding… There's a lot to be done and not much time to do it in.'

'Find the time.' He tugged her more fully into his arms. 'I have to go,' he said, and kissed her.

His touch drove out all thought and reason, banishing the ghosts that lingered from that other time and place. And no matter how hard she wanted to oppose him, to keep a small piece of herself safe and protected, he stripped her of all resistance with consummate ease. Deepening the kiss, he cupped her breast, teasing the tender peak through the thin cotton. And she let him…let him touch her as he wished, let him explore where he willed, let him drive her toward that sweet crest she'd once shared exclusively with him.

For a moment Leah was able to pretend that she meant something to him again, that he really cared for her more than he cared for her ranch. But as hard as she tried to lose herself in his embrace, the knowledge that this was in all probability a game of revenge intruded, and finally drove her from his arms.

He released her without protest. 'Call me with the details,' he instructed, and headed for the door. 'We'll need to get the license as soon as possible.'

'There's one last thing,' she suddenly remembered. He

paused, waiting for her to continue and, almost stumbling over the words, she said, 'Conrad...Conrad Michaels. He retired.' Hunter didn't say anything, prompting her to state her concerns more openly. 'Are you responsible for his retirement?'

'Yes.'

She'd suspected as much, but it still shocked her to hear him admit it. '*Why?*' He didn't reply. Instead he walked outside, forcing her to give chase. Without breaking stride, he gathered up his buckskin's reins and mounted. She clung to his saddle-skirt, hindering his departure, desperate for an answer. 'Hunter, please. Tell me why. Why did you force Conrad to retire?'

After a momentary hesitation he leaned across the horn, fixing her with hard black eyes. 'Because he put you at risk.'

Alarmed, she took a step back. 'What are you talking about?'

'I'm talking about the ad.'

'But I placed the ad, not Conrad.'

'He knew about it, and not only did he not try and stop it he encouraged you to go ahead with it while in his capacity as your banker.' His face might have been carved from granite. 'You still don't have a clue as to how dangerous that was, do you?'

'We were very selective,' she defended.

'You were a fool,' he stated succinctly. 'You might as well have painted a bullseye on your backside, stuck your pinfeathers in the air and proclaimed it open hunting season. Count yourself lucky that you and that old harridan of a grandmother weren't murdered in your beds.'

'So you had Conrad fired.'

'I wanted to!' he bit out. 'Believe me, more than anything I wanted to have him fired for planting such a criminal suggestion in your head. Considering he's an old family friend, I let him off easy. I agreed to an early retirement.'

A sudden thought struck her. 'If you're that powerful—powerful enough to force Conrad's retirement—what do you need with this ranch?' She spoke urgently. 'It has to be small potatoes to you. Why are you doing this, Hunter?'

A grim smile touched his mouth and he yanked the brim of his stetson low over his brow. 'That, my sweet bride-to-be, is one question I have no intention of answering.'

And with that he rode off into the approaching storm, the dark, angry clouds sweeping across the sky ahead of him, full of flash and fury. A portent of things to come? Leah wondered uneasily. Or a promise?

CHAPTER FOUR

WITH only five days to prepare for her wedding, Leah realized that the simplest solution would be to hold the ceremony at the ranch. She also decided to make it an evening affair and keep it small, inviting only her closest friends and employees.

Her reasons were twofold. She didn't think she could handle a day-long celebration—the mere thought of celebrating a marriage that was in all actuality a business deal struck her as vulgar. And by holding an evening ceremony they'd entertain the guests for dinner and it would be over quickly. No fuss, no muss.

Her grandmother didn't offer a single word of argument in regard to Leah's wedding-plans. On only one matter did she remain adamant. She insisted that Leah invite Conrad Michaels. 'He's a close friend and should give you away. If that makes Hunter uncomfortable, that's his tough luck.'

'I don't think it's Hunter who will feel uncomfortable,' Leah observed wryly. 'Let me call Conrad and see what he wants to do. If he chooses to decline, I won't pressure him.'

As it turned out, Conrad sounded quite anxious to attend. 'I'd appreciate the opportunity to improve my relationship with Hunter,' he confessed. 'I deserved every harsh word he dished out, and then some.'

'Harsh word?' she repeated in alarm. 'What did he say?'

After a long, awkward silence, Conrad admitted, 'Oh, this and that. Let's just describe the conversation as strained and forget I ever mentioned it. He did make several valid points, though—particularly about your ad.'

So Hunter *had* taken Conrad to task about that. She'd wondered. 'What points?' she questioned.

'I never should have encouraged you to advertise for a husband,' came the prompt reply. 'Looking back, I realize it was foolish in the extreme. It didn't occur to me until Hunter suggested the possibility, but a crazy person could have responded and we wouldn't have known until too late. I never would have forgiven myself if anything had happened to you.'

Unfortunately, something *had* happened. Hunter had answered the ad. To her disgust, she seemed to be the only one to appreciate the irony of that fact. 'It's all worked out for the best,' she lied through her teeth. 'So don't worry about it.' Securing Conrad's agreement to give her away, she ended the conversation and hung up.

The next two days passed in a whirl of confusion. Leah spent her time deciding on caterers and flowers, food and decorations, and obtaining the all-important wedding-license. Finally she threw her hands in the air and dropped the entire mess in the laps of her grandmother and Inez Arroya. 'You decide,' she begged. 'Just keep it simple.'

'But, *señorita, por favor*...' Inez protested. 'The wedding, it should be perfect. What if we make a mistake? You will be very unhappy. Don't you care?'

Didn't she care? Leah turned away. She cared too much. That was the problem. How could she plan for the wedding of her dreams when the ceremony on Friday would be anything but? 'Whatever you decide will be perfect,' she said flatly. 'Just remember. Keep it simple.'

'What about your dress?' Rose reminded, before Leah

could escape. 'You've deliberately ignored that minor detail, haven't you?'

'I thought I could pick something up on Thursday,' Leah said, refusing to acknowledge the truth in her grandmother's words.

But on this one point Rose became surprisingly obstinate. 'Oh, no, you don't, my girl. I have the perfect gown for you. Your mother wore it for her wedding and it's the most unusual dress I've ever laid eyes on. It's packed away in the attic, if memory serves. Find it and see if it fits. Though considering how much you resemble your momma, I'd be surprised if it didn't.'

Reluctantly, Leah obeyed. It took a good bit of searching, but she eventually found a huge, sealed box with her mother's name and the date of her wedding scrawled across one end. Wiping away the dust, she carried it downstairs. She didn't return to the kitchen, needing a moment alone in the privacy of her bedroom to examine her mother's wedding-dress. Closing and locking the door, she settled on the floor and carefully cut open the box.

Lifting off the lid, she sank back on her heels, her breath catching in her throat. Her grandmother had been right. It was the most unusual dress Leah had ever seen. Her mother had been a teacher of medieval history and her dress reflected her obsession, right down to the filmy veil with its accompanying silver circlet. It was beautiful and romantic, the sort of dress young women dreamed of wearing.

And Leah hated it with a passion that left her shaking.

The dress promised joy and happiness, not the businesslike relationship soon to be hers. The dress promised a lifetime of laughter and companionship, not the strife and friction that was all she could expect from an empty marriage. But most of all the dress promised everlasting love, not the bitterness and pain that consumed her husband-to-be. She ached for the future the dress suggested, but knew it could never be hers.

This marriage would be an act of vengeance, and she nothing more than a pawn in Hunter's game. It was a way to even up old scores for the abuse he'd suffered at her father's hands. Soon he would be master of his enemy's castle and she'd be at his mercy. How long would it take before he had it all? How long before he controlled not just the ranch but her heart and soul as well?

How long before he had his final revenge?

Gently she replaced the lid of the box. She couldn't wear her mother's wedding-gown. It wouldn't be right. It would be...sacrilegious. She'd drive into town and find a chic ivory suit that spoke of modern marriages and easy divorces. And instead of a gauzy veil she'd purchase a pert little hat that no one would dream of referring to as 'romantic'.

Not giving herself time to reconsider, she shoved the box beneath her bed. Then she ran outside and whistled for Dreamseeker, needing just for an instant to feel what her stallion felt—free and wild and unfettered. But the horse didn't respond to her call. And in that instant Leah felt more alone than she ever had before in her life.

'What do you mean, I can't wear the suit?' Leah demanded of Inez. 'Why can't I? Where is it?'

'*Arrunina, señorita. Lo siento.*'

'Ruined! How?'

'The iron, it burned your dress.'

'But the dress didn't need ironing.'

The housekeeper looked close to tears. 'I'm sorry. I

wanted everything to be perfect for your special day. I was excited and…' She wrung her hands. 'Forgive me.'

'It's all right, Inez,' Leah said with a sigh. 'But I get married in less than an hour. What am I supposed to wear? I can't go down in this.' She indicated the wisps of silk and lace beneath her robe.

'Señora Rose, she suggests the dress of your *madre. Es perfecta, sí?*'

Leah closed her eyes, understanding finally dawning. Of all the conniving, meddling, devious… Before she could gather the courage to yank the first outfit that came to hand from her closet, Inez draped the wedding-dress across the bed. In a swirl of featherlight pleats the silvery-white silk billowed over the quilted spread, the hem trailing to the floor.

In that instant, Leah was lost. She touched the form-fitting bodice—a corset-like affair, decorated with a honey-combed network of tiny seed pearls and silver thread—thinking that it resembled nothing more than a gossamer-fine cobweb. It really was an enchanting gown. And it had been her mother's.

Knowing further arguing would prove fruitless, Leah allowed the housekeeper to help her into the gown. It fit perfectly, as she'd known it would. Thin white ribbons accentuated the puffed sleeves, the deep, flowing points almost brushing the carpet.

'The belt, *señorita*,' Inez said.

The housekeeper lifted the silver linked chain from the bed and wound it twice around Leah's waist and hips, the pearl-studded clasp fastening in front. The ends of the chain, decorated with tiny unicorn charms, fell to her knees, the links whispering like golden-toned chimes with her every movement.

'For purity,' the housekeeper murmured, touching the unicorns.

'Not terribly appropriate,' Leah said in a dry voice. 'I wonder if it's too late to change them.'

'You are pure of heart, which is all that counts,' Inez maintained stoutly. 'I will do your hair now. You wish to wear it loose?'

'I thought I'd braid it.'

'Oh, no, *señorita*. Perhaps a compromise?' Without waiting for a response, she swiftly braided two narrow sections on each side of Leah's face, threading a silver cord into each as she went. Pulling the braids to the back of Leah's head, the housekeeper pinned them into an intricate knot.

'That looks very nice,' Leah admitted.

'We leave the rest loose,' Inez said, brushing the hip-length curls into some semblance of order. Finally she draped the veil over Leah's hair and affixed the circlet to her brow. Stepping back, she clasped her hands and sighed. '*Qué hermosa*. Señor Hunter, he is a lucky man.'

Leah didn't reply. What could she say? That luck had nothing to do with it, unless it was bad luck? Her bad luck. 'How much time is left?' she asked instead.

'A few minutes, no more. Señor Michaels is waiting for you at the bottom of the stairs.'

'I'm ready,' she announced. She picked up her bouquet of freshly picked wild flowers—courtesy of the Arroya children—and kissed Inez's cheek. 'Thank you for all your help. Go on downstairs. I'll follow in a minute.'

The door closed behind the housekeeper and, finally alone, Leah glanced at the stranger in the mirror. What would Hunter think? she wondered. Would he find her gown ridiculous? Attractive? Would her appearance even matter to him? She shut her eyes and whispered an urgent prayer, a prayer that Hunter might some day find happiness and peace in their marriage…that maybe, just maybe, he'd find love. Slightly more relaxed, she turned away from the mirror. She couldn't delay any longer. It was time to go.

As she descended the stairs, the pleated skirt of her dress swirled around her like wisps of silver fog. Conrad waited at the bottom. He looked up at her, and his reaction was all she could have asked. He stared in stunned disbelief, his mouth agape.

'Leah,' he murmured gruffly, his voice rough and choked. 'My dear, you're a vision. You make me wish…'

She traversed the final few steps, a small smile playing about her mouth. 'Wish what?'

'Wish that I hadn't so foolishly encouraged you to place that ad,' he confessed. 'Are you sure this marriage is what you want? It's not too late to change your mind.'

She didn't hesitate for an instant. 'It's much too late and you know it. Not that it matters. I haven't changed my mind.'

He nodded without argument. 'Then this is it.' He offered his elbow. 'Shall we?'

She slipped her hand into the crook of his arm and walked with him to the great room, an area used for entertaining that stretched the full length of the ranch-house. It was her turn to stare in disbelief. Huge urns of flowers filled the room, their delicate perfume heavy in the air. And everywhere was the radiant glow of candlelight, not a single light-bulb disturbing the soft, romantic scene.

Her gaze flew to the far side of the room where Hunter stood, and her heart pounded in her breast. The wrangler she'd always known had disappeared and in his place stood a man who wore a tuxedo with the same ease as he wore jeans. She'd never seen him look so sophisticated, nor so aloof.

His hair reflected the candlelight, gleaming with blue-black highlights, and his eyes glittered like obsidian, burning with the fire of passion held barely in check. Despite that, he remained detached from his surroundings, the high, taut cheekbones and squared chin set in cool, distant lines.

The sudden hush that greeted her arrival drew his attention and his gaze settled on her with piercing intensity. Her hands tightened around her bouquet, sudden fear turning her fingers to ice. With that single glance his air of detachment fell away and his expression came alive, frightening in its ferocity. He looked like a warrior who'd fixed his sights on his next conquest. And she was that prize. It took all her willpower not to gather up her skirts and run.

Conrad started to move and she had no choice but to fall into step beside him. In keeping with the medieval theme, soft stringed instruments played in the background. She focused on Hunter, barely aware of her passage down the aisle, even more dimly aware of Conrad releasing her and stepping back. But every part of her leapt to life the instant Hunter took possession of her hand.

The minister began the ceremony. She didn't hear a word he said; she didn't even remember making her marriage vows. Afterward, she wondered if she'd actually promised to obey her husband or if the minister had thoughtfully omitted that rather antiquated phrase. She didn't doubt that Hunter would refresh her memory at some point.

The ring he eventually slid on her finger felt strange on her hand, the unaccustomed weight a visible reminder of all the changes soon to come. She stared at the ring for a long time, studying the simple scrollwork and wondering why he'd chosen such an interesting design. Did it have any particular significance or had it been a simple matter of expediency?

'Leah.' Hunter's soft prompt captured her full attention.

She glanced up at him in bewilderment. 'Did I miss something?' she asked. Quiet laughter broke out among the guests and brought a flush to her cheeks. Even Hunter grinned, and she found herself riveted by that smile, aware that it had been eight long years since she'd last seen it.

'We've just been pronounced man and wife,' he told her. 'Which means...' He swung her into his embrace and lowered his head. 'It's time to kiss the bride.'

And he proceeded to do so with great expertise and thoroughness. It was her first kiss as his wife and the warm caress held all the magic she could desire. She was lost in his embrace, swept up in the moment. Yet, as intensely as she craved his touch, she longed to resist with an equal intensity. She couldn't bear the knowledge that this whole situation was nothing more than Hunter's way of gaining control of her ranch...and of her.

At long last he released her, his look of satisfaction stirring a flash of anger. Fortunately her irritation swiftly disappeared beneath the flurry of congratulations from the press of friends and employees. By the time Inez announced dinner, she'd fully regained her composure.

Like the great room, the dining-room glowed with candlelight, flowers running the length of the oak table and overflowing the side tables and buffet. To her relief she and Hunter were seated at opposite ends, though as dinner progressed she discovered her relief short-lived. Throughout the meal she felt his gaze fixed on her. And as the evening passed her awareness of him grew, along with an unbearable tension.

As the caterers cleared away the final course, Hunter

rose, glass in hand. 'A toast,' he announced. Silence descended and all eyes turned in his direction.

'A toast for the bride?' Conrad questioned.

'A toast to my wife.' Hunter lifted the glass. 'To the most beautiful woman I've ever known. May all her dreams come true...and may they be worth the price she pays for them.'

There was a momentary confused silence and then the guests lifted their glasses in tribute, murmuring, 'Hear, hear.'

Slowly Leah stood, well aware of the double edge to Hunter's toast. Lifting her own glass in salute, she said, 'And to my husband. The answer to all my dreams.' And let him make what he wished of that, she thought, drinking deeply.

The party broke up not long after. Rose had arranged to stay with friends for the weekend and all the staff had been given the days off as a paid vacation. Only Patrick would remain, to care for the animals. But, knowing her foreman's sensitivity, he'd make himself scarce. They wouldn't see any sign of him until Monday morning.

Sending the last few guests on their way, Leah stood with Hunter in the front hall. The tension between them threatened to overwhelm her and she twisted her hands together, feeling again the unexpected weight of her wedding-ring.

She glanced at it and asked the question that had troubled her during the ceremony. 'Did you choose it or...?'

'I chose it. Did you really think I'd leave it to my secretary to take care of?'

'I didn't even know you had a secretary,' she confessed. 'What do...did you do?'

He hesitated. 'Mostly I worked as a sort of troubleshooter

for a large consortium, taking care of problem situations no one else could handle.'

She drifted toward the great room, snuffing candles as she went. 'I imagine you'd be good at that sort of thing. What made you decide to give it up and return to ranching?'

'What makes you think I've quit?' he asked from directly behind.

Startled, she spun around, her gown flaring out around her. 'Haven't you?'

'They know to call if something urgent comes up. I'll find a way to fit it in.' He drew her away from a low bracket of candles. 'Be careful. I'd hate to see this go up in flames.'

'It was my mother's,' she admitted self-consciously. 'I wasn't sure whether you'd like it.'

His voice deepened. 'I like it.'

She caught her breath, finally managed to say, 'You still haven't answered my question.'

'What question?' A lazy gleam sparked in his eyes and she knew his thoughts were elsewhere. Precisely where, she didn't care to contemplate.

'Why,' she persisted, 'if you had such a good job, did you decide to come back?'

'Let's just call it unfinished business and leave it at that. Do you really want to start an argument tonight?'

She glanced at him in alarm. 'Would it? Start an argument, I mean?'

'Without a doubt.' He pinched out the remaining few candles, leaving them in semi-darkness, the night enclosing them in a cloak of intimacy. 'I have a wedding-gift for you.' He picked up a small package tucked among a basket of flowers and handed it to her.

She took it, staring in wonder. 'A wedding-gift?'

'Open it.'

Carefully, she ripped the paper from the jewelry box and removed the lid. Beneath a layer of cotton lay an odd blue stone with a thin gold band wrapped around it, securing it to a delicate herringbone chain. 'It's just like yours!' she exclaimed, tears starting to her eyes.

The only identifying article left with Hunter at the orphanage had been the strange gold-encased stone identical to the one he'd duplicated for a wedding-present. He'd worn it like a talisman all the time she'd known him, though he'd never been able to trace its origin successfully.

'I thought a gold chain a better choice than the leather thong I use.'

'Thank you. It's beautiful.' She handed him the box and turned her back to him. 'Will you put it on?' She lifted her hair and veil out of the way while he fastened the chain around her neck. The stone nestled between her breasts, cool and heavy against her skin.

Before she realized what he intended, Hunter turned her around and swung her into his arms. She clutched at his shoulders, her heart beating frantically, knowing that she couldn't delay the inevitable any longer. He strode across the entrance hall and climbed the stairs, booting open the door to the master bedroom.

She started to protest, but stopped when she saw the candles and flowers that festooned the room. At a guess, it was more of her grandmother's fine handiwork. This time, though, Leah approved. Giving them the master bedroom was Rose's tacit acknowledgement of Hunter's position in the household.

'Where's Rose's room?' he asked, as though reading her mind.

'Downstairs. She had a private wing built when my father married. She said the only smart way for an extended family to cohabit was to live apart.'

A reluctant smile touched his mouth. 'There may be hope for our relationship yet.'

He set her down, his smile fading, a dark, intense expression growing in his eyes. He removed the circlet from her brow and swept the veil from her hair. It floated to the floor, a gauzy slip of silver against the burgundy carpet.

He stepped back. 'Take off the dress. I don't want to rip it.'

Fumbling awkwardly with the belt links, she unfastened the chain at her waist and placed it among the flowers on the walnut bureau. She slipped off her heels, wondering why removing her shoes always made her feel small and vulnerable. Finally she gathered the hem of her gown and slowly lifted it to her waist.

The next instant she felt Hunter's hands beside her own, easing the dress over her head. He laid it across a chair and turned back to her. She stood in the center of the room, horribly self-conscious in the sheer wisps of silk and lace that were her only covering.

'Hunter,' she whispered. 'I don't think I'm ready for this.'

'Relax,' he murmured. 'There's no rush. We have all the time in the world.' He approached, wrapping her in his embrace. 'Remember how good it was between us?'

She clung to his jacket lapel. 'But we're not the same people any more. Our…our feelings have changed.'

'Some things never change. And this is one of them.' His eyes were so black, full of heat and hunger, his face, tight and drawn, reflecting his desire. He lifted her against him, tracing the length of her jaw with the edge of his thumb.

She shuddered beneath the delicate caress. He'd always been incredibly tender with her, a lover who combined a sensitive awareness of a woman's needs with a forceful passion that had made loving him an experience she'd never forgotten. It would be so easy to succumb, to be swept into believing he loved her still—a fantasy she found all too appealing.

'I can make it so good for you,' he said, his mouth drifting from her earlobe to the tiny pulse throbbing in her neck. 'Let me show you.' He found the clasp of her bra and unhooked it, sliding the silk from her body.

She closed her eyes, her breathing shallow and rapid. He didn't lie. She knew from experience that making love to him would be wonderful. It was the morning after that concerned her, when she'd have to face the knowledge that he'd come one step closer to achieving his goal—of winning both the ranch and her. His hand closed over her breast and her heart pounded beneath the warmth of his palm. For an endless instant she hung in the balance between conceding defeat and allowing her emotions free rein, or fighting for what mattered most. Because if she couldn't protect *herself* from his determined assault, how could she ever expect to protect the ranch and all those who depended on her?

She shifted within his grasp. 'It's too soon,' she protested in a low voice.

'We'll take it slow.' He traced her curves with a callused hand, scalding her with his touch. 'We can always stop.' But we won't want to. The words lay unvoiced between them, his thoughts as clear to her as if he'd spoken them aloud, and she shuddered.

Stepping back, he stripped off his jacket and tie. Ripping open the buttons of his shirt, he swept her into his arms and carried her to the petal-adorned bed. Once there he lowered her to the soft mattress and followed her down.

His fingers sank into her hair, filling his hands with long silvery curls. 'I've wanted to do this ever since I saw that picture of you,' he muttered.

She stirred uneasily. 'What picture?'

He tensed, and for a long moment neither of them moved. Her question had caught him unawares and she struggled to focus on it, to figure out why he'd reacted so strongly. He'd seen a recent picture of her. The knowledge was inescapable and she withdrew slightly, confused, questions hammering at her brain. Where and when had he seen the photo...in the study, perhaps? If so, why the strange reaction?

'The picture on your father's desk,' he explained quietly. 'It shows you with long hair.'

'It was shorter when you worked here.'

'Yeah, well. I like it long.'

But the mood had been broken and she rolled away from him, drawing her knees up against her chest. There was more to his idle comment than she had the strength or energy to analyze. 'Hunter,' she said in a low tone. 'I can't.'

'It's only natural to feel nervous,' he said in a cool voice, making no attempt to touch her.

'It's not just nerves.' She swept up the sheet, wrapping herself in its concealing folds. Shoving her hair back over her shoulders, she met his watchful gaze. 'You've gotten your way, Hunter. We're married and there's no going back. You said yourself that we have all the time in the world. Why rush this part of it and risk damaging our relationship?'

A muscle leapt in his jaw. 'You think making love will damage our relationship?'

She caught her lower lip between her lip and nodded. 'It will if we're not both ready for this. And, in all honesty, I'm not ready.'

'When will you be?' he asked bluntly.

She shrugged uneasily. 'I couldn't say.'

'Give it your best guess. I don't have an infinite amount of patience.'

'That's not what you told me five minutes ago,' she flashed back.

He clasped her shoulders, hauling her close. 'Five minutes ago you were as anxious as I to consummate this marriage. You want me every bit as much as I want you. I know it and you know it.'

'That's lust, not love. And lust isn't enough for me.' Aware of how much she'd inadvertently revealed, she fought free of his hold and scrambled off the bed. 'I...I just need a little bit of time, that's all. Can't you understand? Am I asking so much?'

He laughed harshly, running a hand through his hair. 'What will happen between us is inevitable. Tonight, tomorrow or the next night... What's the difference?'

She peeked at him through long lashes. 'Forty-eight hours,' she said with a hesitant smile. For a minute she didn't think he'd respond. Then he relaxed, his tension dissipating, and he nodded, though she sensed a strong undercurrent of anger just beneath his surface calm.

'Okay, Leah. I'll wait.' His gaze held a warning. 'Just don't push it. My tolerance has limits.'

'I'm well aware of that.' She backed toward the door. 'I'd like to change.'

'Don't be long.'

Striving for as much dignity as possible, considering that she kept tripping over the sheet, she left Hunter and hurried to her own room. There she stripped off her few remaining clothes. Pawing through her dresser drawers, she pulled out the most modest nightgown she possessed and tugged it on.

Covered from head to toe in yards and yards of baby-fine linen, she sat on the edge of the bed and nibbled on her fingertip. Had she made her situation better or worse? she wondered. She wasn't quite sure. Perhaps it would have been wiser to make love with him and be done with it, regardless of his motivations for marrying her. Only, in her heart of hearts, she knew it wouldn't truly be lovemaking, at least not on his part. It would be sex, pure and not so simple. Or, worse…it would be revenge.

She curled up on the bed, hugging a pillow to her chest. If only he cared. If only he loved her. Her hand closed around his wedding-gift, the talisman he'd so unexpectedly given her. His love would make all the difference in the world. But he no longer felt that way about her. And the sooner she accepted that, the better off she'd be.

But telling herself that didn't prevent a wistful tear from sliding down her cheek.

CHAPTER FIVE

LEAH stirred just as dawn broke the horizon. Confused by the unexpected weight pinning her legs to the mattress, she turned her head and found herself face to face with Hunter—a sleeping Hunter. It brought her fully awake. She risked a quick glance around, confirming her suspicions. So she hadn't dreamed it. She was back in the master bedroom.

Vaguely she remembered Hunter coming to her old room where she'd drifted off on top of the bed, a pillow clutched to her breast. He'd gently pried it free, and at her drowsy protest rasped, 'We sleep together, wife.' With that, he'd lifted her into his arms and carried her from the room. She hadn't fought. Instead, she'd wound her arms around his neck and snuggled against his chest as though she belonged, as though she never wanted to let go.

When he'd put her into his bed she'd been greeted by the sweet aroma of crushed flowers, followed by a stronger, muskier scent as Hunter had joined her on the mattress. All she recalled after that was a delicious warmth and peace invading her, body and soul, as he'd enclosed her in his embrace, wrapping her in a protective cocoon of strong arms and taut, muscular legs.

She glanced at him again, studying his imposing features with an acute curiosity. Even sleep couldn't blunt his tough, masculine edge, a night's growth of beard only serving to intensify the aura of danger and male aggression that clung to him like a second skin. The sheet skimmed his waist, baring his broad chest to her view, and she drank in the clean, powerful lines, wondered if he slept nude. Somehow she suspected that he did, though she didn't have the nerve to peek.

In all their times together, never had they been able to spend a night in each other's arms. Their joining had been passionate and earth-shattering and the most wondrous experience of her life. But it had also consisted of brief, stolen moments away from the suspicious eyes of her father and grandmother and the other ranch employees.

The irony of their current situation didn't escape her. Years ago she'd have given anything to spend a single night with him. To know, just once, the rapture of greeting the dawn safe and secure within his sheltering hold. Finally given her dearest wish, all she felt was apprehension and dismay—and an overwhelming desire to escape before he awoke.

Cautiously she slipped from his loose grasp and eased off the bed. Only then did she realize that some time during the early morning hours her nightgown had become trapped beneath him, and that he'd entwined her hair in his fingers as though, even in his sleep, he couldn't bear to let her go. Precious moments flew by as she untangled her hair and freed her gown. Gathering up the voluminous skirt, she tiptoed from the room.

A quick stop in the kitchen to grab an apple and a handful of sugar cubes, and she was outside and free. She raced across the dew-laden grass to the south pasture fence, the wind catching her hair and sweeping it into the air behind her like long, silver streamers. Whistling for Dreamseeker, she wondered if she'd ever tame such a wild and willful beast.

He came to her then, bursting across the pasture, a streak of jet against a cornflower-blue sky. Forming a deep pocket for the apple and sugar with the excess material of her nightgown, she awkwardly climbed the fence and sat on the top rail, the thin cotton affording little protection from the splintered wood beneath.

Dreamseeker joined her, snatching greedily at the apple she offered. Not satisfied, he butted her shoulder until she relented and gave him the sugar as well. He waited, muscles quivering, head cocked at an arrogant angle, allowing her to scratch and caress his gleaming coat. She crooned in delight, rubbing his withers, thrilled by his show of trust.

'What the *hell* are you doing?'

Leah didn't know who was more startled, she or Dreamseeker. Springing from her grasp, the horse shot away from the fence, leaving her teetering on the rail. With a cry of alarm, she tumbled to the ground at Hunter's feet, the hem of her gown snagging on a protruding nail. She tugged impatiently at it, the sound of ripping cloth making her wince.

She glared up at him, placing the blame where it belonged—square on his broad shoulders. 'Dammit, Hunter! This is all your fault. What do you mean, sneaking around like that?'

He folded his arms across his chest and lifted an eyebrow. 'Sneaking?'

'Yes, sneaking. You scared Dreamseeker and you scared me.' She shook out her nightgown, lifting the dew-soaked hem clear of the grass. Peering over her shoulder, she searched for the source of the ripping sound. Finding it, she muttered in disgust, 'Just look at the size of that hole.'

'I'm looking.'

The hint of amusement in his voice brought her head around with a jerk. His eyes weren't on the tear but on her. Realization came swiftly. With the sun at her back, the thin cotton she wore might as well have been transparent. And Hunter, his thumbs once again thrust in his belt-loops, was enjoying every minute of the show.

'There are times, Hunter Pryde, when I think I hate you,' she declared vehemently. With that, she grabbed a fistful of skirt, lifted her nightgown to her knees and lit off across the pastureland. She didn't get far.

In two swift strides he overtook her, and swept her clean off her feet. 'Hate me all you want, wife. It won't change a damned thing. The sooner you realize that, the better off you'll be.'

She shrieked in fury, lashing out at him, hampered by yards of damp cotton. Her hair, seeming to have acquired a life of its own, further hindered her efforts, wrapping around her arms and torso in a tangle of unruly silver curls. She stopped struggling, battering him with words instead. 'You don't fool me. You may have married me because it was the only way to get your hands on the ranch, but that doesn't mean you've won. I'll never give in.'

'Won't you?' A hint of sardonic amusement touched his aquiline features. 'We'll see.'

She had to convince him. She had to convince herself. 'You won't win, Hunter. I won't let you!'

'So much passion. So much energy,' he murmured, his arms tightening around her. 'And all of it wasted out here. Why don't we take it inside where we can put it to good use?'

She stiffened, quick to catch his meaning, quicker still to voice her objections. 'You promised. You promised to wait until I was ready. And I'm not ready.'

'No?' His mouth twisted, and a cynical gleam sparked in his jet-black eyes. 'Listen up, wife. It wouldn't take much for me to break that promise. And when I do, count on it, you won't complain for long.'

Without another word he carried her inside. In the front hallway he dumped her on to her feet, forcing her to cling to him while she regained her balance. His biceps were like rock beneath her hands, the breadth of his chest and shoulders an impenetrable wall between her and escape.

'Hunter, let me go,' she whispered, the words an aching plea. She didn't dare look him in the eye, didn't dare see the passion that she knew marked his strong, determined features. If she did, she'd never make it up those steps alone.

'Not a chance.' Then he further destroyed her equilibrium with a single hard, fiery kiss. At last he released her, and she stared at him with wide, anguished eyes. She didn't want him touching her, kissing her, forcing her back to life. She didn't want to feel, to experience anew the pain loving him would bring.

But she suspected that he didn't care what she wanted, or how much he hurt her. He had his own agenda. And she was low on his list of priorities—a minor detail he'd address when he found it convenient.

He snagged the bodice of her nightgown with his finger and tugged her close. 'I warned you last night. I won't wait forever. I catch you running around like this ever again and I won't be responsible for my actions. You hear me?'

She wrenched the gown from his grasp, but all she got for her trouble was a ripped shoulder seam. She gritted her teeth. 'Don't worry,' she muttered, clutching the drooping neckline with one hand and lifting the trailing hem with the other. 'I'm throwing this one out as soon as I get upstairs.'

His mouth curved at the corners, and he plucked a

crushed flower petal from her tangled hair. 'Feel free to trash any others while you're at it. They won't be of much use to you...not for long.' Before she could give vent to her outrage, he instructed, 'Hurry up and get dressed. I'm going to inspect the ranch this morning. I leave in five minutes—with you...or without you.'

Leah didn't lose any time changing. Throwing on jeans and a T-shirt, she stuffed her feet into boots. Securing her hair into one long braid, she grabbed a hat from her bedpost and raced downstairs. At some point she'd have to move her things into the bedroom she now shared with Hunter. But there would be plenty of opportunity for that. Weeks. Months. She bit down on her lip. *Years.*

She found Hunter in the barn, saddling the horses. He passed her a paper sack. 'Here. Thought you might be hungry.'

'Thanks. I am.' Peeking inside, she found a half-dozen of Inez's cinnamon and apple muffins. 'I don't suppose you thought to bring coffee.'

'Thermos is in my saddlebag. Help yourself.' He tightened the cinch on his buckskin and glanced at her. 'I moved that Appaloosa mare with the pulled tendon to another stall. There's a leak at that end of the barn. Looks like we'll need a new roof.'

She bit into a muffin. 'I'll have Patrick and a couple of the men patch it,' she said, taking a quick gulp of coffee.

'No.' He yanked the brim of his hat lower on his forehead. 'I said the barn needs a new roof.'

She sighed, capping the Thermos and shoving it and the sack of muffins back into his saddlebag. 'This is one of those marital tests, isn't it?'

'Come again?'

'You know. A test. You say we need a new roof. I say no we don't. You say, I'm the boss and we're getting a new roof. And I say, but we can't afford a roof. And you say, well, we're getting one anyway, even if we have to eat dirt for the next month to pay for it. And if I say anything further you start reminding me that before we married I promised this and I agreed to that, and that you're the boss and what you say goes. Does that about sum up what's happening here?'

He nodded, amusement lightening his expression. 'That about sums it up. Glad to see you catch on so fast.' He tossed her a bright yellow slicker. 'Here. Take this. Forecast calls for rain.'

'Hunter, we really can't afford a new roof.' She rolled the slicker and tied it to the back of her saddle. 'If we could, I'd have stuck one on last spring, or the spring before that, or even the spring before that.'

'We're getting a new roof.' He mounted. 'Though if it eases your mind any you won't have to eat dirt for the next month to pay for it.'

After a momentary hesitation she followed suit and climbed into the saddle. 'I won't?'

'Nope. Just for the next week.' He clicked his tongue, urging his horse into an easy trot.

They spent the morning investigating the eastern portion of the Hampton spread and Leah began to see the ranch through Hunter's eyes. And what she saw didn't please her. Signs of neglect were everywhere. Fence-lines sagged. Line-shacks had fallen into disrepair. A few of the cattle showed evidence of screw-worm and the majority of the calves they came across hadn't been branded or vaccinated.

At the south-eastern tip of the range Hunter stopped by a small stream and dismounted. 'What the hell have your men been doing, Leah?' he asked, disgust heavy in his voice. 'There's no excuse for the condition of this place.'

'Money's been tight,' she protested defensively. 'We don't have a large work crew.'

'I've got news for you. You don't have a work crew, period. Leastwise they don't seem to be working worth a damn.'

'A lot of what we've seen isn't their fault, but mine,' she claimed, evading his searching stare. 'I haven't had the time recently to stay on top of everything.'

Hunter shook his head. 'Not good enough, Leah. Any foreman worth his salt would have caught most of these problems for you.'

'You told me you wouldn't fire anyone until they'd had an opportunity to prove themselves,' she said, taking a different tack. 'I know things look bad, but give us a chance. Tell us what you want done and we'll do it.'

He stripped off his gloves and tucked them in his belt. 'What I want is for you to get off that horse and sit down and discuss the situation with me. One way or another we're going to come to a meeting of the minds, and I can't think of a better time or place than right here and now.'

Still she resisted. 'If we sit under that pecan tree, we'll get ticks.'

He took off his hat and slapped the dust from the brim. 'Did you last time?'

So he did remember this spot. She'd wondered if his stopping here had been coincidental or deliberate. Now she knew. She closed her eyes. How much longer would she have to pay? she wondered in despair. When would it be enough? 'I might have found a tick or two,' she finally admitted.

'Then I'll look you over tonight,' he offered. 'Just to be on the safe side.'

'Thanks all the same,' she said drily. 'But I'll pass.'

He held out a hand. 'Let's go, Leah. I didn't bring you here to go skinny-dipping again. I brought you here to talk. We'll save a return trip down memory lane for another visit.'

Reluctantly, she dismounted. 'What do you want to discuss?'

'The repairs we need to make and your employees,' he stated succinctly.

'I vote we start with the repairs,' she said. 'Have you gotten the loan? Is that why you plan to replace the barn roof?'

'And fix up the line-shacks, and restring fence-line and increase the size of the herd. Yes, the loan's taken care of, and we have enough money to put the ranch back on its feet. But it isn't just lack of repairs that contribute to a ranch going downhill.'

She sank to the grass with a grimace, shifting to one side so he could join her. 'Time to discuss the employees?'

'Time to discuss the employees. I made a point of meeting most of them before we married.'

She gave him a direct look. 'Then you know why I hired them.'

'Leah—'

'Don't say another thing, Hunter! For once you're going to listen and I'm going to talk.' She fought to find the words to convince him, desperate to protect her workers. 'Not a single one of my employees has been able to find jobs anywhere else. The Arroyas were living out of a station wagon when I found them. Lenny's a veteran who doesn't care to sit around collecting government handouts. And

Patrick risked his own life to save a child about to be run down by a drunk driver. He shattered his ankle doing it. A week later he got a pink slip because Lyon Enterprises didn't want to be bothered with an employee who might not be able to pull his own weight.'

Hunter shot her a sharp glance. 'He worked for Lyon Enterprises?'

'He used to be foreman of the Circle P. Bull Jones replaced him.'

'And you took Patrick in.'

'I've given them all a home,' she acknowledged. 'I've given them a life. And, as a result, they earn a living. More importantly, they've regained their self-respect. So their work isn't always perfect. I can assure you that it's the best they're capable of doing. But if you ask for more they'll do everything in their power to give it to you. That's how much working here means to them. They're family. Don't ask me to turn my back on family, because I can't do it.'

He stared out across the pastureland. 'You always were a sucker for an underdog. I often thought that was what attracted you to me.'

'That's not true.' She stopped, afraid of revealing too much. She'd never seen him as an underdog. A champion, a man of drive and determination, someone filled with an intense passion and strength. But not once had she ever seen him as an underdog.

His mouth tightened, as though he'd mistakenly allowed her to get too close—revealed too much of himself. 'That still doesn't change the facts. And the facts are that you can't run a ranch without competent help.'

'Hunter,' she pleaded. 'Give them a fair chance. No more, no less. I swear I won't ask you for anything else.'

His expression turned skeptical. 'Won't you?'

'No. I won't. Because saving the ranch isn't worth it to me if I can't save them as well.'

That caught his attention. 'You'd give up the ranch if it came to a choice between running at a profit or replacing the help?'

She considered his question at length, a frown creasing her brow. 'I suspect I would,' she admitted at last. 'Because otherwise I'd be no better than Lyon Enterprises. And if I wanted to be like them, I'd have sold out long ago.'

'You're that serious about it?'

She nodded. 'I'm that serious.'

It was his turn to consider. Slowly he nodded. 'Okay. We'll do it your way. For now. But I can't make any guarantees about the future. Will that do?'

'I guess it'll have to,' she said with a shrug.

'Why don't we swing south next, and inspect that side of the ranch? Then we'll call it a day.'

'I'm ready,' she claimed, happy to agree now that she'd been granted a reprieve. 'Let's go.'

He shook his head. 'Not yet. There's just one more thing I want before we head out. And I want it from you.'

'What?' she asked warily, his tone warning her that she wouldn't like his request.

'I want you to kiss me.'

'What?' she repeated in a fainter voice.

'You heard me. I want a kiss. I'm willing to wait until you're ready before we go any further, but there's no reason we can't enjoy a preview of coming attractions.' He held her with a searing gaze. 'Come on, Leah. It's not a lot to ask.'

It wasn't, and she knew it. Not giving herself a chance to reconsider, she leaned closer, resting her hands on his chest. She stared up at him, at the features that were almost as familiar as her own. The changes time had wrought were few, more of a strengthening, a fulfillment of what was once a promise. The lines furrowing his brow and radiating from the corners of his eyes reflected a deepening of character that had come with age and experience.

Tenderly she cupped his face, exploring anew the taut, high-boned planes of his cheeks. It had been so long, so very long. Slowly, she allowed her fingers to sink into his thick black hair and, tilting her head just slightly, she feathered a soft, teasing kiss across his mouth. She half expected him to grab her, to crush her in his arms and take what he so clearly wanted. But he didn't. He remained perfectly still, allowing her to set the pace.

She continued to tease, dropping tiny kisses across his jaw and neck before returning to explore his lips. And then she kissed him, really kissed him, the way a woman kissed her man. And for the first time he responded, not with his hands and arms, but with his mouth alone, returning her urgent, eager caresses with a mind-drugging thoroughness that left her shaken and defenseless. He had to know how she felt—had to be aware of how much she gave away with that kiss, how her protective barrier lay in total ruin. At long last his arms closed around her, enfolding her in the sweetest of embraces, and she knew in that moment that she'd willingly give him anything he asked.

How much time passed, Leah wasn't sure. One minute she existed in a sensual haze, secure in his arms, the next Hunter thrust her from him, tumbling her to the ground. In a move so swift that she barely registered it he spun around, crouching protectively in front of her. To her horror, a wickedly curved knife appeared in his hand.

'You're trespassing, Jones. What's your business here?' Hunter demanded.

It wasn't until then that Leah noticed the foreman of the Circle P, mounted on a bay, not more than fifteen feet away. She hadn't heard his approach. But Hunter had.

'Tell your guard-dog to drop the knife, Leah,' Bull Jones called, his gaze riveted to the glinting length of steel in Hunter's hand. 'Or I'll have to get serious with some buckshot.' His hand inched toward his rifle. 'You *comprende* what I'm saying, *hombre*? You have no business threatening me. I'd only be defending myself if I was forced to shoot.'

The expression in Hunter's eyes burned with unmistakable menace. 'You'll feel the hurting end of this blade long before that Remington clears your scabbard. You *comprende* me, *muchacho*? Play it smart. Ride out now.'

For a minute Leah feared that Bull would pull his gun. His hand wavered over the rifle butt for an endless moment, before settling on his thigh. 'Since you're new to the Hampton spread I'll cut you some slack,' he addressed Hunter. 'But nobody threatens me. Ever. Somebody'd better explain that to you pronto, because next time I won't let you off so easy.'

'Last warning.' The blade quivered in Hunter's hand. 'Ride. Now.'

'You'll regret this, Leah,' Bull hollered. Swearing beneath his breath, he sawed at his mount's bit and rode off.

'Oh, God,' Leah moaned, and she began to tremble. In one supple move, Hunter sheathed his knife in his boot and pulled her into his arms.

'It's okay,' he murmured against the top of her head. 'He's gone.'

She clung to him, unable to stop shaking, reaction setting in fast and hard. He didn't release her, just stood silently, enveloping her in a tight, inviolable hold. Yet she'd have had him hold her closer if she thought her ribs would stand the strain. Slowly the warmth of his body and the strength of his arms calmed her, soothing her terror.

'He could have shot you,' she whispered, fighting to hold back her tears.

He tucked a strand of hair behind her ear. 'Not a chance. I had him dead to rights and he knew it.' His mouth brushed her cheek, her jaw, her lips. 'It's over, Leah. He's gone.'

She melted against him, needing his touch more desperately than she'd ever needed anything before in her life. As though sensing it, he kissed her. But it wasn't like the passionate embrace they'd shared earlier. This caress was so gentle and tender that it nearly broke her heart.

'He frightens me, Hunter,' she confessed in a low voice.

He glanced at the thin cloud of dust disappearing to the south. 'Tell me about him.' It was an order.

She fought to gather her thoughts enough to give him a coherent answer. 'I've told you most of it. Although I can't prove anything, I suspect he's responsible for our fence-lines being cut. We've had a couple of suspicious stampedes and one or two of the wells have been fouled.' She shrugged. 'That sort of thing.'

'He's the reason this place is so neglected.' It wasn't a question. 'You don't ride out here alone, do you? That's why you haven't seen the problems until now.'

She bowed her head. 'I don't let the others come either,' she admitted. 'Unless they're in a group. I've been terrified of something happening.'

'Have you reported any of this to Lyon Enterprises?'

She flashed him a bitter glare. 'Who do you think he's getting his instructions from?'

'Do you know that for a fact?'

She whirled free of his arms, anger replacing her fear. 'I

don't know anything for a fact. If I did, Bull Jones would be in jail and I'd have a nice, fat lawsuit pending against Lyon Enterprises. You married me to get your hands on this ranch, didn't you? If you want to keep it, you're going to have to defend it. Otherwise we both lose.'

Hunter bent down and retrieved his hat. 'Mount up.'

She stared in disbelief. 'Now? Just like that? End of discussion?'

'I want to check the south pasture before dark.'

'That's the direction Bull took. What if we run into him again?' she asked nervously.

The brim of his hat threw Hunter's face into shadow, making his expression unreadable. 'Then I'll make a point of introducing myself.'

She clung to him, checking his move toward his horse. 'Please, Hunter. Can't we go home? We can check the south pasture tomorrow. There's no point in looking for trouble.'

A humorless smile cut across his face. 'You've got it backward. Seems trouble has come looking for us.' For a minute she thought he'd insist they explore the south pasture. But at long last he nodded. 'Okay. I've seen enough. But tomorrow I ride south.' And with that she had to be satisfied.

In the study, Hunter lifted the phone receiver and stared at it for a long minute before punching in a series of numbers. After several clicks the call was connected.

'Kevin Anderson.'

'It's Hunter. Give me an update.' He listened to the lengthy recitation with a frown and jotted down a few notes. 'Okay. Don't do anything for now. We don't want to tip our hand. The rest can wait until I come in.'

'Any problems at your end?' Kevin asked.

'You might say that.' Hunter poured himself a shot of whiskey, and downed it in a single swallow. 'I had another run-in with Bull Jones.'

Alarm sounded in Kevin's voice. 'Does he know who you are yet?'

'Not yet. Our marriage has been kept pretty much under wraps. Not a lot of people know. But Jones could be a problem once he finds out—depending on how much talking he decides to do.'

'What do you want me to do?'

'Send me his file. Overnight it.'

'Will do. Then what? You want him...out of the picture?'

Hunter thought about it, rubbing a weary hand across the back of his neck. 'No. Don't do anything for now. We act too soon and it'll give the whole game away.'

'Whatever you say. You're the boss.'

'Thanks, Kevin.'

Hanging up, Hunter poured a final shot of whiskey and stared at the ceiling. Time to bed down with his beautiful bride. Time to pull that soft, sweet piece of feminine delight into his arms and...sleep. He downed the liquor, praying that it would numb him—at least the parts in dire need of numbing. Patience. He only needed a little more patience. And then that soft, sweet piece of feminine delight would be all his.

CHAPTER SIX

LEAH slipped from Hunter's arms at the crack of dawn the next morning. This time she kept yesterday's warning firmly in mind, and dressed before going to the kitchen for an apple. Running to the south pasture fence, she whistled for her stallion. But instead of the horse all she found was a white-tailed deer and a family of jackrabbits who, startled by her sudden appearance, burst across the grassland and disappeared from view. She climbed on to the top rail and waited for a while, but Dreamseeker proved surprisingly elusive.

Concluding that she'd been stood up in favor of a patch of fresh clover, she bit into the apple. Then she watched as the sun gathered strength, spreading its warm April rays across a nearby field splattered with the vivid purple of bluebonnets and neon-orange of Indian paintbrush. Without question this had to be her favorite time of the day—as well as her favorite season of the year.

A twig snapped behind her. 'Beautiful, isn't it?' she asked in a conversational tone of voice.

'Yes.' Hunter folded his arms across the top rail and glanced at her. 'No accusations of sneaking up on you this morning?'

'You banged the kitchen door.'

'And stomped across the yard.'

A tiny grin touched her mouth. 'I almost turned around to look, but you were being so considerate that I didn't want to spoil it.'

'I appreciate your restraint,' he said, with a touch of wry humor. 'Your horse hasn't shown up yet?'

She frowned, tossing her apple core into the meadow. 'He didn't answer my whistle. But if we're exploring the south pasture we're bound to come across him. Ready to go?' She vaulted off the fence, wanting to get Hunter's inspection tour over and done with. Perhaps if they made an early start they'd avoid Bull Jones.

'No. I'm not ready.' He caught her arm, tugging her to a standstill. 'Not quite yet.'

'Why?' she asked in apprehension. 'Is there something wrong?'

'You might say that.' His hold lightened, though he didn't release her. 'You were gone again this morning.'

She bridled at the hint of censure in his voice. She'd agreed to sleep with him without too much argument; surely he didn't intend to choose which hours that would encompass. If so, he'd soon learn differently. 'Is that a problem?'

'Yes. I don't like it. Tomorrow you start the day in my arms.'

She eased from his grip and a took a quick step back, something in his expression filling her with a discomfiting awareness. 'What difference does it make if I'm there or not?' she asked.

Her question seemed to amuse him. 'If you wake me tomorrow, you'll learn the difference.'

She didn't doubt it for a minute. But that didn't mean she'd go along. 'I'll consider it,' she conceded. 'But I like having mornings to myself.'

'You'll have other times to yourself,' he informed her. 'I want time alone with you. All marriages need privacy...intimacy.'

Understanding dawned and she fought to breathe normally. So the moment of truth had finally arrived. If she read his request correctly, tomorrow morning she'd fulfill her duties as his wife and make their marriage a real, fully functioning union—no matter how much she wanted to resist. No matter how much that final act alarmed her. That was what she'd committed herself to when they'd exchanged their vows, and that was what she'd soon have to face. If only the thought didn't fill her with dread—dread that she'd couldn't keep a small part of herself safe from his possession; dread that when he took her body he'd take her heart as well.

'All right,' she said at last. 'Mornings can be our time.'

He inclined his head. 'We'll discuss the afternoons and evenings later.'

'Hunter—'

'Time to get to work.' He cut her off, amusement gleaming in his dark eyes. 'Are there any more of those muffins we had yesterday?'

'Plenty,' she admitted grudgingly. 'Inez left us well-stocked. I'll go get them.'

'And a Thermos of coffee, if you would. I'll saddle the horses.'

Fifteen minutes later they rode out, heading south along the fence-line. Hunter's buckskin seemed particularly agitated, fighting the bit and shying at the least little movement. Not that he had any trouble controlling the animal, but Leah could tell that their battle of wills wasn't the norm. As though in response, her mare fidgeted as well.

'Is it something in the air?' she asked uneasily. 'Lady-finger never acts up like this.'

'Something has them spooked,' he agreed. 'Have your men noticed any sign of cougar recently?'

'None.' She felt a sudden stabbing concern for Dreamseeker. 'It wasn't that hard a winter. There's no reason for one to come this close when the pickings are so easy further out.' But she knew her protests were more to convince herself than to convince him.

'Don't panic. I didn't say it was a cougar. I just thought we should consider the possibility.' He regarded her intently. 'I want you to stay alert, you got me? In the meantime, we have fence-line to inspect. So, let's get to it.'

They didn't converse much after that. Leah kept an eye open for anything out of the ordinary. And, though the animals remained skittish, she couldn't determine what caused their strange behavior.

A short time later Hunter stopped to examine a drooping length of barbed wire. 'This next section abuts Lyon Enterprises' property, doesn't it?' he asked, clearly annoyed with the condition of the fence.

'From here onward,' she confirmed.

'You're just asking for trouble, letting it fall into such a state of disrepair. One good shove and you'll have a week's worth of work combing Circle P hills for your herd. It gets top priority come Monday morning.'

'What about Bull Jones?' she asked uneasily.

A muscle tightened in his jaw. 'You let me worry about him. I don't expect it'll take long to reach an understanding.'

By noon they'd almost finished their inspection. Riding over a low hill, they suddenly discovered the reason for their horses' agitation. The fence between the two ranches lay on the ground. And down a steep grade, on Lyon property, grazed Dreamseeker...with the Circle P mare he'd corralled.

Hunter reined to a stop and shot Leah a sharp look. 'He's a stallion? That horse you were with yesterday morning?'

She glanced at him in surprise. 'Didn't you notice?'

'No, I didn't notice,' came the blunt retort. 'Because it wasn't the damned horse that caught my eye.'

Then what...? Realization swiftly dawned, and color mounted her cheeks. Not what. Who. He'd been distracted by her...and the fact that she'd only been wearing a night-gown. Well, she couldn't help that. Nor did it change anything. 'I don't see what difference it makes whether or not he's a stallion—'

'There's a big difference,' he cut her off. 'Not many geldings I know are going to bust through a fence to get to a mare in heat. But you can count on a stallion doing it every time.' He shoved his hat to the back of his head, apparently debating his options.

Leah didn't show any such hesitation. As far as she was concerned, only one option existed. Without giving thought to the consequences, she charged across the smashed fence and started after her stallion. Or she would have, if Hunter hadn't been quite so quick. He spurred his horse into action and blocked her path.

'What the hell do you think you're doing?' he shouted, grabbing her horse's bridle and jerking her to a stop.

As much as she wanted to fight his hold, she didn't dare risk injuring Ladyfinger's delicate mouth. 'What does it look like I'm doing?' she flashed back. 'I'm getting my horse. Let go, Hunter. We don't have much time.'

He stared in disbelief. 'You can't be serious.'

'I'm very serious.' Responding to her agitation, Ladyfinger attempted to rear, but a soft word and a gentle hand brought her under control. Leah spoke urgently. 'If Bull Jones finds Dreamseeker on his property, he'll shoot first and ask questions later. I have to get my horse out of there before that happens.' She gathered up the reins, prepared to rip free at the first opportunity.

As though he sensed her intentions, his hold tightened on Ladyfinger's bridle, preventing any sudden movement on her part. 'You try and rope that animal and he'll kill you—which won't matter because I'll have killed you long before he has the chance.'

'Hunter,' she interrupted, prepared to dismount and go after Dreamseeker on foot, 'we're wasting precious time.'

'Tough. You have two choices,' he informed her. 'You can keep fighting me in which case that stallion will stay down there until hell freezes over. Or...'

'Or?' she prompted impatiently.

'Or you can do exactly what I say and we might get him out of there. But I'm telling you, Leah. You ever do anything as stupid as coming between a stallion and his mare and I won't be responsible for my actions.'

'Not responsible...' Anger flared and she made no attempt to curb it. 'That's what you said about my running around in my nightgown! That's a pretty broad range you've got going there. Maybe you'd better tell me what other actions alleviate you of your responsibilities. Just so there won't be any doubt in my mind.'

'Believe me, the second you commit one, you'll be the first to know.'

She didn't miss the implication. He'd let her know in his own distinctive manner—and chances were excellent that it would involve another of those mind-splintering kisses. She opened her mouth to argue, and was instantly cut off.

'Well? What's it going to be? My way or no way.'

More than anything she wanted to tell him to go to hell. But one quick glance at Dreamseeker and she knew she didn't have any other choice. 'Your way,' she gave in grudgingly. 'How hard will it be to get him back?'

'That depends on how long he's been down there with that mare. With any luck it's been all morning, and he's expended most of his...enthusiasm.'

She eyed the seemingly placid animal. 'By the look of him I'd say he's expended plenty of enthusiasm.'

Hunter didn't appear as certain. 'We'll see. Tie Ladyfinger out of the way and stand by the fence. I'm going to rope the mare and try and bring her across. Dreamseeker will give chase. The second they're both on our property, you get that fence-line back up. If anything goes wrong, stand clear and *don't interfere.*' Serious dark eyes held her with an implacable gaze. 'Got it?'

'Got it.' Following his instructions, she tied her horse out of the way and stuck her fence tool and staples into her utility belt. Pulling on work-gloves, she took up a stance by the downed lines and gave him a nod. 'Ready when you are.'

Jamming his hat low on his brow, he released his rope and slowly rode down the hill. He waited near the bottom. Not wanting to arouse Dreamseeker's territorial instincts, he kept his distance from the mare, and though Leah could barely contain her impatience she knew that Hunter hoped the stallion would make things easy and move off a ways, allowing for a clear shot at the mare. Everything considered, the throw would be a difficult one.

Ten long minutes ticked by before an opportunity presented itself. Gently, he swung the rope overhead and tossed. Leah held her breath as it soared through the air...and landed directly on target. With a swiftness born of both experience and a strong desire to get the deed done before Dreamseeker caught wind of his intentions, Hunter dallied the rope around the horn and began to pull the mare up the hill.

The trapped animal fought him, rearing and pawing the air. Dragging a horse in the exact opposite direction from where she wanted to go was bad enough, but having to do it up a hill made it near impossible. Leah could hear Hunter swearing beneath his breath, the sound of his saddle creaking and his horse blowing carrying to her as they inched their way toward Hampton property.

About halfway up the hill Dreamseeker suddenly realized what they were about. With a shriek of outrage, the stallion gave chase. Hunter's buckskin didn't need any more encouragement than that. The sight of seventeen hundred pounds of rampaging stallion barreling straight for them apparently inspired the gelding to redouble his efforts. Even the mare seemed to lose her reluctance.

All too quickly Dreamseeker reached them. Instead of attacking Hunter, the stallion nipped at the mare, who stopped fighting the rope and abruptly changed direction, charging up the hill, the stallion on her heels. It was all Hunter could do to get out of the way.

'Leah, stand clear!' he shouted.

Intent on regaining his own territory, Dreamseeker drove the frightened mare before him up the hill and on to Hampton property. As the horses stormed past Hunter released the rope and followed close behind.

'Get that fence up fast, before he changes his mind,' Hunter bellowed over his shoulder, positioning himself between Leah and the threatening stallion. An agitated Dreamseeker milled nearby, clearly uncertain whether to challenge the intruders or escape with his prize. Hunter tensed, prepared for either eventuality.

Not wasting a single second, Leah slammed staples into

the post, securing the barbed wire. Not that it would stop
Dreamseeker if he decided to head back to the Circle P.
But maybe now that he'd successfully captured a mare and
returned to his own domain he'd be less inclined to break
through again. She cast an uneasy glance at her horse. At
least, he wouldn't break through unless there were more
mares to be had.

With a shrill whinny, Dreamseeker finally chose to retreat. Racing away from them, he hustled the mare toward
the far side of the pasture. Assured that the danger had
passed, Hunter climbed off his buckskin and tied him to
the fence.

'Where's Ladyfinger?' he asked, freeing his fence tool
from its holster.

She spared him a quick look. 'Broke the reins and took
off. I guess she figured that Dreamseeker meant business
and didn't want to get between him and whatever that business might be.'

He made a sound of impatience. 'You'll have to ride with
me. Once we're done here, we'll head on in.'

'Right.' She didn't dare say more, not until he'd had a
chance to cool off. He joined her at the fence, helping to
string wire and reinforce the posts. They worked side by
side for several minutes before Leah thought to ask, 'What
do we do about that mare?'

'We aren't going to do anything. When she isn't such a
bone of contention I'll cut her loose and return her to the
Circle P.'

Leah paused in her efforts. 'What about Bull Jones?'

To her surprise a slight smile touched Hunter's mouth.
'I'll send him a bill for stud service.' He strung the final
line of wire and glanced at her. 'Is that stallion saddle-
broken?'

She shook her head. 'Not yet, but—'

'He's wild?' Hunter didn't wait for her confirmation. 'He goes.'

She straightened, wiping perspiration from her brow. 'You can't be serious!'

'I'm dead serious. He's dangerous and I won't risk your safety on a dangerous animal.'

'Then you'll have to get rid of the bulls, the cows and every other critter around here,' she retorted in exasperation. 'Because in the right circumstances any one of them could be considered dangerous, too.'

'I'm not changing my mind,' he stated unequivocally, stamping the ground around a listing post.

How could she explain Dreamseeker's importance? Hunter would never understand. She wasn't sure she understood. All she knew was that the stallion touched a need, fulfilled a fantasy of being unfettered and without responsibilities. Though part of her hoped some day to tame the wild beast, another part longed to allow the stallion his freedom—just as she longed to experience a similar freedom. It was an unrealistic dream, but she didn't care.

Looking Hunter straight in the eye, Leah said, 'Don't do it. Please don't get rid of him. He means the world to me.'

His expression turned grim and remote. 'Another hard luck case?'

'In a way,' she admitted. 'I took him in when others might have put him down. I suspect he's been abused in the past, which would explain his skittishness.'

Hunter leaned his forearms across the post, his plaid shirt pulled tight across his broad chest. A fine sheen of perspiration glinted in the hollow of his throat, and his thick ebony hair clung to his brow—a brow furrowed in displeasure. 'You're doing a poor job persuading me to let him stay. If anything, you've convinced me he's too dangerous. Besides, you used up all your favors yesterday, remember?'

'I remember.' Having him give her employees a chance was still more important to her than any other considera- tion—even saving Dreamseeker. 'I'm not asking for an- other favor. I promised I wouldn't, and I won't.' She of- fered a crooked smile. 'But I'm willing to compromise.'

'You're pushing it.'

She nodded. 'I know. But it's important to me.'

He frowned, and she could sense his struggle between what common sense told him to do and granting her plea. Finally he nodded. 'One month. If I can break him, or at least put some manners on him, he can stay. But you keep clear in the meantime. Agreed?'

Her smile widened. 'Agreed.'

'That's the last time, Leah,' he warned. 'You've pushed me to the limit. Now, mount up.'

'My horse...?' she reminded him.

'I haven't forgotten. We'll ride double.'

He crossed to his buckskin and untied the reins from the fence. Looking from Hunter to the horse, Leah caught her breath in dismay. With her clinging to his back like a lim- pet, dipping and swaying, rubbing and bumping all the way to the ranch, it would be a long ride home. She shivered.

Real long.

Leah began to ease from the bed the next day, as she had each of the other two mornings, but then remembered her promise to stay. With a tiny sigh she lay down again, and yanked the sheet to her chin. Instantly Hunter caught hold of her, ripped the sheet free and tumbled her into a warm embrace.

'Good morning, wife,' he muttered close to her ear.

'Good morning,' she responded cautiously, waiting for him to pounce, to force himself on her. Considering her forty-eight-hour deadline had expired last night, he'd be well within his rights. Instead he enclosed her hair in a possessive fist and, dropping an arm across her waist, shut his eyes. His breathing deepened and she frowned. 'The sun's up,' she prompted, fighting nervous anticipation.

'Uh-huh.'

He nuzzled her cheek and she drew back. 'This is our time together, remember?'

'I remember.'

'Well?' She could hear the strain in her voice, but couldn't help it. She wanted to get whatever he had planned over and done with. 'You said this time together would make a difference. The only difference I've noticed is that I'm late starting my chores.'

He sighed, opening one eye. 'The chores can wait. Relax. You're stiff as a board.' He slid an arm around her hips and tucked her back against his chest, spoon-fashion. Resting his chin on top of her head, he said, 'Now just relax and talk to me.'

'Talk.' This wasn't quite what she'd expected when he'd made his demand. She'd suspected that he intended to…to do a whole lot more than talk. 'What should I talk about?'

'Anything. Everything. Whatever comes to mind.'

'Okay,' she agreed, knowing she sounded stilted and uncomfortable. 'What are your plans for this morning?'

'I'll start by working with Dreamseeker.'

'And…and the fence-line? The one that runs alongside of the Circle P?'

'It gets fixed today.'

'You'll be careful?' She hesitated to mention her fears, but couldn't help herself. 'I don't trust Bull.'

'I'll take care of it.'

'It's just—' He brushed a length of hair from her brow and she realized that at some point during their conversation she'd rolled over to face him. And with the realization her words died away, and her earlier nervousness returned.

He noticed. She suspected that his sharp, black-eyed gaze noticed everything. Gently, he cupped her cheek, his callused thumb stroking the corner of her mouth. 'I'll take care of it,' he repeated, and kissed her warmly, deeply, sparking an instant response.

She didn't reply—couldn't, in fact. He seemed to sense that, for he pressed his advantage, his kiss becoming more intense, more urgent. Sensing her capitulation, he pressed her into the mattress. Instantly her body reacted, softening as his hardened, moving in concert with his, shifting to accommodate his size and weight.

Her nightgown provided no barrier at all. He unbuttoned the small pearl buttons that ran from neck to waist and swept the cotton from her shoulders. Drawing back, he gazed down at her, the early morning light playing across the taut, drawn lines of his face. Kneeling above her, he seemed like some bold conqueror of old, a bronzed warrior poised to take what he willed, and giving no quarter. Slowly, he reached for her, his black eyes burning like twin flames. His fists closed around her nightgown, and in one swift move he stripped it from her.

Reacting instinctively, she fought to cover herself, the expression on his face frightening her. She shouldn't struggle. She knew she shouldn't, but sudden blind panic overrode all other thought and emotion.

'No!' The tiny urgent whisper escaped before she could prevent it.

'Don't fight me,' he demanded, trapping her beneath him

and staring down with intense, passion-filled eyes. 'I won't hurt you. Dammit, Leah! You know how good it was between us, how good it can be again.'

'I know, I know,' she moaned, a sob catching in her throat. 'I can't help it. It's not the same any more. I can't make myself feel what I did before just because we're married now…just because it's what you want.'

'And you don't?' he bit out. His hand swept across the rigid peak of her breast. 'You're only fooling yourself if that's what you think. You can't deny your body's response to me.'

'No, I can't.' The confession, raw and painful, was torn from her. How she wished she could open herself to his embrace and enjoy the momentary pleasure he offered, regardless of the consequences. But something instinctively held her back, making the gesture impossible. He'd taken so much already. She didn't dare allow him to take more. Not yet.

'Give yourself to me, Leah.' His words were raspy, heavy with desire. 'You want to. Stop resisting.'

Urgently, she shook her head. 'I won't be a pawn in your game of revenge. You have the ranch. You can't have me. Not this easily. And not with such casual disregard.'

'You call this casual?' He gripped her hand, drawing it to his body, encouraging the hesitant stroke of her fingers against his heated skin. 'Touch me and then try and call what I feel casual.'

Unable to resist, her hand followed the sinewy contours from chest to abdomen. 'If you feel something, then say the words,' she pleaded. 'Tell me our lovemaking isn't just sex. Tell me honestly that there isn't some deep, secret part of you settling an old score.' Tears filled her eyes. 'Tell me that, Hunter, so I don't feel used.'

He tensed above her, his hands tightening on her shoulders in automatic reaction. Then his head dropped to her breast, a day's growth of whiskers rasping across her skin, branding her. A tear escaped from the corner of her eye. She had her answer. She'd gambled and lost. His very silence condemned him, told her more clearly than any words that his motivations were far from pure, that his actions weren't inspired by anything as noble as love.

'I could take you by force.' His voice was raw and harsh against her breast.

She prayed that it was only frustration speaking, that his threat was an empty one. 'You once told me force wouldn't be necessary. Have you changed your mind?' She attempted to slip from beneath him, but his hands closed around her shoulders, holding her in place. 'Taking what you want won't help our situation any,' she tried to reason with him.

'The hell it won't! It would help my situation a great deal. And I'd bet my last dollar that it would do a world of good for yours.'

She couldn't deny the truth. She turned her face into the pillow, retreating from the accusation in his eyes. Helpless tears escaped despite her attempts to control them. 'I'm sorry. I wish I could give myself to you and be done with it. But I can't. I can't be that detached about making love.'

'I don't expect you to be detached. I do expect you to resign yourself to the inevitable and face facts.' He threaded his fingers through her hair, forcing her to face him. 'And the fact is, we will be lovers. It will happen whether it's tomorrow or the next day or the one after that. Before long, wife, you'll want my touch. I guarantee it.'

'You're wrong,' she insisted, but they both knew she lied.

With an unexpectedly calming hand he brushed the tears from her cheeks. 'I won't force the issue this time. But understand me; I don't make any promises for the next.'

Then he rolled off her and left the bed…left Leah to her thoughts and to the inescapable knowledge that resisting him would prove futile. Soon her body would betray her and she'd be unable to stop him from completing what he'd started today. And once that happened, he'd have won it all.

Leah headed for the corral a short time later, to observe Hunter work with Dreamseeker. She wasn't alone. The Arroya children and a number of the employees all found excuses to line up along the fence and watch the coming confrontation. But if they had thought that Hunter would simply climb on to the stallion's back and attempt to bust him, they were mistaken. Instead, he lifted a piece of saddle-blanket from the corral fence and, after letting the horse sniff it, ran it over Dreamseeker's shoulders.

'Easy, boy. Easy.' His deep voice carried on the early morning breeze as he calmed the nervous animal.

Leah watched his hands and listened to his low reassurances, uncomfortably aware that his gentling of the nervous animal was remarkably similar to the way he'd soothed her before leaving their bed. She didn't doubt for a minute who would win this battle of wills…any more than she doubted who would ultimately win the age-old battle waged in their bedroom. It was as inevitable as the changing of the seasons; time was the only variable.

Once done with Dreamseeker, he spent until sundown laboring with the men, starting to set the ranch to rights.

As the days winged by, Leah began to relax. He didn't press her to commit to him physically and, contrary to her earlier fears, he also didn't make any sweeping changes. Instead he did just as he'd promised. He gave her employees a chance.

Or so she thought until Inez came tearing up to the corral fence.

'*Señora*, come quick! The men, they are fighting.'

Leah leapt from the horse she'd been training and ducked beneath the fence-rails. 'Where?'

'Behind the barn.'

She ran flat out, skidding to a stop as she came around the corner of the barn. Sprawled in the dust lay one of her more recent hard luck cases; a huge, brawny youngster barely past his teens by the name of Orrie. Above him towered Hunter, his fists cocked, his stance threatening. The rest of the employees stood in a loose circle around the two.

'Hunter!' she called, horrified that he'd actually fight one of her workers, especially one so young.

He spared her a brief glance. 'Stay out of it, Leah,' he warned. 'This doesn't concern you.'

Orrie scrambled to his feet, careful to keep clear of Hunter's reach. 'He fired me, Miz Hampton. He had no call to do that. You have to help me.'

Uncertain, she looked from Orrie to her husband. 'What's this about?'

Hunter's mouth tightened. 'You heard me, Leah. Stay out of it.'

'You have to do something, Miz Hampton,' Orrie insisted, bolting to her side. 'You can't let him get away with it. He's trying to change things.'

'You must be mistaken. He promised to give everyone a fair shot,' she hastened to reassure. 'Do your job and you stay.' She searched the sea of faces for confirmation. 'That was the agreement, right?'

Bitterness filled Orrie's expression. 'Then he strung you along with his lies as well as the rest of us, 'cause he fired me. And that ain't all!' The words were tumbling from him, as though he feared being stopped. Forcibly. 'Lenny's gonna have to leave, too. And he's made Mateo give up the horses.'

She couldn't hide her disbelief. 'Hunter, you can't do that!'

'I can and I have.' He motioned to the men. 'You have your orders. Get to it.' Without a word, they drifted away from the scene.

Orrie stared at her with the saddest, most pathetic eyes she'd ever seen. 'You won't let him fire me, will you, Miz Hampton?'

'Her name is Pryde. *Mrs* Pryde,' Hunter stated coldly. He snagged his hat from the dirt and slapped the dust from the brim. 'And she has no say in this. You have your wages, which is more than you deserve. Pick up your bedroll and clear out.' He started toward them. 'Now.'

Orrie hesitated, shifting so that Leah stood between him and trouble. 'Miz Hampton...Pryde?'

She switched her attention from her employee to Hunter. 'Perhaps if I understood the reason?' she suggested, hoping he'd take the hint and explain himself.

Instead he folded his arms across his chest. 'There's nothing to understand. This is between me and the boy. I suggest you go to the house.'

She stared in shock. 'What?'

'You heard me. You're interfering. So, say goodbye to your friend here and get up to the house. Believe me. I'll be right behind.'

It sounded more like a threat than a promise. For a long minute she stood glaring at him, too furious to speak and too uncertain of the possible consequences to stand her ground. With a muffled exclamation, she turned and walked away, knowing that her cheeks burned with outrage. She could only pray that none of her other employees had been close enough to witness their battle of wills. Especially when she'd been so thoroughly defeated.

'Miz Hampton,' Orrie cried, dogging her retreat. 'Please. You gotta do something.'

She paused, glancing at him apologetically. 'It's out of my hands,' she admitted, risking a quick nervous look over her shoulder.

'That's it? You're going to let him fire me? You're going to give in to that…that half-breed?'

She pulled away in distaste. 'Don't *ever* use that expression around me.'

He'd made a mistake, and apparently knew it. He hastened to correct the situation. 'I…I didn't mean to say that,' he apologized. 'You gotta understand. I'm desperate. I have nowhere else to go.'

It took all her willpower to resist his pleas. 'I'm sorry. There's nothing I can do,' she said, and continued walking.

She didn't turn around again. Once at the house, she stormed into the study and stood helplessly by the window, watching Orrie's departure. Hunter watched too, remaining dead center in the middle of the drive while the youngster packed his things into Patrick's pick-up and finally left. Then Hunter turned and faced the house, grim intent marking every line of his body.

Leah didn't even realize that she'd backed from the window until she found herself up against her father's desk. Not taking time to analyze her reasons, she put the width of the oak tabletop between her and the study door. A minute later it crashed open.

Hunter strode in, slamming the door behind him so hard that it rocked on its hinges. 'You and I,' he announced in a furious voice, 'have a small matter to set straight.'

CHAPTER SEVEN

'YOU'RE angry,' she said, stating the obvious...stating the *very* obvious.

He started across the room. 'Good guess.'

'Well, I'm angry too.' She swallowed hard. 'I suggest we discuss this.'

He kept coming.

'Calmly.'

He knocked a mahogany hat rack from his path.

'Rationally.'

He stalked around the desk.

'Like two civilized adults.' She retreated, using her father's swivel chair as a shield. 'Okay?'

In response, he kicked the chair out of the way and trapped her against the wall.

'That's a yes, right?' she said with a gasp.

A muscle jerked in his cheek and he made a small growling sound low in his throat that told her more clearly than anything else just how furious he was. It took every ounce of willpower not to panic and bolt from the room. He grabbed her wrist in one hand and yanked. Bending low, he clipped her across the hips and tossed her over his shoulder.

'*Hunter*! No, don't!' she had time to shriek, before her entire world turned upside-down.

He clamped an arm around her legs just above the knees, effectively immobilizing her. 'We're going to discuss this all right. But not here where everyone and her grandmother can listen in,' he announced.

'Put me down!' She planted her palms in the middle of his back and attempted to wiggle free. Not that it did any good. His grip was as strong as a steel band.

'We could continue this conversation at the line-shack, if you'd prefer.' He shrugged his shoulders, bouncing her like a sack of potatoes. The breath whooshed from her lungs and she stopped bucking.

'No! Why not here? The study is an excellent place for a discussion. You start discussing and you'll see how good a place it is.'

'I say it's not.'

He'd reached the door and Leah began to panic seriously. 'Hunter, please. Put me down.'

He ignored her, stepping into the hallway. Heading for the entrance, he tipped his hat and said, 'Afternoon, Rose. Glad you could drop in. Or should I say eavesdrop in? My bride and I are going for a little drive.'

'You don't say.' Rose folded her arms across her chest. 'You're going to have trouble driving like that.'

'It's amazing the things you can accomplish when you set your mind to it. Don't wait dinner for us.' With that, he left the house. Beside his pick-up, he dropped Leah to her feet, and held the truck door open. 'Your choice. You can get in under your own steam, or I can help you.'

She planted her hands on her hips. 'I am perfectly capable of getting into a truck all on my own, thank you very much.'

'Wrong answer.' The next thing she knew, he'd scooped her up and dumped her on the passenger seat. Slamming the door closed, he leaned in the window. 'This conversation may take longer than I thought. Stay here.'

Before she could say a single word, he'd started off toward the barn. He returned several minutes later, carrying two fishing poles and a tackle-box. She stared at the rods in disbelief. 'What's all that for?' she questioned, the second he climbed into the cab.

'Fishing.'

'I know that!' Loath as she was to mention the fact, she forced herself to remind him, 'I meant... I thought we were going to have a discussion.' She gave him a hopeful smile. 'But if you'd rather fish...'

'Believe me,' he said, shooting her a sharp look, 'we'll have that talk. Consider the drive to our...discussion site as a short reprieve.'

She struggled to hide her disappointment. 'And the poles?'

'My reward for not killing you.' He gunned the engine. 'If you were smart, you'd stay real quiet and hope it takes a long time to get there.'

'But—'

'Not another word!' His words exploded with a fury that left her in no doubt as to how tenuous a hold he had on his temper. 'Woman, you are inches away from disaster. I guarantee, you don't want to push me any further.'

Taking his suggestion to heart, she didn't open her mouth the entire length of the ride. She soon realized what destination he had in mind. The rough dirt track that he turned on to led to a small, secluded lake in the far western section of the ranch. It had been one of their favorite meeting-spots eight years ago. It was also about as far from curious eyes and ears as they could get. As much as she dreaded the coming confrontation, she appreciated his determination to keep it as private as possible.

'Hunter,' she began as they neared the lake.

'Not yet,' he bit out. 'I'm still not calm enough to deal with you.'

Pulling the truck to a stop at the end of the track, he climbed from the cab and gathered up the poles, tackle-box and a plastic bucket. 'Let's go,' he called over his shoulder.

Reluctantly Leah left the truck, and rummaged in the back for something to sit on. If they were going to stay a while—and she suspected that they were—she intended to be comfortable. Spreading the colorful Mexican blanket in the grass at the edge of the shore, she removed her boots and socks and rolled her jeans to her knees. Sticking her feet into the cool water, she asked, 'Are we going to talk first or fish?'

He spared her a brief glance. 'Both. You want a rod?'

'Might as well,' she muttered.

She searched the surrounding bermuda grass until she found a good-sized cricket. Carrying it back to the blanket, she knelt beside her pole, closed her eyes, and stuck the insect on the end of the hook. Ready to catch a catfish or two, she cast toward the middle of the lake. A bright yellow and red bobber marked her spot and she settled back on the blanket, wishing she could truly relax and enjoy a lazy afternoon of fishing. But she was all too aware of their coming 'discussion'.

Hunter attached his spinner bait to his line and cast into a marshy, partially shaded section of water known to attract bass. 'I've told you before, you can't bait a hook without looking,' he informed her in a taut voice.

'I just did.'

He yanked on his line. 'One of these times, you're going to set the hook in your finger instead of the cricket. It's going to hurt. It's going to bleed. And I'm going to have to cut the damned thing out.'

'*If* that fine day ever arrives, you can say "I told you so".' Until then, I'd rather not see what I'm murdering.' She cupped her chin in her hand and rested her elbow on a bent knee. 'Are we going to fight over fishing, or are we going to fight over the real problem?'

He turned his head and studied her. More than a hint of anger lingered in the depths of his eyes. 'Do you even know what that is?'

'Sure,' she said with a shrug. 'You hit Orrie.'

'You're damned right, I hit him. All things considered, he got off easy.' Hunter slowly reeled in his line. 'But that's not the issue.'

She knew it wasn't, though he'd never get her to admit it. 'Mateo loves working with the horses,' she said instead. 'Did you have to make him give it up? And why fire Lenny? He's a good worker and a wonderful man.'

Hunter cast his line again, his mouth tightening. 'Nor is that the issue.'

'It is so,' she disagreed, her frustration flaring out of control. 'It's why we're arguing.'

'No, it's not. It's why you're annoyed, but it's not why we're arguing,' he corrected harshly. 'You're annoyed because I didn't consult with you before making changes and we're arguing because I won't explain my decision.'

He'd hit the nail on the head, and she focused her attention on that particular aspect of the discussion. 'Why did you do it? Why did you fire Orrie and Lenny and change Mateo's job?' He remained stubbornly silent and she wanted to scream in exasperation. 'You're not going to tell me, are you?'

'No, I'm not.'

'Because it's not the *issue*?' she demanded, tossing her pole to the grass and scrambling to her feet. 'It's my ranch, too. I have a right to know. You promised to give everyone a fair chance. You promised!'

Setting his rod on the blanket, he reached out and swept her feet from under her, catching her before she hit the ground. '*That's* the issue,' he practically snarled. 'I made a promise to you—which I kept. And you made a promise to me—which you didn't keep.'

She fought his hold, with no success. His strength was too great. 'I don't know what you're talking about,' she insisted.

He pushed her back on to the blanket and knelt above her, planting his hands on either side of her head. 'Who's in charge of this ranch?'

'That's not the point.'

'It's precisely the point. Answer me. Who's in charge of this ranch?'

It galled her to say it. 'You are,' she forced herself to admit. She pushed against his chest, struggling to sit up. To her relief, he rocked back on to his heels, allowing her to wriggle out from beneath him.

'So you do remember our conversation at the line-shack,' he said in satisfaction.

She wrapped her arms around her waist. 'Very funny. How could I forget?' It wasn't one of her more pleasant recollections. Every last, painful detail had been burned into her memory.

'And do you also remember the promises we exchanged?'

'Of course.'

'So do I.' He ticked them off on his fingers. 'I promised to give your employees a fair chance. I promised to give your grandmother a home. And I promised to sign a pre-nuptial agreement. Is that everything?'

She glanced at him uneasily. 'Yes.'

'You promised one thing. What was it?'

She knew where he was headed with this and she didn't like it. 'I seem to remember there being more than one,' she temporized.

'Fine,' he said evenly. 'Name any that you remember.'

Time to face the music. She should be grateful that he wasn't rending her limb from limb. She looked him straight in the eye and said, 'I promised you'd be in charge of the ranch.'

'Which means?'

She sighed. 'That what you say goes. That I'm not to question you in front of the employees or second-guess your decisions. You don't work by committee,' she repeated his demands by rote.

'And did you do that? Did you keep your promise?'

Reluctantly she shook her head. 'No.' Nor had she kept her agreement to make their marriage a fully functioning one. She should be grateful that he hadn't pointed that out as well.

'*That's* why I'm angry. One of these days you'll trust me to do what's right for you and for the ranch. You'll trust me without question.'

'You mean blindly.'

'Okay. That's what I mean.'

She bit down on her lip. How could she do what he asked when it might all be part of an elaborate game of revenge, an attempt to even the score for old wrongs? 'I don't think I can do that, Hunter. You're asking me to risk everything.'

'Yes. I am.'

'It's too much,' she whispered, staring down at the blanket, running the wool fringe through her fingers. 'I can't give it to you. Not yet.'

A long minute ticked by before he inclined his head. 'All right. I'll answer your questions—this time.'

She glanced up in surprise. 'You'll tell me why you fired Orrie and Lenny? Why you made Mateo give up the horses?'

'Yes. This once I'll explain myself. Next time you either trust me or you don't; I don't care which. But don't expect me to defend my actions again. You understand?' At her nod, he said, 'I put Mateo in charge of the haying operation. It meant an increase in wages—something he and his family need. Plus he knows more about mechanics than he does about horses.'

'But…he knows everything about horses.'

'He knows more about repairing our equipment. As for Lenny… He wasn't happy working on a ranch. But employment meant more to him than his dislike of ranching, which says a lot about the man's character, so I recommended him for a job as a security-guard at your godfather's bank. Lenny jumped at the opportunity.'

She could hardly take it in. 'And Orrie?'

He frowned. 'Orrie was a thief,' he told her reluctantly.

'A thief! I don't believe it. What did he steal?' An obstinate look appeared in his eyes, a look she didn't doubt he'd find reflected in her own. 'Hunter?' she prompted, refusing to let it drop.

'He took your silver circlet.'

She stared in shock. 'From my wedding-gown? But that was in our…'

'Bedroom,' he finished for her.

The full implication gradually sank in. Without a word she turned away and reached for her pole. It felt as if she'd been stabbed in the back by a family member. Her betrayal went so deep that she couldn't even find the words to express it. Slowly, she brought in the line, blinking hard. The cricket was long-gone and she didn't have the stomach to kill another. At some point during their conversation she'd lost her enthusiasm for fishing.

As though sensing her distress, Hunter caught her braid and used it to reel her in. She didn't resist. Right now she needed all the comfort she could get. He folded his arms around her and she snuggled into his embrace. 'You okay?' he asked.

'No,' she replied, her voice muffled against his shirt. 'See what happens when you trust people?'

'Yes, I see. But I'm not Orrie.'

She sighed. 'No, you're not. I'm sorry, Hunter. I should have trusted you to do the right thing for the ranch.'

'Yes, you should have.'

'And I shouldn't have questioned your judgement in front of the men.'

'No, you shouldn't have. Apology accepted.' Without warning he released her, and stripped off his shirt and boots. Then, snatching her high in his arms, he walked into the lake, holding her above the water.

She clung to him, laughing. 'Don't! Don't drop me.'

'Do you trust me?'

'Blindly?'

'Is there any other way?'

She bit her lower lip. 'Okay. I trust you. Blindly.'

'Close your eyes.'

'They're closed.'

'And take a deep breath.'

'Hunter, no!' she yelped. He tossed her into the air and she tumbled, shrieking, landing in the water with a huge splash. An instant later Hunter dived in beside her, kicking with her to the surface. She gasped for air. 'I thought you said I could trust you.'

A slow grin drifted across his lean face and he caught her close. 'I never said what you could trust me to do.'

And therein lay the real crux of the matter. She knew he'd do what he thought best—but would it be right for her? As much as she wanted to believe, she couldn't. Not yet.

As they drifted toward shore her hair floated free of its braid, wrapping them in a net of long silvery tendrils. He beached them in the grass and gazed down at her, his attention snared by the wet shirt clinging to her breasts. His palm settled on the taut, supple lines of her midriff, where her shirt had parted company with her jeans. As though unable to resist he lowered his head, and gently bit the rigid peak of her breast through the wet cotton.

Her breath stopped in her throat and her nails bit into his shoulders, marking him with tiny crescent scars of passion. 'Hunter!' His name escaped her as though ripped from her throat, filled with an undeniable urgency.

He responded instantly, releasing her breast and plundering her mouth, parting her lips in search of the sweet warmth within. She couldn't seem to get enough of him. Her hands swept down his back, stroking him, needing to absorb him into her very pores, the seductive brush of cloth against skin an almost painful stimulation. His taste filled her mouth, his unique musky scent her lungs. She felt him tug at the fastening of his jeans... And then he hesitated.

Slowly he lifted his head, his angled features stark with want, dark with intent. She knew that expression, knew how close to the edge he must be. She stared at him uncertainly, caught between completing the intimacy he so clearly craved and she so desperately needed, and retreating from an act that would enable him to wrest the final bit of control from her possession. And she waited, waited for him to give in to his desire, to strip away the wet clothes and make her his wife in fact as well as name. But instead he drew away, and she could only imagine the amount of willpower it must have taken him.

He kissed her again, the caress hard and swift. 'Not here. Not like this. But soon,' he warned in a determined voice. 'Very soon. When there are no more doubts in your mind...when there's no chance of turning back, we will finish this and you will be mine.'

She didn't argue. How could she? He was right. Soon they would be lovers, and if she wasn't very, very careful she'd lose her heart as surely as she was losing control of the ranch. And, when that happened, Hunter would finally have his revenge.

The next few days passed with a comfortable ease that gave Leah hope for the future. Hunter continued to work with Dreamseeker, though whether or not he'd made any headway with the stallion was a topic of hot debate. Still, she didn't doubt who would eventually win their battle of wills.

To her relief, the employees seemed quite content working under Hunter's management. Losing two wranglers left ample work for everyone, and she suspected that the fear of being laid off had finally dissipated. Mateo was far happier than she'd ever seen him. And dropping in on Lenny in his new position as security-guard proved that Hunter had been right about that change as well.

Returning from the bank late one cloudy afternoon, she was surprised to discover Hunter Rototilling the ground around the porch. The powerful blades bit into the dark soil, grinding up the crushed remains of Grandmother Rose's begonias.

'What are you doing?' she called. He didn't answer, merely lifted a hand in greeting and resumed his work. Inez stood on the porch and Leah joined her. 'What's he doing?' she asked the housekeeper. 'Or perhaps I should ask why. Why is he plowing the garden under?'

'*No sé*,' Inez replied with a shrug. 'Abuela Rosa, she took one look, said a nasty word, and stomped off to the kitchen. I don't think she is happy that Señor Pryde has decided to ruin her garden.'

Leah frowned. 'Hunter isn't ruining her garden; Bull Jones took care of that already. Hunter's just finishing the job.'

Rose appeared in the doorway, carrying a tray with a pitcher of iced tea and glasses. 'If we're going to stand around and watch all my hard work being ground into mulch, we might as well be comfortable.'

Leah hastened to take the tray, setting it on a low wrought-iron table. 'There wasn't much left to mulch,' she reassured, pouring drinks and handing them around. 'Our neighboring foreman made sure of that.'

With a noisy humph, Rose sat in a rocker. 'If Hunter thinks I'm starting over again, he's got another think coming. That garden can grow rocks and weeds for all I care.' She took a sip of tea. 'What's he doing over there? What's in those bags?'

'*Es abono, sí?*' Inez suggested.

'Fertilizer, huh?' Rose slowly rocked in her chair. 'Yes, sir. That'll give him a fine crop of weeds. A truly fine crop.' She craned her neck. 'Where's he going now?'

Leah shrugged, frowning as Hunter walked toward the

rear of the house. 'I don't know. Maybe he's through for the day.'

'Through!' Rose rocked a little faster. 'With everything such a mess? He'd better not leave my garden like that, or I'll have a thing or two to say about it. See if I don't.'

Leah jumped to her feet and leaned over the rail. 'False alarm. Here he comes. He was just pulling the pick-up around.' He climbed out of the cab and crossed to the back of the truck. Lowering the tailgate, he removed an assortment of bedding plants. She glanced over her shoulder at Rose. 'He bought jasmine for the trellis. I adore jasmine.'

Inez joined her at the railing, beaming in delight. '*Y mira*!'

Slowly Rose stood. 'Well, I'll be. He bought some roses.'

Leah began to laugh. 'How appropriate. They're peace roses.'

Hunter lined the plants around the perimeter of the house, then approached, carrying a shovel. He stood at the bottom of the porch steps and looked directly at Rose. 'Well? You going to play lady of the manor, or do you want to get your hands dirty and help?'

Rose lifted her chin. 'Whose garden is it?' she demanded.

Hunter shrugged. 'I'm no gardener. Just thought I'd get it started.'

'In that case, I'll fetch my gloves,' she agreed. At the door she paused, and with a crotchety glare demanded, 'Don't you break ground without me. Hear?'

Leah waited until Rose was out of earshot before approaching Hunter, offering him a glass of iced tea. 'This is very thoughtful of you. When Bull destroyed her last flowerbed, she gave in to the inevitable and didn't try again.'

He drank the tea and handed her the empty glass. 'He won't destroy another.'

She didn't doubt it for a minute. 'Peace roses?' she asked, raising an eyebrow.

He tipped his hat to the back of his head with a gloved finger, and in that moment, Leah didn't think she'd ever seen him look more attractive. 'Yeah, well. I figured it was past time we came to terms. We'll stick in a few rose bushes and talk. Before we're done we'll have worked out our differences.'

Leah smiled. 'I'm sure you will,' she said softly. 'It's just difficult for her to adjust to all the changes.'

'I'm not done making them, you know,' he warned.

She nodded. 'I know.'

He'd never promised not to make changes. But they were for the better. And more and more she realized how important he'd become—to her employees, to the ranch... even to her grandmother, loath as Rose might be to admit it.

But most of all, he'd become important to her, perhaps even vital. And before much longer she'd have to deal with that knowledge.

Leah watched in concern the next morning as Hunter and his men drove one of the ranch bulls into a pen in preparation for transporting him to his new owner. She'd nicknamed the animal 'Red' because of his tendency to charge anything or anyone foolish enough to wear that color. After nearly being gored by the bull, Hunter had decided to sell the animal.

He'd also flatly refused to allow her to help move Red to the pen, saying it was 'much too dangerous'. She'd heard that phrase used more than once and had rapidly grown to hate it. But she didn't dare argue, especially in front of the employees and especially when—in this particular case— he was right. The bull was very dangerous.

She climbed to the top rail of the corral fence and looked on from a safe distance. With Red secure and peaceful in the holding-pen, the men only awaited the arrival of the truck to move the bull to his new home.

'Señora Leah!' came a childish shout from behind her. 'Silkie! Get Silkie.'

She turned in time to see all six Arroya children chasing after their new sheepdog puppy. The tiny animal, yapping for all she was worth, streaked beneath the rail of the corral, barreling straight toward the holding-pen...and the bull. And around her neck, bouncing in the dust, hung a huge, red floppy bow.

'Stay there!' she called over her shoulder, hopping off the rail. 'Don't you dare come into the corral. You understand?'

The children obediently skidded to a halt and nodded as one. Six pairs of huge dark eyes stared at her, wide with mingled fear and hope. Wincing at their trusting expressions, Leah hotfooted it after the wayward puppy.

Across the corral the dog ran, and Leah realized that she'd have only one chance to catch the animal before it was too late. At the last possible second, just as they reached the holding-pen, she flung herself at Silkie. Belly-flopping to a dusty halt, inches from the bottom rail, her hand closed around the furry, struggling puppy. For a brief second she held the animal safely in her grasp. Then, with a frantic wiggle, Silkie scrambled free and scooted beneath the rail.

'Silkie, no!' she yelled.

Set on a course of total annihilation, the puppy darted

toward the bull. Taking a deep breath and whispering a fervent prayer, Leah ducked beneath the rail, hoping she could snag the animal and escape unscathed. A hard, relentless hand landed on her arm and jerked her back, spinning her around. She stared up into Hunter's furious face.

'Are you nuts?' he practically roared.

'The puppy!' she cried, fighting his hold. 'I've got to save the puppy!'

He glanced from Leah to the Arroya children. 'Open the gates!' he shouted to his men. 'Get the bull out of there!'

Yelling and whistling, the wranglers unlatched the gate between the holding-pen and the pasture. But the bull didn't notice. Focused entirely on Silkie, he lowered his head, pawing at the ground and bellowing in fury. He scored the ground with his horns, just missing the dog.

Swearing beneath his breath, Hunter tossed his hat to the ground and ripped off his shirt. Before anyone could stop him, he climbed beneath the rail and entered the holding-pen.

'Hunter, don't do it!' Leah started to follow, but the look on his face stopped her. If she moved another step, she'd divert his attention and the bull would kill him. It was that simple. She clasped her trembling hands together, hardly daring to breathe. With a fervor bordering on hysteria, she began to pray.

Waving his shirt in the air, Hunter caught the bull's attention. Distracted by this new, more accessible target, the huge animal instantly charged. At the last possible second Hunter threw his shirt at the bull's head and, diving to one side, rolled clear of the vicious hooves and horns. Red pounded by and Hunter leapt to his feet. Snagging the puppy by the scruff of her neck, he vaulted over the fence to safety.

Blinded, Red crashed into the fence between the holding-pen and the corral, the rails splintering beneath the impact. Keeping Silkie tucked safely under his arm, Hunter grabbed Leah by the wrist and ran flat out for the far side of the corral. The bull stood close to the splintered rails, blowing hard. With several shakes of his head he reduced the shirt covering him to rags. Then he looked around for his next victim. At long last, he spied the open gate and, to Leah's eternal relief, he barreled through it, racing into the pasture.

Leaving her side, Hunter carried the dog over to the Arroya children and dropped to one knee in the dirt in front of them. Leah watched anxiously, wondering what he intended to say to them, hoping he wouldn't be too rough.

'Is this your puppy?' he asked the children.

'Yes, sir.' The oldest, Ernesto, stepped forward, swallowing hard. 'She sort of got away from us. We're sorry.'

'You know what could have happened?'

Every last one of them nodded. The youngest, Tina, clung to Ernesto, tears streaking her cheeks. 'We'll be more careful next time,' the boy said solemnly. 'I promise.'

'Promise,' Tina repeated. After a brief hesitation, she held her arms out for Silkie.

Hunter handed over the dog. 'Tie her up until she's old enough to mind. Okay?'

Tina wrapped her arms around the puppy, burying her face in the dog's fluffy coat. With a playful yip, Silkie washed the dirt and tears from the little girl's face. Satisfied that her pet was indeed safe, she peeked up at Hunter from beneath long, dark lashes. 'Promise,' she repeated and offered a gap-toothed smile.

Hunter ruffled her hair and stood. He glanced at Leah and lifted an eyebrow. Without a word, she ran to his side and threw her arms around him, blinking back the tears that threatened to fall. His skin felt warm and hard beneath her hands, and she drew in a ragged breath, picturing what he might have looked like had he not been quite so agile. She clung to him, not wanting ever to let go.

In that instant she realized that she loved him…had always loved him and always would. If he'd died beneath the bull's horns, a part of her would have died as well. For weeks now she'd held him at a distance, reluctant to commit herself fully, because deep in her heart of hearts she knew that, once she did, he'd own her body and soul.

Held in the safe harbor of his arms, she surrendered to the inevitable.

'You do anything that stupid again and *I* won't be responsible for *my* actions,' she whispered fiercely, repeating the words he'd so often used when taking her to task. 'You hear me, Hunter Pryde?'

He held her tight against him. 'I didn't have a choice. You and the children were counting on me to save that damned dog.'

And suddenly she realized he was right. As frightened as she'd been, she hadn't doubted for a minute that he'd save Silkie. Nor had the children. She glanced over Hunter's shoulder, seeing the men laughing and slapping each other on the back. The men hadn't doubted either. They all trusted him, all believed in him. Every last one.

'And you did save her. But then, I…I knew you would,' she confessed.

He stiffened. 'Blind trust, Leah? You?'

She lifted a shaky hand to swipe at an escaped tear. 'A temporary aberration, I'm sure.'

A laugh rumbled deep in his chest. 'Of course. Come on. Let's get that fence fixed. We've got a bull to bring in.'

Reluctantly, she slid her arms from around his neck and

stepped back. 'I'll be right there.' She watched him return to the corral and snag his hat from the dirt. She did trust him, she realized. She trusted him every bit as much as she loved him. Blindly. Totally. Completely.

And she'd never been more frightened in her life. For Hunter had it all now...the ranch and her heart. The only question was...what would he do when he found out?

CHAPTER EIGHT

EARLY the next morning Lyon Enterprises' latest offer arrived by special messenger. Gazing in fury at the papers, Leah knocked back the kitchen chair and went in search of Hunter. Eventually she tracked him down in the barn, running a curry-comb over his buckskin.

'Look at this,' she said, holding out the white embossed envelope.

He set aside his equipment and took the papers, scanning them. His mouth tightened briefly, then he shrugged. 'So? Either write your acceptance or trash it.'

She stared in disbelief as he guided his gelding from the grooming-box and returned the horse to his stall. 'That's it? That's all you're going to say?' she demanded, trailing behind.

He shouldered past her and crossed the barn aisle to a stack of hay bales. Using two large hooks, he lifted a bale and carried it to the stall. 'What do you want me to say?'

She regarded him with frustration. 'Something more than what you have. I'm tired of their pestering me. I'd think you would be, too. Or don't you care if I sell out to them?'

He released a gusty sigh and glanced over his shoulder at her. 'Is that what you want? To sell? I thought the whole point of marrying was to prevent Lyon from getting their hands on your ranch.'

'It was, but you seem so...' She shrugged. 'I don't know. Detached.'

'I am. It's not my ranch.'

She wasn't sure why she kept pushing it. But something about his careless indifference didn't quite ring true. After all, he'd also married in order to secure the ranch. She didn't believe for one minute that he was as unconcerned about her accepting Lyon's offer as he claimed. 'So you wouldn't object if I sold to them.'

'No.' He paused in his labors. 'Though legally you can't without offering me first refusal.'

She blinked, momentarily sidetracked. 'Come again?'

He rolled up his sleeves and leaned his arms on the stall door, exposing the powerful muscles of his forearms. 'The prenup, remember? You retain title of the ranch in the event of a divorce. But if you choose to sell, I have right of first refusal.' He frowned at her, tilting his hat to the back of his head. 'You're the one who insisted we sign the damned thing. Didn't you even bother to read it?'

'Yes.' No. She'd just signed where her lawyer had told her in order to get it over and done with.

'Yeah, right,' he said, clearly not believing her. 'You should have read it, Leah. There are one or two other important clauses in there that you should be familiar with. If that's the way you conduct all your business, it's a wonder you weren't bankrupt years ago.'

She hadn't come to argue. She'd come to vent her anger over Lyon Enterprises' non-stop harassment—an anger that had finally reached the boiling point. 'That's not what's at issue,' she said, determined to get the conversation back on track. 'I'd like to discuss this offer.'

'So discuss it. I'm listening.'

She took a deep breath. 'I plan to drive to Houston this week and talk to them.'

That stopped him. 'You *what*?'

'I want to have it out once and for all—tell them I won't sell.'

He stared at her as though she'd lost her mind. 'If you don't want to sell, just trash the thing. You don't need to drive all the way to Houston to do that. Last time I looked you kept a wastebasket in the study. Use that one.'

'Very funny. I have to go to Houston.'

'Why?'

'So I can address the Lyon Enterprises board.'

He froze for a split-second, the check in his movements so brief she almost missed it. Leaving the stall, he slung the remains of the bale on to the stack and crossed to her side. His hat brim threw his face into shadow, but she could see the dark glitter of his eyes and the taut line of his jaw. Was he angry? She couldn't quite tell.

'And why,' he asked softly, 'would you want to address the board of Lyon Enterprises?'

Her voice sharpened. 'I've had it with these people. As far as I'm concerned this latest offer is the final straw. I'm not putting up with it any more. I'm going to make it clear that I won't be entertaining any future offers and that I won't sell to them. Ever. If necessary I'll even tell them what you said—that our prenuptial agreement gives you first right of refusal.'

He shook his head. 'Over my dead body. That's no-body's business but ours.'

'Okay,' she conceded, uncertain of his temperament. Any time his voice dropped to such a low, husky note she tended to tread warily. 'But I still want to go to Houston and talk to them. And I want you to go with me.'

'Why?' he said again.

She glanced at him uncertainly. 'To support me, if you're willing.'

He turned away, resting a booted foot on the haystack. She could tell from the tense set of his shoulders that she'd thrown him, and she studied his expressionless profile in concern. Perhaps she'd pushed it by requesting his support. If only she could read his thoughts, she'd know. But he'd always been exceptionally successful at keeping them hidden from her.

Finally he nodded. 'Okay. I'll go. We'll leave Friday and spend the weekend at my apartment.'

'You have an apartment in Houston?' she asked in astonishment.

'You can see for yourself when we get there.' His brows drew together. 'Leah, I need you to agree to something.'

She eyed him warily. 'What?'

He stripped off his gloves and tucked them into his belt. 'Once you've confronted the board, I want to handle the situation from then on.'

'But it's not your problem.'

'Yes, it is. Anything that affects this ranch is my problem. And dealing with companies like Lyon Enterprises is my area of expertise—my former area of expertise.'

'Do you think you can get them to leave me alone?'

'No. But I can do a good job of holding them at bay. I'm better equipped than you to wage this war.'

Suddenly she recalled her need for a knight on a white charger, battling the nasty dragon in order to save the damsel in distress. When Hunter had shown up she'd been sure he was the dragon, and that she'd have to fight her own battles. Now she wondered. Perhaps they'd fight those battles together, and Lyon Enterprises would be vanquished once and for all.

'Let me have my say, and then it's your problem,' she promised.

'Fine.' He dropped an arm across her shoulders. 'I'm starved. How about you?'

She grinned. It felt as though the weight of the world had been lifted from her shoulders. 'I think I could eat a horse,' she confessed, and walked with him to the house.

Late that night Hunter lifted the phone receiver and punched in a series of numbers. A minute later Kevin answered.

'It's me,' Hunter said. 'I'm coming in. Call the board together.'

'What's wrong?' Kevin demanded. 'What happened?'

'Leah received Lyon's latest offer and wants to meet with them.'

'She *what*?'

'You heard me.'

'What the hell are you going to do?'

'Introduce her to the board of Lyon Enterprises, what else?'

'I mean…what are *you* going to do? What if…what if she finds out?'

'She won't.' Hunter spoke with absolute confidence.

'Why not?'

'Because no one would dare tell her anything.'

'If they think it'll help with the sale—'

'Once they meet her, they'll see that she trusts me,' Hunter cut in briskly. 'And they'll realize it's to their advantage to keep quiet. Telling her who I am won't help their cause any, and they're smart enough to know it.'

A long moment of silence followed while Kevin mulled over Hunter's words. 'You could be right. You usually are. I'll tell everyone you're coming.'

'And open up the apartment. We'll be spending the weekend there.'

'Won't she be suspicious? It's not precisely a poor man's pad.'

'She'll have other things on her mind by that time.'

Kevin gave a knowing chuckle. 'Understood. See you Friday.'

'Right.'

Hunter hung up and leaned back in the chair. Matters were rapidly coming to a head. More than anything he'd like to get this situation over and done with, but some things just couldn't be rushed. And this, though he'd prefer it otherwise, was one of them.

He heard a soft knock and Leah opened the door. 'Busy?' she asked.

'No. Come on in.'

She stepped into the room, standing just outside the spill of lamplight and wearing a knee-length cotton nightshirt. Unfortunately, this one wasn't the least transparent. His mouth tightened. As much as he enjoyed seeing his wife in next to nothing, he couldn't have her running around half-dressed. One of these days he'd need to make a serious effort to break her of the habit.

'Who were you talking to?' she asked.

'A business associate.'

She came closer. Her hair, cascading past her waist, caught the light from the desk lamp and gleamed like fallen moonbeams. 'Is there a problem?'

He shook his head. 'Just thought I'd tell him I'd be in town at the end of the week.'

'Oh.' She stood a little uncertainly in the middle of the room. 'Are you coming to bed soon?'

He shoved back the chair and walked toward her. 'Is now soon enough?'

'Yes.' She couldn't quite meet his eyes and he felt her sudden tension.

He reached her side and stared down into her face. He'd never seen such perfection. Her eyes glowed like amethysts, her heart-shaped face full of strength and character and determination. 'I want to make love to you,' he told her bluntly, thrusting his fingers into the silken fall of her hair. 'I've been patient long enough.'

She twisted her hands together. 'I know. But...'

'Friday,' he stated, catching her chin with his knuckle and forcing her to look at him. 'I want a decision by Friday, Leah. You have to commit at some point.'

Slowly she nodded. 'Okay. Friday. We'll meet with the Lyon board and then have the rest of the weekend to ourselves.'

He smiled in satisfaction. 'Done. And now, wife, it's time for bed.' He slid an arm around her and lifted her close. She trembled in his arms, which told him more than anything his effect on her.

'Hunter—'

He sensed that her nervousness had gotten the better of her, that given the opportunity she'd rescind her agreement. He stopped her words with a swift, rough kiss, then took her mouth again in a second, slower, more thorough kiss— a precursory taste of the pleasure he intended to share with her over the weekend.

They left early on Friday, arranging to meet with the Lyon personnel after lunch. Leah had dressed carefully, choosing a pearl-gray suit, matching pumps and a white silk blouse. To add a touch of sophistication, she'd looped her hair into

a businesslike chignon, and as a morale booster displayed
the necklace Hunter had given her as a wedding-gift.

To her surprise, Hunter dressed casually, exchanging his
jeans for cotton trousers, his plaid shirt no different from
the ones he wore when working. The boa tie he'd strung
around his neck was his only concession to the occasion.

'Relax,' he said, driving toward the Post Oak section of
Houston. 'They won't eat you.'

Her expression felt stiff and unnatural. 'I'm more concerned about them slitting my throat,' she attempted to
joke. 'Especially after I tell them not to contact me ever
again.'

'Too obvious. They'll just sell you off to white slavers.'
He looked at her and sighed. 'I'm kidding, honey.'

'Oh.' She grinned weakly and her hand closed over the
pendant; she was hoping it would give her even a minus-
cule amount of Hunter's strength and perseverance. 'I'm
beginning to think this isn't such a great idea.'

He spared her another brief glance. 'You want to turn
back?'

'No. Maybe if I do this they'll finally leave me alone.'
She shifted in her seat and studied Hunter's profile. 'Do
you think they will? Leave me alone, I mean?'

He shrugged. 'They might. But don't count on it. They're
businessmen. All they care about is the bottom line on the
balance sheet. If buying your ranch means a substantial
profit, then no. They won't leave you alone.'

A small frown knit her brow. 'I'll have to think of a way
to convince them I mean business.'

'Short of a stick of dynamite between their ears, I don't
know how.'

His comment gave her an idea and a secretive smile crept
across her mouth. 'I'm not so sure about the dynamite,

although the idea has merit. Perhaps a slightly less drastic demonstration would be in order.' Opening the glove compartment, she rummaged around until she found what she sought. Without a word, she pocketed the item, hoping Hunter hadn't noticed the furtive act.

A few minutes later he pointed out a tall, modern glass building with smoked windows. 'That's where we're headed,' he told her, pulling into an underground parking-lot.

Leaving the car, they took the garage elevator to the lobby. 'Which floor is Lyon Enterprises?' Leah asked.

'All of them.'

She stopped dead in her tracks. 'They own the *building*?'

'They're a large company. Lots of companies own entire buildings.' He cupped her elbow and ushered her along. 'Come on. We want the executive level.'

She clutched her purse and the large white envelope with Lyon's offer to her chest. She hadn't realized. She'd had no idea they were such an immense concern. Suddenly she felt very small and vulnerable. How could she ever hope to defeat this Goliath of a company? She was no David. She glanced at Hunter. But he was. He'd protect her. All she had to do was trust him.

Filled with renewed confidence, she walked with him to the security desk. After presenting their credentials, they were escorted to a private bank of elevators that carried them directly to the executive level. Inside the car, she tucked back an escaped wisp of hair and straightened her skirt.

Hunter caught her hand, stilling her nervous exertions. 'Listen to me, Leah. These corporate types eat people like you for a midnight snack. So, don't fidget. Keep your arms relaxed at your side unless you're handing them something.

Look them straight in the eye. Think before you speak. Don't answer any question you don't want to. And above all don't lose your temper. Got it?'

Her tension eased. 'Got it.'

His mouth curled to one side and she realized in amazement that he actually relished the coming confrontation. 'Remember, I'll support you every step of the way. The instant you get in too deep, I'll bail you out. Otherwise, it's your show.'

'Hunter?'

He lifted an eyebrow. 'What?'

She squeezed his hand. 'Thanks.'

'Don't thank me, Leah,' he said, and the seriousness of his tone gave his words an ominous weight. 'Not yet.'

The doors slid open and she released her death grip on him. It wouldn't do for the Lyon board to think that she needed his assistance, even if she did. Stepping from the car, they found a secretary awaiting their arrival.

'Welcome to Lyon Enterprises,' she said. 'You're expected, of course. If you'd follow me?'

She led the way to a pair of wide, double doors. Pushing them open, she gestured for Hunter and Leah to enter. As though in a calculated gesture, the doors banged closed behind, barring their exit. A huge glass table dominated the conference room, and around the table sat a dozen men and women. The man at the far end rose to his feet.

'Miss Hampton,' he said. 'A pleasure to finally meet you. I'm Buddy Peterson. Our chairman requested that I conduct these proceedings, if you have no objections.'

She did object. She wanted to speak directly to the head honcho. 'He's not here?'

'He preferred that I negotiate in his place.' It didn't quite answer her question, but from long experience with Hunter she knew she wouldn't get a more direct response. 'Pryde,' Peterson said, switching his attention to Hunter. 'We were somewhat surprised to hear you'd be attending this meeting—with Miss Hampton, that is.'

'Were you?' Hunter replied. 'I don't know why, considering Leah's my wife.'

'Your *wife*!' The board members exchanged quick glances and Peterson slowly sank back into his seat. 'This puts a slightly different complexion on matters.'

Hunter inclined his head. 'Yes, it does, doesn't it?'

Peterson laughed, a cynical expression gleaming in his eyes. 'Congratulations... I'm impressed. I couldn't have done better myself.'

Leah looked up at Hunter in confusion. 'They know you?' she murmured.

'We're acquainted.'

'You didn't tell me.'

'It wasn't important.' His dark, unfathomable gaze captured hers. 'Do you have something to say to these people?'

She nodded. 'Yes.'

'Then get to it.'

She felt like a pawn in a game without rules. She glanced at Hunter, sudden doubts assailing her, acutely aware that she'd missed a vital piece of information, a clue that would help explain the mysterious undercurrents shifting through the room. She also suspected that what had to be said already had been, though in a language she couldn't hope to decipher. What she chose to contribute would be considered, at best, an empty gesture. Still, she wouldn't have this opportunity ever again. She wanted to say something they'd remember...do something they'd remember. She wanted them to know that Leah Hampton Pryde had been here and made a statement.

Taking a deep breath, she stepped to the table and held out the envelope. 'This arrived the other day.'

'Yes, our offer,' Peterson said with an impatient edge. 'Don't tell me you plan to accept?' He glanced at Hunter. 'It would certainly save much of this board's time and energy if you would.'

'Not only do I not accept, I don't want to hear from you ever again. You people have harassed me for the last time. I'm not the vulnerable woman struggling on my own any more.' She spared Hunter a quick, searching look. At his brief nod, she added, 'I have help now. We won't allow Bull Jones to foul our wells or stampede our herd. We won't be intimidated by you any longer.'

'Yes, yes,' Buddy Peterson interrupted, 'you've made your point.'

'Not yet, I haven't.'

She reached into her suit jacket pocket and pulled out the lighter she'd taken from the glove compartment. With a flick of her thumb she spun the wheel, and a small flame leapt to life. Stepping closer, she held the flame beneath the corner of the envelope and waited until it caught fire. Then she tossed the burning packet into the center of the glass table. Flames and smoke billowed. Frantic executives scrambled from their seats, shouting and cursing.

Beside her, Hunter sighed. 'You really shouldn't have done that.'

She lifted her chin. 'Yes, I should have. *Now* I've made my point.'

'That…and more.'

'Good. Are you ready to leave?'

To her bewilderment, he shot a chary glance at the ceiling, pulled his hat lower over his brow and raised the collar of his shirt. 'In a minute. Go to the car. I'll be right behind.'

The instant the door closed behind her an alarm bell began to scream and the overhead sprinklers burst to life. In a mad dash the executives scurried from the room, like rats deserting a sinking ship.

'Get these sprinklers turned off!' Buddy Peterson bellowed. He continued to sit at the table, his arms folded across his chest, ignoring the drenching spray. 'That was damned clever, Hunter,' he called above the screeching siren.

'She does have a certain…flair, doesn't she?' Hunter said, impervious to the water funneling in a small waterfall from his hat brim.

Peterson stood and approached. 'That's not what I meant, and you know it. How long are you going to keep her in the dark—not tell her who you really are?'

'As long as it takes.'

'You're playing a dangerous game. You could lose everything,' Peterson advised.

'I don't lose.' Hunter's voice dropped, a hard, threatening note coloring his words. 'Fair warning. One leak from anyone at this table and you'll all suffer the consequences. I'll be in touch soon.' He didn't wait for a response. Turning, he left.

'I still don't understand how you got so wet.'

'I told you. A freak shower.'

'Where? There isn't a cloud in the sky.' Sarcasm crept into her voice. 'Or perhaps it rained somewhere between the executive floor and the garage.'

He released a soft laugh. 'Something like that.'

She gave up. Hunter could be incredibly close-mouthed when he chose. If he'd decided that he wouldn't tell her, then he wouldn't. It was that simple. 'What did you say to the board after I left?'

He swung into another parking garage, this one beneath a brand-new, high-rise apartment complex. 'Not much. They didn't hang around for long.'

'Hunter!' she exclaimed in exasperation. 'Why won't you give me a straight answer? What did you say? How do you know them? For that matter, how did you know your way around their building? And why all the secrecy?'

He pulled into a wide parking space with H. Pryde stencilled on to the wall above it. Switching off the engine, he rested his arms on the steering-wheel and turned and looked at her. 'I know the Lyon board through work, which is also how I knew my way around their complex. I told Peterson that I'd be in touch soon. And I'm not being in the least secretive—just selective in what I tell you.'

'Why?'

'Because Lyon is my problem now, and I'll handle it.'

She could accept that. Having to deal all these years with the constant stream of difficulties on the ranch, it was a welcome change to have a second set of shoulders to help carry the burden. 'Why did you tell Buddy Peterson you'd be in touch?'

'To make certain he doesn't bother you again.'

'And he'll agree to that?' she asked in amazement.

'I won't give him any choice.' He opened his door. 'Coming?'

After unloading their overnight bags, Hunter led the way to the bank of elevators. Once there, he keyed the security lock for the penthouse and Leah stiffened. 'The penthouse?'

He paused before answering, and for some reason his momentary hesitation made her think of his advice about addressing the board members of Lyon Enterprises. 'Think before you speak,' he'd told her. 'Don't answer any question you don't want to.' Perhaps that advice didn't apply solely to board members. Perhaps it applied to recalcitrant wives as well.

'They paid me well in my previous job,' he finally said.

'I guess so. I'm surprised you left.' The car glided rapidly upward and she peeked at him from beneath her lashes. 'But that's right... You said you'd still do occasional jobs for them if they called. Troubleshooting, isn't that your speciality?'

'Yes.'

'What did you say the name of the company was?'

'I didn't.' He leaned back against the wall and folded his arms across his chest. 'Why all the questions, Leah?'

'You can't expect me not to have questions.' Her grip on her purse tightened. 'I'm...surprised.'

'Because I'm not the dirt-poor ranch-hand I once was?'

She shot him a sharp look. 'We've been over this before. That's not the problem and you know it. You ask me to trust you. To trust you blindly. But you tell me nothing about yourself, which means *you* don't trust *me*.'

'Point taken,' he conceded.

The doors slid silently apart, opening on to a huge entrance hall. Swallowing nervously, she stepped out of the car. 'Good heavens, Hunter, look at this place!'

'I've seen it before, remember?' he said gently. 'Make yourself at home.'

Her heels clicked on the oak parquet flooring as she crossed to the sunken living-room. 'Why didn't you tell me?' she asked quietly. 'Why the games?'

His hat sailed past her, skimming the coffee-table and landing dead-center in the middle of the *chaise longue*. 'All right. I admit I may have omitted a detail or two about my life these past eight years.'

'A detail or two?' she questioned with irony.

'Or three. What difference does it make? I have money. And I have an apartment in Houston. So what?'

'It's a penthouse apartment,' she was quick to remind him.

He shrugged irritably. 'Fine. It's a penthouse apartment. It doesn't change a damned thing. We're still married. I still work the ranch. And you're still my wife.'

'Am I?'

He thrust a hand through his hair. 'What the hell is that supposed to mean?'

'Why did you marry me, Hunter?'

'You know why.'

She nodded. 'For the ranch. Perhaps also for a bit of revenge. But what I don't understand is…why? Why would you care about such a small concern when you have all this?' He didn't respond, and she realized that she could stand there until doomsday and he wouldn't answer her questions. She picked up her overnight bag. 'I'd like to freshen up. Where do I go?'

'Down the hallway. Third door on the right.'

She didn't look back. Walking away, she fought an unease—an unease she couldn't express and chose not to analyze fully. The door he'd indicated was to the master bedroom. She closed herself in the adjoining bathroom and stripped off her clothes, indulging in a quick, refreshing shower. Slipping on a bathrobe, she returned to the bedroom.

She stood beside the bed for several minutes before giving into temptation. Climbing on top of the down coverlet, she curled up in the center and shut her eyes. A short catnap would do her a world of good. But, despite the best of intentions, her thoughts kept returning to Hunter and their conversation.

The situation between them grew more and more confusing with each passing day. Standing in the middle of the penthouse living-room, seeing the visual proof of the wealth and power she'd long suspected, had forced her to face facts. Hunter Pryde had returned to the ranch for a reason…a reason he'd chosen not to share with her.

And no matter how hard she tried to fight it, the same question drummed incessantly in the back of her mind. Having so much, what in heaven's name did he want with her and Hampton Homestead…if not revenge?

CHAPTER NINE

'LEAH? Wake up, sweetheart.'

She stirred, pulled from the most delicious dream of laughter and peace roses and babies with ebony hair and eyes. She looked up to find Hunter sitting beside her on the bed. He must have showered recently; his hair was damp and slicked back from his brow, drawing attention to his angled bone-structure. He'd also discarded his shirt and wore faded jeans that rode low on his hips and emphasized his lean, muscular build. He bent closer, smoothing her hair from her eyes, and his amulet caught the light, glowing a rich blue against his deeply bronzed chest.

'What time is it?' she murmured, stretching.

'Time for dinner. You've been sleeping for two hours.'

'That long?' She sat up, adjusting the gaping robe. 'I should get dressed.'

'Don't bother on my account,' he said with a slow grin. 'I thought we'd go casual tonight.'

She wrinkled her nose. 'I suspect this might be considered a little too casual.'

'Only one person will see.' He held out his hand. 'Let me show you.'

Curious, she slipped her fingers into his and clambered off the bed. He returned to the living-room and gestured toward a spiral staircase she'd failed to notice earlier. 'Follow me.' At the top he blocked her path. 'Close your eyes and hold on,' he instructed.

'Why?'

'You'll see.'

'Okay. Don't let me fall.'

Before she knew what he intended, he scooped her up into his arms. 'Trust, remember?' he murmured against her ear. A few minutes later he set her on her feet. 'You can look now.'

She opened her eyes and gasped in disbelief. They stood on the roof of the apartment building, but it was unlike any rooftop she'd ever seen. If she hadn't known better, she'd have sworn they stood in the middle of a park. Grass grew beneath her feet and everywhere she glanced were flowers—barrels of petunias, pansies and impatiens. Even irises and tulips bloomed in profusion.

'I thought you said you weren't a gardener,' she accused.

'I lied,' he said with a careless shrug. He indicated a greenhouse occupying one end of the roof. 'Some of the more delicate flowers are grown there. But I've had an outside concern take over since I moved to the ranch. They prepared everything for our visit.'

'It's…it's incredible.'

'Hungry?'

Suddenly she realized that she was. 'Starving,' she admitted.

'I thought we'd eat here. You can change if you want, but it isn't necessary.'

She caught the underlying message. She could dine in nothing but a robe, just as he dined in nothing but jeans, or she could dress and use her clothes as a shield, a subtle way of distancing herself.

'This is fine,' she said casually. 'Satisfy my curiosity, though. What sort of meal goes with scruffiness and bare feet?'

'A picnic, of course.'

He pointed to a secluded corner where a blanket had already been spread on the grass. All around the sheltered nook were pots and pots of azaleas, heavy with blossoms in every conceivable shade. A bucket anchored one corner of the blanket, the top of a champagne bottle thrusting out of the ice. Next to the champagne she saw a huge wicker basket covered with a red-checked square of linen.

She chuckled at the cliché. 'Fried chicken?' she guessed.

'Coleslaw and potato salad,' he confirmed.

'Fast food?'

He looked insulted. 'Catered.' Crossing to their picnic spot, he knelt beside the basket and unloaded the goodies on to china.

'You're kidding,' she said in disbelief, joining him on the blanket. 'China? For a picnic?'

He gave her a bland smile. 'Isn't that what you use?'

'Not likely.' She examined the champagne. 'Perrier Jouet flower bottle? Lalique flutes? Hunter, I'm almost afraid to touch anything.' She stared at him helplessly. 'Why are you doing this?'

'It seemed…appropriate.'

She bowed her head, her emotions threatening to shatter her self-control. 'Thank you,' she whispered. 'It's beautiful.'

'You're hungry,' he said, and she wondered if she just imagined the tenderness in his voice. 'Try this.'

He held out a succulent sliver of chicken that he'd stripped from the bone. She took it from him and almost groaned aloud. He was right. This didn't come close to fast food. She'd never tasted chicken with such a light, delicate flavor. Drawing her knees up against her chest, she tucked into the next piece he offered.

'Don't you trust me with the china?' she teased.

He extended a forkful of potato salad. 'Not when I'm seducing you.'

'With potatoes and fried chicken?' She nibbled the potato salad and this time did groan aloud. 'Ignore that question. This is delicious.'

'Want more?' At her eager nod, he patted the spot next to him. 'Then come closer.'

With a laugh she scrambled across the blanket to his side, and before long they shared a plate between them, exchanging finger food and dispensing with silverware whenever possible. Finally replete, she didn't resist when he drew her down so her head rested in his lap.

'Look at the sunset,' she said, gesturing at the vivid colors streaking across the sky above them.

'That's one of the reasons we're eating out here.' He filled a flute with champagne. Impaling a strawberry on the rim, he handed it to her. 'There's dessert.'

'No, thanks.' She sipped the champagne. 'This is all I need.' His fingers slipped into her hair and she closed her eyes beneath the delicate stroke of his hand, his abdomen warm against her cheek.

'Leah, watch,' he murmured.

She glanced up at the sky. As the last touch of purple faded into black, tiny pinpricks of light flickered to life around the rooftop. It was as though the stars had fallen from the heavens and been scattered like glittering dewdrops among the flowers. She raised a trembling hand to her mouth.

'Hunter, why?' She couldn't phrase the question any clearer, but he seemed to understand what she asked.

'I wanted tonight to be perfect.'

She released a shaky laugh. 'You succeeded.'

'Good. Because I'm going to make love to you and I

want it to be special. Very special.' He made no move to carry out his promise. Instead he sat motionless, apparently enjoying the serenity of the evening. 'Eight years ago you told your grandmother about our meeting at the line-shack, didn't you?' he asked unexpectedly.

It was the last question she had ever envisioned him broaching. She didn't even consider lying to protect Rose. 'Yes.'

'You came to the line-shack and waited for me.'

'Yes,' she admitted again.

'When did you find out I'd been arrested?'

'When you told me.'

'I was afraid of that.' He released a long sigh. 'I owe you an apology, Leah. I didn't believe you. I thought you were lying about what happened back then.'

'Did Grandmother Rose tell you the truth?'

'Yes. She told me.'

'I'm glad.' Leah hesitated, then said, 'There's also an explanation for why I wouldn't leave with you—if you're willing to listen.'

The muscles in his jaw tightened, but he nodded. 'I'm listening.'

'I told my grandmother about our meeting because I couldn't leave without saying goodbye to her. That was when I learned about Dad. He was dying of cancer, Hunter. I had to stay and help take care of him. That's why I wouldn't have gone with you. But I would have asked you to come back…afterward.' She stared at him with nervous dread. 'I hope you believe me, because it's the truth.'

For a long time he remained silent. Then he spoke in a low, rough voice, the words sounding as though they were torn from him. 'Growing up in an orphanage, honesty came in short supply. So did trust. No one cared much about the truth, just about finding a culprit.'

'And were you usually the culprit?' she asked compassionately.

'Not always. But often enough.'

'Didn't you try and explain?'

'Why?' he asked simply. 'No one would have believed me. I was a mongrel. Not that I was innocent, you understand. I provoked my share of trouble.'

She could believe he had, though she suspected that the trouble he'd provoked had never been undeserved. 'And then one day...' she prompted.

'How did you know there was a "one day"?'

She shrugged. 'It makes sense.' She felt his laugh rumble beneath her ear.

'You're right. Okay. One day—on my fifteenth birthday, as a matter of fact—they accused me of doing something I didn't. It was the last time that happened.'

'What did they accuse you of?'

'Breaking a snow crystal—remember, those globes you shake and the little flakes swirl around inside? This one had a knight fighting a dragon.'

She stilled. 'A knight and a dragon?'

'Yes. I'd always been fascinated by the crystal, but it belonged to one of the live-in workers and was off-limits. When it broke, I took the rap.'

'But you didn't break it.'

'No.'

'Why was that the last time they accused you?'

'I left. For good.'

'Blind trust,' she whispered.

'Blind trust,' he confirmed. 'I've never had anyone give me unconditional trust before—never had anyone stand by me in the face of overwhelming odds. I guess it's a futile dream. Still…it's my dream.'

She sat up and slipped her arms around his neck. 'If I could wrap my trust in a box, I'd give it to you as my wedding-gift,' she told him. 'But all I have is words.'

'Don't make promises you can't keep,' he warned.

Her brows drew together and she nodded. 'Then I'll promise to try. That's the best I can offer right now.'

'It's a start.'

He cupped her face and, after what seemed an endless moment, he lowered his mouth to hers. It was as though she'd been waiting an eternity for his possession. There'd be no further reprieve, no postponing the inevitable. After tonight she'd belong to him, joined with bonds more permanent than his ring on her finger.

Champagne and strawberries flavored his kiss, a kiss he ended all too soon, leaving her desperately hungry for more. 'Hunter,' she pleaded.

'Easy,' he answered, his lips drifting the length of her jaw. 'Slow and easy, love.'

And he did take it slow, seducing her with long, deep kisses, igniting the fires that burned so hotly between them. Slipping her robe from her shoulders, he cupped the pendant that had become a permanent fixture about her neck and in silent homage his mouth found the spot between her breasts where it so often nestled.

She gripped his shoulders, her eyes falling shut, blocking out the pagan sight of his dark head against her white skin. All she could do after that was feel…feel the touch of his tongue and teeth on her breasts, feel the hard, possessive sweep of his hands as he stripped off her robe, baring her to his gaze.

'You're even more beautiful than I remember,' he told her.

'Make love to me, Hunter. Now.' She shifted in his grasp, wanting to be closer, trembling with the strength of her need.

He lowered her to the blanket and she opened her eyes, staring up at him. He held himself above her, the embodiment of lean, masculine grace and raw power—a power muted only by the tenderness reflected in the black depths of his gaze. Then he came to her, joined with her, his body a welcome weight, hard and angled and taut beneath her hands.

And there, sequestered within their tiny slice of heaven, he showed her anew the true meaning of ecstasy. She didn't hold back. She couldn't. For, if she gave him nothing else, she'd give him all the love she possessed.

They spent the entire weekend at the apartment, relearning their roles as lovers. For Leah it deepened a love that had never truly died. Unfortunately, Hunter's reaction proved more difficult to read. He wanted her; she didn't doubt that for a minute. She could inflame him with the simplest of touches—his dark eyes burning with a hunger that stole her breath. Nor could she complain of his treatment, his gentleness revealing a certain level of caring. But love? If he experienced such an emotion, he kept it well-hidden.

To Leah's dismay, leaving the seclusion of the apartment and returning to the ranch proved to be the hardest thing she'd ever done.

Worse, the morning after their return Hunter rode Dreamseeker, the stallion at long last surrendering to the stronger, more determined force. Leah couldn't help drawing a comparison, feeling as though she, too, had surrendered to Hunter's perseverance, giving everything while he remained aloof and independent and in control. Never had she felt so defenseless, so aware of her own vulnerability— nor had she ever felt so afraid. As much as she'd have liked to protect herself, she suspected it was far too late.

The morning after Hunter broke the stallion, her fears took a new direction. Dreamseeker was missing from the pasture.

'Saddle Ladyfinger,' Hunter directed. 'And grab your slicker. It looks like more rain.'

Struggling to hide her concern, she did as he'd ordered, lashing the yellow oilskin to the back of her saddle. 'Could he have smashed down the fence again?' she asked apprehensively.

Hunter shook his head. 'Not a chance.'

He mounted his buckskin and they started out, riding toward the area the horse had broken through before. They'd almost reached the southernmost point of Hampton land when the first scream reverberated across the pasture.

Leah had heard that sound only twice before in her life, and it was one she'd never forget. It turned her blood to ice. Throwing a panicked glance in Hunter's direction, she dug her heels into Ladyfinger's flanks and charged toward the sound, Hunter at her side. Throughout the tense moments of that mad dash to the Circle P she prayed she'd be wrong. Prayed that Dreamseeker was safe.

Arriving at the property line, they paused briefly. The fence separating the two ranches had indeed been knocked down again, and Leah's heart sank. There was no doubt now as to what had happened…nor what was about to happen. Another scream echoed from over the next ridge, answered by an equally infuriated trumpeting. Crossing on to Circle P land, they sprinted to the top of the hill and discovered Bull Jones sitting on his mount, watching the scene below unfold.

Dreamseeker stood at one end of a small, tree-enclosed meadow, circling a chestnut thoroughbred stallion. Off to one side milled a nervous herd of mares, undoubtedly the motivation for the fight. Dreamseeker reared on to his hind legs, gnashing his teeth and striking out with his hooves. The chestnut joined in the ritualistic dance, copying each threatening move.

'You did this, Leah,' Bull growled, gimlet-eyed. 'I told you to secure your fence-line. Now it's too late. If that stallion of yours injures our thoroughbred, you'll pay big. Real big. Baby Blue's worth a fortune. If he goes down, it'll cost you your ranch.'

Leah glared at the foreman. 'You deliberately moved Baby Blue and those mares to this pasture in order to rile up our stallion. As to the fence…we reinforced it just last week. The only way Dreamseeker could have broken through is if you cut the wire.'

He laughed. 'Knowing something's one thing. Proving it is a whole different story.'

'She won't have to,' Hunter said in a clipped voice. 'I will.'

With a shrill roar, Dreamseeker reared back, then dropped to the ground with a bone-jarring thud and charged. Baby Blue, his eyes rolling back in his head, raced to meet his challenger.

'No!' Leah shrieked. Without thought or consideration of the danger, she slammed her heels into her horse's flanks, slipping and sliding down the hill.

'Leah!' she heard Hunter shout.

She ignored him, fighting to stay in the saddle while forcing her mare toward the heat of battle. Halfway down the hill, she realized that the terrified animal would go no further. Leah reined to a stop and flung herself out of the saddle. In two seconds flat she'd ripped her rain-slicker free. Screaming at the top of her lungs, she ran straight at the stallions, slapping the bright yellow oilskin in the air as hard as she could.

Just as she reached them the thoroughbred went down, and a sudden image of Hunter distracting the bull with his shirt flashed through her mind. Before Dreamseeker could move in for the kill she threw the slicker directly into her horse's face. He shied wildly, dropping his head and shaking it in an attempt to rid himself of the entrapping coat.

'Leah, move!' Hunter yelled, sprinting to her side. Clamping an arm around her waist, he threw her clear of the danger. Without a moment's hesitation he planted himself between her and imminent peril, nothing at hand with which to protect himself but his rope.

Dreamseeker bucked madly and finally succeeded in flinging the slicker off his head. He froze for an instant, as though trying to decide whether to charge the man or the downed stallion. It was all the opportunity Hunter needed. In one swift move his rope ripped through the air, snagging the stallion's forefeet. Throwing every ounce of mass and muscle behind the effort, Hunter wrenched the rope taut, dropping the horse in his tracks.

Spinning around, he ran flat out toward Leah. Snatching her to her feet with one hand, he hurled the rope around the nearest tree with the other. With more speed than artistry he secured the rope, effectively hobbling the horse.

Breathing hard, he slowly turned to face Leah. 'Woman, you and I are going to have a serious conversation. And, when it's done, your sit-down may be a little the worse for wear.'

162   MAIL-ORDER BRIDEGROOM

'Are you threatening me with physical violence?' Leah asked in disbelief.

His wrath shredded his rigid control. 'You're damned right I'm threatening you with physical violence!' he bit out. 'After what you pulled you'll be lucky if that's all I threaten you with.'

'I couldn't just wait while one of those stallions killed the other!'

He towered over her, his hands clenched, a muscle leaping in his jaw. 'Oh, yes, you could have, and you damned well should have. Before this day is through I intend to explain it to you in terms you won't soon forget. For now, you have a more pressing matter to take care of.'

'What's that?'

He gestured. 'Your horse,' he said flatly.

She couldn't believe she'd been so easily side-tracked. To her relief, she saw that Baby Blue had regained his feet and abandoned the field of battle, driving his harem of mares before him. She ran toward Dreamseeker, careful to keep a safe distance. Slowly she circled the downed animal, searching for any serious damage. He lay on his side, blowing hard and trembling, but without apparent injury. Before she could decide how to handle the stallion's safe return to his pasture, Bull Jones rode up.

'Move out of the way, Leah,' he ordered furiously. She looked up, horrified to discover Bull's Remington free of his scabbard and aimed at her stallion. 'I'm gonna shoot that bronco right between the eyes. If you don't want to get hurt, you'll stand clear.'

Leah never saw Hunter move. One minute Bull sat astride his horse, the next minute he lay flat on his back, his gun thrown out of reach and Hunter's foot planted in the center of his chest.

'We never had the chance to introduce ourselves,' Hunter said in a soft, menacing voice. 'It's time to correct that oversight.'

'I don't care who you are, *hombre*. Get the hell off me and get the hell off my land.' He squirmed in the dirt, attempting to worm his way out of his predicament. Not that it did him any good. Leah could tell he'd remain where he was until Hunter decided otherwise.

'First, it's not your land.' The boot pressed a little harder. 'And second, the name's Pryde. Hunter Pryde. You call me *hombre* once more and you won't be talking—or chewing—any time soon.'

'*Pryde*!' Bull's eyes bulged. 'I know you! You're—'

'Leah's husband,' Hunter interrupted smoothly.

'Aw, shoot. I didn't know *you* were Pryde...' Bull protested. 'You shoulda said something.'

'Being a fair and reasonable man, I'm going to give you two choices. You can get up, climb on your horse, and ride out of here, nice and friendly-like, or you can stay and we'll discuss the situation further. Well, *muchacho*? What's it going to be?'

'Let me up. I'll leave.'

Hunter removed his foot and stepped back. And though he seemed relaxed—his hands at his sides, his legs slightly spread—Leah knew that he stood poised for action should Bull offer any further threat. The foreman slowly gained his feet and reached for his rifle.

'Don't bother. You won't be needing it,' Hunter said, an unmistakable warning in his voice. 'And one more thing.'

'What's that?' Bull asked warily.

'As you ride out of here, take a final, long look around.'

Understanding dawned and a heavy flush crept up Bull's neck. 'You can't do that. I have pull, you know.'

Hunter's chilly smile was empty of humor. 'I have more.'

'You haven't heard the last of this,' Bull growled, mounting up.

'Any time you want to finish the discussion, feel free to drop by. I'll be happy to accommodate you.' Hunter waited until the foreman had ridden out of earshot before switching his attention to Leah. 'Your turn.'

'How can you do that?' she demanded, gesturing toward Bull's rapidly retreating back. 'How can *you* fire him?'

Hunter's gaze became enigmatic. 'Let's just say that Buddy Peterson will find it in his best interest to follow through with my…suggestion.'

A tiny frown creased her brow. After a moment's consideration she nodded. 'Let's hope you're right.'

'I am.'

He took a step in her direction and she froze. As much as she'd have liked to run for the hills, she refused to back down. 'I know. I know. It's my turn. Well, go ahead. Yell at me some more. Stomp around and cuss if you want. Just get it over with.'

'This isn't some sort of joke, Leah.' He snatched her close, practically shaking her. 'You could have been killed. And there wouldn't have been a damned thing I could have done to prevent it. I'd never have reached you in time.'

'I had to save Dreamseeker,' she protested.

He thrust her away, as though afraid of what he might do if he continued to touch her. 'You don't get it, do you? That horse is nothing compared to your safety. I should have let Jones shoot the damned animal and be done with it.'

She caught her breath in disbelief. 'You can't be serious.'

His eyes burned with barely suppressed rage, his features set in stark, remote lines. 'I'm dead serious. You promise me here and now that you won't ever, for any reason, risk your life for that horse again, or he goes.'

He wasn't kidding. She could tell when a man had reached the end of his rope and, without question, Hunter had reached it. Slowly she nodded. 'I promise.'

'I intend to hold you to that promise,' he warned.

She twisted her hands together. 'But you won't sell Dreamseeker?'

His voice turned dry, the rage slowly dying from his eyes. 'Don't worry, Leah. Your horse is safe for now, even if you aren't. Mount up. Let's get this bronco home. And when we get there, and my temper has had a chance to cool, you and I will finish this conversation.'

'That'll be some time next week, right?' she dared to suggest.

He yanked the brim of his stetson low over his brow. 'Try next month.' And with that he headed for his horse.

Hunter placed a call to Kevin Anderson, not bothering to waste time on preliminaries. 'I fired Bull Jones today.'

Kevin swore softly. 'What do you want me to do?'

'Take care of it. Make sure there aren't any... complications.'

'Is it Leah? Has she found out?'

'No. I don't think so. But considering I gave Jones his walking papers in front of her, it'll be a miracle if she doesn't at least suspect.'

'If she does—'

'Don't worry,' Hunter interrupted sharply. 'I'll handle my wife.'

A small sound brought his head around. Leah stood at the door, looking nervous and uncertain. Had she heard? he wondered, keeping his expression impassive. He gestured for her to come in.

'Listen, I have to go, Kevin. I'll be in touch.'

He hung up, not waiting for an answer. He stood up and walked around the desk, leaning against the edge. There he stayed, silent and watchful, as she approached. Catching her braid, he tugged her close. He wanted her. God, he wanted her. And he knew without a doubt that she wanted him as well. He could see it in her eyes, in the faint trembling of her lips and the rapid pounding of her heart.

Not bothering to conceal the strength of his desire, he pulled her roughly between his legs. Her eyes widened, the color almost violet with emotion. Her breath came swiftly between her parted lips, a delicate flush tinting her cheeks. It took only a minute to unbraid her hair, spreading the silvery curls around them like a silken cloak.

Unable to resist, he kissed her, taking her softness with a desire fast flaring out of control. 'Don't fight me,' he muttered against her mouth. 'Not now. Not any more.'

'Fight you?' she said, her voice wavering between laughter and passion. 'I wish I could.'

'Then kiss me, Leah. Kiss me like you mean it.'

She seemed to melt into him. 'I've always meant it. Haven't you realized that by now?' she whispered. And, wrapping her arms around his neck, she gave herself to him.

Leah stared at the ceiling, the moon throwing a shadowed pattern of branches across the smooth surface. What had he meant? she wondered uneasily.

She turned her head and studied Hunter as he slept. His passion tonight had exceeded anything that had ever gone before. More than once she'd nearly said the words, almost told him how much she loved him. But something had held her back. His conversation with 'Kevin', perhaps?

She frowned up at the ceiling again. So what had Hunter meant? What, precisely, did 'I'll handle my wife' signify? And why did it fill her with such an overwhelming dread?

CHAPTER TEN

LEAH awoke the next morning and for the first time found herself alone in bed. She sat up in a panic, not liking the sensation of having been deserted. Hunter was right. Waking in his arms made a difference to her entire day and she didn't appreciate the abrupt change.

She got up and went in search of him, only to discover that he'd left a brief note explaining he'd been unexpectedly called to Houston. The knowledge filled her with a vague alarm. She'd hoped to talk to him, to be held by him, to be reassured that his conversation with this…Kevin had nothing to do with their marriage—or the ranch.

So much for blind trust, she thought with a guilty pang. Let one small incident a little out of the ordinary happen and her trust evaporated like mist before the morning sun.

'I think I'll go into town and do some shopping,' she told her grandmother, needing an outlet for her restlessness.

'Stop by the jewelers and see if my watch is fixed,' Rose requested. 'They've had it a full week and my wrist feels naked.'

'Sure thing,' Leah agreed.

Not long after, she climbed into the ranch pick-up and drove the thirty minutes to the small town of Crossroads. She spent a full hour window-shopping and indulging in an éclair at Cindy's Sinful Pastries before coming upon a new antiques store. Intrigued, she went in, and after much diligent poking around unearthed a small statue that she knew she'd purchase regardless of the price.

Made of pewter, a dull silver knight rode a rearing charger. In one hand he clasped a lance, holding a fierce, ruby-eyed dragon at bay. With his other he pulled a veiled damsel to safety. The damsel's flowing gown reminded Leah of her own wedding-dress and she grinned. Considering the snow crystal story he'd told her, it was perfect. She'd put it in the study and see how long it took Hunter to notice—and whether he caught the significance of the gesture. After paying for the statue she crossed the street to the jewelers.

'Morning, Leah.' Clyde, the owner, greeted her, with a familiar smile. 'I just finished Rose's repair job last night.' He punched the charge into his register and handed her the boxed watch. Eyeing the imprinted shopping bag she carried, he said, 'I see you visited our new antiques store. Find something you liked?'

'Sure did. Want to see?' At his interested nod she carefully unwrapped her purchase, and proudly displayed it for the jeweler.

'My, that's a fine piece.' He peered at it over his wire-rimmed spectacles. 'A belated wedding-gift?' he asked, with the presumptuousness of a lifelong friendship. At her shy acknowledgement he beamed. 'I'm glad. Hunter's a good man.'

A sudden idea occurred to her and she pulled Hunter's pendant from beneath her blouse. 'Clyde... Can you make a miniature of this?'

'To go around the knight's neck?' he guessed. His mouth puckered in a thoughtful frown. 'Shouldn't be too difficult. Actually, I have a stone that would be ideal.'

'How long would it take?' she asked anxiously.

His eyes twinkled with amusement. 'I think Mrs

Whitehaven's ring adjustment can wait. How does an hour sound?'

She sighed in relief. 'It sounds ideal.'

'And if I can make one small suggestion?' He crossed to a display of pewter charms and removed one of the larger pieces—a cowboy hat. It fit the knight as though made for him. 'I could snip off the link and smooth it down, fix it to the knight's head so it won't come off. What do you think?'

It was perfect. 'Do it,' she directed. 'I'll be back in an hour. And Clyde?' He glanced up from the statue and she grinned. 'Thanks.'

'Any time, Leah. Any time.'

Precisely sixty minutes later she left the jewelers for the second time, her statue—complete with cowboy hat and pendant—gift-wrapped and safely tucked away in her handbag. To her dismay, the first person she ran into was Bull Jones. Before she could evade him, he blocked her path.

'Why, if it isn't Miz Hampton.' He removed his cigar from between his teeth. 'Oh, excuse me. That's Mrs Pryde, isn't it?'

'Yes, it is,' she retorted sharply. 'If you were smart, you'd remember that and stay clear, before Hunter hears you've been bothering me again.'

'I'm not worried. Your husband isn't here. And by the time he returns, I'll be long gone.'

Her blood ran cold and she glanced around, reassured to see that their confrontation had witnesses. She glared at Bull. 'You have something to say to me? Then say it. Otherwise, move out of my way before I bring the whole town down around your ears.'

'You always were a feisty little shrew. Okay. Why beat around the bush? Your husband's in Houston, isn't he?' He laughed at her expression. 'What, nothing to say? Aren't you even going to ask how I know?'

'I couldn't care less.' She refused to play into this man's hands. Not that it stopped him.

'I'll tell you anyway,' he offered with mock generosity. 'He's there because he's called the Lyon Enterprises' board together.'

She shrugged indifferently. 'He knows the board. That's not news to me,' she claimed.

But Bull shook his head. 'He doesn't just know the board. He *runs* the board.'

She jerked as though slapped. 'What are you talking about?' she demanded.

'That got your attention, didn't it?' He laughed, the sound hard-edged and rough. 'Hunter Pryde *is* Lyon Enterprises. Course I didn't find that out until he had me fired.'

'I don't believe you.'

'Suit yourself. But think about it.' His cigar jabbed the air, making small smoky punctuation marks. 'Lyon… Pryde…the Circle *P*. It all fits. And if you wanted to confirm it, it'd be easy enough to check out.'

'How?' The question was dragged from her.

'Call Lyon Enterprises. Ask for Pryde's office. If he has one there, you'll have your answer. You'll know he married you to get his hands on your ranch.'

'All I'll know is that he has an office,' she said scornfully. 'That doesn't mean he owns Lyon Enterprises. Nor does it mean he married me to get the ranch.' She wondered if he heard the edge of desperation in her voice. Probably.

'He owns it,' Bull said with absolute confidence. 'And when he realized he couldn't buy you out or force you out, he married you.'

She had to leave. She wouldn't stand here and be poisoned by any more of this man's filth. 'Get away from me, Jones. I'm not listening to you.' She attempted to push past him, but he grabbed her arm and jerked her to a stop.

He spoke fast, his words striking with a deadly accuracy. 'You were all set to marry some joe so that you wouldn't lose your spread. If you had, Lyon would have been permanently blocked. The second Pryde heard about it, he shows up, and marries you himself. Pretty shrewd move. He gets the girl and the land without paying one red cent.'

'I still own the ranch, not Hunter.'

'Do you?' He leaned closer and she turned her head away in revulsion. 'Maybe you do now. But for how much longer? Those business types will find a way around that little problem. They always do. And then you and your granny will be out on your collective backsides.'

With that he released her and, clamping his cigar between his teeth, walked away. She stood in the middle of the sidewalk for an endless moment. Then she practically ran to the truck. Sitting safely in the cab, she gripped the steering-wheel as though her life depended on it, struggling for a measure of calm.

Putting the conversation into perspective, she knew Bull had an ax to grind and so she needed to weigh his comments accordingly. But what horrified her so was that every word he had uttered made perfect sense, playing on her most intrinsic fears. Hunter *had* wanted the ranch above all else. And never once had he been willing to tell her why.

Because he knew she'd never marry him if he did?

She stared blindly out the front windshield for several minutes. She had to think, had to keep a clear head. Either Bull spoke the truth or he lied. It was that simple. All she had to do was figure out which.

Conrad Michaels. The name came to her from nowhere and she seized it with relief. Of course! He had contacts. He could do some digging…off the record. Without giving it further consideration, she started the engine and pointed the truck in the direction of home. She'd call Conrad. He'd help her.

So much for blind trust, she thought in anguish. But how could she be expected to trust when her knight had suddenly turned back into the dragon?

Leah took a deep breath and spoke brightly into the phone, 'Conrad? It's Leah. I'm fine, thanks. And you?' She listened for several minutes while he told her, then admitted, 'Yes, I did call for a reason. I was curious about something and thought you could help.'

'Of course, Leah,' Conrad said agreeably enough. 'What can I do for you?'

She tapped her pencil against the desk blotter. 'It's…it's about our loan. The ranch loan. Did Hunter arrange for it with your bank? I mean… You had the old one and I thought…'

'It's not with our bank,' Conrad informed her bluntly. 'Not any more. Your lawyer insisted that Hunter initially place it with us as part of your prenuptial agreement. But I heard that shortly after your marriage it was bought out by an independent concern. All perfectly legal, you understand.'

'But it was with you originally?'

'Yes.'

Now for the hard part. After a brief pause, she asked, 'Do you know who bought it out?'

'What's this about, Leah? Why aren't you asking Hunter these questions?'

She heard the tension in his voice and regretted putting him in such an uncomfortable position. Unfortunately, she had to know. 'I'm asking you, Connie,' she said evenly, deliberately used the family nickname. 'I need to make sure the payments are current, that I'm not in arrears.'

'I see.' He sounded old and tired.

She closed her eyes, hating herself for involving him. But there'd been no one else she could turn to. 'I realize you're retired and out of the loop. Still, I'd hoped you'd have contacts who could give you the information. I'm sorry to ask for such a big favor. I wouldn't, unless it was important,' she apologized.

'Of course. I'll look into it.'

'You'll be discreet?'

'Don't worry. I'll be discreet.'

She thanked him and hung up, checking his name off the list she'd composed. One down. Studying the piece of paper in front of her, she eyed the second name and number. This next would take even more nerve. She forced herself to reach for the phone again and dial the number. An operator answered almost immediately.

'Lyon Enterprises. How may I direct your call?'

'Hunter Pryde, please.'

'One moment.'

After a brief delay a secretary answered. 'Felicia Carter speaking. May I help you?'

Leah frowned. 'I'm sorry. I asked for Hunter Pryde's office.'

'I can help you,' the secretary hastened to assure. 'May I ask who's calling?'

'Is he in?' Leah persisted.

'He's tied up with the board all day. I can give him a message if you'd like.'

Leah closed her eyes. 'No message.' She started to hang up, then froze. 'Wait! His title. Could you tell me his title with the company?'

'I'm afraid you'll have to discuss that with Mr Pryde.' A hint of suspicion tinged Felicia's voice. 'Could I have your name, please?'

Without another word, Leah cradled the receiver. So. Part of Bull's story checked out. Hunter could be reached at Lyon Enterprises. But that didn't mean he had an office there; it didn't even mean he worked there. And it was far from indisputable evidence that he owned the company. There's no need to panic, she told herself, breathing a little easier. She'd managed to glean two facts. He had business in Houston with Lyon and their meeting was ongoing.

Beneath her hand the phone rang and she lifted it. 'Yes? Hello?'

'It's Conrad.'

From the reluctance in his voice she could tell that she wouldn't appreciate the information he'd gathered. 'Get it over with. I can take it,' she told him.

'It's not anything definitive,' he was quick to explain, 'so don't jump to any conclusions. The company that bought out your note is named HP, Inc.'

'HP, Inc? As in…Hunter Pryde, Incorporated?'

'It's…possible, I suppose. I couldn't get the status of the loan itself. But I have their number in Houston, if you want it.'

'I want it.' She jotted down the information and thanked him.

'Let me know if you need me,' Conrad said. 'I had hoped…' He didn't finish his sentence. He didn't have to.

'Me, too,' she said in a soft voice.

This time she didn't delay placing the call. Asking for

Hunter's office, the operator once again put her through, and once again a secretary offered to take a message.

'This is Felicia Carter at Lyon Enterprises,' Leah said. 'I'm trying to track down Mr Pryde.'

'Why... I believe he's working over there today, Ms Carter.'

Leah managed a careless laugh. 'How silly of me. I must have gotten my days mixed up.' Then on impulse she said, 'I don't know how he keeps it straight. It must be difficult owning two such large companies.'

'Yes, it is. But Mr Pryde's an unusual man. And he only hires the best. Delegation. It makes his life much easier. One minute, please.' Leah could hear a brief, muffled conversation before the secretary came back on the line. 'Mr Pryde's assistant just came in. Would you like to speak to him?'

'Kevin?' she asked casually.

'Oh, you know him?'

She ducked the question. 'That won't be necessary. I'll get the information I need at this end.' To her horror, her voice broke. 'Thank you for your help,' she managed to say, and hung up.

The tears, once started, couldn't be stopped. She despised herself for being so weak. It wasn't the end of all her dreams. She still had her grandmother and the ranch. She still had her employees and Dreamseeker. But somehow it wasn't enough. She wanted Hunter. Most of all, she wanted Hunter's love.

Too bad all Hunter wanted was her ranch.

'What's going on, Leah?'

Leah looked up, distressed to see her grandmother standing in the doorway. Silently she shook her head, swiping at her damp cheeks and struggling to bring her emotions under control.

'Is it Hunter?' Rose asked, stepping into the room. 'Has something happened to him?'

'No! Yes!' Leah covered her face with her hands, fighting to maintain control. She couldn't afford to break down again. 'His health is fine, if that's what you mean.'

Rose crossed to the desk. 'Then, what's wrong?'

'Hunter owns Lyon Enterprises, that's what's wrong.' She slumped in the chair. 'I'm…I'm sorry. I didn't mean to blurt it out like that.'

'Hunter owns Lyon Enterprises,' Rose repeated. 'You're joking.'

'It's true,' Leah said in a tired voice. 'I just got off the phone with his office. Dammit! What am I going to do?'

'You're going to talk to him, of course.'

'*Talk*?' She stared at her grandmother in disbelief. 'What's to say? "Oh, by the way, did you really marry me just to get your hands on my ranch?" That's why he proposed. He never made any secret of the fact.'

Rose planted her hands on her hips. 'Then why act so betrayed?' she snapped. 'What's the difference if he wanted the ranch for himself or for his business? If you married the owner of Lyon Enterprises it sounds to me like you were the one to get the better end of that deal.'

That brought her up short. 'Excuse me?'

'You heard me. Think about it. Hunter's gotten one thing out of this so-called bargain—a lot of hard work and darned little thanks. But if he's Lyon, you get the ranch, the Circle P, and anything else he cares to throw into the hat…' She cackled. 'Best of all, you get Hunter. Yessir. Sounds like a damned good trade to me.'

'Until he manages to obtain title to the ranch and forecloses on us. Next comes the divorce and then we're begging on the streets.'

Rose snorted. 'You really are a ninny. Get your butt out of that chair, climb into the pick-up and drive to Houston. Talk to the man. Ask him why he married you. Flat out.'

'I already know—'

'He actually told you he married you for the ranch?' Rose asked with raised eyebrows. 'Or did you assume it?'

Leah shook her head in bewilderment. 'I don't remember. I…I don't think he said. Every time I asked, he'd just stand there.'

'Looking insulted, maybe? I would have.'

'Why?' she demanded. 'That's the reason we married. It's not a secret. No matter how much you try to wrap it up in pretty ribbons and bows, I married for business, not love. And so did Hunter.'

'I'm sure you're right. A man as rich as Croesus, as smart as a whip and as handsome as ever came down the pike is going to sacrifice himself in marriage in order to get his hands on one little old Texas ranch.' She heaved a sigh. 'Sounds reasonable to me.'

Leah bit down on her lip. 'Stop making so much sense! You're confusing me.'

'Good. Now for the punchline. Do you love him?'

There was only one possible answer to that question. 'Yes,' she said without a moment's hesitation. 'More than anything.'

Her grandmother grinned. 'That's all you need to remember. Here's your purse. Here's the keys to the pick-up. Go to Houston. I'll see you tomorrow. Or the next day. Or the one after that. Go hide out in that apartment of Hunter's and make some babies. I want to be a great-grandma. Soon. You hear me, girl?'

'I hear you. Judging by how loud you're shouting I'm sure Inez, her children and at least two-thirds of our wranglers heard you, too.'

But she obeyed. Without another word of argument, Leah took the keys and her purse and walked out of the study. Not giving herself a chance to reconsider and chicken out, she climbed into the pick-up and started the engine. Pulling a Bull Jones, she spun the wheel and stomped on the gas, kicking up an impressive rooster tail of dirt and gravel as she headed down the drive.

Half a dozen times she almost turned back. But something kept her going. One way or another she'd have her answers—whether she liked them or not. And maybe—just maybe—she could convince Hunter to give their marriage a chance. A real chance. She loved him. And she intended to fight for that love.

She only got lost twice, but the delay added to her growing tension. Finally she found the Lyon Enterprises building and pulled into the underground garage. She didn't know how she'd talk her way into the board meeting, but somehow she'd do it. Stopping at the security desk, she showed her credentials.

'Leah Pryde,' she told the guard. 'Mrs Hunter Pryde. I'm supposed to meet my husband.'

'Certainly, Mrs Pryde. I'll ring upstairs and let him know you're here.'

'I'd rather you didn't,' she said, offering her most persuasive smile. 'I'd like to surprise him.'

He looked momentarily uncertain, then nodded. 'Sure. I suppose that would be all right.'

'Thanks.'

With a calm that she was far from feeling she walked to the bank of elevators, and all too soon arrived on the executive floor. This time no secretary waited to greet her. She glanced down at her clothes and wished she'd thought to change before leaving home. Jeans and a cotton blouse didn't seem quite appropriate. Did they have dress codes on executive floors? At the very least she should have brushed her hair. Her braid was almost nonexistent, loose curls drifting into her face.

She peeked up and down the deserted hallway, aware that it wouldn't be wise to delay much longer. Someone would soon stop her and she didn't doubt for a minute that they'd call security or, worse...Hunter. Looking neither right nor left, she started for the boardroom. If she was going to get thrown out of the place, she'd rather have done something to earn it.

Five yards from the huge double doors, the first road-block appeared. 'Excuse me,' the tall, perfectly groomed woman said. 'May I help you?'

'No,' Leah replied and kept walking.

The persistent woman scooted ahead, planting herself square in front of the boardroom doors. 'I'm Felicia Carter,' she tried again, offering her hand. 'And you are?'

'Late. Excuse me.' Leah brushed past the secretary and reached for the door, but Felicia proved too quick. The woman grasped Leah's hand and shook it.

'It's a pleasure, Miss...?'

'Leah.'

'Leah.' The handshake turned to an iron-like clasp. 'If you'd come this way, we can find out what your situation is and we can get it taken care of right away.'

'*We* appreciate your help,' Leah said with an amiable smile, and turned in the direction Felicia indicated. The second the woman moved from the door Leah broke free, and lunged for the knob. An instant later she scooted inside the boardroom and slammed the huge door in Felicia's face, locking it.

'Take care of that,' she muttered beneath her breath, and turned to face the board members.

To her horror there were about twice the number there'd been on her last visit. And every last one of them stared at her as though she'd just pulled up in a flying saucer. At the far end, where Buddy Peterson had last been, sat Hunter, his chair pushed back, his feet propped on the glass table. Buddy now sat to Hunter's right.

'Don't be shy.' Hunter's words, gentle and yet oddly menacing, dropped into the deafening silence. 'Come on in.'

'Okay.' She took a single step forward. 'I think that's far enough.'

For an endless minute their gazes met and held—and if his was implacably black and remote, she didn't doubt for an instant that hers was filled with a mixture of defiance and fear.

The phone at Hunter's elbow emitted a muted beep and he picked it up. 'Yes, Felicia, she's here. Relax. I'll take care of it.' He hung up and addressed the board members. 'Ladies. Gentlemen. My wife.' Cautious murmurs of greeting drifted around the room and after a long, tense moment, he asked, 'What can we do for you, Leah?'

She swallowed hard. Maybe she should have rehearsed this part at some point during the drive. She glanced at him uncertainly. 'I wondered...' She took a deep breath. 'I wondered if there was something you have to tell me.'

His eyes narrowed and he removed his feet from the table and straightened in his chair. 'No. Is there something you have to tell me?'

So, he wasn't going to admit who he really was. He'd

warned her that he'd never explain himself again. Still, he had to know that she wouldn't be here if she didn't at least suspect the truth. He had to know that the cards were stacked against him. And yet he expected her to trust him…or not. It was that simple. And suddenly she realized that despite everything she'd been told, despite all the facts that proved his duplicity, she did trust him. And she loved him.

'No,' she whispered. 'I don't have anything to tell you.'

His mouth tightened. 'Then if you'd excuse us?'

With a passion that brought tears to her eyes she wished she'd never come, that she'd never listened to Bull Jones, that she'd never given an ounce of weight to any of the despicable suggestions he'd made. Did she believe Jones more than Hunter? Never. Now she'd failed. She'd failed her husband, and she'd failed herself. When it came to a choice, she'd chosen to doubt him. And he'd never forgive her for that.

Her shoulders sagged in defeat and she started to turn away. Then she froze. What had he said that night at his apartment? 'I've never had anyone give me unconditional trust before—never had anyone stand by me in the face of overwhelming odds. I guess it's a futile dream. Still…it's my dream.'

She set her jaw. No. She wouldn't walk away. She wouldn't give up. She loved him. She loved him more than anything in her life. More than Dreamseeker, more than her employees, even more than the damned ranch. He wanted blind trust? Fine. She'd give it to him.

'Yes,' she said, turning around again. 'I do have something to say. In private, if you don't mind.'

'Ladies, gentlemen. Sign the papers,' Hunter ordered, snapping his briefcase closed and lifting it from the table.

'If you'll excuse us. My wife and I have a few matters to discuss in private.' He stood and walked to a door that opened on to a small office off the conference-room. Shutting them in the restrictive confines, he tossed his briefcase on to the desk and turned to her. 'What the hell is this about, Leah?'

She gathered her nerve to speak, to say the words that were long, long overdue. 'The whole time we've been married you've asked for only one thing from me. You told me that it's more precious to you than anything else. I offered to box it up for a wedding-gift if I could. Well... Here it is. My gift to you. It's up to you what you do with it.' She opened her purse and pulled out the gift-box from the jewelers.

He stared at it, making no move to take what she offered. 'What is it?'

'Open it and find out.'

He took the box then, and ripped it apart, removing the statue. She heard the swift intake of his breath, saw the lines of his jaw tighten. And then he looked at her, his black eyes aflame with a fierce, raw joy. 'Do you mean this?' he demanded. 'You trust me?'

She nodded, biting down on her lip. 'With all my heart.'

A brief knock sounded at the door and Buddy Peterson stuck his head in the office. 'Papers are signed and the boardroom's all yours. By the way, that was a gutsy move. Some might call it chivalrous. You could have lost everything you own.'

Hunter inclined his head in acknowledgement. 'Instead I won.' He glanced at Leah. 'Everything.'

Buddy grinned. 'I guess things will change now that you own the whole shooting-match.'

'Count on it,' Hunter agreed.

The door closed behind the executive and they were alone again. 'I don't understand,' she whispered. 'I thought you already owned Lyon Enterprises.'

He shook his head. 'Not until two minutes ago.'

'And before that?'

'I was their chief rival…and their worst nightmare.'

She could hardly take it in. 'Why didn't you tell me?'

'Because until the papers were signed there was nothing to tell. Like the man said, I could have failed in my take-over bid and lost everything.'

'Not everything,' she suddenly realized, tears starting to her eyes. 'Not the ranch.'

'No,' he conceded. 'I made sure that was protected by our prenuptial agreement.'

'You told me to read it. I guess I should have.' She gazed up at him a little uncertainly. 'Hunter?'

His eyes glittered with amusement. 'Yes, Leah? Could it be there's something you forgot to tell me after all?' He reached for her braid, releasing the strands and draping the curls across her shoulders.

'I believe there is.' A slow smile crept across her mouth and she tilted her head to one side. 'Yes, now that I think about it, I'm positive there is.' She stepped into his arms and rested her cheek against his chest. 'Have I told you yet how much I love you?'

He dragged the air into his lungs, releasing his breath in a long, gusty sigh. 'No. I believe you forgot to mention that part.'

'I have another question, and this time you have to answer,' she said, pulling back to look up at him. 'Why did you marry me?'

He didn't hesitate. 'Because you were going to marry the next man who walked through your door. And I couldn't let you do that unless I was that next man.' His tone reflected his determination. 'Fact is, I planned to be the only man to walk through your door.'

'But you wanted to buy the ranch.' It wasn't a question.

'True. At first, I wanted it in order to block Lyon and force them into a vulnerable position. Later it was so that I could protect you from them.'

'That's what Buddy Peterson meant when he said that the takeover attempt was a chivalrous move?'

Hunter shook his head. 'It wasn't. Buying the ranch would have facilitated my takeover. Marrying you…'

'Was riskier?' she guessed.

'A little. But worth it.' He reached behind her and removed a file folder from his briefcase, handing it to her.

'What's this?'

'Open it and find out,' he said, throwing her own words back at her.

She flipped open the file. Inside she found the deed to Hampton Homestead—free and clear, and in her name. The date on the title was the day before their wedding. 'Hunter…' she whispered.

'I love you, Leah. I've always loved you. How could I not? You've given me my dream.'

She managed a wobbly smile, tears clinging to her lashes. 'I think it's time for some new dreams, don't you?'

He enfolded her in his arms. 'Only if they're made with you,' he said.

And he kissed her. He kissed her with a love and passion that she couldn't mistake. And wrapped in his embrace she knew she'd found her life, her heart and her soul. She'd found her knight in shining armor.

At long last her dragon had been vanquished.

EPILOGUE

LEAH took a sip of coffee as she leafed through the morning paper. And then she saw it—the ad practically jumping off the page at her.

WIFE WANTED!
Male rancher in immediate and desperate need of his woman! Interested applicant should:
1. *Be 27 today and have eyes the color of Texas blue-bonnets—a feisty and ornery personality is a plus!*
2. *Have extensive ranching background—and the good sense to know when not to use it!*
3. *Have solid business know-how—particularly the ability to dampen the tempers of bullheaded board members.*
4. *Be pregnant. Did I mention the doctor called?*
I am a thirty-four-year-old man and can offer you a comfortable bed and an occasional rooftop picnic with all the stars a Texas sky can hold. (Details of a more intimate nature are open to negotiation as soon as you hightail it upstairs). Your husband awaits. Impatiently!

Tossing the ad to one side, Leah leapt from her chair and ran...ran to her husband, the love of her life...but, most important of all, to the father of her baby.

Margaret Way takes great pleasure in her work and works hard at her pleasure. She enjoys tearing off to the beach with her family on weekends, loves haunting galleries and auctions and is completely given over to French champagne "for every possible joyous occasion." Her home, perched high on a hill overlooking Brisbane, Australia, is her haven.

Margaret started writing when her son was a baby, and now she finds there is no better way to spend her time. She had her first book published by Mills & Boon® in 1970 and since then she has written 75 books, which have been distributed worldwide.

A FAULKNER
POSSESSION
by
MARGARET WAY

CHAPTER ONE

END of school. It invoked so many memories, exquisite and painful, time was suspended while Roslyn became lost in them. Students and fellow teachers were mostly long gone, but she continued to sit at her desk staring out broodingly over the beautifully manicured lawns and gardens of Seymour College for Girls. There were many jacarandas in bloom in the grounds, but instead of emerald sweeps of lawn and a glorious, lavender blue haze, her inner eye was possessed by her old visions....

The immensity of the desert...a burning sun going down over infinite miles of red sand...towering, windswept dunes transformed by the sunset into pyramids of gold...a raven-haired young man—how beautiful he was astride a wonderful, palomino horse—a small girl up before him, her enormous topaz eyes full of wonder and adoration for all the vast chasm between them.

Macumba. Marsh Faulkner. It gave her no peace to think of them. Marsh, once her idol, now the man she struggled daily to keep from her thoughts. The old, remarkable friendship? Banished without a trace. Except for memories. Memories had the power to return at any time, like old passions that refused to die.

Roslyn's eyes clouded with melancholy. She slumped back in her chair unaware her hands were gripping the mahogany arms. It wasn't as though she hadn't tried. Even now she blinked furiously in an effort to dispel those haunting images, but they continued to possess

her; so vivid, so immediate, she felt nostalgia and pain
in every cell of her heart.

For most of her childhood and adolescence, the end
of term meant only one thing. The return to Macumba.
Stronghold of the Faulkners. Flagship of Faulkner Holdings, a beef cattle empire that spread its operations over
the giant state of Queensland, from its desert heartland
to the lush jungles of the tropic north and into the vast
wilderness of the Northern Territory, one of the world's
last great frontiers. The Faulkners, descendants of the
founding fathers, were the landed establishment, enormously rich and powerful, and heirs to a splendid, his-
toric homestead that had in its history entertained roy-
alty, Indian maharajahs and countless VIP's.

And my mother is the housekeeper, Roslyn thought.
The whole thing just broke her to pieces. Her beautiful,
hardworking, incredibly loyal and long-suffering mother
was housekeeper to the Faulkners and had been for the
past ten years. She would never come to terms with it,
her nature behind the cool facade, bright, passionate and
above all, proud. My mother, all I have in this world, is
just another Faulkner possession. She could be here with
me, free and independent, yet she chooses to remain in
service. It didn't bear thinking about, and most of the
time Roslyn couldn't. Her great purpose in life since
she'd been able to earn money was to provide for her
mother: to repay all her mother's endless sacrifices. She
had a house: there was room: they could live together.
Except for the grievous fact her mother chose to remain
on Macumba.

Oh, hell!

Roslyn stood up so precipitously she sent a pile of
textbooks on the edge of her desk flying. Sighing, she
bent to retrieve them and as she did so, Dave Arnold,

the junior science master came into the room. He took one look at her and hurried around the desk.

"Here, let me get those, Ros!"

This was the colleague who had lit up Dave's year. Roslyn Earnshaw. A slender, graceful young woman, average height, great legs, slight but sensual curves, wonderful dark hair he had sometimes seen in a cloud, now neatly confined at the nape; large, faintly slanted topaz eyes, a flawless magnolia skin that was the envy of all Seymour. Dave, like everyone else, thought Roslyn a natural beauty who played down her looks. She was always beautifully groomed in good, classic clothes, but Dave thought quite another person lurked behind the contained exterior. A witching, passionate person with a volatility just below the surface. Not that her pupils didn't love her. They adored her like an older, more beautiful and clever sister. But then, Roslyn showed another side to her students. It was with staff that she maintained a pleasant, but impenetrable reserve. She was highly regarded as a teacher, but no one knew much about her private life. Roslyn Earnshaw was something of an enigma, which greatly endeared her to Dave who found mysterious young women terribly glamorous.

He stacked the books on the desk and Roslyn thanked him with a smile. Sadness to sunshine! It entranced Dave, who asked, as if he didn't already know, "Your car is being serviced, isn't it?"

Roslyn pulled down the window and locked it. "Don't worry about me, Dave. I thought you long gone."

"Without saying goodbye?"

She looked at him with gentle wryness. "You *did* say goodbye. At the staff party."

"That was public. This is private. Besides, someone has to drive you home."

"You do have a kind heart, Dave. Thank you. I'm very grateful."

A few minutes later they were walking through the empty corridors and out to the staff parking lot, its functionalism masked by tall borders of flowering oleanders. Seymour was justifiably proud of its magnificent grounds. The annual Spring garden party drew huge crowds.

"What do you intend to do with yourself over the holidays?" Dave asked as they were driving away.

"I haven't decided yet." Roslyn gave a faint sigh. "My mother wants me to visit her, but there are complications."

"Such as?" Dave was curious.

"Other people, Dave. Other people to spoil things."

Dave took a moment to digest that. "I see." He glanced at her quickly. "You never talk much about your family. In fact, you never talk about them at all."

"I haven't got much of a family, that's why. I'm an only child. My father was killed when I was fourteen."

"I'm sorry, Roslyn," Dave said with genuine sympathy. "That accounts for the sad look."

"I didn't know I had one."

"You do. The reverse of the super-efficient look we all know. But getting back to your mother, has she remarried? Is that it?"

She should have remarried. She should have had someone to love her, Roslyn thought. "Mother never remarried," she told Dave. "My father was something of an adventurer. As a young man he packed a bag and headed for the outback to become a jackaroo. He thrived on station life, tough as it is. Eventually he got to manage an outstation. When he was twenty-six he met my mother. She was an English girl working her way around

Australia with a friend. Her mother died when she was three. Her father remarried a year later and started another family. According to my mother, her stepmother never wanted her and things got worse as my mother grew up. I should tell you, she's beautiful, and that doesn't always make for a happy life. Her upbringing made her very vulnerable. Sometimes I think she's still a lost child.

"Anyway, she left home as soon as she was able and came to Australia with her friend, Ruth. They've kept in touch through the years. My father fell in love with my mother at first sight. He could never get over the wonder of getting her to marry him, he said. She was so refined and gently spoken and he was very much the prototype of Crocodile Dundee, funny, gritty, very direct. I loved him and he adored his two girls. Once he was settled, he started stepping up the ladder. When I was about ten, he became head stockman of a very grand station indeed. Life was a lot easier and settled for my mother. A nice bungalow, more money, permanency if things worked out. They did. Dad did become overseer, but he was killed a little over a year later."

Dave took his eyes off the road to stare at her. "How did it happen?"

"He was thrown from his horse and broke his neck. He had lived in the saddle, that was the tragic irony. My mother never got over it. For me the pain has dulled with the years, but I've always been conscious of *loss*, of missing him. An expression, a song, the scent of the bush makes it all come rushing back. Life is so *sad*!"

"It is for a lot of people. Where is your mother now?"

"Still at the same place." Roslyn couldn't control the strain in her voice. "After Dad was killed, the owner offered her a job and she took it."

"You don't sound too happy about it?"

"Not then and not now," Roslyn admitted. "We could have made it on our own."

"But you said yourself your mother is a vulnerable woman. She would have been devastated at the time. Widowed so early with a young daughter. Times like that, people either make a complete break or stick with what they know. What job was it?"

"Housekeeper," Roslyn announced flatly.

"So?" Dave turned his head in surprise. "You're not a snob, are you?"

"I am and you'd better believe it! Where my *mother* is concerned. I can't bear to see her at anyone's beck and call. Especially not them. I worked like a demon all through school and university. I graduated in the top three of my class. Seymour took me on and they don't take just anybody, as you know. I make good money and I can look after my mother." There I go again, she thought. A fixation. I can't leave the subject alone.

"Are you quite sure she can't look after herself?" Dave asked as gently as he could.

Roslyn closed her eyes. "Oh, Dave, you *can't* know. One has to experience what I'm talking about. These people are enormously rich and powerful. They aren't like you and me. They say the rich are different. They *are*. They have super and often unwarranted confidence in themselves and their opinions. They move through life like the lords of creation. Some of the women can be unbearable. I've known a few who were affronted I would dare speak to them. Others found me quaint. Some women like throwing their menfolk's power around." She gave a little embarrassed laugh. "I know I sound like I've got a giant chip on my shoulder. I have. But I grew up a kid people could, and did, hurt."

"Well, it doesn't show," Dave said comfortingly. "Hardly a girl in the school doesn't dream of looking and sounding like Miss Earnshaw."

Roslyn shook her head, smiling slightly. "It's my skin they like, Dave. Spots can make the teen years a torment. Don't think too badly of me. It's just that I want a better life for my mother."

"It hurts she won't come and live with you?"

"It does. Rather badly. It's all I've worked for, but she says I must be free to live my own life. She's content where she is."

"So why don't you accept it?"

Roslyn shrugged. "You wouldn't, either, Dave. This isn't a nice family situation like the Brady Bunch. Anyway, I don't believe her. My mother is only fifty years old. She's a beautiful woman but she's had such a hard life. At least, not one of her own. Think what other women are doing at her age. She hasn't really lived at all."

There was a short pause while Dave considered. "I can see your point, Ros," he said finally, "but it's *your* point, isn't it? Your mother's tragedies may have robbed her of a lot of fight. So, what is this place we're talking about? You're terribly secretive."

Roslyn glanced down at her locked hands. "I suppose I am. I like to keep my private life private, but end of term depletes my reserves. I start harking back to the old days. Always a mistake. They're there waiting for me if I let down my guard. I've told you more than I've told most people. The name of the station is Macumba. Macumba Downs."

Dave looked flabbergasted. "But that's the *Faulkner* place!"

"Snap out of it, Dave. They're human."

"They're *not*! Why, the old guy—the founding father—is an icon. I'll be honest with you, Ros, I'm
amazed. Wasn't a Faulkner killed in a plane crash a few
years ago?"

"Sir Charles, the owner," Roslyn said, her expression
turning sad. "His plane came down in a freak electrical
storm en route to one of their northern properties. Sir
Charles and Lady Faulkner were killed, along with two
passengers. One was a lifelong American friend. The
other was Sir Charles's younger brother, Hugo." She
didn't say Marsh had been scheduled to go with them
but some crisis had kept him on the station. She often
had nightmares about Marsh dying in that crash.

Dave was engrossed. "What a tragedy!" he breathed.
"It must have been the son on television recently. Something to do with beef cattle exports to Japan and South-
East Asia. I haven't a lot of interest in the subject, but
he made me sit up and take notice. Electrifying kind of
guy. Founding family. Old money. Doesn't have to
prove anything. Is he married? Bound to be."

Roslyn shook her head. "No, he isn't."

"He must be the biggest catch in the country!" Dave
chortled.

"He knows it."

"I imagine he might. His name is Charles, too, as I
recall."

Roslyn looked out the window. "Everyone calls him
Marsh. Marshall is his middle name. It was Lady
Faulkner's maiden name. The Marshalls still control the
Mossvale Pastoral Company."

Dave made another little howling sound. "Mossvale!
Gosh, isn't it always the way. Money marries money."

"It keeps it all together."

"And how do you feel about Marsh Faulkner?" Dave

asked. "He seems like the kind of guy to arouse powerful feelings."

Roslyn smoothed her skirt over her knee. "He is."

Dave was intrigued by the thread of steel in Roslyn's attractive, low-pitched voice. "Can you elaborate on that?"

"Not a chance! Let's get off the subject, Dave."

"It does have a disturbing ring," he agreed.

Ten minutes later they turned onto Roslyn's quiet, tree-lined street made a glory by the summer flowering of the poincianas. Dave commented on their spectacular beauty as they drove past the comfortable, modern homes until he came to Roslyn's low-set house. Once the most ordinary house on the street, she had transformed it with a stylish brick and wrought-iron fence and a replanted garden.

"I'll bring the carton of books in, shall I?" Dave asked hopefully.

There was absolutely no point in encouraging him. "Thanks, Dave, but it's not heavy," Roslyn said gently.

"Then I'll be off!" Dave answered breezily, covering up his disappointment. "Take care, Ros. Enjoy your holidays." He bent quickly, kissed her cheek, then lopped back to his car.

Roslyn stood at the front gate, waving him off. Dave was nice. A pleasant companion on several occasions this past year. What did she want? Another bolt of lightning?

There was mail and she skimmed through it. Her head was aching from too much talk about Macumba. She unfastened the clip at her nape, shaking her dark cloud of hair free. Ah, that was better! She always thought of her prim knot as a form of disguise.

The gardenia bushes she had planted in a shady corner

of the garden were smothered in blossom. She veered off to pick one, twirling it appreciatively beneath her nose. If only camellias had this wonderful scent! When she had changed her clothes, she would turn the sprinklers on. She loved her garden. Everything she had planted was thriving thanks to all her hard work. It was hard to believe she had her own home even if it would take her a lot of years to pay it off.

Her mother had wanted her to buy a home unit, thinking she would be more secure, but Roslyn, reared to the vast, open spaces, couldn't bear the thought of being cooped up. Besides, she loved a garden and she had to have somewhere for her piano. An accomplished pianist, the piano, a baby grand, had been her mother's twenty-first birthday present to her. Roslyn treasured it, even if it never ceased to bother her that her mother had spent so much of her savings on it. Yet, wasn't it part of the pattern? Her parents had lavished their last penny on her. She had gone to an excellent boarding school from age ten to seventeen. A straight-A student, her mother had insisted she go on to university, which was what Roslyn desperately wanted but had accepted as out of the question. Where was the money to come from?

Somehow, between the two of them, they had managed. Roslyn had worked her way through university, waitressing in a friend's mother's restaurant and tutoring at a coaching college; an exhausting grind with all her assignments, but she was young, eager, and she had a goal. To look after her mother. She had gone straight from university to Seymour, a top-rated private school for girls. She considered herself one of the lucky ones. She had several good friends from her university days and as much social life as she wanted. So why did she feel so empty, so unfulfilled? Teaching wasn't enough,

though it did give her a sense of satisfaction and purpose.

The great sadness of her life was that her mother had
chosen the Faulkners over her. She had endured all those
years under Lady Faulkner. Dreadful to speak ill of the
dead, but Lady Faulkner had been an unbearable woman.
Imperious, brook-no-nonsense, full of demands that were
never properly met. Roslyn had a stark vision of herself
as a child sprawling in the dust because Lady Faulkner
had struck her with a riding crop.

She could see Lady Faulkner now, her strong, high-
boned features too severe for beauty, but handsome, as
a lioness is handsome, tawny-haired, ice-blue eyes,
freckled, weathered skin, in her riding boots, six feet tall.
A terrifying sight to a child, yet Roslyn had shouted up
at her, "You horrible, nasty woman! I did not frighten
Rajah!"

A stockman's child to dare answer back the mistress
of Macumba and in such a fashion! Sir Charles coming
on them, had broken up the incident, shocked and stern.
Marsh had raced to her, picked her up and brushed her
down. From that day he had placed himself between
Roslyn and his mother. A state of affairs that had continued right up until Lady Faulkner's death. Lady Faulkner had never struck her again, but there had been barbs
galore and a chilling condescension. The whole outback
had mourned Sir Charles's death. Lady Faulkner's passing had elicited private sighs of relief. Sybill Faulkner
had always been deferred to in her lifetime, but never
liked. All the warmth in her had been reserved for her
only son. Even her daughters had understood they could
not compete with Marsh for their mother's love and attention. Yet both of them had inherited her height, her
tawny colouring and autocratic ways. The Marshall In-

heritance, most people called it. It had made Macumba no place for Roslyn and a difficult one for her mother. Yet her mother had stayed. Why? What had been the hold? Mostly Roslyn closed her eyes to it as though investigation would only open a Pandora's box.

Lost in her reflections Roslyn was almost at the short flight of steps that led to the veranda, when her heart gave a great, warning leap. A man who had been sitting in one of the wicker chairs suddenly rose to his feet, giving Roslyn a glimpse of a tall, rangy figure in elegant, city clothes.

Yet hadn't she been expecting it?

He moved along the veranda with indolent grace, out of the cool, golden-green shadows into the full sunlight, a saturnine expression on his marvellous face.

Marsh. A man no woman could forget. Certainly not Roslyn.

The old, dark excitement struck. *"You!"* She was aware, as always, of the magnetism that passed between them.

"Me. Sweet Rosa!" His dazzling, bluer than blue eyes moved over her as if reminding her they knew every inch of her and she'd been his for the taking.

"What are you doing here?" she asked in her coolest tone.

"Never mind that. What do you think you're doing with another man?"

"I'm a free agent, Marsh. Just like you."

"Fine words, Rosa. Come closer." Blue eyes narrowed and a taunting smile played around the beautiful, sardonic mouth.

"Thank you, Marsh." She shrugged. "This *is* my house." Studiously casual, she tossed the gardenia into the shrubbery and walked quickly up the steps. Into, as she thought, the lion's den. Her whole body was warming as the dark flames moved through her and she hoped the telltale colour wasn't showing in her cheeks.

"And very nice it is, too," Marsh was saying in a mock conciliatory voice. "I love the garden. All your work? I was thinking maybe a small sculpture?"

Her dark cloud of hair flew around her face as her quick temper sizzled. "Don't start patronising me. I can't stand that."

"Goodness, no!" he answered, and there was an infuriating little hint of laughter in the vibrant tones. "It's like waving a red flag in front of a bull. Settle down, poppet. I haven't seen you in months. The last time a bare ten minutes at your school and you were *freezing*!"

"What were you expecting? A dazzling display of affection?"

"Easy enough in the old days," he reminded her with more than a touch of cruelty.

The days when he had total dominion over her. Roslyn flushed. "I stopped caring about you a long time ago."

He only smiled at her, his teeth a flash of white against a dark tan. "I'll live with it, Rosa. So why are *you* so miserable?"

Roslyn touched a quick hand to her forehead. It seemed to be burning. "That's the whole point, Marsh. I'm not. The only thing that bugs me is not having Mother."

"Her choice, Rosa. Don't keep blaming me. Liv's not like you. Life has sobered her. She's not determined and headstrong, like you. She's a gentle, retiring person. Not an argumentative, prickly little fire-eater. Liv feels safe at Macumba."

"More like you have some hold on her, like your

father before you!'' Roslyn blurted, wanting to strike him physically she was so angry at his easy, instant effect on her. "And who said you could call her Liv?"

"She likes it," he snapped. "I'm the new regime, Roslyn. You can't seem to get that into your head. Now, I'd like to go into the house, if you don't mind. One of your neighbours has been eyeing me suspiciously for the past fifteen minutes."

"That's no surprise! Most women give you open-mouthed attention." Roslyn moved down along the veranda. "It's a wonder you didn't find the key."

"As a matter of fact, I did. Casually pushed down the side of that basket of orchids you're making for. Not a good idea, poppet. A beautiful young woman living alone can't be too careful."

"Who said I was living alone?" The key retrieved, she swept past him, her every movement as mettlesome as a high-stepping filly.

"*Aren't* you?" Without appearing to move, he had her by the arm. A touch that weakened her knees and brought back a terrifying leap of rapture.

"Take your hands off me, Marsh," she managed with commendable calm. "What I do is none of your business."

The mesmeric gaze sharpened into irony. "After all these years? Face it, Rosa. I'm always going to keep an eye on you."

"You'll get tired of it." Cold reason demanded she pull away. "What are you really in town for? I'm sure it's not to see me."

"Come on," he lightly jeered. "Would I pass up the chance? It so happens I'm meeting up with a few of my colleagues. Business and pleasure. Liv explained your reluctance to come to us."

"I think I put it with more vigour." Roslyn inserted the key in the lock. "The truth is, Marsh, I've had enough of you and your precious Macumba to last me a lifetime."

"You don't mean that." He followed her in. "What's regressive about you is, you keep harking back to the past. You're not the only one who felt pain."

Inside the quiet house his presence was doubly disturbing. "So you admit it? There *was* pain?" Her question was a challenge.

"Of course I admit it. Stop working yourself up. You always were too damned sensitive to everything. Offer me a cup of coffee before I'm forced to make it myself."

"When did you ever make yourself anything?" she flared.

He stared at her so she felt the full weight of his natural authority. "Are you trying to tell me I don't do a day's work?"

"All right, so I put that unfairly." Roslyn shook her head as though to clear it of little demons. "I know how hard you work, Marsh. Incredibly hard. I only meant you get waited on, as well."

"Rosa, you're a worse snob than any of us. I consider having a housekeeper to prepare my meals perfectly normal. For one thing, I don't have the time or inclination and it gives someone a job. You've always taken the view your mother was sold into slavery. We've always had household staff. Is that a sin? We can afford it and the homestead is huge. I can't think of anyone who would care to run it on their own. All in all, we have hundreds of employees. None of them forced to stay. Most of them I would think, happy enough. And that includes Liv. She takes great pride in her efficiency."

"In fact, she's had an awful time and you know that

perfectly well," Roslyn said in a tight voice. "When my father was killed she was too bereft to think for herself. I wasn't old enough to be much use. I bitterly regret that. Your father offered her the job and not even your mother would go against him but she never liked us."

"My mother never liked anyone," Marsh answered with bleak humour.

"Except *you*. She adored you. You were the only person in her life. I used to feel so sorry for your sisters. Anyone else but your mother would have been besotted with Sir Charles."

Marsh gave a harsh sigh. "My parents' marriage wasn't a love match. You know that. They were paired off almost from the day they were born. It's not all that unusual. Everyone thought it would work. It didn't. My mother and father led separate lives but they elected to stay under one roof. My father didn't believe in divorce. He'd made his commitment and that was that. You know what he was like."

Roslyn lowered her head, feeling a quiver of shame. "An honorable man but not a happy one. Like you, he was laden with too many responsibilities. Too much expectation. Old school. Old values. Isn't it better to split up than live a lie?"

Marsh gave her a hard, impatient glance. "And what about the children, family, the continuity of tradition? There are worse things than staying together. Like pulling everyone apart. All we have to do, Roslyn, is solve our own problems. Not everyone else's. Not even your mother's. People don't always do what we want. My father had powerful reasons for doing all the things he did. That's good enough for me."

"Well, it's not good enough for me!" Roslyn announced dramatically. "Sir Charles blackmailed my mother into staying."

Inflammatory words! Goaded, Marsh grasped her by the shoulders. "So he cared about what happened to her? There was no relationship, if that's what you're implying."

So profoundly protective of her mother, Roslyn decided to take affront. "Dear me, no!" she cried. "How could such a thing happen? The exalted Sir Charles Faulkner, pillar of the establishment, a genuine gentleman, and his housekeeper? We're talking sacrilege here!"

The blue eyes blazed. Blue. Blue, bluer. "Don't say another word, Roslyn," he growled.

It was insanity to ignore him. "You're hurting me," she said, looking pointedly at his hands.

"I'm sorry." Abruptly he released her. With a characteristic upthrust of his head he walked away down the hallway with its polished floor and bright Indian runner, glancing left and right before turning into the kitchen at the rear of the house.

Roslyn stood for a moment, trying to cool down. The last time they had been together their meeting had ended in bitter argument. Mostly her fault. She acknowledged her guilts, but she had received too many painful blows from Faulkner hands.

When she walked into the kitchen, Marsh was looking moodily around. Roslyn was rather proud of the way she had transformed the kitchen with sunshine yellow paint and a glossy white trim. Filmy white curtains adorned the windows, a circular pine table and chairs occupied the center of the room, an old pine dresser she used to display a very pretty Victorian dinner set against the wall. A mixed bunch of flowers stood on the table, another at the window behind the sink. Everything was spick-and-span as was her way. Her mother had trained her well.

Not that she expected Marsh to notice. He was used to grandeur. He had known it from the cot. Her first cot had been a washing basket. It came to her, looking at him, big men needed big rooms. Marsh, like his father before him, was six-three. At nearing thirty, very lean and athletic, whereas Sir Charles who had never appeared to carry an extra pound had somehow filled out with age. Both of them big men. Marsh's everyday gear was a bush shirt and jeans, a pearl-grey Akubra tilted at a rakish angle, his Cuban-heeled riding boots making him tower over the men. Today he wore a beautiful dark grey suit with a blue shirt and a silk tie, predominantly red, a matching kerchief in his breast pocket. In the city, as at home, he had the perfect male frame for hanging clothes on. Not that Marsh had ever shown the slightest vanity about his astounding good looks. His looks were almost irrelevant to performance. He had to shine academically, on the sports field, in the company of the rich and powerful. The focus had been on carrying on the Faulkner proud tradition. His mother and father, for all the differences between them, had been as one in their pride. Everything Marsh attempted he excelled at. Roslyn could not imagine what life would have been like for him had he not. Through the grace of God and bloodlines he was a born leader with a natural presence and an enviable capacity for getting the best out of everyone without friction.

Except *me*. Well, I'm not about to fall down and adore him, Roslyn thought. Those days are over.

"Quite the little achiever, aren't you?" Marsh broke into her thoughts.

"Why not? You showed me that, if nothing else. Sit down, Marsh, instead of towering over me. You make the place look like a doll's house."

"Sweet Rosa, it is, but it's pretty and comfortable and it's all you need. For now."

"And what is that supposed to mean?" She busied herself with the preparations for making coffee, thankful she had the best coffee beans at hand.

"Even you, Rosa, will get married. You vinegary little thing."

"I'll think about it when *you* walk up the aisle," she retorted dryly. "What's happened to Kim Petersen?"

"She's around." Idly he stroked the petals of a pink gerbera.

"No pride!" Roslyn clicked her tongue. "You've led her a merry dance."

"The hell I have! I made no promises to Kim."

Roslyn shrugged. "If that makes you feel better."

"I can't help it, Rosa, if women have only one thing on their minds. Not everyone is a dedicated career woman like you."

"My own woman," Roslyn told him with satisfaction. "Your sisters would have been all the better for a job."

"I agree." The tautness of his smile conveyed she had scored a point. "Being heiresses didn't help. I know you wanted them to feel guilty. Anyway they're married now and out of range of your tart tongue and superior IQ. You're a basket case feminist."

Roslyn paused with a hand on the coffee grinder. "You bet I am! All thinking women should have that in common. Your sisters are a throwback to the nineteenth century. So intelligent, yet with closed minds."

"Young women with large trust funds aren't always interested in making the most of their talents."

"Such a shame!" Roslyn sighed. "Anyway, they made sure I didn't dream above my station. I'm not likely to forget how Dianne behaved at her engagement party."

"I don't suppose the fact her fiancé was paying you too much attention had anything to do with it." Marsh stood up. "As always, your judgments are too trenchant. Here, I'll do that. You get the cups and saucers."

"I barely noticed him." Roslyn turned away to the cupboard. "I was only there at all to help Mumma." And glimpse *you*. Marsh, who had filled her eyes and heart.

"Well, I might accept that, but poor old Di couldn't," Marsh said. "The trouble with you, Rosa, you don't know anything about sexual jealousy. It's my bet you've sworn off sex altogether."

"I'm not prepared to talk to you about that!" she said tartly.

"So you're not going to tell me about the school-teacher?"

Roslyn swung round with a look of surprise. "How do you know Dave is a colleague?"

"Come on, Rosa, wouldn't I check him out?" His tone was like silk.

"Sure you would. No problem, except you've never laid eyes on him."

Marsh ground the coffee before he answered, sniffing appreciatively at the rich aroma. "Darling, I spotted him on my last visit to school. A caring guy with a baby face. He was coming out the main doorway as you were charging in like a baby rhino. Obviously you were show-ing your temper because he looked most solicitous. I can't think he knows what a little firebrand you really are. Crisp little skirts and button-up blouses aren't you at all. He should see you on Macumba riding like the wind. You might say you hate it, but it brings out your true colours.''

"Would you like anything with your coffee?" Roslyn asked in an abrupt change of subject.

"A little pleasant conversation." His blue eyes so riveting with his tanned skin and black hair never left hers. "Liv is most unhappy you've decided against coming. She's been looking forward to it immensely.''

"Then why don't you give her time off so she can come to me?" Roslyn placed the coffeepot on the hotplate.

His dynamic face tightened. "You know perfectly well we have a full house at Christmas with a lot of entertaining."

"Ah, yes, the busy social scene!" she purred.

"Business and pleasure. There are people to be thanked. I couldn't do without Liv and she doesn't want to leave me in the lurch. No one will dare to give you a hard time."

"You bet they won't!" Roslyn replied with some aggression. "I'm a big girl now. Able to stick up for myself. Sock it back to them if I have to, but I don't want to live like that. No, Marsh, the further I keep away from you all, the better. I'll miss Mother terribly, but that seems to be my lot. Macumba comes first. It's been drilled into her. Sir Charles first. Now you. I should be used to it."

"Hang on a minute, Rosa," he said flatly.

"No, it's *true*!"

"What can I say to change your mind?"

"Absolutely nothing!" she maintained. "I'd like a little peace over Christmas. Christmas *is* peace, after all.

Not a renewal of hostilities. The girls will be coming home, won't they?"

"For part of the time, yes. Would you like me to tell them to stay away?"

Roslyn shook her head, exasperated by his tone. "Never! They love you. They want you all to themselves. Part of the reason I don't plan on darkening your door."

"Because the past is with you at all times."

Roslyn poured the coffee and pushed it towards him. "Surely you're not suggesting we make a fresh start?"

"I'll even throw in the kiss of peace."

She could not focus on his face, the glittering, sapphire eyes. "No, thanks, Marsh. I remember your kisses. They're lethal. So far as I'm concerned, the past is always with us. Maybe not always on the surface but ready to spring to life at the slightest jolt. Our relationship is beyond repair. We came at life from opposite ends of the spectrum. You with a silver spoon in your mouth, the adored object of everyone's hopes and dreams. Me, the offspring of very ordinary folk. I know I'm easily given to anger where you're concerned, but I can't change that any more than you could have changed your mother's attitude. It impinged on us all. It colours Macumba to this day. There never was and never will be any question of my fitting in. It doesn't have everything to do with the fact you were the elite and we were so far down the social scale as to be off it. Your mother detested us. My mother and me. The way she used to look at us was just terrible. Anyone would have thought we were a threat to her. I was always waiting for the day she would accuse me of stealing—"

"Her son?" Marsh suggested abrasively.

"I don't think anyone would have stood for that. I

was going to say the family silver. There was no rational explanation for it.''

Marsh took a quick gulp of his steaming hot coffee and set it down. "Maybe for my mother there was. You could be too one-eyed on the subject, Rosa. Have you thought of that? My mother's life wasn't absolutely perfect. As a young woman like you, she would have started off her married life with high hopes, but somehow it all turned to ashes. When that kind of thing happens, it can have devastating results. I know my mother had a harsh tongue. She was very high-handed. But have you ever considered she might have felt herself a failure?''

In her total confusion Roslyn laughed. "A failure! Why, your mother considered herself quite extraordinary and in her way, she was. You Faulkners were the rightful rulers of this world.''

"Leave it be, Ros,'' Marsh said, a decided edge to his voice. "If you want me to give it all up and go join a monastery practising poverty, I'm not doing it. You'd only find something else to chew on. You like to hate me. It makes you burn. And speaking of burning, would you mind putting the coffeepot down. Your hand is shaking so badly you're going to pour it all over the table.''

"I'll do no such thing!'' Regardless of her brisk denial Roslyn filled her own cup and returned the coffeepot to the stove.

"And while we're on the subject,'' Marsh continued, "you're too hard on Di and Justine. They're more vulnerable than you think. You said yourself Mother didn't take a whole lot of notice of them and Dad was far from demonstrative. *You* were the one he noticed. The girls didn't like it, either, when you grew more beautiful by the day. There's heartache in a face full of freckles and being too tall. Having a brother who supposedly got the lot. Mother was never gentle and loving with them. They felt her tongue just as you did, but unlike you, they never challenged her. I know you're not going to believe this, but Di in particular was terrified of bringing a guy back in case he caught sight of you. As it turned out, her worst fears were realised when Chris made an ass of himself at the engagement party. Face it, sweet Rosa, like it or not, you have a witching side to your nature.''

She looked at him gravely, even sadly. ''I was totally innocent of any charge of trying to 'bewitch' Chris, as your mother put it. I'm just glad she didn't have a stake handy she reacted so terribly. I've never set out to deliberately hurt anyone outside *you*. I'm pleased Di and Justine are happily married. They deserve some joy. I expect you to love and defend them. I'm even glad they'll be back on Macumba for Christmas, but I'm not running the risk of trying to hang out with them. They don't want me. The barriers remain.''

''They will for as long as you let them. Do you know how bitter you sound, Rosa?''

That hurt her and she nodded wearily. ''Unfortunately, yes, but unlike you, Marsh, I was wounded daily in my self-esteem. You'll never know what I'm talking about. It hasn't and will never happen to you. My scars don't heal. If I could get Mother to come to me, maybe they would. I love her so much but she seems to have some form of agoraphobia. She won't leave Macumba. It seems like the only place she's safe. Yet most of it has been terrible. I'll never, never, understand it. Ever since Dad was killed all I've ever wanted is to look after her.''

His expression was brushed with compassion. ''I understand that, Rosa, but you could hardly afford to keep her.''

"I'd give it my best shot. We don't live like you. We live quietly within our means. Besides, if she wanted to, she could take another job. Something interesting, part-time.''

"Like what?'' Marsh asked bluntly. "Your mother is excellent at running a large house but she's had no experience in the workforce. Unemployment is running high and she's not the right age. You must realise she wants to be independent. Life is a lot different for her these days, Rosa. You should check that out.''

Roslyn took a deep, calming breath. "No, thanks, Marsh. Charming as you undoubtedly know how to be, my mother is still your servant.''

"We don't use words like that anymore, Rosa,'' he said crisply. "Haven't you learned?''

"My mother might appreciate that. *I* don't.'' She shrugged. "I've carved out a life for myself, Marsh. A good life. I've bought a house and I have a secure, rewarding career. At this point I'm reasonably happy when happy is a mighty big word. It would be foolish and dangerous to allow myself to be drawn back to Macumba.''

"Yet you loved it,'' Marsh said, his expression faraway. "There were times you were extravagantly happy. No one saw the magic of Macumba more than you. You knew all its secrets. You were addicted to the life, Rosa. That can't have changed.''

There was so much emotion in just being in the same room as him, Roslyn felt stifled. "I've confronted that realisation, Marsh, but I've had to remove myself from the scene of so much pain and humiliation. Most of all,

I've removed myself from *you*. You wounded me more than anyone.''

''You were a child, Rosa.'' His voice reflected a bitter regret.

''Old enough to give you pleasure.''

Her arrogant Marsh visibly winced. ''You wanted me as much as I wanted you.''

''Yet you drove me away!''

''I *had* to!'' Air hissed through his teeth. ''It was a dangerous situation. The timing was all wrong. You were sixteen and I wasn't truly adult, either. Violent delights have violent ends, so they say, Rosa. How could I take you—''

''You *did* take me!'' she cried, her voice rising passionately.

''I haven't forgotten. I was a savage then and wild for you. No one knew better how to tempt me.''

''Of course!'' She threw up her hands in disgust. ''Woman, the eternal temptress. Woman destroying a good man's willpower. I *know* what I did, Marsh. How I acted. I abandoned myself to a fiery relationship. But I paid for it. God, how I paid for it. Afterwards you made sure I was kept out of the way. Macumba shut its doors. You started wooing a whole string of suitable girls. You even went to infinite pains to make sure I knew. Well, it didn't take me long to overthrow the old idolatry. Everything I felt for you sickened and died. You used me and I let you. I acknowledge that. But all that is left is remorse.''

''Then it must be pretty powerful,'' Marsh challenged her bluntly. ''You'd rather hate me than love anyone else.''

The truth. The whole truth. And nothing but the truth.

It cut straight to Roslyn's heart. She sprang up, in her

agitation knocking her coffee so that some of the hot liquid splashed across her hand. Instantly the fine skin turned red.

"For God's sake!" Marsh moved like lightning, overcoming her resistance and drawing her to the kitchen sink. He ran the cold water and held her hand under it. "Why do you fight me all the time? Fight yourself?" There was an angry, haunted look on his face.

"Maybe conflict is my natural milieu." His skin on hers was sending little tingles up her arm.

"Quiet, Rosa. Quiet." With infinite gentleness he dabbed a paper towel to her hand, miraculously as ever, concerned for the delicacy of her skin.

Put your hat on, poppet, and keep it on! How often had she heard him say that and adoringly obeyed? She felt such a longing for him; for the best days of her life, she almost cried out. The old magical link was running between them. Indestructible. She could see it in his eyes; echoes of a passion that had caused nothing but upset and pain. His nearness was intoxicating, trapping her. She wanted to touch him…hold him…take him to her breast.

"Rosa?"

He had broken her heart once. He would do it again.

Come to me, Rosa, my little love!

The way he had talked to her! The world of ecstasy and wonderful dreams! What she had felt for him was a flame that had never gone out.

"Look at me," Marsh urged. "The pain will go away if you let it."

It might have been the devil himself at his most seductive and charming. A younger Marsh had been a tempestuous lover. Now he was beguiling her with such tender depth in his voice.

A fierce quaking gripped her. She could not move or speak. She knew it for what it was. An erotic spell. Under compulsion she raised her mouth and, as if at a signal, a look of triumph blazed into his eyes.

"My beautiful Rosa!"

He was drawing her closer and closer, filling her with a consuming passion. She made no outcry. Lean, caressing fingers bent her head back over his arm. Gentle, but *insistent*. No guilt at all at having her at his mercy. He was looking at her with such a mixture of feelings.

Conquest? Oh, yes!

Possession? Why not? Wasn't she Rosa, his little captive love? It was her special role to please him.

This was the stuff of her dreams. The night-time visions that fanned the terrible storms in her. She didn't realise it, but her knees had buckled so badly he was forced to take her weight.

A single lock had fallen away from his ink-black hair, lying in a crisp curl on the polished bronze of his forehead. His eyes were achingly blue, like the sky over the desert.

"Rosa. Oh, Rosa," he whispered, looking—could it be possible?—*vulnerable*.

It was all that she needed. She had waited a long time for this. Pride and resolve streamed into her. She went as rigid as a statue, revenge burning fiercer than love. Once she had been a wild thing in his arms. Young, untamed, clamouring for the rapture he had shown her one perilous, desert night. Now she was breaking his power. Exorcising him and the terrible fascination that had bedevilled her for so long.

"Let me love you," he begged, frustrated by her withdrawal. His free hand had found the curve of her breast, cupping it. An ancient ritual that dredged up an involuntary moan. Eddies of dark pleasure began cascading in, lapping at her willpower.

"What is it?" he asked urgently. "Trust me, Rosa."

Trust him when he had dealt her such a terrible blow? Was he *mad*? Was *she*? The tenderness was no more than a manifestation of his mastery. An angry little sob escaped her and instantly he buried her open mouth beneath his.

Fever and delirium. All it had ever been. Trying to resist Marsh was like getting caught in a rip-tide. She would never have her freedom. Loving him, hating him, gave meaning to her life. For the moment she surrendered while ecstasy was repossessed.

"Rosa!" His low, agonised whisper came against her throat. "Don't tremble like that. I don't mean to—"

At that she jerked her head back. "You *do* mean to!" Her voice cracked with emotion. "As soon as you touch me, you mean to. You think I'm still a Faulkner possession. You can have me any time you choose."

"That's not true!" He denied it vehemently. "If it were, why haven't I laid a finger on you in years?"

"Because I've taken good care you don't!" She stared up at him, her arousal equal to his own. "Good grief, Marsh, don't you know how I hate you?"

"*Hate* me?" He almost spat it out. "Hate me, love me, what's the difference? Hell, I even like your kind of hate. You're a lost soul, Rosa, but you won't let anyone save you."

"Not *you*! I was your unquestioning victim once. Never again. I won't do *anything* to have you. Contrary to your expectations."

"Don't say any more, Rosa." There was a warning sparkle in his eyes.

"But there *is* more," she continued, quite unable to

stop. "I'm fearful of coming to Macumba. I've said it's because of your extended family, who, with few exceptions, treated me and my mother like a sub-species. They took the view, of course, that they didn't have to bother their heads over the servants. But really, it's all to do with *you*. I don't give a damn about them and their place in the sun. You knew I was in love with you, long before I knew what being in love was. You were a god to me. Surely you saw that? The sun danced in the heavens every time you smiled at me. You had such powers. I placed all my trust in you. My life. If you looked into your soul, you would know that you had the power to destroy me."

A tremendous tension was all around them. His blue eyes glittered like gems. "You, Rosa?" he returned scornfully. "You call yourself a victim? You're strong and you're clever. You've fought your way out of a background you apparently detested. You were always too proud. Too ready to see insult where it wasn't really intended. So people are careless, insensitive? They don't always intend to wound. You've been as toey as a boxer since you were a child. If you imagine I've treated you badly, how do you think you've treated me? I'm sick to death of your bitter tongue. The way you want to lash me whenever I come near. I let you go. I had to. Both of us were thrown into a terrible, painful situation. The timing couldn't have been worse. So I was weak, with no thought in my head but having all the beauty and innocence you offered. I've suffered for it. Don't think I haven't. There's heartache and regret in every corner of my mind. If *you* loved me, *I* worshipped at your altar. There was no limit to my passion. But it was wrong and audacious. It had to stop."

"So you could feel virtuous again? In control?" Roslyn stared into his eyes, saturated in their blueness. ''Besides, the scandal might have travelled far and wide. The heir to Macumba, Sir Charles and Lady Faulkner's adored only son having it off with the housekeeper's daughter. My God, who of the elite could grapple with that? Grounded in conservatism and doing the done thing.''

Marsh's striking face tightened. ''As far as I remember, correct me if I'm wrong, the housekeeper's precious daughter did everything in her considerable power to delight me. Venus herself couldn't have been more alluring. You held me in your palm, yet you insist on playing the tragic victim. You always were a great one for histrionics. These past couple of years you've never let me near you. But you won't let go, either. What is it, the goddess syndrome? Believe me, I'm at the end of my tether. What is it you want, Rosa? Spell it out. *Marriage*?''

For a moment Roslyn looked as though the sky had fallen in on her. ''Never in my wildest dreams did I expect that,'' she said finally.

''What did you expect?'' he demanded. ''A lifetime of being my mistress?''

She visibly paled. Her nerves were worn ragged. ''For a while...nothing...more. I was crazy with love for you. So young, so ardent, I couldn't hold back. We had unforgettable times. Secrets between us, but it's long gone. You hurt me too much and I can never forgive you. Right or wrong, that's the way it is. I can't even bear to be in the same room as you.''

''What about the same bed?'' he asked on a hard rasp.

She shook her head. ''We never shared the same bed.''

"Only the two of us locked under the desert stars. So what does it all mean? Liv has to suffer, too?"

Roslyn turned away, looking her strain. "We've been over and over this, Marsh. Even for my mother I can't walk back into the lion's cage."

He looked over at her, his blue gaze detached, even distant. "Not even as my wife?"

CHAPTER TWO

Shock immobilised her. Her heart rocked wildly, then seemed to shudder to a stop.

"I know," he said flatly. "It didn't sound romantic." In fact he was looking at her like a long-time opponent who had thrown down a challenge. "Maybe these last years have beaten the romance out of me. At any rate, I'm serious."

Roslyn, for all her intelligence, was looking as though she was having extreme difficulty tracking the conversation. "You're serious?" Her voice came out oddly pitched and full of confusion.

Marsh's brief laugh conveyed anything but humour. "Why the hell are you looking so stunned? For my sins, I am."

"Sins? Atonement? You must be mad!"

He nodded in perfect agreement. "For better or worse, you're the woman I want."

"Passion, Marsh. Nothing more." Her tone was pained and very subdued.

"I wouldn't knock the passion if I were you," he said sardonically. "In my experience it's pretty rare. I've never had a woman raise such hell in me. You've brains, courage, toughness. I admire your style. I even admire your wild nature though you do your level best to keep it under wraps. Under that satin skin lurks a primitive."

"Takes one to know one," she retorted instantly, but still in that subdued tone. Her eyes scanned his face, marvelling at the precise arrangement of features that made it so compelling. "This is madness, Marsh. You made your decision. So did I. They can't be unmade. Why, if your parents were still alive, you'd never propose such a thing."

He hated that. How he hated that, for his eyes flashed blue lightning. "I could have sworn you knew me. Now I realise you don't. I've never proposed to a woman in my life, but if I had, no one would have prevented the marriage. No one runs *me*!"

"So *you* say!" She reacted fierily. "Times might have changed, but your family didn't change with them. They believed in the old feudal system."

"Listen to me, Ros!" He took hold of her forcibly, fairly shimmering with rage. "Macumba has changed already. I'm the boss now. Chairman of the board."

She pulled away blindly. "I'm going into the living room, Marsh. It's too claustrophobic in here."

She rushed away while he followed her more slowly, taking the armchair opposite her. "I didn't realise you'd be so shocked." He studied her pale face.

"Not even a little bit?" Her topaz gaze was quietly ironic. "All we've been these past years is sparring partners."

He shrugged. "Be that as it may, I can't exorcise what we had together. Neither can you."

"Maybe we should see a psychiatrist to help us out?" Her lips twitched.

His expression lightened, as well. "I don't have the time to work on that. Neither, apparently, do I have the self-control to stay away. I need a wife and, in due course, an heir. It might seem like a big challenge for us to marry, but we're not afraid of challenges, are we? I can give you back the life you loved. The splendid thing we shared and understood. You used to call us twin

souls, remember? Maybe if we try hard enough we can
have that back. I promise you a free rein. Your own
money.''

"Don't try to buy me, Marsh," she said with quiet
dignity. "I'm not interested in your money."

"To hell with my money, then! In your case, it counts
against me. But it could make life easier and fuller for
Liv.''

"So now we come to it. *Blackmail*!''

His mouth compressed. "Not a terribly attractive
view. All's fair in love and war. Liv is your mother.
Aren't you the same girl who used to rail because she
didn't have lots of nice clothes and places to go? We
could take care of all that. You might get all up in arms
about money, but having it does make people a whole
lot more confident. Liv is a beautiful woman. She should
give life and maybe the right man a chance.''

Her thoughts exactly, but Roslyn wasn't about to
agree with him. "Aren't you the one who told me you
desperately needed her services for the holidays?''

Marsh gave her a sardonic look. "Maybe I exaggerated a little. I could always get staff. No one like Liv,
of course, but competent enough. I'm really after *you*."

"Goodness knows why!" She sighed deeply.

"A blind obsession." His voice was spiked with self-
derision. "You're just hiding out as a schoolteacher. I've
seen your face all painted with ochres, parrot feathers
on your head. Who nagged Leelya for the recipe for a
love potion? I know I refused to drink it, but you could
have slipped it to me at another time. You were a tricky
little thing.''

At his words, nostalgia swept sweetly across her mind.
Leelya, an aboriginal woman who wandered the station,
had been the great friend and mentor of her childhood.

Leelya had been a vast source of information about humans, animals, the birds of the air and the fish in the streams. Leelya had taught her all about the timeless land, the red desert, how to play the clapsticks and dance in mime. Because of Leelya, she knew scores of myths and legends from the Dreamtime, how to gather food, find water, so vital to desert life. Leelya had taught her how to make that love potion and she remembered the recipe to this day. She had been quite a herbalist, mixing it perfectly, but Marsh had made her deeply unhappy by refusing point-blank to drink it. She'd been around fifteen at the time. They were down by the sacred lake with its flotilla of pink waterlilies and black swans. She had never forgotten his amusement. The way he had teased her, not knowing a young girl could fall in love.

After that failure, she and Leelya had put their heads together to create a special spell. Powerful woman magic that really worked. They had shared their secrets silently, the old gin and the precocious, self-dramatising white child. It was Leelya who had painted her face and body with bright ochres. Leelya who had arranged brilliantly coloured bird feathers in a crown around her head. Again her plan misfired because Marsh had burst out laughing, asking where was the corroboree?

"Rosa?" Marsh's voice catapulted her back to the present. "Where have you gone off to?"

She gave her head a little shake. "I was just thinking about Leelya. How is she?"

Marsh shrugged. "I haven't seen her for ages. She's gone walkabout."

"She was a great friend to me."

"Co-conspirator, more like it! You and she were always cooking up spells."

"Some of them worked. Perhaps not in the way we intended."

"That's the danger with magic, Rosa. Leelya should have warned you. I'm flying back to Macumba on Monday. I'd like you to come with me."

"You were always driven, weren't you, Marsh?" she asked reflectively.

"Let's say, I don't like to lose. I'm asking you to be my wife. You're not going to find anyone else in this life."

He said it lightly, but she found it significant. "Isn't that a bit melodramatic?" She, too, played it coolly.

"You're not getting any younger, poppet. Twenty-five in January. For all your beauty, you could just get left on the shelf. You want children. I know you do. You're very good with kids. It's all very well waiting for Prince Charming, but you must have a few fears he mightn't even exist. Besides, you are so damned hard to please. I don't think any man could measure up to your exacting standards. Better the devil you know than the devil you don't know. I'm approaching the deadline myself. I can't find a single woman to delight me for more than a week at the outside. You're the one with that unholy knack. I know these past years have been rough, but I'm prepared to take you traumas and all."

"The question is, am I prepared to take you?" Roslyn returned. "I'd cut myself off from you."

"So why are the scars too much to live with?"

Roslyn blanched and immediately he closed the distance between them, sitting beside her on the couch. "The things we say and the things we mean! We humans are terrified of exposing our hearts." He drew her into his arms. "You still care about me, Rosa, just as I care about you."

"No!" She shook her head in denial.

"I have trouble with that."

She buried her head against his jacket. "It's all about what you want, Marsh. Always *you*."

"I want the glory days back, Rosa. I admit it. This standoff could go on forever. I have to make the decision for both of us. But I'm not going down on bended knee and I'm not taking any more hell for the past, either. We have to bury it to survive. If you like, we can draw up a marriage contract. You can keep referring back to it. I'll give you time, but if you decide yes, you'd better know I'll never let you go. No running off. No divorce. You and me for all time. No one else. No lovers. Treat that very seriously. I could bring myself to shoot anyone you got involved with. I'm serious, sweet Rosa. Mess with me and you've made a huge mistake. On the other hand, if you honour our agreement I'll do everything in my power to make you happy. I remember holding you in my arms and promising you the moon and stars."

"Wild words, Marsh." She turned up her face, her voice husky.

"I remember." His expression was intimate, intense, a little brutal. "So do you. Marriage might put us out of our misery."

"It could leave us worse off than we've ever been."

"*I* don't intend to walk out," he announced, almost grimly. "Think about that. Get it right. I won't let you go, Rosa. Our marriage will be forever. Rooted in the soil of Macumba."

Her eyes were liquid amber, her thick black lashes spiked with tears she couldn't control. She let her whirring head rest back against his shoulder. "And in true, dynastic style you'll want a son?"

"I want a family," he said. "I want sons and I want

a daughter just like you so I can spoil her."

"This is *real*, isn't it, Marsh? I'm not dreaming?"

He tugged her hair very gently. "It's real."

"It's the last thing I expected to happen," she said. "I have to think about it very seriously. You've taken me totally by surprise. You broke my heart once. There's no possible excuse for me if I allow it to happen again."

"Try to be more positive, Rosa," he jeered softly. "We can't let the past warp our lives. The future is full of hope. Besides, you're my favourite girl. What more can I say?"

"Maybe you love me dearly?" she responded with a return to irony.

The dazzling blue eyes became hooded. "Love is a danger, Ros. It makes fools of us. A man can lose control and you know me. I like being master of the game. Besides, I haven't heard any love words from you. Let's stick with what we know. We have a long, shared history. You're at the center of my life until I die. I never asked for it. It just happened like something preordained. Neither of us is going to beat this thing and we've both tried. For all that, we speak the same language. Come back to Macumba with me. Enjoy all the things you used to love. You'll have Liv's company and mine. Once, I was able to speak to your heart."

She stared up at him, searching for words. "Marsh, you scare me," was all she eventually managed.

He lowered his head and pressed a hard, fierce kiss on her mouth. "That's the way it should be. A woman should be a little scared of her man."

His philosophy in essence. She'd been warned.

Long after Marsh had gone, Roslyn lay on her bed feeling totally strung out. Marsh's proposal had literally taken her breath. She couldn't believe it, given they had done everything possible to avoid one another these past two years. Marsh had spoken ironically of a "blind obsession." No piece of theatre, but a well-documented human condition. She could vouch for its existence. Passion...obsession...bound them together as much now as at any time in the past. Its grip was unrelenting. Only, if the truth were faced, she loved him. But the truth threatened her. Once confided, it put her instantly back into the position of suppliant. Marsh simply wanted her, like he acquired desirable properties and made no bones about it. Not that they weren't compatible in other ways but she was convinced he would never have proposed had his mother been alive. The violence of Lady Faulkner's opposition would have caused tremendous upset. Marsh's sisters would have felt compelled to follow their mother's lead. Likewise the extended family with a few exceptions. The housekeeper's daughter, child of a stockman who had been killed on the station, was hardly the sort of person to invite into a family whose position in society went back to the earliest days of settlement.

Except Lady Faulkner wasn't around. No one would have to bear her violent opposition. Roslyn groaned aloud. She was so confounded by the turn of events she couldn't seem to think properly. She imagined her reaction was pretty much the same as someone who inherited a fortune right out of the blue. She had spent years trying to get over Marsh. Years of building up a defensive shield. It had been an absolute waste of time. She had only to see him, to hear his voice, for all the old longing to start up again. Her heart defeated her every time. Even her acquired persona of coolness and competence was unravelling at breathtaking speed.

"I'm in shock, damn it!" she told the empty room.

How could she seriously be considering a marriage between them? A monstrous thought in the old days, what had suddenly changed? Marsh had thrown off the constraints of family? Didn't she still *burn* with resentment? Their past was complex and painful; their future promised stormy times. She would always be the butt of someone's snide little joke, human nature being what it was. There was something else, as well. She was forced to consider it with some trepidation. Marsh was one of the richest men in the country. Not only did he control Faulkner Holdings, he had inherited the bulk of his mother's fortune, which stood at some 50 million dollars at her death.

There was a whole side to Marsh's life she knew absolutely nothing about. A side she didn't want to know about. Great wealth wasn't a great blessing in her view. No one could have called the Faulkners a happy family though even Lady Faulkner had played down the exact size of the family fortune. Strictly speaking, the beef cattle chain was down the list of interests. There was a massive investment portfolio. Marsh was one of the biggest shareholders in the giant Mossvale Pastoral Company. It was common knowledge. She didn't give a hoot about any of it, but Marsh was deeply involved in all Faulkner operations. Business trips took up a great deal of his time. In his own way, he was a celebrity even if he took great care to keep a low media profile. The Faulkners she knew were private people, hiding their wealth, not splashing out on a lavish lifestyle. Nevertheless, Faulkner money had built hospitals, schools, townships. They funded numerous charities, scholarships, and a major art prize. As heir to the trust, Marsh had worked for and acquired degrees in economics and law. In many ways he had been brought up like a prince in a castle, but immense pressure had always been placed on him from the earliest age. It was a heavy burden he had been forced to carry, but necessary for someone who would one day wield a lot of power.

That day had arrived. In keeping with tradition he was expected to take the right wife and raise a family. The right wife surely meant someone of similar background; in other words, one of the ruling classes. Not a schoolteacher of no social distinction at all. Worse, a skeleton in the family closet. Roslyn murmured aloud her distress. Once, as a child, she had overheard Lady Faulkner and Elaine Petersen discussing quite seriously and calmly a possible marriage between their children. Marsh would have been sixteen at the time. Kim, a year or so younger. It would bring two prominent families together. Cement already-rock-solid fortunes. Even then, Roslyn had been appalled. Did these women think they owned their children? Marsh didn't even like Kim Petersen. He had told her so.

That was *then*. Marsh and Kim had been an item only a few years back, when his parents had been alive. Lady Faulkner had long since given Kim her stamp of approval and she was a lifelong friend of his sisters'. One hundred per cent suitable. Absolutely top drawer. Kim wouldn't sit idly by while she trapped their adored Marsh. She would be branded the ultimate opportunist. Was she equal to the battle that surely lay ahead? If only he had said he *loved* her. If only…

Saturday morning she went shopping for presents for her mother. Saturday afternoon she spent in the garden in the warm sun planting out masses of white petunias along a border. At least she no longer felt stunned. Marsh had asked her to marry him. He had asked no one else. Hadn't she always prided herself on her fighting qualities? She would make him love her. She would bear his children. She could do absolutely anything so long as he backed her. She could return pride and happiness to her mother. Warmth and hospitality to a Macumba that had felt Lady Faulkner's brand of rigid exclusivity for too long. Nothing worth having was achieved easily. It all took hard work and commitment.

She glanced with pride around her garden. It was very pretty, if of necessity, small. The gardens at Macumba were magnificent, watered by bores sunk into the Great Artesian Basin. Lady Faulkner had had no time for the garden, preferring to leave all decision-making to Harry Wallace, a roving Englishman who had come to Macumba to play polo and stayed on as the resident landscaper.

She supposed in a way she hadn't been a *containable* child, because she had seen herself as absolutely free to roam the station at all times. Lady Faulkner had positively discouraged her. Sir Charles and Marsh had been extraordinarily indulgent, almost applauding her audacity. If only Lady Faulkner had been a kindly woman! Life would have been very different for all of them.

CHAPTER THREE

IT WASN'T until they were flying into the Faulkner desert stronghold that Roslyn fully realised what she was letting herself in for. She had come to Macumba all those years ago as a humble stockman's daughter, now she was seriously contemplating becoming its mistress. A rags-to-riches story. Something one might read in romantic fiction. It seldom happened in real life.

Seen from the air, the blood-red terrain was extraordinary. It stretched away to the rainbow-hued mesas on the horizon, the hills a vast network of caves that were the repositories of aboriginal art many tens of thousands of years old. Macumba was fabulous. Even in drought savagely beautiful but so empty and isolated after her quiet leafy suburb it might have been a strange, new planet. Down beneath them were knife-edged rising temples of shimmering red sand, crystal-clear rock pools, swamps and billabongs that were a major breeding ground for nomadic water birds. Where the coolibahs stretched their long limbs over the water, colonies of ibis, spoonbills, shags and herons built their nests and the brolgas performed their wonderful dance on the sands. In the good seasons countless thousands of ducks invaded the swamps, becoming a common sight.

The outback *was* birds. The phenomenon of the west, the budgerigars in their chattering millions, the brilliant parrots, the soft galahs, the zebra finches, crimson chats, variegated wrens and huge flocks of white corellas that often appeared to decorate trees like giant white flowers.

So often she had sat and watched the soaring flight of the great wedge-tailed eagle over the dunes. This was the place she loved most in the world and always thought of as the real Australia. The land of whirlwinds and mirage, its ancient plains crisscrossed with a vast natural irrigation system that allowed the country's huge cattle kingdoms to support their stock. Roslyn thrilled to it in every fibre. But as they flew in, Marsh at the controls, she braced herself for conflict. What they were considering was a radical shift from tradition. She could bring no fortune with her. No powerful family alliance. She could only bring herself. She was of the mind and generation to think it ought to be enough. She had no inflated ego, but she knew she was good-looking, intelligent, healthy. Most people found her pleasant. She was highly regarded as a teacher. She hadn't anything to be defensive about. Times had changed. She was entitled to a better life than her mother, yet she knew the instant Kim Petersen found out she was back on Macumba, Kim would fly in ready to do battle in her cool, superior way. Kim was the natural successor to Lady Faulkner. Kim was one of the self-styled Higher Order.

"We're home!"

Marsh's announcement brought her out of her reverie. His voice was filled with great satisfaction. *You're* home, she thought.

"No premature announcements, Marsh," she begged. "I want to gauge reaction to my return in my own way. Once the family arrives, it's bound to be forthcoming."

"You're not marrying the family, you're marrying *me*."

"It's never as easy as that." She sighed. "You and your relatives are very close. You're bound in so many ways. Blood, business, shared heritage. You're the anointed heir. They all love you. They don't love *me*. I don't expect them to, but I do want to be seen as a person in my own right. Not the little kid who tagged after you.''

"Give it a rest, poppet," he said.

"I want nothing more. At the same time I'm compelled to defend my own position.''

"You're good at that, Rosa," he drawled. "You always were as sharp as a tack. While we're laying things on the line, might I suggest you lighten up. You're too ready to fly off the handle. The girls would have made friends with you long ago were you not so touchy. They admire you, in fact. Your beauty and your brains, the way you've made a career for yourself. Marriage has improved both of them, you'll find. They've matured and mellowed. *Mellow*, you ain't!''

"A subjective view, Marsh. I don't have trouble with other people. It will do you no good to criticise me.''

He made a grab for her hand and kissed it. "Forgive me, my lady. Tolerance is the wisest course for both of us. Anyway, there's Aggie.'' He referred casually to his distinguished grand-aunt Dame Agatha Faulkner, author and historian. "You and she usually get on like a house on fire.''

Roslyn smiled with uncomplicated pleasure. "Dame Agatha is a true lady. She brings out the best in everyone. Everything was so much nicer when she visited. She was even interested in what I was doing. She's a great feminist. Always championing the rights of women. She was the one who discovered I was musical, remember? She always asked me up to the house to play for her.''

"Darling, take it I'll carry on the tradition," Marsh said suavely. "I can just picture us. You with your lovely head bent to the keys. Me, relaxing in my favourite armchair, a single malt whisky in my right hand. Peace. Harmony. I like anything you play.''

"I thought you said it was torture listening to me practice," Roslyn accused him.

He glanced sideways, blue eyes sparkling. "I lied. Secretly I was envious of your talent." Lined up with the all weather runway, he released the landing gear. "This is a great day for us, Rosa. Be happy."

The late Lady Faulkner had been a splendid horsewoman and a champion show jumper in her youth and had continued Macumba's tradition of breeding and training high-quality polo ponies for the home and international market. It had proved a lucrative sideline to Macumba's beef trade. The breeding and training program continued under Joe Moore, head of Macumba's veterinarian laboratory. It was a venture Roslyn the horse lover had always been interested in, but Lady Faulkner had made sure she was barred from the stables complex except for the times Sir Charles himself had intervened on her behalf. It was Sir Charles who had once said she could sweet-talk any horse on the station, a gift she had inherited from her own hapless father.

Her father's grave was in the station cemetery. She had looked down on it as they flew in. Her thoughts spiralled back to the day they had buried him. It had been the worst of times, two days before Christmas. Her beautiful mother had been white to the lips, so overcome by grief she had to be led away. An image of herself arose, huddled against Marsh, a devastated young girl just home on holidays. She had tried desperately not to break down. Her father had always called her his ''little cobber'' and she told herself she had to be brave for him. It was Marsh who had drawn her quite unselfcons-

ciously into his arms, telling her to let the tears come
out. She might have been his little sister so closely did
they remain, she sobbing and sobbing, he stroking her
long curly mop of hair tied with a black ribbon. Marsh
had been there at every turn. Woven into the fabric of
her life. Marsh had listened endlessly to her dreams *and*
her rages. They shared the same sense of humour. They
had been the greatest of friends.

Adolescence and the swift onset of sexuality had
changed all that. One day she was an innocent child.
The next, a budding woman barely able to cope with the
intensity of her changed feelings. The Marsh she had
looked on with great pride and pleasure, her dearest
friend, her hero, was now the person she was terrified
of being close to because of the tumultuous feelings that
engulfed her. Marsh had often given her a fleeting kiss
on the cheek, coming and going, or when she had been
especially helpful around the place; now she wanted to
turn up her mouth to him. To feel the delicious edges of
his sculpted lips. She wanted his hands on her flowering
body. He was totally, perfectly, acceptable to her. He
could do what he liked.

Such a situation had only one consequence. He *had*.
It was only when he turned away from her, she wanted
vengeance. Even contemplating marriage she still
wanted it at some subterranean level. It was a dilemma
of the heart she would have to address. On the trip up
to the homestead Roslyn looked around her with hungry
eyes. There was no disrepair, no neglect on Macumba.
The bungalows, sheds, the men's kitchen and canteen,
the schoolhouse, the huge stables complex with its
white-railed rings and horse paddocks were maintained
in prime condition.

Silver-boled ghost gums grew in abundance as they

approached the main compound, the homestead set like a pearl in many acres of formal and informal gardens. A small stream, a tributary of Macumba Creek, which in flood became a river, girdled the house, widening out to a lake in front and several ornamental pools as it wandered on its way. It was an enterprise begun by Marsh's great-grandmother, Charlotte, Surrey born and widely travelled. The indomitable Charlotte, horrified by the vastness and "utter savagery" of her new environment had taken to conquering it with a passion. She had worked tirelessly to create a wild garden. Any thoughts of a decent garden in a semi-desert environment was plainly out of the question. Yet she had succeeded so well her name had become legend. Over the years the gardens had become more formalised with built-up terraces, archways, fountains, beautiful statuary and an Indian summerhouse by the lake.

The effect was quite extraordinary coming as it did on the desert approaches. But nothing could surpass the sheer romance of the homestead for Roslyn. She had loved it as a child. She loved it still. Her blood always quickened when she saw it. It rose out of the grassed terraces like a great white bird with its wings outstretched. There was the central colonnaded core, two long projecting wings. The stone pillars were perpetually wreathed in a white trumpet flower that blossomed prodigiously. It was only looking directly towards the portico that Roslyn was assailed by one of her visions.

The shade of Lady Faulkner. She stood just outside the front door with its lovely fan lights and side lights, tall and imperious in her riding clothes, swishing that well-remembered riding crop.

Don't come in here, my girl, she warned. *You are not and never will be good enough for my son.*

Roslyn's slender body tensed as it had done so many times in the past. What a powerful woman Lady Faulkner had been. Despising frailty in others but driven by her own devils.

"What *is* it?" Marsh demanded, catching sight of her expression.

"I thought I saw your mother. She was standing right outside the door."

"You and your imagination, Rosa," Marsh said in a neutral voice. "There's no one and nothing to hurt you."

"I never did feel comfortable walking into the homestead."

"I thought you loved it?"

She shook her head. "I didn't say I didn't love it. It mightn't love me."

"Nonsense!" Marsh drew the Jeep to a halt. "Nothing is beyond you, Rosa. You're a million times stronger than you know." He turned to her, his blue eyes glazing with vitality. He looked profoundly pleased to be home. He swooped on her luggage and pulled it out onto the driveway and as he did so a middle-aged man in khaki trousers and a matching bush shirt came through the front door and hurried down the short flight of stone steps.

"Don't you bother with those, Mr. Marsh. I'll take 'em."

Roslyn swung around, extending her hand. "Ernie! How good to see you."

"Good to see *you*, Roslyn." Ernie Walker, part aboriginal, and a fixture around the homestead, gave Roslyn his white, infectious grin. "The place ain't the same without you."

"I've brought you something." She met the liquid, dancing eyes.

"Don't tell me. The latest Slim Dusty?" Ernie named his favourite country and western singer.

"Don't tell me you've got it?"

Ernie shook his head. "Woulda had it, though. Thanks a lot, Roslyn."

Roslyn held up her hand. "A present for all the kindnesses you poured out on me."

"Saved your hide plenty of times and that's a fact!" Ernie agreed. "You were one hair-raisin' kid."

They all looked back as Olivia Earnshaw, "Mrs. E." to just about everyone on the station, rushed through the front door, arms outstretched.

Roslyn immediately took off like a gazelle, so the two women fell into one another's arms at the top of the stairs. Roslyn rained kisses on her mother's cheeks, while the ready tears collected in Olivia's eyes.

"Darling, let me look at you!" Olivia peered beyond Roslyn to Marsh. "I just knew you'd bring her back."

"He's not a man to take no for an answer. You look wonderful, Mumma," Roslyn said. "You never age a minute."

And it was almost true. Seen in the streaming sunlight, Olivia Earnshaw looked a decade younger than her fifty years and still beautiful. Her skin was unlined except for a few fine wrinkles around her sherry-coloured eyes. Her thick black hair worn carelessly short was as glossy as her daughter's and only lightly dusted with silver. Her body was as slim and erect as a girl's. Looking at mother and daughter, one was struck by the extraordinary resemblance, but whereas Roslyn's face hinted at banked-up passions, Olivia's conveyed a certain natural docility.

Marsh looked from one to the other, his thick black lashes veiling his expression. Roslyn could be as obdurate as a Shetland pony but there was nothing she wouldn't do for her mother. Liv was as enchanted with her daughter as ever. Both women were equally protective of the other. Both had suffered under his mother's hands. Though he had loved his mother and understood the demons that drove her, he had to accept she had done a lot of damage. It was for Roslyn to decide if she would allow the scars to heal.

They had a marvellous evening together with Marsh playing host. Harry Wallace, resplendent in a cream safari suit with a silk cravat rakishly tied at the throat, came up from his bungalow to join them, delighted to see Roslyn and savouring Olivia's company for all she chose to misinterpret it. They had drinks and a platter of delicious canapes in the cool of the veranda and an hour or so later, dinner, which Olivia set up in the family room, a lovely spacious room half the size of the formal dining room, made all the more beautiful since Marsh had had the rear wall demolished and replaced with floor-to-ceiling French doors and Palladian fanlights.

Tonight all the doors were open to the wide expanse of terrace and the breeze drifted in, totally seductive with the wonderful aromatic scents of exotic and native flowers.

"That was a marvellous meal, Liv!" Harry proclaimed, admiration in his hazel eyes. "Cooking is an art form."

"So's landscaping. You're a genius, Harry."

"Am I ever!" Harry accepted Olivia's accolade as his due. He was a very *interesting*-looking man in his late fifties, not handsome, but whipcord lean, his good English skin tanned to leather by the elements, rapidly thinning fair hair but a luxuriant moustache; a man women would always find attractive. His speaking voice

was one of his greatest assets, cultured, resonant, full of
a dry, tolerant humour. From his earliest days on Macumba he had been treated more as a family friend than
an employee, even by Lady Faulkner. Roslyn always
thought it had a lot to do with his voice, so upper crust,
and his easy, self-assured manner. Later on she suspected it was her mother as much as polo that kept Harry
on the station.

"You know, Liv," he now confided, "it's always
been an ambition of mine to open a restaurant in some
fabulously beautiful place. North Queensland possibly.
Glorious country. A clifftop overlooking the blue sea
and the off-shore islands. I could build it and create a
beautiful garden. You could supervise the cooking. Of
course, you'd have to marry me."

"The things you say, Harry!" Olivia brushed the suggestion off as a joke.

"I think he's serious, Liv," Marsh said dryly.

Olivia only responded with a gurgle of laughter. "He
tells me something different each time he sees me."

"Marriage is always the bottom line, m'dear," Harry
said gently. "Sooner or later you'll take that in."

Roslyn glanced quickly at Marsh, vivid as a flame,
and he winked, obviously used to these exchanges. Roslyn looked back at her mother. Olivia's head was bent,
her creamy cheeks flushed with the wine and sheer pleasure. She looked especially lovely tonight, Roslyn
thought proudly. She could take her place anywhere. She
was wearing the dress Roslyn had bought her, a simple
wrap dress with little cap sleeves and a longer skirt, but
the printed silk was beautiful; multicoloured sprigs of
pansylike flowers on a white ground. It had been very
expensive and it looked it. Mumma deserves the best,
Roslyn thought fiercely. She had bombarded her mother

with presents, but her main present was still tucked away for Christmas. Olivia wore her new Lancome makeup, too. Giggling like a couple of schoolgirls, Roslyn had made her mother sit still while she'd applied it. It brought Olivia's lovely gentle features to full life. Even her expression had the dreamy tenderness of a film star.

What a waste! Roslyn thought for perhaps the umpteenth million time. My mother is a beautiful woman. She should have a full life. Perhaps it could still happen. If Roslyn married Marsh, her mother would be assured of comfort and security. She could travel, do anything she liked.

They talked until nearing midnight when Marsh and Roslyn decided to take a stroll down to the lake. A huge, copper moon hung low in the sky and the white summerhouse took on a magical, romantic aspect.

"You know Harry's serious," Marsh said as they walked. "He's been in love with Liv for years."

"Mumma doesn't think of him in that way," Roslyn answered, not without regret. "We can't love to order."

"She's very fond of him just the same. She could be even fonder but she won't let him close."

"Surely Macumba's housekeeper, if not respectably married, has to live like a nun?"

"You don't quit, do you?" Marsh said, with no bitterness in his voice but a question.

"I'm sorry." Roslyn took a deep breath, feeling remorse. "We've had such a lovely night. Mumma is so happy."

"But unfortunately for Harry her thoughts don't encompass remarriage."

"Love is grief, Marsh," she said. "Maybe Mumma, like me, yearned for the stars."

"What does that mean?" He glanced down at the dark head near his shoulder.

"Are you sure you don't know?"

She waited for his reaction and it wasn't long in coming. "Let it lie." They had been walking arm in arm and she felt his muscles bunch.

"That's no answer, Marsh. Just something else to be swept under the carpet. Sir Charles was the fixed star in Mumma's firmament."

"As *I* recall, Liv was devastated by your father's death."

"I'm talking about *after* my father died. Mumma was so bereft and lonely. She wasn't exactly surrounded by a supportive family. She was virtually an orphan with an orphan's mentality. And there was your father. A man among men. You could hardly blame her. She made a decision and in a split second lives changed. Your father became too important to us. We orbited around his star. But he couldn't give Mumma anything. He was a married man with a family. A deeply conventional man. A pillar of society. He'd made his commitment and I accept that as right and proper. I pay full reverence to the sacrament of marriage. I'm only saying *our* lives were ruined. My mother somehow sidestepped life, while mine has been overflowing with conflict and resentment."

"God knows that's true," Marsh agreed with bleak humour. "We're none of us angels, Rosa. If Liv sometimes wept for the impossible, you might consider my father had his bad days, too. No one had to open my mother's eyes, either. She knew she had been found wanting quite early in her marriage."

Roslyn threw up her head, quite agitated by his words and their implication. "What are you saying, Marsh?"

He shrugged, backing off. "All families have secrets, Rosa. Unhappiness can make people cruel."

"But your mother was unkind to her own daughters!" Roslyn, a witness to countless incidents, stated.

"Maybe she saw them as an extension of herself."

"How, in what way?"

Marsh let a moment pass. "The knowledge that they were like her," he said. "You thought my mother didn't love my father. You got that wrong. He dominated her every waking moment. Theirs might have been as close to an arranged marriage as one can get, but my mother never could accept my father hadn't come to love her as she loved him. There was no visible alienation, but she needed to take her unhappiness out on someone. And there was Liv. Liv and her beautiful little daughter. Right under her nose and in a position of deference."

"It was cruel, Marsh."

"Lord, yes!"

"There *was* no relationship, either!" Her voice trembled traitorously. "My mother had a clear conscience. She has never done anything dishonourable in her life."

"I hope you're not suggesting my father might have made life difficult for her?" he said curtly. Worse, with some arrogance. *His* exalted father could do no wrong. *His* mother's sins could be easily pardoned.

Incensed, Roslyn broke away, walking rapidly towards the lake. "Heaven forbid!" she called.

Marsh caught up with her, turning her to face him. "Can't we take this calmly for once?"

"It seems not. And don't call yourself calm. You're as arrogant as the devil. The fact is, Mumma wasn't grand enough, anyway. She was a *servant*. There was always that as a powerful deterrent." She stopped abruptly on the hard constriction in her throat.

"It's impossible for you to let go, isn't it?"

Roslyn felt something akin to frenzy run through her blood. Why was *she* always in the wrong? "Listen, that's no news flash," she proclaimed angrily. "I don't say to the past, 'come back and haunt me.' It does. Your way seems to be to put a lid on it, but you can't keep it from simmering away. We have to address this, Marsh."

"When it might destroy us? It's already robbed us of years. My parents, God rest their troubled souls, are dead."

Sudden tears swam into Roslyn's eyes. She shook her head. "I'm sorry, Marsh. I want so much for things to be right between us, but my mind is full of trepidation. I'm on the classic emotional roller-coaster. Nothing is going to be easy for us. Particularly me. I'll be the target. We can't simply go off and get married. Just the two of us. Everyone will expect a big ceremony. The media will have a field day with my rags-to-riches story, my whole background. The gossip mongers will have plenty to say in private about your father and my mother. There will be plenty of ugly speculation. Honourable as they might have been, any halfway observant person could have detected they really cared for each other."

Marsh lifted his head and looked away across the lake. "There's little enough caring in the world, Rosa. I have to tell you I don't give a damn about what people think. The people that matter anyway will understand. You'll have to be the same. If you want us to be married privately, we will. I'll marry you any way you like."

She heard the resolution in his voice. "Then the word will go around I'm pregnant. I really can't win. By the same token, I don't feel inclined to duck anything, either."

"That's my girl!" He drew her to him and kissed her hair. "Besides, I think I'm entitled to see my wife as a bride. It would give me infinite pride and pleasure. I want everyone to see you, Rosa. The whole world!"

It was the reassurance she wanted. Harmony was restored. By common accord they walked into the summerhouse, its romantic ambience increased by the fragrance and starry profusion of the King Jasmine. It twined through the white latticework and climbed the slim, elegant supports.

"How beautiful it is here!" Roslyn leaned her hands against the railings, staring out over the shining expanse of water. The lake was alive with myriad little sounds and the incessant throbbing song of the cicadas.

"Beautiful!" Marsh came behind her, wrapping his arms around her.

Marsh, the sun in splendour. Marsh, the moon at night. At his slightest touch, the heat of desire blazed up. In the soft, purple darkness she could make out the outline of two swans, probably Sirius and his mate, Bella, asleep on the water, their necks bent over their backs. The other swans were somewhere on the banks, their black plumage hiding them from sight. The lake was deceptively deep. Once she had given in to a craze to dive in and Sirius, the most splendid and aggressive of the swans, had chased her.

"Do you remember when—"

"Sirius chased you? Yes, I do. I don't know how many times I told you he would." He pushed the shining cascade of her hair to one side, revealing a profile traced by the starlight in silver.

A soft, smouldering sensation was licking along her veins. "You promised, Marsh."

He kissed the exposed side of her neck, one hand

roving the sweet curve of her breast. "I certainly didn't promise not to put my arms around you."

"That's all it takes."

"With *you*. No one else. You're a creature of fire and air. You know how to weave spells." His mouth began nuzzling her ear, the tip of his tongue tracing the delicate inner whorls.

"It's late," she said.

"Yes, I know."

Her hands half floated up to stop his, then dropped as yearning overcame her. She rested her head back, savouring afresh his marvellous, male scent. It had always aroused her. She had a boundless urge to turn into his arms, to feel the fused lengths of their bodies. He continued to kiss her as though famished, dozens of kisses, light, delicate, pressing. She let him, her mind reliving the old splendour in total recall. The very same stars looked down on them then as now. Brilliant, eternal, their radiance lightening the black velvet sky to a soft, mysterious dark lavender. No other sky looked like the sky over the vast, empty outback. The air was so pure, so unpolluted, there scarcely seemed a barrier to reach up and pluck a star. A perfect jewel.

She gave a dreamy, spellbound sigh. "Marsh, this has to stop."

"When did I ever force you to do anything you never wanted?" he murmured.

She could think of no time at all. The fire in the blood had been mutual. Her magnetism for him had been as electric as his magnetism for her. She knew she was brushing too close to danger. Only when he told her he loved her could she cast off the final constraints.

She was suffocating with emotion now, her feelings building to crisis point after the long deprivation. Water lapped against the giant grasses and reeds. A breeze shook out the jasmine, spilling blossom and scent.

"Kiss me," Marsh said, nudging her face up to him. "Kiss me and don't stop. It's been too long."

Her breath fluttered. Her lips parted. She turned her body slowly, a near balletic movement that had him reaching for her, his body hard. Masterfully he sought and found her mouth spreading a white-hot illumination that enveloped them both.

"Sleep with me, Rosa. Sleep with me. I'm afraid to let you go."

At his words, the sound of passion in his voice, she felt herself at the brink of a chasm. She had done what he wanted before and lost everything. She could risk it all now. She pressed her hands against his chest, immediately fending him off.

"I'm no sex object, Marsh."

From lovers to instant antagonists. A pair of aliens.

"Here we go again," he said harshly. "You're a lot more than that."

"Tell me, *please*. I have to know. What has *changed* exactly that you now want to marry me?"

"Why *exactly* are you considering my proposal?" he countered in a suave, cutting voice. "I thought we had this out?"

She felt tendrils of the jasmine clutch at her hair and she brushed it off. "I'm sorry, but we've never had *anything* out. Not since you drove me away. I certainly wasn't good enough for you then."

"Don't talk like a fool," he said angrily. "You were a schoolgirl."

"Well, there's *that*," she said, her voice deceptively benign. "I had an excellent education. That helps."

He heard the hard mockery behind the dulcet tone.

"Indeed it does. Then there's the way you look. The way you speak. The radiant flash of your smile. There's not a man alive immune to the spell of a beautiful woman. Men are erotic creatures, Roslyn. Violently erotic at times. I can't promise to keep you up there in your ivory tower. I want you badly. You, on the other hand, won't be truly satisfied until you bring me to my knees."

"How repulsive!" Roslyn actually recoiled.

"And too damned close to the truth. You'll never admit to it, Rosa, but revenge drives you. I was hopelessly in love with you, but you saw yourself as a woman scorned. Damn it, girl, you were a teenager. *Sixteen*!"

"I was a woman in all else. I knew how to suffer. I'm damaged, Marsh," she said in a hurt, aching voice. "Can't you see that? Damaged people are dangerous, so they say."

"Hell, Rosa, you talk as though you've stumbled on a secret. Lots of us are damaged. I was fairly well damaged myself. There wasn't a lot of love in our house and what there was wasn't normal. In my parents' eyes I had to be perfect. The perfect heir. I wasn't a medal to be worn with great pride. I was just a boy like any other. Many the time I would have swapped places with my friends. To hell with my inheritance if it was going to cost me my only chance at happiness."

Roslyn shut her eyes to all the emotion in his voice. "I know the pressures that were put on you, Marsh."

"So stop hammering away at me. I want to marry you, Rosa," he said, revealing the ruthless, imperious streak that was in him. "Not only that, I'm going to. You're *mine*!"

CHAPTER FOUR

LATER that night, alone in her bedroom, Roslyn sat on the bed trying to think how best to tackle the difficulties that lay ahead of her. The very first thing she had to do was liberate the minds of Marsh's family who had never recognised her worth, but had chosen to see her through Lady Faulkner's jaundiced eyes. In the old days, she would scarcely have been allowed a place at the table. Now the fact that Marsh had asked her to marry him represented an overwhelming triumph. The only trouble was, there was lots of pain behind the triumph and lost time.

Engulfed in her thoughts Roslyn gave a start when her mother tapped on the bedroom door, then put her head around it.

"Sorry, darling. You gave a little jump. I just wanted to say goodnight and tell you how wonderful it is you're here."

"Come and talk to me, Mumma," Roslyn begged, patting a place on the bed beside her.

"Just for a little while," Olivia smiled. "You must be tired out after all that travelling?"

"I ought to be, but I'm not. Too many things on my mind." As Olivia found herself a comfortable place on the bed Roslyn slipped a pillow behind her mother's head. "You looked beautiful tonight, Mumma," she said proudly. "The dress suited you perfectly. Harry couldn't take his eyes off you."

"Harry enjoys women," Olivia said in a complacent voice, taking her daughter's hand.

"Of course he does, bless him, but don't hide your head in the sand, Mumma. He's very fond of you."

"Harry knows he's perfectly safe with me," Olivia said, as she always did, but added another piece of information. "He was married. Did you know?"

Roslyn was astonished. "He's never said a word."

"Well, it's a sad story." Olivia gave a sigh. "His wife left him for his best friend. She was awarded custody of their two sons. They were six and eight at the time. Harry hung in for some years but somehow his ex-wife managed to turn the boys against him. He had access, of course, but mostly when he wanted to see them she had the boys doing something else. She blocked his calls, made his visits a nightmare. The younger boy started having tantrums. When the children started calling his former friend "Daddy" he decided he would have to try for a life of his own. He was 'someone in the city', whatever that might be. He didn't elaborate and I didn't ask. He left the boys well provided for, then he took off. There doesn't seem to be a place on earth he hasn't visited. Even Antarctica. He spent a lot of time in Kenya then he travelled on to Australia. He's attracted to the wide, open spaces."

"So poor old Harry is one of the walking wounded," Roslyn said with sympathy. "He must have been heartbroken."

"He was. Still is. The bonds weren't broken entirely. The children became men. They wanted to repair the relationship. Harry sees them when he goes back to England. One's in law, the other works for a merchant bank. Neither is anxious to get married."

"It does happen to the children of broken homes."

Olivia gave her daughter a tender look. "You've got something on your mind, haven't you?"

"Am I that transparent?" Roslyn smiled.

"I'm your mother, darling. I know all the signs."

"My beautiful mother!" Roslyn lifted her mother's hand and kissed it. "I don't know how you're going to take this, but Marsh has asked me to marry him."

"Roslyn!" Olivia's nostrils flared and a look of acute unease spread over her gentle face.

"I thought that might be your reaction." Roslyn let out a deep sigh. "It's been a long, long attachment."

Olivia frowned. "As if I didn't know! It was quite terrifying the way you two were so crazy about each other. I expected at any moment Lady Faulkner would cast us out into the desert."

Roslyn smiled wanly. "She just didn't have enough clout. Sir Charles would have said no. He wasn't a man to argue with."

"Nevertheless he was worried. You, particularly, were so *young*. It had to stop."

"Yes, indeed!" Roslyn said in a cynical voice. "We all know about these old families. So very closely knit and so conservative. They don't favour the nouveau riche joining the family let alone the daughter of people who work for them."

"No matter how beautiful and well-educated," Olivia added sadly. "You have to consider, Rosa, Marsh's family is important to him. He's tied to them in every possible way. Macumba is only a small part of the Faulkner interests now. They knew the benefits of diversity before a lot of their friends started to think about it. There's a huge property portfolio. There's Mossvale. The family has a major holding in Westfield Mines. There's a whole lot more, I'm sure. They're very private people."

"I'm not marrying Marsh for the money. It doesn't concern me."

"Then it should!" Olivia looked at her daughter almost sternly. "You could be thrust into a whole lot of responsibilities, even a lifestyle you mightn't want to handle. You won't be living quietly here at Macumba. Increasingly it will become a more public life. It would be easier, too, if Marsh or even his father were self-made men. New Money. But they're the Old Rich."

"Mumma, I hate these labels."

Olivia shook her glossy head. "Unfortunately they exist. We know that better than anyone. The Old Rich have a well-developed herd instinct. They like to stick together. They don't favour outsiders. As soon as an announcement is made, the press will be onto it in a flash."

"So none of us led a life of crime. What do we have to hide, Mumma? We're perfectly respectable."

"Maybe we won't be by the time they tell the whole story. You know it won't be easy, Rosa. You *know*."

"So you're saying, don't marry him?" Roslyn asked wryly.

"I'm saying my main concern is your happiness. You've had a hard enough time of it."

"I thought you loved Marsh?"

"I do!" Olivia compressed her soft lips. "He has never in all these long years offered me the slightest hurt. He shielded us both from his mother's tongue. The girls, of course, followed their mother's lead…"

"I think they were afraid *not* to."

"Possibly. But can't you see, darling, Marsh has always lived like a feudal prince. What Marsh wants, he gets. He even has his own private kingdom. He's uncompromising when it comes to his possessions. I know how the two of you suffered when your affair was bro-

ken up. I know how you worked to put it all behind you.
I know the determination and the pain. Marsh seemed
to want a clean break, as well. He courted Kim Petersen
for a time. She was Lady Faulkner's choice for her son's
bride. Yet here you are! The two of you can't seem to
leave one another alone.''

"That's passion, Mumma."

"Then passion is a damnable thing!"

"It doesn't make for an easy life. I've tried to form
other relationships, Mumma. They didn't work out.
Marsh was always there standing in the shadows. No
one could come near him let alone surpass him."

Olivia's white brow furrowed. "But can he make you
happy?"

"If we put aside his family, Mumma, we're two of a
kind."

Olivia continued to brood. "Not just his family, Rosa.
A wide circle of friends. Your news is dazzling, darling,
but I can't say I'm happy about it. Some will try very
hard to break it up."

"Would they dare with Marsh?"

"They'll go behind his back. You know how it works.
You've been the target of so much unkindness," Olivia
reflected with some foreboding.

"So have you! Why didn't we go, Mumma, while we
had the chance?"

"You're strong, Rosa. You're a fighter. I never was.
So I did nothing."

"And afterwards you came to care for Sir Charles?"

"Ah, don't!" Olivia made an agitated little movement.

"We can be honest with each other, Mumma."

"I loved your father, Roslyn."

"I know you did. I'm talking about later, Mumma. I

understand. Our lives were caught up with the Faulkners.
You were young, beautiful. There was too much prox-
imity. The Faulkners didn't have a happy marriage.
Everyone thinks Sir Charles was a great man. I say he
should have set you free!''

There was sadness and old despair in Olivia's eyes.
''The decision was *mine*, Rosa. I wanted to remain. I
told myself I needed the job. And I did. But in a way it
was self-deception. Sir Charles offered me a job out of
the goodness of his heart. It was a genuine act of kindness. I mourned your father. I still do, I will never lose
his memory. I will never lose the memory of Charles.
There was nothing dishonorable between us. You must
believe that.''

''I do, Mumma.''

''We cared for each other, but we were separated by
a great chasm.''

''Sir Charles was *married*, Mumma. Marsh isn't.''

''No, but he's practically supporting the whole damn
lot of them. I'm telling you, Rosa, if the family can
figure a way to stop this marriage, they will!''

''Then they're in for a few shocks,'' Roslyn said determinedly. ''I know there'll be stormy days ahead, but
Marsh has asked me to marry him and I've told him
yes.''

''Then if that's your decision you have my total support.'' Olivia's beautiful eyes suddenly filled with tears.
''You're a hundred times brighter and stronger than I
am.''

This lack of self-confidence in her mother affected
Roslyn deeply. ''I wish I'd met that stepmother of yours.
I'd have given her a piece of my mind.''

Knowing her daughter Olivia could see precisely how.

"She would never have crushed you the way she crushed me. You have your father in you. Lots of grit."

"It's an easy matter for an adult to crush a child, Mumma," Roslyn pointed out gently.

"I suppose!" Olivia's mind turned inwards. "She used to play games. She was sweet to me in front of my father and so unkind and critical in his absence. My father thought I was the one who wasn't trying. That's what separated us in the end. He took her part against me. People do play games, darling. Especially women. You'll have to be on your guard."

"Why do you think I was sitting upright in bed? I was trying to figure out the best way to go."

"Well, you won't have much time. The family arrives next week. As Christmas comes closer we can expect lots of visitors. The Petersens among others. When are you going to make an announcement? I don't even know if you're engaged."

"I told Marsh I wanted a little time. I want to gauge their reaction to my being back."

"Are you sure that's wise? Why not present them with a fait accompli?"

"No." Roslyn shook her head. "I want them to *reveal* themselves first."

"Count on them to do that," said Olivia. "And count on an uproar when you make your announcement."

"Well, I am expecting a few adverse comments," Roslyn drawled.

"So what's going to happen to *me*? I don't imagine Marsh will want his mother-in-law around the place?"

"Why ever not?" Roslyn looked startled.

Olivia had to laugh. "Not the three of us, darling. I just can't see it. A young couple, newly married. You'll want to be on your own."

"But I want you here, Mumma," Roslyn said in dismay. "This is a *huge* house! If we wanted to, we needn't meet up for months."

"Oh, darling," Olivia shook her head. "I'm finished as a housekeeper. Am I right?"

"Absolutely!" Roslyn sprang up from a lying position to kiss her mother's cheek. "You've worked for the Faulkners long enough. I want you to be able to enjoy yourself. I want you to be financially secure."

"Ho, ho!" Olivia said warily.

"No 'ho, ho,' about it! Marsh wants to settle my own money on me. I'm entitled to it as his wife. What's mine is yours. You've always wanted to take an overseas trip with Ruth. Now you can do it. You can do anything you like."

"Oh, lord!" Olivia moaned. "I'm a quiet person. This is going to change everything."

"Yes it is, Mumma. We'll have to convert overnight to grand ladies." She laughed aloud, an infectious sound that made her mother laugh, as well. "Personally I don't believe we have to do much converting. Maybe a new wardrobe."

"Promise me I wasn't part of it, Rosa?" Olivia asked in a low voice.

"What do you *mean* Mumma? Looking after you wasn't part of a package deal. It's a side benefit. I've always loved Marsh. I always will. Consider it something neither of us can do anything about."

"It can happen like that. So when exactly do I cease my duties?"

"I wonder if you can get breakfast?" Roslyn joked. "No, seriously, Mumma, as of now. I can cook almost as well as you can. We'll share things until we get a capable woman or perhaps a couple. The house girls are used to me. There'll be no problems.''

"Except you won't be 'little Rosie' anymore. You'll be Mrs. Faulkner. All the station staff will have to adjust to that. Harry will take it in his stride. He's always said you could take your place anywhere. For myself I'd just as soon stay 'Mrs. E.' when the family arrives. Going social could give me severe palpitations.''

"You can do it, Mumma.''

Olivia thought for a moment. "Darling, it's quite possible I could find it a nightmare. It's too big a change. I'm the housekeeper. Not an old friend. Am I allowed to talk to Marsh about this?''

"Of course!'' Roslyn exclaimed. "We want your blessing, Mumma.''

"If only my blessing would make a difference!'' Olivia sighed. "I'm not the matriarch of the family.''

"You don't have to be so modest, either.'' Roslyn clicked her tongue. "You're a lady, Mumma. A *real* lady. You're the dearest, most important woman in the world.''

"My baby!'' Olivia pulled Roslyn to her and held her. "I've succeeded with you, if nothing else. So when *is* it you're going to make your announcement? Knowing Marsh, I'm amazed he's giving you any time at all.''

"He plans to tell them Christmas Eve.''

For a long moment they remained wrapped in each other's arms.

"Then look out for the shock waves,'' Olivia said finally.

The week before the family arrived was undoubtedly a happy one. For the first time Roslyn had the complete freedom of the station, which she and Marsh toured from dawn to dusk as business partners, a new thing in Roslyn's life. Marsh had already begun a crash course of instruction. She was given an overview of the station's current management plan and the horse breeding program. As well, he had taken to filling her in on the seemingly endless list of family business interests, which for the most part she had been unaware of it. It had all been part of a far-removed dreamworld the Faulkners lived in. It had nothing to do with her.

Now she discovered with Marsh as her mentor she was able to assimilate a whole mine of information and ask the sorts of penetrating questions that clearly pleased him. She had a good mind and Marsh made it all sound so *interesting* she was able to absorb a surprising amount of fact and figures as well as a few cautionary tales. The money Marsh talked was mind-boggling. How could anyone possibly spend it? Marsh didn't see it that way. He was the custodian for future generations. There was a serious philanthropic program in place, part of which she already knew, but it would be a long time before she felt she would have a good working grasp of the Faulkner money making machine.

One thing had emerged. Marsh had an unswerving dedication to what he saw as his destiny. Was destiny for males alone? Roslyn was thrilled and reassured Marsh had decided to take her into his confidence, but she wanted to use her own voice. She had sailed through her arts degree and diploma of education. It wouldn't hurt her to undertake further external study in the coming year. Business management or commerce. The Faulkner business holdings were ten times bigger than she had imagined. If she really wanted to involve herself in Marsh's life, and it seemed that was what he wanted, she had better prepare herself for a share of the power.

Someday their child would take on the custodian role. The Faulkners had held strictly to the old feudal rule of primogeniture.

Roslyn was of the generation to believe women were capable of big things. Why shouldn't a *daughter* assume the role of custodian when the time came? A daughter could do it. For herself Roslyn didn't want to sit back and become one of the Faulkner pampered women. That would be the worst thing. Excluded from the 'men's talk'. She knew for a fact Marsh's sisters had not been encouraged to take an active interest in the family's business affairs. Not only that, they hadn't been reared to think of themselves as achievers. Roslyn didn't want that to happen to her and it certainly wasn't going to happen to any daughter she might have. Further study was in order. If she wanted to be listened to, she had better know what she was talking about. The prospect didn't scare her. With Marsh so much on her side she saw lifting her game as a challenge. It was the others who would do their best to shoot her down. Well, good luck to them! She had lived a lifetime subjected to unkind and unfair criticism. It might have made her prickly but it had also made her strong.

Marsh and Roslyn were out on one of their exhilarating dawn rides when Marsh brought up the subject of his sisters' pending arrival. They were riding parallel to the silvery green waters of Mali Creek with the breeze skittering around like a happy child, fluttering the leaves and the swamp grasses, scattering blossom—a pure white bauhinia clung like a symbol to the fine cotton covering Roslyn's left breast—and ruffling the glassy surface of the water breaking up reflections of the flowering trees. Both of them had slackened the reins of their horses,

allowing the spirited animals to walk, and now Marsh
seemed anxious to talk.

"It could be, Rosa, you're making things more difficult for yourself," he remarked, adjusting the rakish angle of his Akubra as the sun gleamed across his sapphire
eyes.

"You're like Mumma." Roslyn shrugged. "You want
to present them with a fait accompli."

"I don't need my sisters' permission to marry."

"You'd like their approval, though."

"Of course, but I'm not going to crack up if they're
not absolutely thrilled."

"Let's face it! They won't be *pleased*."

"I had a sinking feeling when Di decided to marry
Chris. As far as that goes, Justine's husband nearly puts
me to sleep, but I've had to accept them."

"But they are very *very* establishment."

"Times change, Rosa."

"For anyone in the real world."

"You're saying my sisters are locked away?"

"It's a closed world of privilege, Marsh. You know
that."

His handsome mouth went wry. "I guess when you
get right down to it they don't know how the other half
live. It's the luck of the draw, Rosa. To compensate we
do our bit as a family."

Roslyn nodded. "The rich have a moral obligation to
help out as best they can."

"Then do allow us to take some credit," Marsh said
in a dry voice.

"For heaven's sake, I *do*!" Roslyn looked up as a
flight of parrots as brilliant as flowers streaked from the
sweet-saped trees. "I don't expect you to sell off everything."

"I'm not going to. Even to oblige you," Marsh said lazily, reaching down to pluck a wild plum which contained more vitamin C than any other fruit. "Isn't it a glorious morning?" Beneath the wide brim of his Akubra his eyes glittered like gems. "Here, have a bite."

Roslyn took the plum and tasted of its tangy, dark gold flesh. "Have you thought the girls are bound to ask Kim Petersen over?"

"I can't see that will do any great harm. They've been friends forever." He leaned sideways in the saddle, caught her face and turned it to him. "You've got juice on your chin."

"Lick it off."

"I intend to." His tongue collected the pearls of moisture then moved over her parted mouth. "When are you going to sleep with me?"

She let him kiss her, a convulsive little shiver moving through her body.

"When we're *married*."

He drew away and laughed. "What if I run right out of control?"

"You won't!" She gave him a challenging smile.

He continued to stare back into her eyes and the smile stole away. "Promise?"

"Not a hope!"

She felt the lick of heat move through her body and enter her cheeks. "Kim will be devastated when she finds out about us."

"Then I'm sorry!" Marsh sat his horse splendid as a feudal king. "These things will happen. Anyway, I got through to Kim long ago. She ought to accept Craig McDonald before he turns to someone else. That's the best offer she's had all year. Lord knows, I never told her I loved her. Or that I wanted to marry her."

"Unfortunately for her she was reared to believe you *did.*"

Marsh clicked his tongue in exasperation. "Blame it on our foolish mothers. What do you really think this holding off is going to achieve?"

Roslyn rapidly veered her horse away so it wouldn't trample a clump of purple, cream-throated lilies. "I *told* you. I want to gauge your sisters' reaction to having me back."

"I'm sure they can handle it if you don't press them too hard."

"What's that supposed to mean?" Roslyn's topaz eyes flashed.

"Now, now, Rosa, you'll have to wrap up that aggression."

"I don't like getting hassled," she said more mildly.

"Do you know anyone who actually *does*? Another thing that concerns me. When is Liv going to give up playing housekeeper?"

"She's shy about her new role. Do you *mind*?"

"Such a feisty little creature!" He glanced at her beautiful face. It was full of feeling; his own fierce joy in the morning. "Tell me, what's happened to the buttoned-in schoolmarm?"

"Scratch me and you'll find she's in."

"So, I'll volunteer."

It was said tauntingly and her body thrummed with response. Many times this past week his arms had gone around her, caressing, possessive, his murmured love talk sweet and hypnotic. Many times she had half expected he would override her soft, stifled protests, but in the end he had always released her, knowing full well she could hardly contain her desire. When he held her there was only his *touch*. His inescapable magic.

Masses of bauhinia blossom tumbled down on their heads. Marsh swept off his Akubra, dislodging the floral butterflies caught in the wide brim. "I'm not going to wait long, Rosa," he told her with a sort of thrilling finality. As always he had read her every expression. "We've wasted enough time. Two months from the engagement, we'll be married."

She felt a frisson of panic, then a great curl of rapture. "How am I going to organise a big wedding in *that* time?"

"I honestly don't know. You *want* a big wedding?"

"Yes, I do!" Her voice shook a little.

"You'll make an unforgettable bride!" His eyes swept over her, amazingly sensual, amazingly blue.

"It's a fantasy, isn't it?" Even now she was experiencing a sensation like dreaming.

"More, it's a marriage," Marsh answered almost tautly. "Two months should be long enough for a clever, well-organised girl like you."

She nodded, her mind racing pleasurably ahead. "It will take a lot of planning but if we know what we're looking at."

"Well, you won't be inhibited by a lack of money," he teased dryly. "I thought we'd be married here on Macumba if you feel the same. We'd have to throw some sort of super party in Sydney for those we can't fit in."

"Macumba will be fine." Who, then, would invite the shade of the late Lady Faulkner? Roslyn thought. "Where would we go for our..." She was aghast she couldn't get out the word.

"Honeymoon, Rosa?" His voice was almost tender. "Don't be shy. Anywhere in the world you want to go.

Our marriage and honeymoon will be a very important part of our lives.''

"Well, then, just the two of us on a tropical island," she said.

He turned his head swiftly. His eyes gave off such brilliance! "You're serious?"

She nodded. "I'm stunned this is happening at all."

"I'm walking around in a bit of a daze myself." His laugh was deep and amused. "If you want a tropical island for two, that could be arranged. On the other hand I'd like to ensure your comfort at all times. Perhaps as an alternative we could cruise the islands of the Great Barrier Reef. The Whitsundays. It's a dazzlingly beautiful world. We could visit your uninhabited islands, anchor in a turquoise lagoon, make love on a secluded beach, pull into one of the luxury islands for a romantic dinner. Actually, it sounds great, but so would a trek across the Great Stony Desert with you as a companion.''

Intense joy flooded her. "So you'll be skipper?"

"Aye, aye, ma'am!" He saluted her lazily, yet the depth of expression in his eyes drenched her in blue. "You can leave it to me to organise the honeymoon. All you have to bring along is you and maybe a pretty dress for when we have dinner.''

"I'll make certain I have one and a swimsuit besides.''

"Throw in a sexy nightgown." He smiled. "Then I'll have the pleasure of taking it off.''

"I never could trust you."

"You can trust me when we're married," he said, very intensely. "Make no mistake about that. But never, never, look at another man.''

"And if I do?"

"You'll regret it," he said promptly.

"I didn't mean it, Marsh." Her response was hardly more than a whisper. "It's always been you."

"And I fell hopelessly under *your* spell. We're going to make this work, Rosa. Our marriage will be forever and ever." Deliberately he lightened the severity of his tone. "Now, I'm on my way home for breakfast. Juice, fruit, steak and eggs, maybe some hash browns thrown in. Plenty of toast and coffee. Are you coming?"

Roslyn's topaz eyes gleamed. "Not only that, I'll beat you back."

"You *think* so?"

Roslyn's hand clasped the reins, gathering them in. "I'm going to give it my best shot!"

The challenge was taken up, ending in a passionate kiss as the victorious Marsh lifted her from the saddle and led her from the stables complex up to the homestead.

CHAPTER FIVE

MARSH was the first to spot the charter flight carrying his sisters when it was only a speck in the cobalt sky.

"That's them now. Right on time!" He thrust up from his planter's chair, his handsome face filled with animation. "I might as well drive down to the strip. Sure you won't come, Rosa?"

Roslyn felt the familiar flutter of nerves in her stomach but her voice was perfectly serene. "No, thank you, Marsh. You go ahead. The girls will like that. We'll wait for you here." She stood to see him off, going to the wrought-iron railing that enclosed the veranda and leaning her slight weight against it.

"Right!" He leaned down and kissed her, the expression in his eyes bringing the heat to her cheeks. "You're not a bad-looking girl, are you?"

"Glad you've noticed."

"Do you remember a time I didn't?" His fingers moved lightly around her magnolia throat.

"Now now, you two!" Olivia called from her comfortable wicker chair.

Marsh gave her a mocking salute. "All right, I'm off. Ten minutes at the outside." He took the front steps of the homestead two at a time.

"Did you ever see such a graceful man!" Olivia sighed. The Jeep swept down the drive before she went to join her daughter at the railing. "Do I really need to stick around, darling? I'm getting bad vibrations already."

"We have to think positive, Mumma," Roslyn said, trying to sound bracing.

"Easy for you, difficult for me." Olivia gave a little wry laugh. "With the exception of Marsh and Dame Agatha, all the Faulkners give me heartburn."

"A teaspoon of apple cider vinegar in a glass of water. That's the cure."

"I've been known to take it occasionally." Olivia smiled. "Marsh is so pleased they've come. Say what you like, the family is very close."

"Tell me about it!" Roslyn invited dryly. "If you're too nervous, Mumma, you don't have to stay."

"Then I'd be leaving my little chick on her own." Olivia slipped an arm around her daughter's waist. "Marsh is right. You look lovely."

"That's good. I went to a bit of trouble."

"You have a natural chic, a natural style," Olivia said, regarding her.

Roslyn was dressed simply in a silk knit sleeveless top and fluid wide-legged pants, both in a subtle shade of gold that placed enormous focus on her eyes. Because of the heat, her dark hair was confined in a Grecian knot, the severity of the hairstyle only serving to draw attention to the purity of her bone structure.

"Of course, it's handy to have a beautiful mother," Olivia said playfully.

"You can say that again! The most beautiful mother in the world."

"Oh, it's lovely being together!" Olivia leaned her head against her daughter's. "You fill my aching heart."

"It does ache, Mumma?" Roslyn turned her head to stare into her mother's eyes.

"That sort of slipped out, darling. What did I want from life anyway?"

"A lot more than you got!" Roslyn's topaz eyes flashed.

"Sometimes when you start off badly, the pattern continues," Olivia said. "Even today I dream of my own mother. So many dreams! So many people in them. All dead."

"It's time to be happy now, Mumma," Roslyn said, gripping her mother's hand. "I want you to enjoy life."

"As long as I wasn't part of the bargain, Rosa. I happen to know you'd do anything for me."

Roslyn didn't answer for a moment. "It's no hardship marrying Marsh."

"It's not going to be easy, either. Why should *you* have to fight for approval?"

"A lot of people have to do it, Mumma. I have to be strong. Prove my worth."

"And they have to prove nothing."

"That's the way of it! The first hurdle is Di's and Justine's visit."

"Then count on a little unpleasantness, darling. I know you never saw it, but the girls were very jealous of you when you were all growing up. They weren't dealt much of a hand when it came to their looks and they had to compete with you for their *father's* as well as their adored brother's, attention. It doesn't make for easy relationships."

"I felt for them, Mumma. I still do. But they never wanted my friendship. Things will have eased now they're married."

"If only I had complete confidence in that!" Olivia sighed. "I'm dreading Chris's arrival. He did make such an ass of himself over you."

"I never *saw* him, that's why. Indifference was the big turn-on."

"Well, don't say I didn't warn you."

Beyond the main compound the Cessna was commencing its descent. Under ten minutes later the Jeep swept back up the drive with Marsh at the wheel, Dianne beside him and Justine in the back seat. Both young women were wearing wide-brimmed straw hats to protect their sensitive skin and both had a hand clamped to the crown.

"Come on, Mumma, enough of this idle chitchat. Let's get this show on the road." Roslyn stood to attention and, smiling wryly, Olivia did the same.

"What do you bet they've got enough luggage for six months?"

"Try ten cents. Ernie will have a big job getting it all into the house. There he is now." Roslyn looked to where their aboriginal houseman was rounding the west wing.

"Ernie's definitely got eyes in the back of his head," Olivia said.

Marsh parked the vehicle and his sisters stepped out. Dianne was the first to look towards the veranda and as she did so she appeared to give a start.

"It doesn't look as though Marsh told them you were here," Olivia remarked in an ironic voice.

"I wanted it to be a surprise."

"A surprise it is, my darling. You saw *that* with your own eyes. Justine was always the nicer girl. Go down now. I'll wait here like a good housekeeper, hands folded quietly in my nonexistent apron."

"You've been getting very cheeky lately, Mumma." With a smile fixed on her face, Roslyn walked down the stairs and out onto the circular driveway where Marsh and his sisters stood in a tightly knit group.

"Why, Roslyn, this is a surprise!" Justine, the perfect lady, held out her hand.

"How nice to see you, Justine." Roslyn took it, her smile including the younger sister who stood almost scowling. "Di, how are you? I hope you both had a pleasant trip?"

"Hi, Roslyn!" Dianne said in her clipped voice. "No, not really. I can't understand how anyone could call Jock Bannister a good pilot. I thought I was going to be sick at least three times." In fact she didn't look well. Her strong-featured face showed strain. She was wearing a smart, tobacco linen dress that should have suited her but somehow didn't. Her one beauty, her thick, curling tawny hair, was cropped to within an inch of its life.

"A cup of tea will soon put you right," Marsh said soothingly. "Go up out of the sun. I'll give Ernie a hand here."

"Anything *I* can take?" Roslyn couldn't keep her eyes from straying around the amazing amount of luggage.

"Ernie will take care of it," Dianne informed her none too politely.

Justine sought to make up for it. She took Roslyn's arm. "Spending the holidays with your mother, Roslyn?" she asked as the three young women walked towards the house. "Marsh didn't think to tell us you were here."

"Mostly it was a surprise."

"It was a bit!" Justine admitted with a faint smile. "I must say you look marvellous. You get more beautiful every time I see you."

"Yes, and isn't it a bore!" Dianne cracked out in her arrogant voice.

"Behave yourself, Di," her sister urged.

"No such thing ever happened to us, did it?" Dianne said almost angrily. "Marsh is the most gorgeous man you ever saw and we turned out two scraggly ugly ducks."

"Which is why you had your hair chopped off," Justine retaliated. "Good hair, too. Don't you think, Ros?"

"Yes, I do!" Roslyn looked at her, her expression both serious and helpful. "That particular tawny shade is quite rare. Both of you have the height and the features to carry off a mane. Men always go for long hair anyway."

"Well, you'd know!" Dianne said with a short laugh. "It must be years since you've visited us. It's a wonder you could *live* without seeing Marsh."

"I don't think he found it easy not seeing me, either," Roslyn replied gently. She kept her expression unflustered while she fought down the little spurt of anger.

"So put that in your pipe and smoke it, Di!" Justine looked at Roslyn almost admiringly. "Don't take too much notice of Di's ill humour. She's been like that for weeks."

"What she means is, I'm preggers," Di announced.

"Why that's wonderful!" Roslyn turned to Dianne with pleasure.

"It might be if I could stop feeling sick."

"Oh, you will!"

"You'd know, would you?" Dianne answered rudely.

"It's generally accepted the first three months are the worst. When is the baby due?" Roslyn asked.

"If I can believe anything my obstetrician tells me, August."

"Chris must be thrilled?"

"He *is*," Dianne confirmed with triumph. "As far as I'm concerned, it's a bit early in the marriage for me. I

wanted a little bit more time alone, but he must have his
son and heir.''

"Let's hope you're not carrying a girl," Justine said
tartly. "It's got to be a *boy*, Ros, didn't you know?"

Dianne sighed. "All I'm hoping for is a healthy
child.''

They had reached the veranda where Olivia, a graceful
figure in a white, sleeveless blouse and a button-through
denim skirt, stood waiting. "Hello there, Mrs. Earnshaw!" Justine called as they mounted the steps to the
veranda. "It must be wonderful for you to have Roslyn
come to visit?"

"Lovely!" Olivia smiled. "How are you both? Well,
I hope?"

"You'll hear about it so I might as well tell you. I'm
pregnant," Dianne announced as though no one else had
ever had that experience.

"I'm delighted for you, Dianne," Olivia responded in
her gentle voice. "You must be a little tired after your
journey. Would you like tea?"

"We'd *love* it, Mrs. E.!" Justine swept off her wide-
brimmed hat embellished with masses of dried flowers.
"What about here in ten minutes?" She indicated the
spacious veranda with its charming arrangements of
white wicker armchairs and glass-topped wicker tables.

"I want to go up to my room," Dianne said in almost
her late mother's tone of voice. "Have Ernie get a move
on with my bags.''

As a consequence of Dianne's attitude Olivia did her
best to cry off sitting down to dinner, but Marsh insisted.

"I won't have you off by yourself," he told her emphatically. They were in the kitchen where Olivia and
Roslyn were making preparations for the evening meal.

"I shouldn't have agreed to this charade in the first place."

Dianne's abrasiveness had thrown them all off balance. Marsh included. "Dianne is pregnant, Marsh." Olivia moved to the oven and popped in a chocolate pecan torte. "I don't want to upset her."

Marsh's handsome face tautened. "She's only been home a few hours and she's succeeded in upsetting everyone else."

Olivia looked more worried than ever. "Can't you see she doesn't want us around, Marsh?"

"Nothing changes," Roslyn said. "Well, that's not true. Justine is really making an effort to be pleasant."

"I'm rendered dumb by such jealousy," Marsh frowned. "Maybe it's genetic and not taught. I don't understand it. I honestly don't!" His eyes gave off an angry shimmer.

Roslyn went to him and put a hand on his arm. "Be gentle, Marsh. Justine told me there was a little pressure put on Dianne to have this baby before she was ready and maybe because of it she's been plagued by morning sickness."

"Then implore her to take her medication!" Marsh sounded exasperated. "Her doctor wouldn't have given it to her unless he was sure it was safe. Di always did like making things difficult for herself. I've asked Harry to join us, as well. Harry can keep the conversation going in the most difficult situations."

But even Harry's amazing conversational powers were put to the test. They were all assembled in the study, Marsh's now, which the family often used for intimate gatherings. It was a large, beautiful room, panelled in English oak with wonderful Pompeian-style frieze, lots of pictures, books and trophies, the armchairs and sofas

upholstered in jewel-bright tapestry weaves to lift the
dark lustre of the woodwork.

"Nothing for me, thank you, Marsh," Dianne said
with exaggerated resolve. "I'm determined to do this
thing right."

"Why do you make so much out of everything, Di?"
Justine groaned. "Marsh was only going to offer you a
Perrier water. You could easily manage it, surely?"

Dianne's long nose quivered. "Maybe a small glass."
She glanced across at Roslyn sitting quietly in a wing-
back chair. The light from a nearby lamp fell in a gleaming crescent across her cloud of dark hair and creamy
skin and Dianne felt the old jealousy bearing down on
her in a giant wave. "Are you joining us this evening,
Roslyn, or are you having dinner with your mother?"

Roslyn felt the familiar bitterness of rejection rise in
her throat. It was downright scary how like Lady Faulkner Dianne had become.

"We're all having dinner together," Marsh said before Roslyn could formulate an answer. For a second he
showed a formidable disapproval to his sister. "Liv and
Harry often keep me company when I'm on my own. I
don't see why they shouldn't now. Friends make things
so much better, don't you think?"

Dianne didn't answer for a minute and Roslyn, for
one, held her breath. "It's *your* house, Marsh." She
sounded as if he'd betrayed her. "I was only *asking*."

"Perhaps you could play for us after dinner, Roslyn?"
Justine intervened hastily. "I've always envied you your
musical talent. Mother was so disappointed in us. Every
time I touched the keys my hands got clammy. Di could
barely squeeze out a tune, yet Grandma Marshall was a
fine pianist. Two of her brothers played to concert standard. The Faulkners were musical. Aggie was supposed

to have been a brilliant pianist in her youth. Her teachers wanted her to make a career of it but her father wouldn't hear of her going away to Europe to study. She had to become a writer instead.''

''Roslyn can certainly thank Aggie she can play now,'' Dianne said in a sharp, superior voice.

''And how is *that*?'' Roslyn was confused and startled. It was an odd sort of remark to pass, even for Dianne.

''Encouragement,'' Marsh supplied, giving his sister a glinting glance. ''Agatha always encouraged you, Rosa. Every time she visited she had you up to the house to play for her.''

''Yes, she did.'' Roslyn's confusion began to recede, but it didn't disappear. ''She was always very kind to me.''

''You make it sound as though you were surrounded by people who weren't?'' Dianne asked, glacier-eyed.

''That's how I *felt*, Dianne.''

''To my intense shame I recall that was so,'' Justine said with a regretful expression. ''We needed to take that line to please Mother, God rest her soul. I've often thought about it and I realise I didn't really want to, but Mother could be fairly terrible if one didn't see things her way.''

''How dare you speak about Mother that way!'' Dianne snapped, shocked.

''Is this all news to you, Di?'' Justine asked in a goaded tone. ''We know exactly the way Mother treated Roslyn.''

''It's all in the past, Ju-Ju.'' Marsh reverted to his childhood name for his sister. ''We can't go back and change anything, but we can all start a new life. That's certainly what I intend to do. Harry, what about another martini?"

"I won't say no." Harry stood up in some relief and offered Marsh his cocktail glass. "You know exactly how to make 'em. Just show the vermouth to the gin."

It was nearly impossible to get Dianne to join the conversation at dinner. Halfway through the main course she suddenly thrust back her chair, holding herself very erect. "You'll have to excuse me," she said in a stilted voice. "I feel very queasy. I'm not used to this *rich* food!"

Olivia laid down her knife and fork, looking acutely distressed. "I'm so sorry, Dianne. It could only be the sauce. I kept the meal light."

"The food is delicious, Liv," Marsh assured her. "Not rich at all." In fact it was simple and elegant, the delicate seafood entrée followed by tender lamb fillets with a selection of fresh vegetables. Olivia had even gone to the trouble of preparing a special dessert for Dianne, a light apricot soufflé, but it was obvious her efforts had failed to please.

"Would you like someone to go up with you, Di?" Marsh asked. "If you're not feeling well in the morning I'll have a doctor fly in."

"I don't need *anyone*!" Dianne insisted with a sharp jut of her chin. It was as if the late Lady Faulkner was standing there. "You all go ahead. You get on so well!" With that, for a queasy woman she stormed away.

"I'll see she's all right." Justine pushed back her chair. "Not that I can say a thing right these days. Being pregnant doesn't seem to suit Di at all."

They all remained fairly silent until Justine returned barely four minutes later. "She's fine!" she said, slipping into her chair. "You look upset, Mrs. Earnshaw.

You needn't be. The meal is delicious just as Marsh said. Di's got a bee in her bonnet about something.''

And we all know what it is, Roslyn thought bleakly.

They had coffee at the table and later retired to the drawing room where Marsh opened up the lid of the Steinway grand. It wasn't the first time Roslyn had played it since her return to Macumba but it was the first time since then she had approached it feeling so upset. Her own idea of allowing Marsh's sisters time to settle in now seemed to make no sense. She should have gone down to the airstrip with Marsh with an engagement ring firmly planted on her finger. It was apparent Marsh was losing patience with the situation. Nevertheless the expression in his eyes as she walked to the piano found an answering chord in her.

'''The Lover and the Nightingale'. For *me*.''

"Lovely!'' Harry took a chair close to Olivia. He tipped his head back and closed his eyes, an expression of pleasure and expectancy on his face. Harry was a connoisseur.

From the moment her fingers touched the keys, Roslyn felt her agitation drain away. Her role was to interpret Granados' famous piece. She liked to think the composers were speaking to her. Sometimes she imagined she could almost see their faces. In her short life she had known tragedy, suffering and abandonment. Her playing, always technically secure, had developed considerable depth. A singing soul that spoke, like the nightingale, to the listener.

She played without interruption for perhaps forty minutes. The Spanish music she loved, several pieces from the Suite Española by Albeniz, on to Debussy's arabesques, ending with one of Harry's favourites, the beautiful D Flat Major nocturne by Chopin.

There was complete silence for a moment, a tribute to the spell, then Justine exclaimed, "It must be wonderful to feel so passionately about something! I enjoyed that immensely, Roslyn. One of your children at least should be so gifted."

"I'll drink to that!" Marsh lifted his brandy goblet and drained it.

While Harry chose to remain with Olivia, Justine decided to accompany Marsh and Roslyn on their after dinner stroll. The night sky above Macumba was enthralling. The stars shone with great brilliance and luminosity, leading Roslyn to recount some of the myths and legends she had learned from Leelya in her childhood. She had just finished a story about the Morning Star when Justine said quite seriously, "You should really write all of this down. Our aboriginal people themselves will be pleased. I'm unhappy now to think we had nothing to do with Leelya or indeed any of the tribal people who regularly crossed the station. Yet Leelya saw you, Roslyn, a white child, as some sort of kindred spirit."

"And I was honoured." Roslyn looked up, tracing the outstanding constellation of the Southern Cross. "I wonder what has happened to her."

"I'd say she's joined her ancestors up there." Marsh pointed to the glittering river of the Milky Way. "She would have been a great age. I'll make more inquiries. One of the boys came back with the story she was walking in the hill country. That was many months ago. Other women were with her. She could have been walking to the spot she wanted to die. Something to do with her dreaming."

"If that's right, I know the spot," Roslyn said. "It's where she believed the rainbow touched the earth."

They parted in perfect harmony shortly before eleven, Roslyn and Justine to go to bed, Marsh to do a little more paperwork in the study.

"Listen, Ros, why don't we go riding tomorrow?" Justine suggested as they parted company in the upstairs gallery.

Roslyn thought swiftly. She treasured her early morning ride with Marsh, but Justine was showing the first signs of friendship. It was too important to be ignored. "Why not first thing in the morning, Justine, if you won't be too tired? It's the coolest part of the day."

"Oh, I can make it." Justine's attractive smile softened the angularity of her face. "Do you think Marsh would join us?"

"I can guarantee it," Roslyn said. "A six o'clock start?"

"Fine!" Justine turned back, bent on healing wounds. "Friends, Ros? How about it?"

On an impulse Roslyn went forward and embraced her. "It's what I've always wanted."

"Me, too. For years. We weren't very nice to you, were we?"

"You were awful. Just awful."

Justine winced. "But Marsh took care of you. He was crazy about you at one time."

"We were crazy together."

"Want to hear something to your advantage?" Justine looked directly into Roslyn's eyes. "He hasn't found anyone else."

It was a buoyant Roslyn who continued on to the room where she found her mother sitting quietly.

"What's up, Mumma?" Olivia's face wore a perturbed expression.

"Sit down, darling. There's something we have to talk about."

"Is it Dianne?" Roslyn asked anxiously. "I thought she'd gone to bed?"

"It's something Dianne *said*." Olivia suddenly slumped forward and rested her face in her hands. "Marsh cut her off, but I don't know for how long. Better I tell you myself."

Something in Roslyn seemed to snap. "Come on, Mumma. Get it out!"

"It's about your piano tuition," Olivia said, looking around her dully.

"Of course it is!" Roslyn threw herself on the bed. "The Faulkners paid for it."

Olivia shrugged forlornly. "Dame Agatha paid for it. It was something she wanted to do. She wanted to do it quietly. She believed you had a gift and she wanted to see it developed." Olivia glanced towards her daughter, who, instead of looking grateful, was alight with outrage. "Justine spoke tonight about her own family's musical abilities. I could have mentioned my own mother played the piano quite beautifully. She taught me up until the time she died. I never had the heart to touch the piano after that. My father couldn't bear to listen to me, either. *I* knew before Dame Agatha you had perfect pitch. But what could your father and I do? It was going to take all we had to send you away to school."

"For God's sake, Mumma, why didn't you tell me?"

Olivia looked mutely at her daughter for a moment. "You'd never have accepted the situation," she said finally. "You'd have rejected Dame Agatha's offer. You wouldn't be able to play today. Think of that!"

"And they all know?" Roslyn felt the sting of humiliation in her throat.

"Charles knew," Olivia said in a guarded voice. "He may have told Marsh later on. I'm certain neither of them would have told the girls, let alone Lady Faulkner. They were painfully aware of their resentments. They wouldn't have wanted to add to them."

"That's all very well, but Di knows now. That's what she was getting at. I thought it was odd."

"What's odd is how she's turning into her mother!" Olivia said sharply. "I would have thought marriage and the prospect of motherhood might make her mature, softer, more tolerant. Justine seems to have managed it, but Di has that same cutting way as her mother."

"What else did they pay for?" Roslyn asked. There was more. She could tell.

"Nothing. Until your father died. I did the best I could. Charles made up the rest. He loved you."

"He loved *you*, Mumma!" Roslyn sprang up from the bed, a whirlwind opening up a floodgate of memories in her mother. Roslyn at all stages. Up in arms. Fighting the hurts.

"Please don't upset yourself, darling," Olivia begged. "Maybe he did. Maybe he even said it. *Once*. We both had our honour. We'd made our commitments. If you're wondering about your piano, I paid for that entirely out of my own money."

"Oh, Mumma," Roslyn moaned, distressed.

"You worked very hard to help put yourself through university. I know what a grind it was. If I was forced to accept a helping hand, it was for your sake, Rosa. You weren't an ordinary child. Your father was thrilled with his little girl. Charles used to say you were like a precious stone. You had to be polished. It would have been a crime not to."

"And in all these years Marsh hasn't spoken one word of it to me."

"Surely you don't blame him?" Olivia was a little frightened of something in Roslyn's tone. "Marsh protected you as much as I did."

"We were bought. Both of us, Faulkner possessions."

Olivia looked stabbed to the heart. "What a way of putting it, Rosa. You always were overly dramatic. It was not bought. I was alone, vulnerable, in need of help. The Faulkners have a big philanthropic program in place. They offer several scholarships to gifted young people. Think of yourself as having received one."

"Not from the Faulkners!" Roslyn said.

"So this is what I get for speaking out? Next time I'll shut my mouth. You have to resolve your ongoing feud with this family, Rosa. What chance have you and Marsh got with this love-hate?"

"Maybe no chance at all!" Roslyn picked up a cushion and threw it.

"You're overreacting, Rosa." Olivia picked up the cushion and laid her aching head against it. "It was Dame Agatha's wish to remain anonymous."

"You mean she knew I suffered from the sin of pride?"

"Rosa, darling, we all knew that. Even Lady Faulkner couldn't break your spirit and she tried. Don't throw Dame Agatha's kindness and generosity in her face. She meant only good to come of this, as did Charles. Neither of them wanted you to feel under any obligation."

"I can't see how that's possible. I *do*."

CHAPTER SIX

ROSLYN waited just long enough for her mother to retire before she found her way downstairs again to the study. She realised she was in an emotional, excitable mood, but she was driven to have this issue out with Marsh. She felt anger, disillusionment, pain and, above all, *pity* for her mother's lack of power and position in life. Her father's early tragic death had forced them into a life of dependency. She *hated* it. She had always hated it. She could never get rid of the inner distress however good her intentions. In a way she identified too much with her mother. It couldn't be an uncommon situation with a lone parent and lone child. Maybe she had even assumed her father's role. She had certainly tried to fight her mother's battles, impose *her* nature on her gentler mother, but she had never succeeded in inciting her mother to revolt. Her mother's love for Charles Faulkner had been the crucial factor in their staying on at Macumba. Not that she could blame her mother for anything, but Olivia's decision had forced them into living under the power and protection of the family she had once called the Enemy. Maybe things would have been better for her had she not been such a bright child. She couldn't remember a time she hadn't wanted to better herself, intellectually, socially. She had spent all her school years *striving*. She had longed to be considered an equal by the Faulkner girls, covering her frustrations with a quick, ironic wit they couldn't match. As for Marsh? Marsh was in her blood. Whether marriage was going to set all the wrongs right was another matter.

She rapped on the door of the study, opening it before he had a chance to respond.

"Rosa, my love!" He laid down his pen, his blue eyes embracing her. "One of these nights I'm going to put you in my pocket and take you up to bed."

"Can we talk?" She crossed the room so swiftly the skirt of her rose-printed chiffon dress swirled around her.

"Damn! I thought you'd come back to kiss me good-night." He rose from behind the desk and came round to her, his long arm gathering her up.

"Don't treat me with amusement," she warned him, tilting her dark head.

"Oh, my God, here we go again!" he said on a slow breath. "What is it this time, rosebud?"

"All these *years* and you've never told me."

"Ah, here it comes!"

"At least you're not going to pretend you don't know."

He released her and sat back on the desk. "All this melodrama, Rosa? There's nothing so terrible about it, is there? I assume you're talking about your piano lessons?"

"I am."

His sapphire eyes rested on her passionate face. "It wasn't Di. It must have been someone else."

"Not one of your precious sisters. Mumma told me. She was waiting for me in my room."

"Poor Liv!" He laughed shortly. "She's got one scary daughter!"

"What a thing to say, and you want to marry me?"

"I didn't say *I* was scared of you, Rosa. You've met your match. Which doesn't mean I'm not expecting lots of crisis situations. So Aggie paid for your piano lessons? Don't read anything indebted into it. Aggie could afford it and your parents couldn't.''

"I should have been *told*!"

"I'm inclined to agree, but all in all we were locked into an explosive household.''

"You mean, your mother's reaction?''

"She would have used it, Rosa.''

She sank her teeth in her full, bottom lip. ''Yes, she would. Let's get to how your *father* subsidized my education.''

His expression assumed an arrogant cast. ''Your mother was all alone in the world. She had no family in this country. No one outside of her friend, Ruth, to care about what happened to her. What did you think my father was going to do? Your father was killed in our employ. My father acted out of kindness and sympathy. Not that you were a charming kid, except when you felt like it, and then you could curl us both around your little finger. You had more prickles than a spiny anteater.''

"I had to grow them for protection.''

"You're just spoiling for a fight, aren't you?'' He put out his hand and laid it along her cheek.

"Why didn't *you* tell me, Marsh? There was a time you could have told me anything and I would have accepted it.''

"Unhappily in the past tense.'' His expression tautened. ''For a long time I didn't *know*. My father didn't tell me everything. It was a private arrangement with your mother. You had to be given every chance. Helping you made him happy.''

Her brilliant eyes flashed upwards. Her tone was hard and steady. ''Are you sure it wasn't to get Mumma to sleep with him?''

"*Don't*!" he said grimly.

"What do we really know what went on?"

"They had their honour."

"So Mumma says."

"Then why don't you accept it?"

"You can't know what it's been like growing up. I love my mother, but I was never stupid. She wasted her life on an impossible dream. It's all so sad I want to scream."

"Then go ahead!" He pulled her to him roughly, his nostrils flaring, a disturbing curve to his mouth. "Scream if you have to, only let it *out*!"

It seemed like an invitation she couldn't resist. A therapeutic answer to the pressure points that plagued her. Her hands made fists. She pounded them against his hard, muscled chest.

"I hate you, Marsh," she gritted, which of course was nonsense. Without Marsh she was half a person but she was awash with emotions Dianne's arrival had set loose.

It was as if a whip had flicked him, raising weals on his flesh. "Maybe you have a right!"

The light gleamed queerly across his bronzed cheekbones, darkened his eyes to an electric blue-violet. For a time he tolerated her pent-up railing, then he grew tired of it, bringing her fists together and holding them still. "It's *loving* you want," he said thickly. "Loving until you can't remember the hurt."

Even as his face swam above her, Roslyn started to shudder. She made a grab for his arm, but he bent her body back in a supple arc, seeking the magenta shadow at the base of her low, scoop-necked dress, moving lower over the sinuous chiffon so her flesh beneath its thin covering *burned*.

Sensation upon sensation was moving through her like

ever-widening ripples on a lake. There was so much between them; their shared history, their passionate loving,
the deep resentments that suddenly flared up and set
them on a collision course. Passion and sexual hostility
was so intermingled it was impossible to say where it
was coming from.

She gasped as he allowed her up, turning his questing
mouth on hers. Her soft lips opened in overwhelming
longing. Their tongues curled, mated, until it became
such a pressure they had to break off to breathe deeply,
then return to the intense sensual exploration that dou-
bled the excitement with every frantic moment....

Marsh grasped a handful of her glistening hair, stared
hard into her eyes. "Sleep with me, Rosa. Now, tonight!"

As if it hadn't been her fantasy more times than she
could possibly count! Yet she said in a kind of desperate
rush, "We go up to your bedroom just like that?"

He looked at her searchingly. "You're ready. Do you
think I don't know that?"

"Always ready for you. That's no secret."

"A rosebud under spring rain." He ran his finger
around the outline of her full lips. "I can't take this
waiting, Rosa. I'm a man, with all a man's needs!"

"Then you must try discipline." She shook her head.
"I can't...I won't sleep with you until I'm your wife!"

For a moment he looked at her, blue fire in his eyes,
then he laughed, self-derision etched into the little brack-
ets around his mouth.

"Them's fightin' words, Rosa," he drawled. "I don't
know that you're going to be able to pull it off."

"We had a bargain."

"Did we now! I said nothing about total abstinence.

I'm *starved* for what we had. In fact I think I'm heading for some sort of crackup."

"Not you, Marsh. You forgot me for years."

His beautiful mouth twisted in a smile. "I thought that was what you wanted. You couldn't tell me enough you'd stopped loving me."

"Love wasn't enough!"

"You wanted marriage. Well, you've got it. So why make it sound as if there's a big question hanging over the whole thing?"

"It's my suspicious nature. You'll have to pardon it."

"More like you want to turn me inside out."

"Whatever it takes! I've learned the hard way it's much better to play hard to get. *You* taught me that."

He caught her hand, carried it to his mouth. "You're a cruel little cat, which makes me wonder why I want you. I could think of at least a dozen women who wouldn't act this way. Kim Petersen included."

"I thought maybe you'd slept with her."

"Sleeping with a woman is easy. Loving her is an entirely different thing. It so happens I'm crazy about you. Emotions tend to obscure the mind. It was a terrible mistake letting you get away from me."

She put out her slender arms, rested them on his wide shoulders. "I'm amazed it wasn't forever."

"Will you *ever* forgive me, Rosa?" There it was, the flash of vulnerability in the stunning self-assuredness.

She could have said no. Instead her extraordinary topaz eyes filled with tears. She didn't lift a finger to wipe them away. They gathered and fell, in shining crystal drops.

"Rosa...darling!" He drew her in utter tenderness against him, his sensitivity as always disarming her. "Why can't we end this futile war? We've been happy since your return, haven't we? So Dianne arrived to create a few problems. She's not behaving well. But I'm not going to let her get away with it for long. On the other hand, why don't we simply tell them we're getting married? The limbo has to end.''

"Oh, I know, Marsh.'' She allowed him to gently dry her tears. ''It's just that your family scramble me up so much.''

"When will a wounded little girl accept her womanhood, her own worth?''

"When your family play fair.''

"You have Justine's vote. That's a beginning. Frankly I don't think you need anyone's vote but mine and you have it overwhelmingly.''

"I still won't sleep with you.'' She smiled. She was feeling so much better. Kisses were ravishing. Comfort was important.

His fine white teeth showed in an ironic grin. ''I hope you don't fancy yourself as another Anne Boleyn?''

"Her end was too unattractive. How did Dianne get to know Dame Agatha paid for my piano lessons?''

Marsh shrugged. ''You know what an avid eavesdropper she was as a girl. Aggie would never have told her. Nor Dad. I certainly didn't. Does her knowing bother you so much?''

"In a way it seems to undermine my self-value. Maybe I wouldn't feel like that if Dianne wasn't so unkind.''

"Then someone has to tell her. That someone is me!''

"She'd see it as a betrayal. I don't want you to say anything unless it all gets too intense. I should be fighting my own battles. A line has to be drawn somewhere with Di. You realise why she jumped up from the table? She was furious Mumma was sitting down with us.''

"That makes her look an appalling snob. I can't defend her. On the other hand, don't let it get to you. It's
Dianne who has to iron out that particular unattractive
kink. It sure as hell would help if you and I got engaged
before Chris gets here. Married or not, you're the sort
of woman he loses his cool over."

"And I'm a total innocent!" Roslyn frowned at the
prospect. "As far as I'm concerned, Chris is a—"

"Don't say it!" Marsh begged, holding up two palms.

"Lord knows I was only going to say 'twit.'"

"Whatever. You can handle it."

"Of course. The one I can't handle is *you*." She
leaned closer and pressed a butterfly kiss on his mouth.

The girls were scarcely home before Kim Petersen flew
over, piloting her own single-engined Cessna, a birthday
present from her father.

"I thought I might stay a day or two," she announced
unnecessarily. Down in the driveway Ernie was bow-
legged under the weight of her two suitcases.

"That will be lovely!" Dianne looked overjoyed to
see her. "I've missed you so much!" She threw her arms
around her friend, kissing her Euro-style.

"Good to see you, Kim!" Justine smiled in turn,
swishing cheeks. "Roslyn is here to join us." She turned
to include Roslyn in the group.

"Yes, I *know*. How are you, Roslyn?" Kim's large
grey-green eyes examined Roslyn from head to toe. Kim
was as tall as her friends, but far better looking. Her sun-
streaked, dark blond hair was precision cut to swing in
a thick, medium-length pageboy. Her clear, tanned skin
was innocent of make-up, except for a natural, dark pink
lip gloss. Her ultra-slim body, fit and tightly muscled
was encased in a white linen shirt and matching wide-

legged pants, stylish leather sandals on her feet, a handsome leather belt around her trim waist. She looked what
she was. A rich young woman, super confident and competent. Unlike Marsh's sisters, she had always taken a
deep interest and active part in the running of her father's cattle and sheep chain.

"I'm very well, Kim. And you?" Roslyn went forward, prepared to take Kim's hand, but it wasn't offered.

"Couldn't be better!" The tanned face smiled, but the
eyes held their familiar condescension.

"Why don't I show you up to your room?" Dianne
was quite pink with pleasure. "It's not your usual one.
For some reason Roslyn's got that, but we've prepared
another."

Just as Roslyn thought. It had all been arranged.

"Any other changes I should know about?" Kim
laughed as she and Dianne walked from the veranda into
the cool of the spacious entrance hall.

"I'll go, too. See she's settled." Justine turned a
vaguely apologetic face to Roslyn. "It's nice to have
Kim here. We've always been great friends."

"Yes, I know." Roslyn smiled, but a kind of sadness
moved through her. She would never be accepted in this
multi-layered world, where friendships went back generations. Better get used to it, she thought. Cultivate your
own inner strengths. Build your own dynasty if you have
to.

Fifteen minutes later all three young women returned
to the veranda where Roslyn was still sitting. She had
committed herself to a course of action. She was prepared to see it through.

"Still here, Ros?" Kim asked casually, as though
Roslyn might have sought refuge in the kitchen.

"I hope that's okay?"

"But of course!" Justine sounded dismayed.

Dianne, however, settled herself back comfortably in a planter's chair.

"Still suffering morning sickness, are you, poor angel?" Kim flopped rather gracelessly into a wicker armchair facing her.

"Strangely enough not for the past two days. It must be something in Macumba's air. The purity and the wonderful, comforting scents." Dianne glanced across at Roslyn, still wearing the elegant riding clothes that became her so well. "Ros, do you think you could ask your mother to bring coffee and tea out here?"

Justine immediately jumped up. "Don't worry, Ros. I'm going back inside for a minute. I'll ask."

Kim looked hugely surprised. "In that case, stay and talk to us," she invited. "I've got to hand it to you, you've certainly got yourself together. You look marvellous. So what brings you back to Macumba? You haven't been here for a couple of years surely?"

Roslyn adjusted her chair so she could join the circle. "Mumma, of course. Then Marsh wanted me to be here." She held Kim's faintly scornful glance unwaveringly, watching it dissipate into ludicrous shock.

"*Marsh*?" Both young women cried out together, making it almost a shout.

"You sound surprised?" Roslyn kept her expression cool and polite.

"Well, *I* am, dear." Kim ran a strong hand through her thick fall of hair. "Considering Marsh never *once* mentioned you."

"You wouldn't have been all that interested in news of me, would you, Kim?"

Kim lifted a linen clad knee then stamped one of her sandals on the floor, rather like a horse. "I certainly would! I don't want anyone trying to muscle in on my man. And that includes you, young Earnshaw. Not that you'd be in the running,'' she added in her insulting fashion.

"Is that a joke?" Roslyn asked.

"Joke?" Kim looked at the younger Roslyn as though she'd gone temporarily mad. "It's a plain statement of fact."

"As *you* see it?"

"I'll say!" Kim looked to Dianne for confirmation and support.

"Then forgive me if I take exception to the implications. You have an embarrassingly large ego. As far as I'm concerned, we're all equal."

Kim eyed her contemptuously. "Come off it, Ros. I have a pedigree. Surely you don't expect me not to take pride in it?"

"You're a horsewoman. You know pedigree is secondary to performance. Call it character if you like. Distinguished people are generally egalitarian."

"It is dreadfully hot," Dianne suddenly said.

"Give your mother a shout," Kim told Roslyn firmly.

"She'll be here presently. Would you like a fan, Di?"

"I'd like you two to stop scrapping at one another."

"I'm sorry," Roslyn apologised. "I don't want any unpleasantness, either, but I can't sit quietly while Kim makes me the target for her somewhat brutal put-downs. I endured too much of that in the past. Now I want things to be different. I'd be glad of a little civility, not this absurd pulling rank. Take it from me, the Colonial era has passed."

"So the word's got around?" Kim barely controlled a supercilious smirk.

"After many discouraging setbacks. Please remember I'm here as Marsh's guest. Maybe a great deal more."

There, she'd almost put it in a nutshell!

As a consequence Dianne gave a little cry of alarm and Kim braced herself as though for battle. "Now you've got us utterly befuddled. What do you *mean*, exactly?"

"I mean, the situation has changed," Roslyn said calmly.

"Interesting!" Kim said grimly. "I had the feeling you were up to something."

"So you lost no time in flying over?"

"My dear, I had advance warning."

"She means *me*!" Dianne looked as though she suddenly detested herself.

"The fact you've always had a thing going with Marsh hasn't bypassed us entirely," Kim said with an insolent lift of her brows. "You *are* beautiful in a cloying sort of way."

Dianne looked thoroughly startled. "Cloying?" she blurted. "Is that what you'd say of a bouquet of red roses? I've always wanted to look like Ros. Naturally I loathed her when I didn't. I still haven't learned to live with it."

"Dearest, what the devil are you babbling about?" Kim cried.

"It's this pregnancy," Dianne laughed weakly. "I wish it would get a move on. Ros, do you think you could be a pal and give your mother a call? You've no idea how I'm longing for a cup of tea."

"No problem!" Roslyn responded. And it wasn't, put like that.

"It's fairly obvious your mother has got a bit slack,"

Kim began severely, but was interrupted by the sound of the trolley being wheeled through the hallway.

Roslyn stood up immediately trying to control her quick temper, but it was Justine who eventually appeared. "Sorry about the delay." She pushed the trolley forwards, her expression positively chirpy. "Poor old Harry cut his hand and Mrs. E. had to dress it. God, it was harrowing! Blood everywhere!"

"Do you *mind*?" The freckles stood out on Dianne's pale skin.

"Sorry, old dear!" Justine gave her sister an apologetic smile. "It looked worse than it was. Mrs. E. dealt with it very efficiently."

"If that's what it takes to make you happy!" Dianne said.

"I'm not telling you *all* I know."

"Obviously you're going to make us wait for it," Kim said, accepting a cup of coffee from Justine while Roslyn attended to Dianne's lemon tea.

"Will you look at these scones!" Justine cried. "I've never been able to make a decent scone in my life. They're supposed to be so *easy*!"

"*Well*?" Dianne looked at her sister fretfully.

Justine sat down. Arranged herself comfortably. "Prepare yourselves for an astonishing tidbit."

"Has it anything to do with Ros?" Kim asked sharply.

Justine shook her tawny head. "Harry cut himself because he's in a state of shock. It appears he stands to inherit a baronetcy. And a stately pile. Some ancient relative of his is dying in England. Lord Marchmont, Mortimer, something like that."

"Good Lord!" Kim sat erect in her chair. "To tell

you the truth, I'm not surprised. Harry has always handled himself in the grand manner."

"He put plain old 'gardener' on his income tax return," Roslyn pointed out mildly. "When did he find out?"

"The news was waiting for him this morning. Faxed to him by one of his sons. He has to return home."

"You mean, he's going to take it up?" Dianne asked eagerly.

"First things first, Di. The old gent has to die. Harry was very fond of him apparently."

"He must have known he was the heir, surely?" Roslyn asked.

"You'll have to ask your mother," Justine responded in an arch voice. "She was the first to know. In fact I wouldn't be a bit surprised if Harry didn't ask her to marry him now."

"Why on earth would you say that?" Dianne looked at her sister sharply to see if she was ribbing them.

"God, you're dense sometimes, Di. Harry's been in love with Mrs. E. for as long as I can remember. Don't you agree, Ros?"

"I think that's what's kept him hanging in."

"You mean, on the station?" Dianne demanded.

"Yes."

"But he'll be a baronet now," Dianne said stonily.

"I wish I knew what you're getting at." Roslyn's topaz eyes started to blaze.

"They don't come more patrician-looking than Mrs. E." Justine said supportively, and touched Roslyn's arm. "So in a little while we'll have a lord in our midst, or Harry won't come back at all."

While the others stayed on the veranda discussing the matter and reminiscing about old times in which Harry largely figured, Roslyn wheeled the trolley back into the kitchen where she found her mother and Harry sitting at the table, drinking coffee, their expressions engrossed.

"So, m'lord, how are you?" Roslyn asked with gentle mockery, looking at his bandaged hand.

Harry turned his kindly face towards her. "Plain shell-shocked, darlin'. Justine told you, obviously?"

"Yes."

"I would have liked to tell you myself only she happened to walk in at a crucial time."

"That's all right, Harry."

"Come and sit down. Join us in our little talk."

"Harry has asked me to marry him," Olivia said, looking at her daughter with half-rueful, half-sparkling eyes.

"What a one he is!" Roslyn put her hands on Harry's shoulders and kissed his cheek. "Taking all things into account, I'm happy to give you my blessing."

"She hasn't accepted me yet, duckie." Harry laughed.

"I haven't said no, either." Olivia smiled. "I want time to think this over, Harry."

"What, another ten years?" he crowed. "No, no, m'love, it's not on. It's now or never!"

"That's it, Harry. Sweep her off her feet."

"It's such a big decision," Olivia said. "I'm not good at making decisions."

"You can say that again!" Harry sighed, his expression turning a little bleak. "Faulkner was a dream, Liv. Nothing could ever have come of it. Now he's gone."

"Harry!" Olivia looked stricken. "Why would you speak of Charles now. And in front of Rosa?"

"Because she knows better than anyone else," he answered in a quiet but blunt voice. "You have to lay your ghost to rest, Liv. *I* love you. I have from the moment

I set eyes on you. I've stayed on Macumba to be near you, now it's time to take up my own heritage.''

"Then you'll want to stay in England, Harry?" Roslyn asked.

"Oh, yes, m'dear. I love this country. It's young and vigorous and it's been kind to me, but England is where my roots are. That's where I want to die.''

"I understand that, Harry," Roslyn told him, "but you'd be taking Mumma away from me.''

"Nonsense!" Harry reached across the table and patted Roslyn's hand. "Liv's told me you and Marsh are to marry. Don't worry, your news is safe with me. I'm absolutely delighted for you both. In my opinion you're splendidly matched. But when you're married, you'll need to be on your own. If your mother honours me by accepting my proposal I'll take her back to England with me, yes. She *is* English lest we all forget. But we would expect you and Marsh to visit us frequently. At the very least, once a year. That should present no problems. Marsh travels a great deal as it is. He has relatives of his own in England. He visits them all the time.''

"But Harry—" Olivia said.

"No buts, darling," he interrupted forcefully. "I'm certain in my heart we could be very happy. You care for me a good deal more than you've been prepared to acknowledge. Who was frantic when I came a cropper at our last polo match?''

"I think you should stop playing polo," Olivia said. "You've had a pretty good run.''

"I promise to stop if you promise to marry me." Harry caught Olivia's hand and carried it to his lips. "Think of it as saving my life.''

The following morning Marsh flew Harry to the nearest domestic airport where he was booked on a flight to

Brisbane, the state capital, which in turn hooked up with a Qantas flight direct to London. Roslyn and Olivia went along for the first leg of the trip, hugging Harry warmly before he was forced to obey the final boarding call.

"Love you, love you!" he called, an unfamiliar figure in a beautifully tailored city suit.

"Why do I have the feeling Harry's proposed?" Marsh glanced over to where Olivia was standing so demurely, waving a silk scarf.

"I wanted to tell you but Mumma hasn't given him her answer yet," Roslyn explained.

"*That* doesn't surprise me," Marsh said dryly.

"I think she loves him." Roslyn's voice trailed away.

"I think she *could* if she gave herself half a chance. They're very good friends. As far as I'm concerned that's a lot!"

"I remember when *we* used to be very good friends."

"I remember, too." He looked down at her, the expression in his sapphire eyes setting up a faint tremble.

In the near distance the jet turned in preparation for the taxi down the runway. "Oh, I do hope he'll be all right!" Olivia moved over to join them, her gentle face anxious. "Such a long, long trip! He'll be exhausted, poor darling."

Marsh gave a casual shrug. "Harry's tough, in excellent condition. I just hope he makes it in time."

"I don't believe what's happening around here anymore," Olivia said in a bemused voice. "You and Rosa to be married. Now Harry wants to marry me." She tilted her head, looking directly into Marsh's eyes.

"Why are you looking at me like that, Liv?" he demanded. "Do you want *my* permission? You've got it. You and Harry are family. I could easily learn to call you Lady Mortimer," he teased.

Olivia didn't smile. She continued to stare up into his striking face with its strong echoes of his father's vivid blue eyes, firm jaw and cleanly defined mouth. "You're so much like your father," she said. "It's impossible to forget him with you around."

To Roslyn it was the most revealing thing her mother had ever said. Marsh must have thought so, too, because he looked down at Olivia in silence for a moment before he answered. "Dad would have approved, Liv. You need a great deal more out of life. In a sense you've been hiding away. I've been very grateful, but it's not what you deserve. Harry is a fine man. When he first came to us he was teetering on the edge of emotional collapse. Macumba took him in, allowed him to heal. His problem of recent times has been getting you to marry him. You must realise he truly loves you?"

"Oh, I *do*!" Olivia looked agonised. "I've done everything but face it. Goodness knows why. I love him, too, as a person. I'm terribly upset he's going away. I'd be devastated if I thought I'd never see him again, it's just…it's just…"

"No explanation to offer?" Marsh prompted gently.

"No explanation I can offer." Olivia's beautiful eyes filled with tears.

Marsh put his arm around her shoulder and they all began to walk on. "It's all got to do with dreams, Liv," he said. "We all have our dreams but it's not always the way life *is*. Harry can give you a good life. At the same time you can make him whole. It seems to me you'll be making a big mistake if you lose him."

"Do you think I could?" Olivia sounded shaken.

"This inheritance thing has forced the issue. Harry's

not the man to give up easily but he will expect an answer.''

Olivia gave a ragged little laugh. ''When you put it like that, Marsh, I've a strong urge to step on a plane.''

''Well, now,'' said Marsh. ''Just say the word.''

CHAPTER SEVEN

ROSLYN sat her horse in the shade of a silvery coolibah looking down on the spectacle of brumby running on the quivering plain below. The ridge was a wonderful vantage point—she was sharing it with two inquisitive kangaroos—but the glare was harsh. It did funny things to the landscape, making it seem to swim in shimmering heat waves. She crammed her Akubra further down on her head, tilting the brim against the shattering brilliance that pierced the light, leafy canopy. Burning ochre dust, the vivid Namatjira red, rose in a great cloud as some fifty brumbies were being driven towards the holding yard at Inga-warri. Inga-warri was an old camping ground and the horses could water there at the large dam.

She waved to the kangaroos who looked at one another then appeared to nod at her gravely. She knew kangaroos could be a terrible menace but they had always charmed her. There were countless aboriginal myths and legends about the travels of Kangaroo and Euro on their journeys through central Australia. They were mythical creatures and there was no question they could look, like now, extraordinarily dignified. Interesting, too, they weren't in the least unsettled by her presence or the ear-splitting noise that came from the plain.

In the old days running and yarding wild horses was considered the greatest of sports. She'd had a lot of fun herself but of recent times motorbikes were being utilised on Macumba to capture the plentiful mobs just as the helicopter was used on the musters. Now the silent

119

plain was split by the spine-tingling roar of four Yamaha
600 cc's herding the bush horses. It was exciting but
very dangerous work, especially in the scrub. Sometimes
the stallion fearing for his mares would try to savage a
rider. The slightest mistake with the bike and the rider
could and often did end up in hospital.

"Lucky" Redding, so called because everyone said
he was lucky he wasn't dead, had crashed four times in
the last eighteen months. Twice on Macumba when the
Royal Flying Doctor had to be called in to rescue him.
"Lucky" was out there today in hot pursuit of the big
bay buck stallion. Roslyn hoped he was wearing his
lucky talisman, a roughly star-shaped stone a part-
aboriginal friend had picked up on one of his ritual walk-
abouts in the gibber desert with its vast pavement of
sparkling coloured stones. Roslyn had dozens of them
Marsh had helped her collect as a child. The gibber
plains are remarkable phenomena, the stones rounded
and polished by windblown sand until they resemble
gemstones. Lying embedded in the ochred clays, they
resemble a fantastic glazed mosaic. "Lucky's" talisman
was a curious semitransparent quartz with a marking like
an Egyptian hieroglyphic in the centre. A spirit stone
Lucky's friend had called it. It seemed to work, though
not totally.

The dust was rising now in a turning, twisting cumu-
lus cloud, blown up by a sudden hot wind that seemed
to come out of nowhere, the willy-willies that were supposed to be sent as a warning. The horses appeared to
be in superb condition. Their muscles rippled in the dazzling light, coats taut against their lean frames. The stallion appeared to have a lot of Thoroughbred in him. His
ancestor had probably escaped from the station at some
stage. There were more than half a million wild horses

in Australia. This mob looked a fine lot. The bikkies had been on the go since dawn. As far as she knew they were to cover the northwestern corner ranging over a few hundred kilometres. They would stop soon for smoko. She wouldn't say no to a cup of billy tea herself. Marsh had a meeting going with an important horse breeder. She had left Kim and the girls lazing the time away beside the pool. Justine had invited her to join them in her new, friendly fashion, but she had taken pity on the glance Kim and Dianne had exchanged. She was feeling much better in herself now. Stronger. When it was all said and done, the only person who really mattered was Marsh. Let the others think what they liked.

As she commenced her descent of the rolling, stony slope, Roslyn saw some of the horses make a break, while the others cunningly bolted in the opposite direction. She held her breath, but within minutes Lucky and his team had wheeled them in. Men on horseback would have had little chance against this lot, she thought. They would have been outrun. The horses were wonderfully fit. They were on their own territory. They knew every inch of the scrub.

She made it into camp at the same time the weary mob were being driven by the tailers, the stockmen on horses, who shepherded the subdued brumbies into a temporary holding yard. The stallion was still looking unpredictable but the bikes were ready to wheel him back into the tailers who were handling them with the ease of long experience.

"Hi, Ros!" Tall, blond, laconic Lucky parked his powerful Yamaha then removed his helmet. His face and clothes were covered in bright red dust that he cheerfully brushed and thumped off. "That was some chase. Hard work."

"At least you're in one piece." She dismounted and tethered her horse, responding with a smile and a wave to the rest of the work party.

"Wearin' m'lucky charm, that's why." He limped over, favouring his gammy leg, courtesy of an 80 m.p.h. flight through the fork of a tree. "So where's the boss?" he asked, easing himself down onto a convenient tree stump.

"He had a meeting. What about a cup of billy tea? That should go down well?"

"Wouldn't even touch the sides!" Lucky turned his tousled, white-gold head. "Blackie," he yelled. "Get the billy on, will ya? Ros wants a cup of tea. The blokes will want one, as well."

"Gotcha!" Blackie bellowed back, making Roslyn think the day-in, day-out roar of the bikes might be making them a little deaf.

"So, long time no see. Tell me what you've been doin'?" Lucky invited. "I don't mean to be cheeky like, but is it possible you're even more beautiful?"

Roslyn sat back, meeting the twinkling gaze. "Come off it, Lucky! You're seeing me through rose-coloured dust."

"I'll be damned if I am." Lucky grinned.

They were all relaxing over their second cup of tea when Marsh drove the Jeep into camp. He had someone with him.

"Well, if it ain't the high-and-mighty Miss Petersen!" Lucky muttered beneath his breath. "Just watch 'er give us the big ignore."

In fact Kim condescended to give them all a regal wave, but chose to remain within the safe confines of the Jeep.

"Who does she think she is, the bloody Queen?" Lucky groaned, and struggled to his feet.

"You couldn't ask for a better wave than that, Lucky," Roslyn teased.

Marsh was crossing the short distance between them, easy and nonchalant, the most graceful male. He had swept the sides of his pearl-grey Akubra up but the front was tilted down rakishly over his eyes.

"Rosa, I thought I might find you here," he said. "How's it going, Lucky?" He lifted an arm in salute to the rest of the men who responded in kind.

"I've been watching the chase," Roslyn told him. "It was quite exciting!"

"I'll bet! The only thing that surprises me is you didn't join in."

"I can't ride the bike yet."

"And you're not going to," he said. "So don't let me catch you trying. Hear, Lucky?"

"Sure, Boss, but she's the gamest girl I ever came across."

"Just think of your own injuries, Lucky. How's the leg?"

Lucky looked down and grimaced. "I'm always amazed it's holdin' me up."

"You really ought to get out of the business." Marsh was frowning, looking towards the railed enclosure.

"I will when I'm thirty," Lucky promised. "Think you could find a job for me?"

"No problem." Marsh looked back. "We could do with another rail. I don't think it's high enough to accommodate the stallion. He's enormous for a brumby and too damned restless for my liking. It's astonishing what an animal like that can do. Some of them even love fences. Get onto it, Lucky.''

''Sure, Boss!'' Lucky limped away, yelling at his mate Blackie at the same time.

''I'll be damned if Lucky's not going deaf,'' Marsh said.

''Blackie, as well,'' Roslyn said ruefully. ''You're right about that extra rail. Will you just look at the glare in the stallion's eye! 'Think you've beaten me! The devil you have!' Come to think of it, he's got a look of Blazer.'' She referred to a magnificent hunter Sir Charles had kept.

''You've got keen eyes, Rosa.'' Marsh nodded approvingly. ''I was just thinking the same thing myself. Blazer got away once for at least half a day. This fellow could well be the produce of a bush mating. He's got Blazer's distinctive mark. Go and talk to Kim until we get the rail up.''

''Could be she doesn't want to talk to me?''

Marsh smiled. ''I've got to tell you she doesn't know what she's missing. Come back in the Jeep with us. One of the men can bring the mare in.''

Roslyn took off her hat and let the breeze ruffle her neatly coiled hair. ''Need protection?''

''One thing I've learned. Never, *ever*, trust a woman.''

''Not when they've been flinging themselves at you since you were fourteen years old.''

''Rosa, darling, more like fifteen,'' he said.

Kim's eyes surveyed her coolly as she approached the Jeep. ''Do you think it's wise being one of the boys?''

''Why not? I find them chivalrous and friendly like most men in the bush.''

''My father always says it's a mistake to come down to that level.''

"But then, he was raised as an old feudal baron. Most of them have got out of the habit."

Kim shrugged. "Well, what you do with your time has nothing to do with me. I was just trying to give you a piece of advice, that's all. You're always *trying* to aim higher."

Roslyn looked at the other young woman thoughtfully. "Why are you always so rude to me? I mean, you really want to *hurt*."

"And you're the perfect target. I figure you're a threat." Kim smiled tightly. "I'm not telling you that to get your hopes up. It's more a warning."

Roslyn sighed. "Not another one!"

"You haven't had any for a *while*. I'm glad you decided to come over. I've been waiting to have a word with you. It's so difficult in front of Dianne and Justine."

"What is?" Roslyn swatted at a flying insect.

Kim stared at her with hard eyes. "What you think you're getting up to," she said finally.

"Any clues?" Roslyn's topaz eyes were shining in her spirited face.

"Don't waste time trying to be smart," Kim answered in an infuriated voice.

"But I *am* smart, Kim. I heard you never got your degree."

"I couldn't be bothered going on with it, that's why. I didn't need to go out and find myself a job."

"What a pity!" Roslyn said lightly. "You might have been all the better for a little struggle."

Kim laughed harshly, narrowing her eyes. "Look, this kind of banter leaves me cold. You say you're smart? Well, be smart enough not to interfere with *my* plans."

"You still won't give me any clues."

"So help me!" Kim pleaded to no one at all. "You know exactly what I'm talking about. I daresay Marsh isn't averse to tumbling you in the hay. You seem to have the patent on that femme fatale stuff. But you'll no more get him to marry you than you were able to in the past. All I can say is, you must really *love* punishment."

"And it seems to make *you* happy doling it out. Can't you come up with something better than a tumble in the hay? Marsh is as fastidious as hell."

"Oh, I know," Kim said softly. "So it's still going on between you two?"

Roslyn glanced up as two brilliantly enamelled parrots landed in a tree. "I don't think it ever stopped."

A ripple passed along Kim's long throat. "And you're happy in the role of a little bit on the side?"

"Actually it's a role I wouldn't consider."

Kim pushed forward sharply in her seat, giving Roslyn the impression Kim would have liked to strike her. Sad, but not impossible. She even braced herself. "My dear, that's how he treats you." Kim sneered.

"You could say that's how he's treated us both. Lift a finger and we come running. Not that he isn't one splendid prize, but I refuse to do it anymore."

"You surely can't think you can get him to marry you?" Kim challenged, at the same time turning a little white.

"I'm working on it." Roslyn shrugged.

"Then you're *mad*!" Kim said with a violent hiss. "I mean, who would accept you? You'd be snubbed at every turn."

"Hey, what's with you and the snobbery?" Roslyn's own voice sharpened. "Only a fool would play that game. Who'd take the risk of insulting Marsh Faulkner's *wife*? Why would they want to? I may not have been born into the establishment, but I'm a long way from unacceptable. I'm young, well-educated, presentable. I don't look like a camel in disguise, which has been said of your friend Suzanne Crawley."

"Suzanne is a sweet girl," Kim said shortly. "She certainly wouldn't bother with someone like you. Isn't it enough for you Lady Faulkner *hated* you?"

"It was rare for Lady Faulkner to like *anyone*. She wasn't overfussed on her own daughters."

"I think she was disappointed they're so plain." Kim permitted herself the remark, then looked like she wished she hadn't said it. "Anyway, she liked me. She approved of me."

"Well it's doubtful she would have looked at someone who was destitute. It's possible she put you and your mother on the wrong track, too. You've put a lot of years and a lot of heartache into trying to land Marsh. It doesn't look like he wants to marry you, though, does it?"

"Look here, how dare you challenge me!" Kim said in a hard, angry voice. "Marsh and I are deeply involved. There are a lot of things you don't know."

"I know you might have been lovers at one time, but unfortunately for you, the allure wore off."

"Boy, have you got that wrong!" Kim retaliated, eyes flashing outrage.

"I don't think so," Roslyn said quietly. "This is a go-nowhere conversation. Why don't we wind it up?"

"On the contrary, I want to get to the bottom of this—" Kim broke off, startled as there was a loud crash close at hand. Roslyn, too, turned her head in alarm, pulling up her bandana against the spiralling cloud of thick dust. When it settled she saw the two stockmen making a desperate attempt to reposition the final top rail. The rest of the men were making a variety of calls, whistles, threats, trying to calm the horses, but it was obvious the stallion with its superior intelligence saw this as its chance for freedom.

It reared wildly, making a weird, screaming sound like a battle cry. The harem moved back respectfully at this spectacle of rearing male pride. Powerful hooves flailed the air then came down thunderously on the red sand. The wild horse backed up, then, while the men dived for cover, flew at the fence, soaring fully extended for a moment before it came down on the other side, unable momentarily to galvanise itself into a gallop.

With a frenzied, "Dear heavens!" Kim threw herself into the driver's seat, hitting the ignition and putting the Jeep into reverse. The swift violence of the action pitched Roslyn, who had been leaning against the Jeep, off balance. She went down hard, thinking fatalistically, *I'm going to die*. No time now to get out of harm's way. It was all happening in seconds. A warm body threw itself over her. *Lucky*.

"God Almighty, what a bastard!" he moaned, trying to drag them to some kind of safety, while his boots kept slipping in the sand. "This is it, luv!"

And it might have been only Marsh in his lightning way had sized up the situation putting himself right where he should be, in the saddle, spinning out a lasso that fell unerringly, miraculously, over the fleeting stallion's neck. It came up with a mighty jolt, in turn almost jerking Marsh out of the saddle. While they all looked on, helpless, he managed to right himself, adhering to the quiet, powerful quarter horse while the brumby reared and bucked frantically, hell-bent on unseating him and mauling the station workhorse.

"If that's not the most brilliant throw of the century,

I'll eat my gloves!'' Lucky yelled in Roslyn's ear. The brumby was careering madly in circles now, unable to break Marsh's domination. Had it been the time to appreciate it instead of lying half stunned with her heart in her mouth Roslyn would have found it a marvellous exhibition of skill and control. Finally the stallion was brought to stand with nothing more than a neck rope, man's authority and iron nerve.

"That's a classic!'' Lucky whooped like a fan at a rodeo. "Ya not gunna see any better!''

"You're pretty fearless yourself, Lucky.'' Roslyn sat up gingerly. "I'm sorry you had to take a tumble trying to save me.''

"You and me are mates,'' he told her cheerfully. "Besides, it was the boss who saved us. He's one daring guy. Rumour has it he'd put his life on the line for you anytime.''

Roslyn looked at him in astonishment. "Where did you hear *that*?''

"Here and there!'' Lucky answered with a grin. "He stopped that horse for ya. No mess, no fuss. Love's what me mum would call it. Here, let me help you up. What Miss Petersen done could be called all sorts of things, but love ain't one o'them.''

"Self-preservation?'' On her feet, Roslyn began to dust herself off.

"I think I'd use something stronger. Speak of the lady and here she comes. No doubt to explain the dastardly deed.''

"I hope not.'' Roslyn didn't want to hear a word from Kim.

If Kim's sickly pallor was any indication, she wasn't altogether happy with her own actions. "Roslyn, are you all right?'' she called, her voice full of anxiety and distress. "There was so little time. I just had to move the Jeep. You understand?"

Roslyn swung around nursing a skinned elbow. "Words fail me."

"I'm so shocked. I got such a fright."

"Couldn't you have yelled *stand clear*!"

"There wasn't time. We would have been trapped between a maddened wild animal and its freedom."

"I *was* trapped, Kim," Roslyn said simply. "In fact, Lucky and I would have been mush without Marsh's intervention."

"He's astonishing," Kim said tearfully. "He threw himself into terrible danger for us."

"Except you managed to get the Jeep thirty feet away. I think you would have kept on going only you backed yourself into a tree."

"At least credit me with quick thinking," Kim pleaded. "There was simply nothing I could do about you. I'm so dreadfully sorry."

"Bunkum!" Roslyn said pleasantly.

"I think I'll get Marsh to take me back to the house." Kim fished out a handkerchief from her pant's pocket and dabbed at her brow. "Horses can be such frightening animals. Especially those brutish brumbies. If I had my way they'd all be sent off to the abattoirs. They're nothing but a nuisance to station owners."

"The stallion doesn't remind you of Blazer?" Roslyn asked curiously.

"Blazer?" Kim's straight brows drew together in a frown. "You surely don't mean Sir Charles's old hunter?"

"Yes."

"Oh, don't be absurd!" Kim said in her brittle voice. "And you're supposed to have a good eye."

"Not only supposed to. *Have*! Marsh thinks the same. Here he comes now looking like Chief Thundercloud."

In fact Marsh was striding towards them, his whole aura radiating a dazzling authority. He had pitched his hat away in a fit of aggravation and one coal-black wave fell onto his dark copper forehead adding to the impression of rugged vitality.

His blue eyes were like lightning as he stared at them, then without a word, he seized Roslyn, pulled her into his arms, and held her in a fierce, biting grip.

"Lord Rosa!" He sounded as though he was under intense pressure. "If I hadn't got a rope to that stallion..."

"You *did*." She stood on tiptoe, getting her mouth to his chin. Her body curved into his, drawing and giving superlative comfort.

Neither of them took account of Kim who stood aghast at the sight of them locked so tightly together. She sucked in her breath, sharply agonised, then blurted, "Don't worry about *me*, Marsh. Worry about her. She's perfectly all right." The muscles of Kim's throat were so tight her voice was almost hoarse. "It was splendid the way you lassoed that murderous brumby."

Marsh threw up his head, looking back at her. "The brumby was doing what all wild horses do. It was taking a desperate chance," he observed harshly. "I can't say much for the way *you* acted. You simply looked after yourself. In the process putting Roslyn in worse danger. The two of you could have taken shelter behind the Jeep, instead you sent her crashing to her knees."

Kim's haughty, high-boned face flushed a mottled red. The colour even stained her throat. "It was an accident, Marsh. It wasn't intentional."

"It was a fearful *mistake*!"

Kim looked at him imploringly, just managing not to cry. "I *told* Roslyn I was sorry."

"Yes, she did, Marsh. Kim didn't have time to think. She had to move." Roslyn had received poor treatment at Kim's hands for years but she found she had no desire to retaliate.

"You're right, Roslyn. You're right." Kim looked at the younger girl with a kind of desperate gratitude. "It was just one of those terrible moments in life."

"The split-second decision that can make or break," Marsh said grimly.

"I do regret it." Kim wrung her hands, her habitual arrogance quite crumpled away.

Looking at her Roslyn decided. "We can and will forget it," she said, applying a little pressure to Marsh's arms in an effort to get him to lighten up. "Friends, Kim, okay?" She held out her hand.

"Yes, indeed!" Kim moved quickly to shake Roslyn's hand. "It's very kind of you to see things my way."

Roslyn's smile was touched with a little irony. "I have my points."

"I might go back to the homestead now." Kim looked back towards the Jeep. "I feel a bit shaky."

"Pour yourself a brandy. A large one," Marsh suggested, sounding less daunting. "I'll have one of the men drive you back. I'll have to stay here and supervise."

"They didn't have the top rails high enough." Kim sought to divert attention from her.

"They would have been only the stallion's no ordinary brumby. He has quite a look of Dad's Blazer."

"I noticed it," Kim answered, more in her ordinary tone. "At least I noticed it after Roslyn pointed it out.

Will you come back with me, Ros? There's no need for you to stay here.''

"She's staying.'' Marsh spoke emphatically. "I don't want her out of my sight until my nerves settle.'' He looked over to the holding yard, where Lucky was perched on the top rail. "Lucky,'' Marsh called. "Get over here, mate.''

"We ought to do something for him,'' Roslyn ventured.

"I intend to.''

"What have you got in mind?''

"Enough to induce him to give up brumby running. He's had one too many crashes for my liking.''

"He's brave!'' Roslyn watched Lucky limp toward them, his face split in a grin.

"Isn't he!'' Marsh's tone left little doubt of his opinion of those who weren't. "Now it's his turn to be rewarded.''

"But it's not necessary,'' Kim said.

"Why don't we walk over to the Jeep while Marsh speaks to Lucky,'' Roslyn suggested.

Lucky was blushing in anticipation of a grateful slap on the back. Roslyn knew it would never enter his head he was about to be assured of a windfall.

"That was good of you to take my part the way you did,'' Kim murmured, almost painfully as they waited beside the Jeep. "Marsh seems to be disgusted with me. I've never, ever, disappointed him before.''

"Don't dwell on it, Kim.''

"I expect I will.'' Kim glanced away. "Do you suppose he'll tell the girls? A recount of the incident could make my part in it look worse than it really was. I was in a genuine, breathless panic. We all know horses but they can be scary creatures.''

Roslyn wasn't prepared to let her off quite so lightly. "Kim, only for Marsh, Lucky and I would have been right in the line of fire."

"Dammit, I know that too well. I can't decide whether the bike rider was brave or he'd taken leave of his senses. It's not as though he was getting anywhere with that busted leg."

"The great thing is, he *tried*."

"Yes." Kim gave a mirthless smile. "All's well that ends well, so they say. I hope the girls are as understanding as you are. They'd hate me forever if anything had happened to Marsh."

"Perish a thought for Lucky and me! Why don't you say one of the brumbies made a break for it and Marsh lassoed it in. They'll accept that. They're used to Marsh and his extraordinary feats."

"Of course, that's it!" Kim ran a hand over her sun-streaked hair, looking down in distaste as her palm came away smeared with red dust. "Lord, I'll have to take a shower and wash my hair. You look a sight, as well. Marsh is a genuine hero all right, but he can be so very intimidating at times, don't you think?"

"No question about it!" Roslyn smiled, realising this was probably the first time Kim had been on the rough side of Marsh's cutting tongue. Well, serve her right!

It was evident at dinner Kim had given her own version of the afternoon's events to Justine and Dianne, but neither Roslyn nor Marsh sought to contradict her.

"The perfect whitewash!" Marsh commented later as he and Roslyn were waiting on the veranda for Justine to join them on their after-dinner walk. "I'm only surprised she didn't make herself out the heroine of the piece."

"Maybe that was due to your rather sardonic expression. Kim's not comfortable being in the wrong."

"She doesn't hesitate to come down strongly on everyone else. Must give her a sense of power. Before Ju-Ju turns up, how about a grateful kiss? It's already hours overdue."

"Sure, a pleasure!" She intended to keep it light but his arm encircled her, drawing her into the shadow of a vine-wreathed white column.

"Marsh, someone might come."

His blue eyes gleamed. "Am I supposed to care? Your place is in my arms and that's where you're going to stay."

"We'll tell them very soon," she promised.

"Why not the hell *now*?"

"Not with Kim here. Not a chance. I don't want to see her pain."

"For a little fire-eater, you're surprisingly tender-hearted." He bent his head and began to trail his lips down her cheek. "Your skin is so smooth...so cool. It's like satin. It has a lustre. I'm waiting for when I can kiss every inch of it!" He turned his attention to her mouth, kissed it roughly, sweetly, until she clung.

"Wild thing!" he muttered, feeling the fever in her.

"You're my hero!"

"I *know*. Also, when you can get your act together, your *husband*."

"What kind of husband are you going to make?"

"Don't expect bashful."

She felt an incredible spring of joy. "Not bashful, *no*!" Ardent, urgent, warm and tender, a flawless, imaginative lover who could make her body dissolve with desire. Just standing within the circle of his arms, having his beautiful, sensuous mouth touch her skin, was dizzying. It created an immense *need*.

"I'm only human, Rosa," he murmured. "I'm even considering sleep walking."

"I'm sorry. I'm stuck with my vow."

"And I'm stuck with *you*."

"Were you ever in love with Kim?"

"What do you think?" he asked crisply, lifting his head.

"Curious, nothing more."

"I don't blab," he said in a dry, laconic voice.

"I don't, either, but I am involved."

"So long as you know that." He grasped a handful of her hair. "If I must tell the truth, *you're* my only passion."

"Yet you found the time to fit in a few others?"

"Rosa, I had to do something to keep myself from going mad."

"Men are the devil!" she said in a soft, helpless undertone, her need for him so desperate it threatened to override all else.

"And I intend to take advantage of it." He touched a hand to her breast, then pulled her into his arms, pressing his marvellous mouth down on her own.

Waves of flame.

Scorching her...searing her.

This was Marsh and he had the power to destroy her.

CHAPTER EIGHT

MIDMORNING of the following day when even the gum leaves were turned edge on to the sun Roslyn went back to the homestead in search of a cold drink only to walk head-on into a confrontation with Kim. She was barely inside the house, her riding boots beating a tattoo on the patterned tiled floor when Kim came flying down the central staircase, her face wearing a furious expression.

"So there you are!" she cried, advancing on Roslyn who stood rooted to the spot in sick dismay. Did it *ever* stop? "It was just too much to expect, wasn't it? That's what comes of a lack of breeding. You can't be trusted to act with honour. Well, you can stop playing your games around me, you devious little bitch!"

Close up Roslyn could feel the heat coming off Kim's tall body. Her own face darkened but she fought hard to hold on to her composure. "What compels you to attack me?" she asked. "What gives you the right? You talk of *breeding*. You're no one to admire."

"And you *had* to tell the girls?"

"What?"

"Oh, don't act the innocent. Don't make me sick!" Kim cried hotly. "How *could* you when you promised? You've humiliated me dreadfully. Perhaps lost me my dearest friends."

"Kim, you'll have to explain yourself," Roslyn said in a quiet voice that lost nothing in intensity. "Otherwise I'm going in search of a cold drink."

"You'll damned well stand still and listen to me!"

137

Kim reached out and grasped Roslyn's arm, her long fingers digging into the skin.

Roslyn shook her head. "Take your hand off me, Kim. I don't respond to this kind of approach."

"Oh, I hate you. I hate you," Kim said. "Why did you ever have to come back? We thought we were shot of you forever!" She threw off Roslyn's arm and immediately Roslyn stepped back.

"But I'm here, Kim and I'm staying," Roslyn said with quiet dignity.

"Then bear in mind you're not *wanted*."

"Marsh is the only one I'm worried about."

"Of course!" Kim gave a discordant laugh. "But when are you going to get it into your head he'll never take you seriously? He doesn't respect you. He doesn't—" She broke off as tyres crunched on the driveway and a moment later Marsh started up the steps, halting on the threshold as he sensed the anger and tension that bound the two women.

"Anything wrong?" he asked briskly, his burning blue eyes moving from Roslyn to Kim.

"No." Roslyn was reluctant to go into it, but Kim laughed incredulously.

"No, she says, when her underhand actions have bitterly hurt and humiliated me."

Marsh's expression went grim. "Hey now!" he protested, moving further into the entrance hall.

Roslyn put out a hand to him, seeking to avert a worse scene. "Kim is upset about something. I don't know what."

"Then she'd better explain herself. What's your problem, Kim? Maybe we can straighten it out?"

Kim turned to him in an attitude of appeal. "You can't trust her, Marsh, as you'll soon discover. You're playing with fire encouraging this girl. She's not one of us.''

"It might be a good idea, Kim, if you minded your own business," Marsh responded in such a cutting voice Kim's face crumpled.

"To say that to *me*!" she cried, unable to conceal her hurt. "After all we've been to each other."

"Kim, we haven't been anything to each other for years," he contradicted her flatly.

"You *loved* me!"

He spread his hands. "I'm sorry, no. You knew what we had the brief time we spent together."

"It was wonderful!" Kim stared at him, her heart in her eyes. "I'll remember it always. Always!"

"That would be downright foolish," Marsh responded, still with that tough slant.

Roslyn found she couldn't bear it. She had never been much good watching someone else's pain. "Please excuse me," she said. "My throat is quite parched."

"Hah!" Kim suddenly cried, blocking Roslyn's way. "It's this girl, isn't it? This little nobody whose mother is in your employ."

Marsh's blue eyes flashed sparks. "Your snobbery is appalling. And it beats me why!"

"What about your sisters, then?" Kim challenged. "Do you know how they feel?"

Marsh shrugged. "I had hoped they'd drop into the twenty-first century. It's long overdue. But so far as Rosa's concerned, my sisters have no say at all. If Rosa and I want to get married, we will."

Kim's imperious, high-boned face blanched. "Married? Whoever mentioned the word? Not even Roslyn would be such a fool."

"I mentioned the word," Marsh told her grimly.

''Rosa's been holding out on you but I don't mind telling you I've asked her to marry me and she's agreed.''

Kim stood like a woman faced with the ungraspable. ''You're joking,'' she said finally. ''It's just a cruel joke. You want to get back at me.''

''That's a big job! Actually, Kim, on this occasion I didn't give you a thought.''

''Ah, *no*!'' Kim wasn't yet persuaded, locked into her own vision.

''What made you tell her, Marsh?'' Roslyn asked, distressed.

''Don't be ridiculous, Rosa!'' he said with crisp impatience. ''It needed saying. I've gone along with your idea long enough. It hasn't come off.''

''I don't believe this!'' Kim stared from one to the other though her gaze seemed unfocused.

''I'm sure you do,'' Marsh responded.

''Not marriage, *no*! Your mother detested this girl. And her mother. She'll be here to haunt you.''

''Oh, my!'' Marsh said with a derisive smile.

''I must go home!'' Kim cried, realising her plans had been shot to pieces.

''Whatever you think best.'' Marsh shrugged.

''Take a little time to calm down, Kim, please,'' Roslyn begged, but Kim turned on her with loathing.

''How can you speak to me like that after all you've done? You couldn't wait to reduce me in Dianne's and Justine's eyes.''

''How is that?'' Marsh asked curtly, infinitely more aggressive than Roslyn.

''I'll tell you how,'' Kim said in a harsh voice. ''She told them about that incident yesterday when she promised she wouldn't. She made me out a coward in the girls' eyes.''

"No!" Roslyn brushed her dark glossy hair off her face. "You're quite mistaken."

Marsh's tall, lithe body went tense. "A liar she is *not*! If Rosa said she didn't say anything, she didn't. Why don't we get to the bottom of the matter right now?"

"Why not?" Kim agreed harshly, breathing fast. "At least you'll find out what your precious *Rosa* is really like."

Marsh's expression turned daunting, but he didn't reply. He turned away, leading them through the house until they found Dianne and Justine deep in conversation on the rear courtyard overlooking the pool.

Both young women broke off in their conversation as the others approached.

"Hi!" Marsh said in such a clipped tone Justine rose to her feet.

"What's up?"

"A little matter to be cleared up." Marsh swooped on the big, fringed umbrella, adjusting it so Dianne was completely in the shade.

"Thanks, Marsh," she said, looking up. "You seem upset?"

"You've got it in one! Kim seems to think she's been shamed by something Roslyn said to you both regarding the incident with the brumby?"

"Oo-oh, need we talk about it?" Dianne nearly wailed. "So unlike Kim. I can scarcely believe it!"

"What makes you think Ros told us, Kim?" Justine demanded.

"Well, didn't she?" The words exploded out of Kim with furious impatience.

"Not at all!" Justine spoke very coldly and distinctly. "Marsh and Ros allowed us to believe your version. It was Mrs. Earnshaw who put us in the picture. She considered your action put Ros into considerble danger. Let alone Marsh! She wasn't about to kowtow to your desire to protect yourself."

"Well, thank you, Justine!" Kim sounded cut to the heart.

"Mumma told you?" Roslyn asked Justine in amazement.

"That's right!" Justine turned to her. "She was very angry about it. She didn't think she was under any obligation to cover for Kim. As far as that goes, Kim's overdue for a setdown. She's been barely civil to Ros and her mother for as long as I can remember. I suppose if Mrs. Earnshaw ever comes back to Macumba as Lady Mortimer, Kim will fall down before her."

"That'll be the day!" Kim gave a hard, ironic laugh. "Harry's probably not serious at all. Once he gets back to his own people he'll forget all about her."

"It just kills me you've done this, Kim," Dianne said sorrowfully. "The consequences could have been dreadful."

"I thought you *wanted* Roslyn out of the way?" Kim gripped a chair and shook it.

Dianne's mouth fell open. "Come off it, Kim! I've always had a problem with Ros. No question about it. I think it started when I kept growing and growing and Ros stayed petite."

"Good God!" Kim said in disgust. "So you'll settle for having her as a sister-in-law, will you?"

Dianne straightened abruptly. "A *what*?" she demanded with some vehemence.

"I would have liked to tell you myself," Marsh interjected, "but Kim is bent on vengeance. Afterwards she's promised to pack up and be on her way. Rosa was giving you time to settle but it seems to be out in the open now. I've asked her to marry me and she's agreed.''

"But you *can't* marry her!" Dianne gasped, and fell back among the cushions. I'll go insane with Roslyn for a sister-in-law.''

"Oh, shut up, Di," Justine said briskly. "You know you're talking rubbish." She turned to Marsh and Roslyn, who had drawn closer together. "I'm offering you both my love and very best wishes right now. I truly believe you'll be very happy together.''

"Thank you, Justine." Roslyn inclined her head as Justine bent to kiss her.

"What a turncoat you are!" Kim cried scathingly. "I'm shocked. *Shocked.* Just you wait until the word gets around.''

"Concerning *what*?" Marsh asked with such asperity Kim sobered abruptly. "I'm not a good man to cross.''

"None of us are!" Dianne said sharply. "So don't go spreading any gossip around.''

"It could be you're all mad!" Kim cried emotionally. "I'm not among friends anymore. I'll go pack.''

Less than twenty minutes later Kim had herself organised to leave.

"You're all going to regret this!" she cried out in the hallway. "There's no way Marsh can marry that girl and have a happy life.''

Despite protests she didn't want them, they weren't friends, Dianne and Justine accompanied her to the airstrip, Justine at the wheel of the Jeep. "Very bad manners not to have," Dianne declared afterwards. "I'd like you to know, Ros, I warned Kim against spreading any malice. If you *must* be part of the family, we'll all have to pull together.''

"That's very kind of you, Di," Roslyn answered politely, trying hard to look suitably grateful.

Olivia wasn't in the least perturbed she had precipitated the crisis. "There's no such thing as keeping something like that quiet on a station," she told Roslyn when Roslyn approached her about it. "Even when she gave her version I somehow didn't believe her. Young Jessie told me in the kitchen this morning. She got it from her dad. He was *there*. I can tell you no one was impressed with the high-and-mighty Miss Petersen. I know you and Marsh were prepared to let it pass, but I saw it more as a strike for us. I've nursed quite a bit of resentment about Kim Petersen's treatment of you."

"I felt sorry for her all the same." Roslyn sighed. "She was mortified in front of the girls and she's still in love with Marsh."

"It's called tunnel vision. I've been guilty of it myself," Olivia murmured wryly.

"So what's the latest on Harry?" Roslyn asked.

Olivia brought tea to the table and poured it. "It appears his cousin has rallied a little but the doctor thinks it was only to keep himself going until Harry arrived. It's quite marvellous the will to hang on. Harry wants me to come over for a bit after Christmas. Out of the question with a big wedding to be arranged."

"Of course it's not, Mumma. It's just what you need and it will settle things for you and Harry. Have you made any decision?"

Olivia shook her head. "You know me, darling. I'm a real ditherer. It's such a *big* decision. I'm very fond of Harry. He's a good friend. We're so comfortable together, but this baronetcy has thrown me a bit. I've known enough snooty people to last me a lifetime."

"There are lots of nice people, too, Mumma. The *real*

people. Besides, there's no need to give everyone a run-down on your life. Let them judge you on how you look and act. I know Harry will be proud of you.''

Olivia gave a worried smile. ''Have you considered, darling, his feelings might have undergone a change?''

''A great big no to that!'' Roslyn answered firmly. ''Harry has a constant heart. He wants you over. My advice is to make a booking.''

''I have a stepbrother and two stepsisters, you know,'' Olivia said, and tears suddenly welled in her eyes. ''I used to love them when they were little.''

''Look them up. It's entirely possible they'll welcome you with open arms.''

''Not if they've turned out like Delia.'' Olivia sighed. ''How have the girls been since Marsh sprang his bomb-shell?''

''Okay,'' Roslyn said. '''We all have to pull together' was the way Di put it.'' Roslyn gave an excellent imi-tation of Dianne's haughty tones.

''Well, Justine is nowhere near as stuffy as she used to be,'' Olivia commented. ''Marriage has improved her no end. Dianne has a way to go. By the way, the Shepards are arriving tomorrow afternoon. You couldn't ask for better references. They'll take up their duties immediately but I'll be on hand to help out. We'll have lots of visitors between now and Christmas.''

''Marsh told me he fully intends to introduce me as his fiancée,'' Roslyn said in slightly troubled tones.

''Good.'' Olivia gave her daughter's hand a sharp pat. ''I never thought he'd go along with all that business of keeping quiet. It's not his style.''

''No. But then Marsh has never been in my position. Anyway, the girls took it a lot better than I thought.''

''I don't know whether to applaud or to cry. You

could take your place anywhere. And you'll have to remember Kim Petersen is bound to try to cause trouble.''

"Then she runs the risk of alienating this family,"
Roslyn retorted sharply, suddenly realizing it was true.

The very next day the first of the visitors descended from
the sky to be followed by dozens more. Once Roslyn
counted thirty light aircraft scattered like birds off the
strip. The girls' husbands arrived in the middle of this
migration, bearing stacks of gifts. It was obvious they
had been informed Marsh and Roslyn were to marry but
Roslyn privately considered both of them had difficulty
taking it in. Only one name had loomed on their horizon.
Kim Petersen. It had generally been agreed she was the
most impressive candidate.

How things had changed!

As for the stream of visitors they professed to a man
to be delighted Marsh had at long last decided to take a
bride. The news had spread like wildfire from station to
station courtesy of Kim Petersen, so all of them had had
plenty of time to absorb the shock. What did fascinate
them was the revelation ''good old Harry'' was now
Lord Mortimer. All gave Olivia their best wishes to pass
on, apparently unsurprised Harry and Olivia were considering making a match of it.

Meanwhile Mr. and Mrs. Shepard went about their
business with a social stiffness and a pompousness that
jarred Roslyn in particular. They were extremely competent as their references had stated, but Roslyn would
have liked more natural behaviour and less formality.
She tried to indicate this, she hoped diplomatically, but
it soon became apparent the Shepards intended to stick
to their inflexible code. The family didn't seem to notice.
They had long been used to having servants around them

and, generally speaking, treated them as though they weren't there. It didn't suit Roslyn at all. Obviously courteous behaviour was essential but the stiffness put her off.

"So change them later on," Olivia advised. "As mistress of Macumba you'll be able to do as you like."

"Mistress of Macumba!" Roslyn cried softly. "Lady Faulkner will turn in her grave."

"Does that scare you?"

"No." Roslyn shook her head. "What really bothers me is the way Chris still likes to hang around me. What an ass! It's no wonder Di gets jealous and resentful. I've tried insulting him but nothing seems to put him off. Not the fact he's married, or this ring." She held up her left hand adorned with a diamond ring of exquisite design.

"The marriage is solid enough," Olivia considered. "It's just that you fascinate him. My own view is he's well on the way to getting a punch in the nose. Marsh is fed up with him. He's fairly well fed up with Justine's husband, as well. All those long boring accounts of his professional brilliance. Maybe the Shepards could go to him. I think they'd suit."

One way and another the festive break turned out to be a stressful time, which somehow got worse as the days rolled on.

"I don't think our holiday is turning out a success," Justine told Roslyn privately as they took a late afternoon ride together. "I never realised how boring we all are. Not you, of course, and heaven knows, not Marsh, but the rest of us. Ian is only thirty-five yet he's starting to sound like an elder statesman. He really is a dear, you know, but taking silk had such an effect on him. I was going along with it, but now I can see he takes himself much too seriously. One can see those Rumpole stories aren't all that exaggerated. And, of course, Chris, if he continues, will set off a calamity. I saw Marsh's face last night. I wondered how he checked himself.''

Roslyn sighed. ''I don't give Chris the slightest encouragement. Rather the reverse.''

''Oh, we know that!'' Justine exclaimed in disgust. ''It's not a serious thing. Of that I haven't got the slightest doubt. It's more a silly moth around a flame sort of thing. You *are* so much more beautiful than the rest of us. It can be very unsettling. I think we'll get away earlier than intended. See the New Year in, then fly off home. One thing I've been meaning to say to you—'' Justine turned a prim face to her ''—with your mother joining Harry in England you *can't* stay here with Marsh. There will be quite enough chatter as it is. I want you to come to *us* until the wedding. You'll need help getting it all arranged. It could be such fun! Organisation is my job. It's where I come into my own.''

''I hadn't thought about it, Justine,'' Roslyn said when she had given the matter a lot of consideration. ''I still have my own house.''

''And I'm sure it's very pretty, but let's face it, ours is better. We're undertaking this as a family. Everything must be done *right*. Marsh told me you're giving a big gala party for everyone we can't fit into the wedding. I can help you with that. I know everyone you will need to get to know. I thought possibly the big reception room at the Beaumont. They do things extremely well and it's so central. Black tie, of course. I'll be your matron of honour. Di will be too far gone to act as an attendant. Don't you worry about Di.'' Justine paused reassuringly. ''Once she gets used to the idea she'll be as excited as I am. You'll have to help us with our outfits. You're so good with that sort of thing.''

And so it went on for almost an hour.

"I don't want you going anywhere," Marsh said when Roslyn attempted to discuss it with him. "Not even for a day."

They had managed to find a moment alone together, taking the four-wheel drive to the edge of the sandhill country. The mirage was abroad, creating fascinating visual effects. In the distance shimmered a long billabong where there was no water to be had, with curious, stick-like figures dancing delicately above the silver glitter.

"I suppose we have to be seen do the right thing," Roslyn reasoned. "There will be enough talk without our being alone together at the homestead."

"How could we possibly be alone with the Shepards in attendance?" Marsh asked with extreme sarcasm.

"I thought you were happy enough with them?"

"Listen, I'd have been better off hiring a couple of actors. They're much too stiff and formal. But I can't see us getting replacements until the New Year. I'll just have to pay them off and mark it down as a mistake. The agency handled it. Next time you'll have to do it."

"They'll be *different*."

"That's all right with me. Macumba is a homestead, not a stately home. Another one I might just consider chucking out is Chris. His behaviour is only tolerated in adolescence. Obviously you've lost nothing of your old witchery."

"I've tried to be as offputting as possible," Roslyn said mildly.

"A little difficult when you haven't got the knack."

"I could try growing a beard," Roslyn joked. "You sound disgruntled."

"Clever you! Actually I'm as mad as hell. If I didn't

have Di to consider I'd bundle him onto the first plane home.''

"It's not serious, Marsh. Justine put her finger on it. It's a sort of harmless crush.''

"It's not harmless and it's not amusing,'' Marsh answered with a little rasp. "Di must be finding it very embarrassing.''

"She hasn't mentioned it to me.''

Marsh shrugged. "Knowing Di, there's no guarantee she's not saving it up. I never thought I'd say this, but I'll be glad when they all go home.''

"Justine thought just after New Year.''

"She's a darling!'' Marsh said feelingly. "I don't go along with her idea of taking you, though.''

"Mumma has offered to stay as chaperone, but I said no. No one is trying to rush her into marrying Harry, but the fact of the matter is, she does need a little push.''

"Come on, a big push,'' Marsh drawled.

"You are out of sorts!'' Roslyn allowed her eyes to linger on his face.

"*I want you.*''

"I want you, too.'' Her voice was husky. There was colour in her creamy skin. She was about a second away from admitting *how* much.

"So what's the stand-off?'' he asked edgily.

"You might abandon me after you have your wicked way.''

"Don't start that again, Rosa,'' he warned in a dangerous voice.

"All right. Let's say I don't want to land us in a crisis situation.''

"Crisis? *What* crisis? God, we're engaged.''

"I have the ring.'' She spread her small, elegant hand, manoeuvring the diamond ring, a central two-carat stone flanked by baguettes, into a beam of sunlight. The glitter was dazzling. "Four carats in all, isn't it?"

"Closer to five."

"It's unbelievably beautiful."

"Nothing beside you." Instead of loverlike it came out as a soft growl.

"You just want to get me into your bed."

"As soon as possible," he assured her crisply. "What do you think is going to happen to you? You'll fall pregnant?"

"Would you want that?"

He looked at her, his eyes drowningly blue. "I surely would," he said in a heart-stopping voice. "I'd even shed a few tears. But I want you to *myself* for a while."

After you abandoned me for years? It sprang into her mind automatically, evidence even now as his promised bride she couldn't overcome the raw pain of the past. Damaged people took a long time to heal, she thought, but managed quite coolly, "That sounds very loverlike, but I, for one, don't want to anticipate our wedding night."

He touched a hand to her cheek, pretended to shiver as if a chill lay on her skin. "Are you sure you won't want to order up a couch for me in the dressing room?"

"No. I'll stick to my side of the bargain."

He was silent for a little while, staring out at the savage beauty of the sweeping plain. A hawk that had been hovering overhead suddenly made a leisurely swoop on a group of zebra finches feeding on the ground. The little birds made no attempt to get away. They never did.

"You're enjoying this, aren't you?" he said.

There was something like a taunt in his vibrant voice. "Why would you say that?" she parried.

"Because I *know* you, Rosa." He held her chin. Made

her look at him directly. "I know your fears and your
resentments. I know what shapes you. Drives you. You
were powerless once. You're not going to allow it to
happen again."

"That's only sensible, isn't it?" The old hostility was
alive around them.

"Being sensible isn't the motivation," he said, and
released her. "It's more like punishment and we both
know why." He switched on the ignition, turned to her.
"Go back with Justine if you think you should. I won't
try to stop you."

CHAPTER NINE

IT TURNED out to be a hectic time. Roslyn had been
staying with Justine and her husband, Ian, in their beautiful harbourside home for just on three weeks and already she had lost count of the number of social gatherings she had attended. Justine was determined on
introducing her to all the people she thought Roslyn
should know. Legions it seemed. She badly missed Macumba. Most of all she missed Marsh. She had spoken to
him on the telephone several times since she'd arrived
but they were strangely stilted conversations that left her
feeling isolated and vulnerable. Their gala party was
scheduled for the coming Saturday night. Marsh had
promised he would be in Sydney by Friday afternoon at
the latest, piloting his own plane. He would be staying
with Justine and Ian, as well, taking advantage of the
large, heritage-listed house Ian had inherited from his
maternal grandmother.

As the house and grounds were so large it had been
decided instead of the Beaumont as originally planned
the party would be held at the house. Something that
pleased Roslyn and Justine took in her stride. They
hadn't seen a lot of Dianne who didn't appear to want
to be a part of all the endless social rounds, the planning
and preparations for the party and the wedding. Her
pregnancy was an excuse in part, but Roslyn had to accept she and Dianne would never really get on. A fact
of life and one she could live with. Justine, on the other

hand, had been a tower of strength. As she'd claimed, organization was her forte and she was thriving on all the excitement and bustle.

"Planning makes perfect!" she told Roslyn constantly, her countdown guide, her blueprint for success, never far from her hand. "Everything is going to be splendid, you'll see. Weddings have a way of catching everyone up."

The invitations would go out the following week, a month before the ceremony would take place on Macumba. All the attendants had been chosen, Roslyn had asked two of her closest friends from her university days to be bridesmaids. Justine would be matron of honour. Not for a moment had Roslyn considered anyone else. Gowns for the bridal party had been settled on and were in the process of being made by a top designer who specialized in exquisitely romantic bridal wear. The same designer had been given the task of making Roslyn's gown for Saturday night but as she was losing weight a small adjustment to the waist and bodice had to be made.

She spent an hour at Bridal House standing tirelessly while her party gown then her wedding dress were refitted. The designer had a wonderful stock of gowns, fabrics and accessories but nothing more beautiful in Roslyn's opinion than her own wedding gown which was nearing completion. It was a midsummer's dream in lace and silk: the long, line-fitted lace bodice, off-the-shoulder and long-sleeved, tapered to a central peak, the wonderful silk skirt billowing from the hip. Bodice and a deep hemline of the skirt featured the same exquisite pearl beading. Her headdress was a very beautiful and delicate circlet of handmade flowers in pinks, palest yellow and magnolia with little sprays of pearls to simulate baby's breath. It was a very romantic look and Roslyn thought it was perfect for her. So did the designer and her clever team who were counting on a lot of publicity.

Justine, who never figured herself the "romantic type" would wear the very flattering fitted sheath with a small hat and a spotted eye veil Roslyn had suggested. It all worked and everyone was delighted with their outfits. Roslyn should have been in a state of euphoria, instead she was conscious of high emotion fraught with pressing anxieties. Justine was being marvellous, indeed they had grown surprisingly close, but Roslyn wanted her mother home. They talked frequently but it wasn't enough. Olivia had given Harry the answer he most wanted in the world. They were to be married in London soon after the "super wedding" as Harry had dubbed it. That meant Roslyn and Marsh could attend. Olivia was due home in a few days. Plenty of time for the wedding but Harry, deep in family business, would remain in England for as long as possible. It was Harry who was to give Roslyn away. Harry, the perfect gentleman. Harry, the English lord. Justine considered this an enormous asset.

When Roslyn arrived back at the house shortly before noon she was told by Justine's housekeeper that Mrs. Herbert and a friend were in the Garden Room where lunch would be served. Justine had a wide circle of friends. Roslyn wondered briefly if she'd already met her. The same people seemed to turn up at every large gathering. She went directly to her room to tidy up then found her way back downstairs to the Garden Room so called by the family because it was filled with lush green plants and marvellous hanging ferns, furnished informally and looked out over the beautiful grounds and the sparkling blue harbour beyond.

Roslyn was almost at the door, arranging her face into a pleasant smile when she heard Justine's friend speak.

"Well, with all *your* help, darling, it should be a wonderful occasion. Roslyn doesn't know just how lucky she is."

Roslyn felt the sudden intense heat of anger. Kim Petersen. She had to have a hide like a rhinoceros! The thought of her still stalked Roslyn. The spite and the rage Kim had displayed. But why should she feel so shocked? It was inevitable they would see Kim Petersen again. The Faulkners and the Petersens had been lifelong friends. Elaine Petersen and Lady Faulkner had been close confidantes, fellow schemers. It was understandable Kim's aberrant behaviour might be forgiven.

Roslyn took a deep breath and entered the room, unaware her golden eyes were *burning* in her face.

"Ah, there you are, Ros!" Justine called from her chair, not exactly looking like she had been enjoying her chat. "You'll never guess who's come to call on us." The tone was slightly dry.

"It couldn't be Kim?"

"Hi, there Ros!" Kim put her blond head around the back of her peacock chair, her voice bright and friendly, her eyes as hard as agates. "I'm in Sydney on a shopping spree so I thought I'd call in and say hello."

Roslyn hid her disgust perfectly. "How are you, Kim?" she asked calmly, taking a chair facing the entrancing view.

"Splendid!" Kim smiled, showing her fine white teeth. "You've lost weight, haven't you? You look tired."

"All the excitement!" Roslyn ignored the little flash of malice.

Justine nodded. "Justine's been telling me all about it. It's quite an achievement to take Sydney by the storm."

"Have I done that?"

"Justine appears to think so. Look, what I really wanted to ask you both, *beg* really, was not to hold my little outburst at Christmas against me. I deeply regret it. I assure you such a thing will never happen again."

"That's good to hear. It was an unpleasant experience," Roslyn said, looking straight at her.

"And I've said I'm sorry." Kim tried her best to look humble but only succeeded in looking dogged. "Justine and I have been friends all our lives. I can't imagine life without her and Di. If you'll allow me, Ros, I'd like to be friends with you."

Roslyn stood up, walked to the French doors, then turned back. "Is that possible, Kim?" she asked in a quiet, reasonable tone.

"Oh, please, do sit down again," Kim implored. "I think so. I hope so. It will be very difficult if we're not. The family is expecting an invitation to the wedding."

Justine, looking perturbed, made a sweep on her countdown guide.

"Is this a joke of some kind?" Roslyn asked.

"I didn't imagine, Kim, you would want to come." Justine stirred restlessly in her chair.

"Of course I want to come!" Kim cried. "There would be too much talk if I wasn't invited. Besides, Mum and Dad were your parents' close friends. It's clear we *have* to be invited."

Roslyn sank back into her chair. "It's not clear to me.

It's *my* wedding after all. It's generally understood I invite the people I like."

Kim seized the legs of her linen slacks and pulled them down over her knees. "All right, I know you have a perfect right to say that, given my behaviour, but you must realise I'm no longer any threat."

"I wouldn't write you off all the same," Roslyn said dryly.

"Surely it would be too painful," Justine asked in a near puritanical voice.

"You overestimate my feelings, Ju-Ju," Kim's grey-green eyes blazed up. "I know I've wasted a great deal of my life hankering after Marsh. That's all over. He's made his choice. He wants Ros. Actually life's picked up for me. Craig and I are thinking of getting engaged."

The relief on Justine's face was enormous. "You *are*? But that's marvellous. Craig's always been in love with you. I couldn't be more delighted. Have you told Di?"

"As a matter of fact I have. I rang her as soon as I arrived. She sounded quite out of sorts, poor darling. Craig is in town right now as a matter of fact. He has business to attend to. Actually his fondest wish would be to meet up with Marsh. Neither of us is doing anything Saturday night. Would it be too much to ask an invitation to the party? If Craig's thinking of a best man he wouldn't go past Marsh. You don't mind, do you, Ros?"

"That's a tough one. I think I do."

"It would mean so much to me. To us both." Kim fished in her Gucci bag, pulled out a handkerchief and actually touched it to her eyes. "You've no idea how our little falling out has weighed on me."

"Please, Kim, don't upset yourself," Justine said, looking distressed.

"I've been punished enough. I knew I had to come to you both and beg your forgiveness. Di's so sweet. She told me she could never turn her back on me."

"That's all right, I wouldn't either," Roslyn said in a wry voice. "You and Craig are welcome to come along Saturday if it's so important to you. Does that suit you, Justine?"

"That would be just fine," Justine murmured, her expression indicating the opposite.

"Lovely. *Lovely*! I'll get myself something extra special to wear." Kim jumped up, insisting on kissing them both. "Marsh due in Friday?" she asked as she resumed her chair.

"How did you know?" Roslyn heard her own voice sharp with challenge.

"Di told me," Kim answered sweetly. "Justine told me your wedding dress is almost finished, Ros. What's it like?"

So you can spread it around as the latest intelligence? Oh, no!

"That's a secret," Justine said before Roslyn could even speak.

"Why not!" Kim gave a merry laugh. "You'll make a beautiful bride, Ros. Ju-Ju's been telling me you've been better than a sister helping her make herself over."

"She's created my new image!" Justine declared with touching gratitude. "I've never bothered much with clothes, as you know, but there's no doubting they make the person. I have an entirely new wardrobe. Ros decided on my hairstyle and my new makeup, as well."

"I swear I couldn't believe my eyes!" Kim declared jarringly.

Justine did, in fact, look striking in just the way her mother's looks had commanded attention. Her thick, wavy hair, her great asset, was beautifully cut and groomed, her skin polished, cared for and deftly made up. Roslyn had steered Justine away from her conservative wardrobe to one with a more dynamic character. It revolutionized Justine's "look" showing to advantage her lean lines and tawny lioness colouring.

"Where did you get that silk shirt?" Kim suddenly demanded, staring hard at the distinctive cinnamon shirt.

"*I* picked it up," Roslyn answered, realizing Justine was momentarily stuck for words. "But I can't remember where." If she'd said where she'd bought it the chances were Kim would be right up there.

"You're staying to lunch, Kim?" Justine asked faintly.

"I'd love to!" Kim nodded her head with enthusiasm. "Something good on the menu?"

"Cheeseburgers," Roslyn said wickedly.

Midmorning Friday the grounds were invaded by workmen who erected three huge, pure white marquees around the garden and pool area. The same firm took care of the linen, crystal, cutlery, china, chandeliers, chairs and the fairy lights for the trees. In the afternoon a floral decorator would arrive to fill the house and the marquees with flowers, various swags and all the indoor plants they would need including tubs of standard ficus. The food would be handled by another service, providing what was confidently expected to be a sumptuous buffet and a bar service. One group of musicians would play under their own canopy in the garden. Another had been hired to play in the old ballroom in the house. In all one hundred guests had been asked, but sadly, in Roslyn's opinion, that number had been upped by two. The weather held perfect.

Roslyn was enjoying a short rest in her bedroom that afternoon when she heard a car sweep up the driveway and come to a stop at the foot of the steps, its engine ticking over. It had to be Marsh. He'd told them he would take a taxi from the light aircraft terminal. She rushed to the window and looked out, her heart racing so fast she actually held a hand to it. It *was* Marsh! She emerged through the front door as he stood out on the driveway paying off the driver. He looked wonderful from all angles. She loved the back of his head, the set of his shoulders, the way their width tapered to his lean, taut waist, terrific butt and long legs. She felt such a flood of love she flew down the steps, hair and pleated skirt whipping in the bay breeze.

Keep what we've got at all costs, she thought. One day he'll tell me he loves me.

Marsh turned, flashed his wonderful smile, threw out an arm.

How to describe his reaction? *Rapture*. She moved into the charmed embrace, feeling his arm close strongly, urgently, around her. Her loneliness lifted miraculously. She turned up a radiant face and he seemed to glide into kissing her; no affectionate greeting but a kiss that left her feverish and clinging.

"So how is my promised bride?" he asked, his blue and brilliant eyes intent on her expression. "Surely you've lost a little weight?"

"All the partying," she explained. "I've lost count of the luncheons and dinner parties. How was your flight?"

"Too slow. I couldn't wait to see my beautiful Rosa."

"I've missed you." Her voice shook a little.

He looked at her for a long moment, touched her hair that in the sun had the sheen of a dark plum. "If that isn't the darnedest thing! I think you mean it." There was a faint twist to his beautifully shaped sensuous mouth.

"Don't you believe me?"

"Convince me when we're on our own."

"In fact I can't wait."

He laughed under his breath. "So, absence does indeed make the heart grow fonder."

"You haven't said you missed me."

"You mean that kiss didn't get through to you?" He lifted his dark head, saw his sister waving as she came through the front door and out onto the veranda. "Say, Ju-Ju looks great!" he exclaimed with some satisfaction.

"Doesn't she!" Roslyn stood away happily as brother and sister exchanged bear hugs.

"You've been hiding your light under a bush," Marsh said after a low whistle.

Justine flushed with pleasure. "Ros can take the credit. She's nothing less than a magician."

Marsh moved back. Seized Roslyn around the waist. "Haven't I always said there was magic about her? You look very stylish, Ju-Ju. Keep it up."

"Ian's thrilled," Justine confided. "He keeps telling me I look compelling."

"And he's not wrong!" Marsh put an arm around both women's waists. "Plenty of activity going on?"

"You're going to pay for it, darling," Justine said

gleefully. "No expense spared for Marsh Faulkner and his divinely beautiful fiancée."

Roslyn laughed a little ruefully. "What exactly *is* the connection? people ask, then rush into the next question before I can tell them. I suppose they'll wake up one day."

"No need for any secrets," Marsh said firmly.

"You can tell everyone Lord Mortimer will be giving you away," Justine said slyly. "A lot of people are still impressed by a title."

"Not *me*," Marsh said crisply. "It's what people *are* that counts."

"As I'm learning," Justine said, leading the way into the house. "I suppose you'd better know Kim Petersen is back in our lives."

Silence for a moment. "Why not?" Marsh said in a jaded tone. "There's something unstoppable about Kim."

"I fear so." Justine moved into the living room and they followed her. "She turned up the other day. Said she was on a shopping spree. Wanted us all to be friends."

"Dear Lord!" Marsh made a derisive sound. "More like she wanted invitations to the wedding."

"How did you guess?" Roslyn gazed up at him.

"*Darling*, it's going to be a big, social event. It may even turn out to be the biggest event of the decade if what's going on here is anything to go by." His glance swept the glorious flower arrangements and the festive appearance of the room. "Kim will certainly want to be there. Her mother, too, even if her nose will be very slightly out of joint. They'd be devastated to be left out."

Justine nodded. "I guess so."

"Well, she won't be the *bride*," Roslyn observed brightly.

Marsh took her hand, carried it to his mouth. "That's *your* role, Rosa. You're the only one who can fill it."

"How gorgeously romantic!" Justine cried, and clasped her hands. "Getting back to Kim—"

"*Must* we?" Marsh groaned. "She can't dictate our lives."

"Here, here!" Roslyn agreed heartily.

"I was only going to say she told us she's getting engaged to poor old Craig, which is a great relief."

"Well, the poor devil has lived in hope. The relief, I doubt. Personally I'll believe it when it happens." Marsh drew Roslyn down onto the sofa beside him. "Black coffee and maybe a sandwich, Ju-Ju, if that's no bother. I haven't eaten since first light."

"*Really*?" Roslyn looked at him with the utmost concern.

"No Shepards to pack a picnic lunch," he said dryly.

"We'll soon fix that!" Justine made immediately for the door. This was her beloved brother. There was nothing she wouldn't do for him. Except tell him Kim had virtually invited herself and Craig to the party the following night. Roslyn would have to do that. She was so happy for them. Surely Kim couldn't come along to spoil it.

At seven o'clock on the night of the party Roslyn stood before her long mirror surveying the effect of her beautiful gown. It had been ruinously expensive but well worth it. She had never looked better, but then, she had never owned such a gown nor indeed been invited to the sort of function where she could wear it.

In keeping with the designer's romantic vision, the dress was almost a ballgown in the grand tradition. Scarlett O'Hara might have worn it! Roslyn couldn't describe the colour of the sumptuous silk taffeta. Fern green, willow green, green shot with gold? It was very unusual, but so soft and seductive. It made her eyes glow strangely. Her "witching" look as Marsh put it. She touched a hand to the full, short sleeves, puffing them still further. The neckline—what was it, portrait?— framed her shoulders, the décolletage a little lower than she'd wanted but the designer wouldn't have it any other way. It was a bravura gown. A tantalising glimpse of bosom was de rigueur.

Because of the *Gone With the Wind* overtones Roslyn had decided to wear her hair in a loose, dark cloud at the back, but drawn up at the sides. She had some very pretty pendant earrings she intended to wear. Her face was a little pale. Perhaps a touch of blusher? She had to admit she was nervous. This was the first time she and Marsh would appear together before all his friends. It struck her now as extremely odd she had given in to Kim Petersen's emotional blackmail and allowed her to come. It had been nothing less than that. For all Kim's avowals of friendship and the news of her pending engagement, which Marsh had taken with a large grain of salt, Roslyn feared there had been something almost sinister in the depths of Kim's eyes.

A little shiver ran through her and she turned away, comforted by the lovely, rich swish of her billowing skirt. What to wear around her neck? She had an Art Nouveau necklace that might do. It didn't match the earrings but she had often worn them together. In fact they'd been much admired. She *did* have good taste. Justine's transformation had been extraordinary. It gave her a great deal of satisfaction. As did their bonding. Of course Justine would do anything for her brother but there was no denying a genuine friendship had sprung up between them. Justine was a kinder, more sensitive person than her sister and light-years away from the late Lady Faulkner. A veil of sadness, of old memories, settled on Roslyn that she tried to shake off. She must take hold of her new life. Recognise her own value. A few people, it was true, had greeted her with speculative eyes. But for the most part she had been welcomed with warmth by all the people Justine had insisted she meet. The fact that she could play the piano extremely well had been a help. When Dame Agatha returned from her overseas lecture tour she would find the right moment to thank her for all she had done. It was a great pity she'd had to grow so many prickles to survive.

A knock at the door interrupted her thought. She went to it expecting Justine, but finding Marsh in evening dress on the threshold. He looked so splendid surely her eyes were exposing her heart?

"Rosa, darling, you're a living dream! Here, stand back. I want to take a look at you."

"You won't believe the bill!" She stretched out her two arms and stepped into a waltz, looking over her shoulder and smiling at him as she dipped and swayed. The bright brilliant light shone on her, struck a dazzling light in her eyes. She felt faintly unreal. Perhaps it was all a dream?

"The awful thing is I can't do what I want," Marsh said in a deep, thrilling tone.

"Which is?" She broke off gracefully to stand before him.

"Kiss you and kiss you and kiss you. Never stop."

"That would be wonderful," she whispered.

"Don't close your eyes or I'll forget everything," Marsh said in a soft warning. "Will we *ever* get a moment together?"

"That's my prayer. That's my dream."

They stood staring into one another's eyes until finally Marsh remembered what he'd come for. "You'll want something to wear around your neck. This should do admirably." He handed her a long, narrow box covered in midnight-blue velvet.

"Jewellery?" Her own eyes shone like gems.

"An expression of my undying love."

"I don't know if I can stand this."

"I think you can. Open it."

Roslyn did so, at the same time giving a soft, little gasp. "Marsh, how exquisite!"

"Not very, beside you. Shall we try it on?"

"*Please!*" She lifted her hair away from her neck and turned. "I've never had such a gift."

"Don't think it's your last." He secured the catch, his fingers warm and tingly at her nape. "Let's take a look." He took her hand, drew her to the long mirror and stood just behind her, his hands on the tips of her shoulders. "I don't think you know how beautiful you are."

Roslyn stood staring at her reflection in some awe. The necklace lay against the creamy skin of her breast; lustrous pearls linked in gold, a diamond centrepiece from which was appended a diamond set opal heart. Brilliant flashes lit the deep glowing black gem. Blues, greens, fiery reds, the topaz of her eyes.

"You've had it specially designed." She brought up a hand to trace the outline of the opal heart.

"Of course, with you in mind. I know you love opals. The heart is symbolic."

"I'll treasure it all my life."

"As I'll treasure the vision of you." He bent his head, his lips finding the little depression above her collarbone. "My beautiful Rosa!"

Sensation was so exquisite, so melting, she let her head fall back as his hands came up gently, but so sensuously beneath her breasts. She put her own hands over his, guiding them higher. Her body craved his so badly the stress was enormous. Her breasts throbbed with pain.

His voice murmured endearments into her ear, soft, intimate, infinitely seductive.

I'm dying with love for you, she thought. Marsh, my destiny!

"Oh, this is impossible," he said. "I can't kiss you. Spoil your makeup. So help me I just could go crazy."

"Love is often described as a madness, didn't you know?" She dropped her hands, giving a shaky little laugh.

"Tell me you love me, Rosa," he said. "We're alone." His expression was taut and brushed with a faint violence.

"Marsh...you can't know...I..."

Whatever she was going to say he was not then to know. The bedroom door was ajar and after the briefest of raps Justine came bustling through. "Darlings!" she cried. "We'll have to take up our positions downstairs to receive our guests." Her eyes fell on Roslyn's necklace and she checked abruptly. "Nice," she said. "Very nice. Glorious but not vulgar. A rare thing, like you,

Roslyn. Now look here, you two! I'm not going to burst into tears. It took me a solid hour to put on my make-up.'' She touched her forehead, gave it a little worried rub. ''Earrings, what about earrings?''

''What's the matter with me!'' Marsh exclaimed. ''They're here in my pocket.''

''Of course they are. I knew they were,'' Justine said. ''You never forget anything.'' She swooped on Roslyn suddenly to kiss her satiny cheek. ''All right? Not nervy?''

''Not now.'' Roslyn clipped the earrings, large pearls surrounded by a twist of gold, to her ears.

''Fan the sides of your hair out a bit,'' Justine advised, a striking figure in a white, one-shouldered, togalike garment. ''Now, come downstairs, darlings. Ian wants us to pose for a few home photographs. Don't expect them to be professional, but he *will* keep at it!''

By nine o'clock the party was in full swing. People roamed the grounds and the main reception rooms to a heady flow of music, laughter and streams of conversation. The buffet tables, covered in starched white damask sagged a little under the wealth of dishes; honey-glazed hams, stuffed roast turkeys, differently prepared chickens. There were silver platters of just about every kind of seafood served on beds of ice; whole smoked salmon, lobsters, prawns, oysters, scallops, crabs and oven-baked mussels. Quails eggs were piled up in bowls and there were salads of all kinds. Hot dishes were served, as well; Thai and Indonesian, splendid in their presentation and accompanied by traditional rice. A separate table had been set up for sweets from delectable, mouth-watering light mousses to the richest, wickedest chocolate gateaus and tortes. Waiters in black trousers and short, natty jackets circled continually with champagne, classic cocktails, Kir, Bellini's, Buck's Fizz and nonalcoholic drinks.

At different times the level of noise almost drowned out the band on the lawn but they continued to play their hearts out to an ever-changing, appreciative audience.

The quality of dressing was superb. The black tie of the male guests complimented the beautiful dresses their wives and girlfriends had chosen. Lots of expensive jewellery had come out of bank vaults for the occasion. There was even one tiara Roslyn thought a bit idiotic until she was presented to a genuine European princess of fabled glamour. She shook Roslyn's hand, smiled at her and said, "So lovely. So very lovely!" The v's were pronounced as deep f's. Roslyn realised she was being honoured.

By ten-thirty she thought she would need at least a week to recover. She drank only mineral water or orange juice so she could keep her mind together. No way was she going to become the slightest bit intoxicated.

Apart from the fact she didn't want to, she knew her every gesture, her every move was under scrutiny. Yet she felt happy, confident, unfazed by all the introductions. Most people seemed delighted to meet her. Not critical at all. Some *did* eye her off speculatively. Older women mostly. Probably friends of the Petersens. But in the main she felt she was making a good impression. Marsh's blue eyes every time they rested on her, conveyed enormous pride and pleasure. How could she *not* shine? Even Dianne smiled happily and waved, every time they passed her. Dianne had taken to growing her hair out. With her pregnancy well established she had gained a soft bloom. Chris must have been threatened with all kinds of things because his manner, though friendly, held none of the usual silly flirtatiousness. Perhaps the thought of fatherhood was maturing him.

Kim and Craig had arrived late. Kim standing a statuesque three inches over Craig's head. She was dressed to kill in bright red chiffon. The dress hung on shoestring straps and the skirt was slit in several places to show her spectacular legs. The colour brought out her golden tan and the gilt streaks in her blond hair. Roslyn thought she looked stunning, but her gaze was a little odd. A surprising mix of supreme self-confidence with a decided dash of defiance. Beside her, Craig faded into nothingness. He was prematurely losing his hair, which was sad, but he had inherited a quarter share of the family business with an estimated personal fortune of around 55 million dollars. He was known to be paranoid about publicity but with Kim on his arm he was beaming broadly.

"For Pete's sake, couldn't you have told me?" Marsh demanded as he and Roslyn moved forward to greet them.

"I tried, but I just couldn't find it in my heart. That doesn't mean I'm not going to keep an eye on you."

"Oh, don't be absurd!" Marsh laughed. "I only hope they're going to spring a surprise and announce their engagement. It'd be just like Kim to break the good news at *our* party."

"It *is* possible," Roslyn said.

Instead Kim took Marsh by the arms, leaned forward and kissed him full on the mouth. "Darling, my congratulations! This is a wonderful occasion."

"Indeed, indeed!" Craig added hastily, giving Roslyn

an uncertain smile. "It was sweet of you both to invite me when you heard I was in town. You look absolutely beautiful, Roslyn. A knock-out!"

"I want to steal your necklace," Kim smiled. "Marsh's present, am I right?"

"Of course!" Roslyn put her hand on Marsh's arm and he hugged her to him so her billowing skirt swayed. "An expression of our love."

"Opals are a bit too unlucky for me," Kim said with a tiny shudder of unease.

"Surely you're not superstitious?" Craig asked, looking embarrassed. "I think it's the loveliest necklace I've seen and it suits Roslyn perfectly."

Kim patted him and rolled her eyes. A kind of what-would-*you*-know? "The house looks splendid, all the decorations and everything. Did Di make it?"

"But of course!" Marsh said, sounding surprised. "Di would never miss an occasion like this."

"Mmm," Kim looked as though she had heard differently.

"Ah, there are the Munros," Marsh said, his gaze going over Kim's head. "Would you both excuse us? I'll catch up, Craig, later on. A few things have happened you might like to know about."

Kim looked momentarily devastated as though some of it could be about her, but it would be business, polo, something like that.

"Watch Kim tonight," Marsh warned Roslyn as they moved off. "She has a decidedly malicious streak. More, with a few drinks in, she's nutty enough to do anything."

"So why did I say she could come?" Roslyn answered in a wry voice.

"I'm sure we'll live to regret it. She gives me the impression she's out to make trouble."

After supper Roslyn retired briefly upstairs to repair her lipstick. She looked fine and that soothed her. So far the party was progressing amazingly well. Kim and Craig had merged in with their friends. Was it possible Craig could control her excesses? He *was* a hard-nosed businessman after all.

Roslyn decided to take the rear staircase to the ground floor. She would be much less on view. As she commenced the descent to the first landing she realised a group of women was having a conversation in the shadowy privacy of beneath the stairs. She hesitated a moment, unsure whether she should keep going or retrace her steps and take the main staircase. For no reason she could understand she had a sinking suspicion Kim might be one of the women. Marsh was right. Kim had a kind of aura tonight. It conveyed a certain "I'm going to have my little revenge." Not exactly smart. Roslyn herself wouldn't care to confront Marsh head-on. Nor Justine and Ian if they considered themselves insulted. But Kim would gossip *in private*.

Before she could take another step Roslyn had her proof. *Kim.*

"Oh, I know she looks good, but she's desperately unsure of herself."

Another woman snapped back, "You'd have fooled me! I thought her incredibly poised. I wouldn't have taken her for a modest little schoolteacher at all. Carol was telling me she plays the piano awfully well. I adore the classical piano. I'd love to hear her play."

"You wouldn't enjoy it as much as you think," Kim came back. "Her style is very over-the-top."

"Darling, would *you* know? You don't know anything about music," another voice said. One Roslyn knew. Anne Fletcher. "It beats me why you wanted to come tonight. We're sorry Marsh has been snatched from you. We know you're very upset, but it's all history now. He's made his choice. Accept it."

"I'd dearly love to but I'm finding it a little hard after all we meant to each other. This marriage would never happen if Lady Faulkner were alive."

"Not that awful woman!" Anne Fletcher moaned with black humour. "Did you ever meet with such coldness and arrogance? The time she gave the girls, yet she was ruthlessly possessive of Marsh. Not that he tolerated it for long."

"Very tragic Sir Charles was killed," another voice said. "Snatched away in the prime of life. Such a pity the marriage wasn't a success."

"You can blame that on the little bride's mother. The housekeeper," Kim said with such vindictiveness it made Roslyn ill. She wasn't going to listen to this. She put her hand to her long skirt, lifted it, but again Anne Fletcher broke in, staying Roslyn's intervention.

"I'm sure we'd all prefer if you didn't mention that, Kim. You're being incredibly bitchy tonight. You and Marsh were never *that* close. Besides, I don't believe that old gossip for a minute."

"Then you *should*!" Kim maintained in a steely voice. "Mother and daughter, both opportunists. Roslyn latched onto Marsh and wouldn't let go. The mother got her hooks into Harry Wallace when all else failed. He's Lord Mortimer now by the way. I suppose you've heard. It's quite bizarre! The Faulkner housekeeper will most certainly become Lady Mortimer."

"Good for her!" yet another voice said. "Why should the rich have all fun!"

"You're not terribly supportive!" Kim complained, obviously stung by the group's reaction.

"Not very," Anne Fletcher agreed. "We've all been friends with the Faulkners since forever. We're not about to fall out now and for *what*? I can't see that they won't be divinely happy together. Now, I'm for a drink. Anyone else coming? Doesn't Justine look marvellous tonight? She's finally got herself together."

The women moved off and Roslyn proceeded down the stairs. She felt upset by what Kim had said, particularly about her mother, yet heartened by the lack of response. Anne Fletcher was a leader in young society and obviously ready to embrace Marsh Faulkner's wife. Kim would have her nose well and truly out of joint.

Sometime later Marsh told her many of their guests had expressed the wish to hear her play the piano. "You don't mind, do you?" He looked at her, his eyes brilliant. "I thought it would be nice if you did."

"I don't mind in the least."

"I'm sure they'd be very appreciative."

"Besides, Ian is already lifting the lid."

Marsh lowered his head suddenly and kissed her cheek. "Show them what you're capable of. You have quite a repertoire. What about the 'Ritual Fire Dance' to start seeing we're all on a roll, then maybe one of the Chopin études? I like the one that goes all up and down the piano."

"The 'Ocean Étude.'" She smiled. "It's a very good thing I haven't touched a drop of alcohol. Bravura performances just don't happen unless one's in total control."

Marsh laughed gently and led her across a sea of smiling, expectant faces. Roslyn arranged herself at the piano, pushed the long piano stool back a little, cleared her long full skirt from the pedals and her feet. Finally she was comfortable and announced in a calm voice her two choices. The "Ritual Fire Dance" by Manuel De Falla and Chopin's famous étude in C minor. Clapping broke in a wave over the large drawing room. All the French doors were open to the veranda so the music would float out over the lawn. Someone had obviously told the band to stop so the level of noise had dropped dramatically. Many of the guests had heard Roslyn was a gifted pianist but only a handful had actually witnessed a performance.

Near the double doors leading to the hallway, Kim hissed in Craig's ear, "For God's sake, how boring! Anyone would think she was a famous concert pianist, when she's strictly an amateur. I'm going for some fresh air. You stay if you want."

"I'd like to," Craig said, sounding shocked. "It might be a good idea, Kimmy, if we toddle off shortly after. You've had one Bellini too many."

Vulnerable to criticism at the best of times, a heated flush rose to Kim's cheeks and she looked back wild-eyed. "Don't tell *me* how to conduct myself, Craig McDonald, you little squirt!"

"Squirt?" Craig savoured that for a moment. "How very delightful!" He turned away deliberately.

Kim waited for no more. She stalked unsteadily into the packed hallway and made for the front door while the thrilling opening bars of the "Ritual Fire Dance" spilled out into the night....

*   *   *

Roslyn sat with Marsh, wonderfully relaxed and happy. Her little recital had been a brainwave. It appeared to have established her in her own right. Marsh was telling a story that had everyone laughing when a waiter came to stand at her shoulder.

"I'm sorry, Miss Earnshaw," he apologised, "but Mrs. Herbert would like to see you for a moment in the Garden Room."

Roslyn left immediately, signalling to Marsh with a little wave of her fingers. Probably it had something to do with the handful of guests who weren't behaving as they should. What Roslyn could do about it she didn't know. Justine mightn't like the idea but she could be forced into suggesting they might like to go home.

When she reached the Garden Room, which wasn't open to their guests, she found it very dimly lit. The great hanging ferns and the golden canes in glazed pots stood out in sharp silhouette against the backlit glass wall which was a blaze of dull gold. Across the hedge of sasanqua camellias she could just see couples walking and beyond that people dancing on the lawn.

"Justine?" she called, just starting to think something was amiss. Justine wouldn't be standing about in the semi-dark.

"Roslyn?" a voice cried back from somewhere in the shadows.

She felt a flash of rising irritation. "Is that you, Chris?" She walked towards the sound. "What are *you* doing here?" Surely to God it couldn't be a replay of his and Dianne's engagement party when he'd cornered her for a kiss. "A bit of fun" as he'd put it then. "Chris?" she repeated sharply.

"Keep your hair on. Here I am." He was suddenly

there, pressing her arm. "Justine sent a message she wanted me. I expect she has a problem with the sillies in the pool."

"Who told you?" Roslyn demanded.

"I'm sorry?" Chris responded in his supercilious tone.

"Who told you Justine wanted you?"

He touched her hair. "Oh, a waiter. I'm sure it was a waiter."

"Well, she's not here. It might be a good idea to find the light switch."

"Just when I was enjoying it in the dark. *I* don't know where it is. You've been living here for weeks."

Roslyn moved back to the door. "I have, but I don't think I've turned the lights on here once. One would expect to find the panel somewhere here, but it's not. Frankly I think we should leave."

"What, when you've done your best to get me here!" He laughed.

"That'll be the day!"

"I wonder. I'd say you planned all this."

"For what purpose?" she asked coldly.

"Trouble-making, I should think. That would suit you. You *are* a troublemaker as we all know. That business at Christmas was your doing. How gauche to imply I was bothering you."

With her eyes adjusted to the gloom Roslyn saw his expression plainly. It disgusted her. "Are you quite mad?" she demanded. "I never said a thing."

"I'm sorry, Ros, I don't believe that. Marsh was just about ready to throw me out. Di was livid. Upsetting her at such a time. I love her. We've never had such unpleasantness."

"That's a downright lie. You'll always have unpleas-antness while you can't seem to stop yourself from chat-ting girls up."

He stared at her in outrage. "Chatting girls up? I as-sure you I'm only being pleasant. Most girls love it."

"Well here's one who doesn't! It's my opinion some-one has set *us* up. It's not me and even you couldn't be so dim-witted."

"Dim-witted? Oh, hell, yes. That's why I'm so suc-cessful. I do believe your little triumph has gone to your head. If there's any mischief going on, probably you have something to do with it. Of course I know what it is. You're put out I haven't paid any attention to you all evening. Kim's right. You muscled in on this family. You've tried to make a fool out of me."

Roslyn saw red. "From where I'm standing, I wouldn't *have* to try!"

He gave a derisive snort. "You don't fool me, Ros. You and your sharp little tongue. Not that it isn't part of your charm. I suspect you're a vixen at heart. I want you to know if you cause any more unpleasantness—"

"You'll do what?"

"I won't have Di upset," Chris said in a pious tone. "You've been causing these upsets for years. I want it to stop."

"Give me strength!" Roslyn exclaimed. "*You* want it to stop when I'm the one who's had to put up with your stupidity. You make me sick!" By now, Roslyn, in a fine temper went to turn on her heel, but Chris caught her arm, the expression on his face equally angry, but excited, too.

"Oh, really? Well, *I* think you've always been at-tracted to me."

"Let go of my arm, Chris," Roslyn snapped.

"We've got a few things to clear up first."

"Then let's clear them up in front of Marsh and Dianne."

"So you've got Marsh in the palm of your hand." Chris jeered unpleasantly. "It's only a temporary thing. He'll start back up with Kim. They understand one another."

"I said *let go*!"

"Shut up. Shut up for a minute," Chris urged. "There's someone coming this way."

In another minute one of the doors leading to the terrace opened and the room was flooded with light.

"Hey, you guys!" a teen-aged, bedraggled apparition cried. "Are we breakin' up a little tryst?"

Chris dropped Roslyn's arm in horror. "What in the world are you doing here, Marcy, and in that condition?" To make it worse, the girl was accompanied by Kim Petersen, who looked at Roslyn and Chris with open disgust in her eyes.

"Just can't leave it alone, can you, Ros!" she said with contempt.

Marcy giggled, obviously intoxicated. "Naughty, naughty, Chris!"

"Don't be ridiculous!" he said, looking devastated.

"It don't look good," Marcy crowed. "Though why in the world anyone would look at you when they had Marsh."

"I think you'd better stop right there, Marcy," Roslyn warned, suddenly producing her most quelling schoolteacher tone, "or repeat what you're saying in front of my fiancée, Dianne and your parents."

It had some effect because Marcy appeared to sober

abruptly. "Hang on, hang on. I was only trying to take the heat off me."

"Then I assure you you haven't succeeded. I take great exception to your implication."

"So I apologise. Absolutely," Marcy replied, peering earnestly through her long, sopping hair. "Hey, wait a couple of ticks. Kim insulted you, as well. Make *her* apologise. Make her apologise, too, for giving me a glass of champagne and daring me to jump in the pool."

"I did nothing of the kind!" Kim protested vigorously, giving Marcy a push in the back.

"You did so, too!" Marcy accused her. "Ask Craig. He fished me out. I've been drinking orange juice all night. Then one drink and it hit me like a bomb."

"You're dripping water all over the floor," Roslyn said dispassionately. "We're of a size. I can lend you something to put on, then maybe we should think about getting you home."

"I've never done anything like this before," Marcy suddenly wailed. "Mum'll kill me."

Just as another wail went up Justine, who had been informed of the incident, appeared. "Gracious, Marcy, what a really foolish thing to do!" Oblivious of her expensive dress she went to the girl and put her arm around her. "You've always been so sensible, too."

"I only had *one* drink, Justine," Marcy said almost indignantly. "Kim gave it to me, but she won't admit it."

"Because it's not *true*!" Kim said coldly. "The first thing you should learn, Marcy, is to admit your own mistakes."

"Where's the bathroom," said Marcy. "I feel sick."

Justine led her away hurriedly and Roslyn decided to speak her mind.

"I knew when you arrived tonight, Kim, you'd planned some little incident to discredit me or spoil the party."

Kim looked unimpressed. "My dear, you have the problem of explaining to Dianne what you were doing here in the *dark* with her husband."

"She sent me a message," Chris said, on Kim's side.

"You're pathetic, Chris!" Roslyn exclaimed. "You don't have to explain anything to Kim. She set the whole thing up. I suppose she popped a little extra into that girl's drink. She's unscrupulous enough. The Garden Room has been off limits to our guests. Why bring her in here? The pool house would have been a better idea. It's well stocked with towels and robes."

"I wanted dry clothes," Kim declared in her superior voice. "I knew perfectly well Justine wouldn't mind. I know the house well."

"You certainly know where the light switches are. I overheard you talking to your friends earlier in the evening, the unkind things you said about me and my mother."

"Well, you know what they say, darling." Kim sneered. "Eavesdroppers et cetera."

"You didn't get much for yourself, either."

"So what's going on?" a voice demanded. They all looked around as Dianne made her way towards them, her forehead creased in a frown. "There's a party out there, doesn't anyone know? Ros, Marsh is looking for you everywhere. Anyone would think you've been kidnapped!"

"I'll go to him," Roslyn said, anxious to avoid any further embarrassment.

"She's going to run, just like she did the last time," Kim said to Dianne in a harsh, ugly voice.

"What are you talking about, Kim?" Marsh, who had combed the house, finally found them in the Garden Room. He spoke forcefully, his handsome face stirred to anger.

"She's going to ruin everything for you," Kim cried. "Do you think I'd be speaking out only the old ties run deep? Roslyn is the catalyst amongst us. She forces change."

"The complications of love!" Dianne cried. "I wish I knew what you're on about now, Kim. This whole business has affected you."

"Then let me explain." Kim's eyes flashed around, her face flushed with drink and recklessness. "It's the old story. Conquest. She's done it before at your engagement party. Some weird trait in her character—"

"As I recall, you were the one to bring it to Mother's attention," Dianne interrupted as though she had suddenly thought of something significant.

"I *had* to. Then as now. Roslyn is the sort of woman who won't let go. She needs all this admiration. She's missed out on so much. She doesn't care you and Chris are happily married. You're pregnant. She arranged to meet Chris here. Alone."

"Incredible!" Marsh made a sound of utter disbelief. "Is that the best you can do? And I imagine you've been working on it for weeks. Rosa stole away to meet *Chris*? You'd better lay off the booze."

"It's the way it happened," Kim said in a furious

voice. "I have a witness. Marcy Hallett. We surprised them."

To Roslyn's utter horror Dianne began to weep. "Di, *please*, this is nonsense. Chris and I haven't the slightest thing to feel guilty about. We were both told Justine wanted to see us here. She didn't. It was a pathetic scheme Kim thought up. I'd say she even brought along something to lace my drink, only I wasn't having any. *Anything* to discredit me."

"Chris believes me," Kim said. "Perhaps he knows Roslyn better than any of us."

"You rattlesnake!" Roslyn went white.

It was the last straw for Marsh. "You might like to leave, Kim," he said in a hard-edged voice. "There's no way I'm going to allow you to ruin *our* night. I'd like to make it perfectly plain I believe that was your intention."

His words and the way he said them filled Roslyn with all the confidence she needed. *Our night.* Their shared happiness. The certainty she was very special. Everything about him spoke of love and commitment!

Yet Kim persisted, locked in to the delusions she had long nourished. "Hate me. Go on, hate me. It can't be helped. I'm your friend, Marsh. Di and Justine have been like my own sisters. There's a lot of feeling in our relationship. I'm vitally interested in the Faulkner good name. Roslyn Earnshaw is a wild card. I admit she looks and acts the part, but she's a *fake*!"

"Fakes get exposed. Rosa is the real thing."

"She's taken every opportunity to drive a wedge between the family." Two hectic spots of colour burned in Kim's face. "I loved you, Marsh. So badly. We were going to spend our lives together. You *promised* me, you know you did. After we made love we used to lie so gently, so quietly, making plans for the future."

"You don't want to sell your story to the newspapers, do you?" Marsh asked in a caustic voice. "They print pure fiction.'"

Kim put a hand to her heart, a gesture that could have been poignant only for the touch of theatre. "I know, too, I'm *not* lying!"

"Ah, God, Kim," Dianne said, and her voice broke. "Why don't you just shut up? There's always been a dark side to you."

"Forgive me, pet." Kim reached over and touched Dianne's tawny hair. "It's as bad a thing as I've ever done upsetting you."

"Excuse me before I throw up," Roslyn said abruptly, turning to leave.

"Not on your life!" Marsh caught her around the waist, holding her to him. "This is *our* party. The others can leave."

Kim threw up her head, lifting her body to its full height. "I'm sorrier than I can say it's turned out like this, Marsh. I only thought to warn you as a lifelong friend."

"*Out!*" Marsh said in no uncertain tone.

"You love me, darling, don't you?" Chris asked as he led his wife away.

"I don't know. I honestly don't know."

"It hurts me to see you so upset, Di," Kim cried, hurrying after them.

"I can imagine!" Dianne's voice floated back, the tone as dry as ashes.

"My poor, sweet Rosa," Marsh groaned, dropping a

kiss on the top of Roslyn's head. "But don't say I didn't warn you."

"It's just obscene the things she says."

"Blame it on her childhood," Marsh said laconically.

"And you. It all goes back to you."

Marsh smiled, his mouth curving ironically. "Not a fight, Rosa. Not now. I couldn't stand it. It's been a perfect evening. You've been wonderful. I'm so proud of you."

His blue eyes were as clear as a rock pool. She could see her own reflection. "That means *everything* to me, Marsh. Your total trust and commitment. You haven't even heard the full story."

"Darling, if it's all the same to you, I really don't want to know," Marsh said with dry humour. "I'd like to drive Kim into the desert and leave her there. She's supposed to be Di's friend yet she couldn't care less about upsetting her."

"I'd say from Di's tone that's truly sunk in. Chris might have a time calming her. It's really terrible the tickets he has on himself."

Marsh looked at her, tipped her chin, smiled. "Hey, it's *our* party remember?"

"I love you," she said, the last barrier down, her most secret thought uttered.

"Say that again!" His blue eyes glittered with such an extraordinary light she felt irradiated.

"I said, I love you. I love you. I love you. Forever and ever!"

His arms closed around her, a little rough, a little fierce. "You've taken your time."

"I was wounded, Marsh."

"Tell me you're healed?"

She stared up at his beloved face; a face of passion and power. "As long as you allow me to become part of you."

His arms tightened urgently. "But, Rosa, you've always been that. You *must* know. You're the flame in my heart. The love of my life. That's all there is to it, what we've always known in our souls. We love each other."

"Why has it been so difficult to *say* it?"

"We lost a little trust in each other for a time. We let too much of the past stand in our way, but that's all over. You're going to bloom as my wife, Rosa. I want to love and cherish you and give you all the things you've been denied. I want you to become my partner in all things. I want you to use and display your gifts. I want our children. Our mutual creations. You're the only woman in my life, my adored Rosa."

"You used to be a *fantastic* lover!" she whispered.

"*Used* to be?" he said, laughing. "I'd better tell you—"

"Kiss me," she begged with loving intensity. "I need you to—"

"Lord, Rosa!" he muttered, his handsome face taut with high emotion. He kissed her then, elated by the response he met. She was beautiful…beautiful…her mouth a flower that opened for him. He had dreamed of the day she would tell him she loved him again. He couldn't fully express his love. Not tonight. Nor the next. Part of the manifestation of their love was something spiritual. In just under a month they would be married on Macumba. Their wedding night would be one they would remember forever…

"Marsh!" Roslyn gasped, almost overcome by the blaze that had sprung up between them.

"Just showing you how it's going to be." He placed his hands on the sides of her face, his thumbs tracing the lovely line of her jaw. "Remember our secret place?" he murmured.

Irresistibly Roslyn's mind turned back. "How lonely I've been for it. A billion desert stars, the white limbs of the ghost gums glowing in the purple night, the scent of the boronia and the lovely little mauve mist that grew in great numbers around the lagoon, the crunch of the sand beneath us, the wind song at intervals whistling through the trees. I used to dream of it endlessly. Our magic place. Our magic time. We belonged then. But we were torn apart."

"We've reclaimed our dream, Rosa," Marsh said with great depth of feeling. "Just as we can reclaim our supremely beautiful secret place. We can go back on our wedding night. It would be easy to slip away."

She was quiet for a moment, afraid she might cry. "That would be *perfect*!"

"So, it's a date?"

"It's a promise!" Her golden eyes filled with a radiant light.

Marsh bent his dark head, claiming her mouth in a kiss that began slowly then surged into desire.

All this Justine saw as she bustled into the room having dealt with young Marcy, who was still feeling the effects of her earlier dip, and Kim and Craig who had made a swift exit on the verge of a few words. Justine had nearly wept with relief. She was an absolute dolt allowing Kim to come.

"Darlings, darlings!" she cried, and got through to them on the fourth try. "Plenty of time for all that. Decades and decades! Everyone wants to know where you are.''

''Just a quiet moment together, Ju-Ju,'' Marsh said languorously, lifting his handsome head.

''And tremendously touching it was, too!'' She smiled indulgently. ''But we must return to our guests. Marsh, would you mind having a word with the band? They don't seem to be paying any attention to Ian. The volume is enough to loosen your fillings. Ros, you might like to touch up your lipstick. Marsh seems to have kissed it off. Honestly, I haven't felt so good in years. Tonight has been wonderful but you've no idea how much I'm looking forward to the wedding.''

Marsh's blue eyes met Roslyn's over his sister's tawny head. ''Never as much as we are,'' he said.

Anne McAllister was born in California. She spent long lazy summers daydreaming on local beaches and studying surfers, swimmers and volleyball players in an effort to find the perfect hero. She finally did, not on the beach, but in a university library where she was working. She, her husband and their four children have since moved to the midwest. She taught, copy-edited, capped deodorant bottles, and ghostwrote sermons before turning to her first love, writing romance fiction.

Anne has now been writing for Mills & Boon® for nearly fifteen years and has published fifteen books, which have been distributed all over the world.

THE ALEXAKIS BRIDE
by
ANNE MCALLISTER

CHAPTER ONE

'A MAN can never have too many women.'

Damon Alexakis could remember his father saying that as far back as he was able to recall. The old man's rich baritone practically caressed the words as he said them. And then he would look at his only son and give him a conspiratorial wink.

At the ripe old age of thirty-four, when a single man in possession of all the right instincts might most likely have been expected to concur wholeheartedly, Damon Alexakis begged to differ.

It wasn't that he didn't like women. He did. The sort he could take to dinner, take to bed, and forget about the next morning.

It was the other women who were the bane of his existence — the women Aristotle Alexakis had most adored.

But then Aristotle had never been surrounded by and responsible for a widowed mother and six — count them, *six* — hellish sisters. Not to mention five-year-old twin nieces.

The old man had died when Damon was only eighteen, while the girls were still charming everyone in sight. His father, Damon often thought grimly, didn't know what he'd missed.

Now, as Damon drummed his pen on the top of his broad teak desk, then stared distractedly out the window at the midtown New York skyline, he wished, not for the first time, that he were an orphaned only child.

He could have done without them all — without his

5

mother, who was trying to settle him down and provide
him with the Perfect Alexakis Bride, without Pandora
who had lately dashed off with a shifty Las Vegas
blackjack dealer, without Electra who was shedding
her clothes in that off-colour, off-off-off Broadway
production in the name of art, without Chloe who had
taken off for darkest Africa without a word, without
Daphne who'd bought all those chinchillas on the hoof
because she was sorry for them and not because they'd
make lovely coats, without Arete who just this morning had stalked into his office and quit to take a job
with Strahan Brothers, Importers, his biggest compet-
itors, and most especially, at the moment, without his
eldest sister, Sophia, whose pregnancy was at present
complicating his life.

Why, Damon lifted his eyes and asked the heavens,
should any man have to worry about his sister's
pregnancy? Why shouldn't it be her husband's
problem?

Because, he answered on behalf of the heavens, her
husband, Stephanos, *was* the problem.

He and Kate McKee.

Kate McKee.

The woman even sounded like trouble. A fiery and
frolicsome Titian-haired temptress — exactly the sort
of woman that his philandering brother-in-law would
be eager to take to bed.

Had no doubt already taken to bed, Damon
reminded himself savagely, stabbing his pen into the
desk blotter.

All those other mother's helpers Stephanos had
hired — Stacy and Tracy and Casey and whoever else
had come and gone keeping an eye on his and Sophia's
impish twins in the last two months — had been mere
red herrings.

It was Kate McKee whom Stephanos had been

intent on installing in his and Sophia's Park Avenue apartment. And in his bed.

Damon knew he should have been suspicious from the moment Stephanos had announced that the doctor recommended a nanny. His brother-in-law was never eager to lay out a penny more than necessary, much less voluntarily pay someone to help not him but his wife.

But Stephanos had been all soulful eyes and deep concern when he'd come into Damon's office that afternoon two months ago. 'The doctor is worried about Sophia. He says she's in danger of miscarrying. She needs someone to keep an eye on the twins.'

'I'll take care of it,' Damon had promised, phone against his ear. He scratched Sophia's name on a pad at the same time he was trying to catch the particulars on a crystal shipment due from Venice that afternoon.

But Stephanos had given Damon an airy wave of his hand. 'It's not your problem. I'm just telling you. I'll interview the girls myself.'

Damon ground his teeth now. He should have known better. Everything that even vaguely affected the lives of any of the Alexakis women ended up being his problem sooner or later!

Kate McKee.

What the hell was he going to do about her?

Fire her tail. That was what he'd like to do. He'd like to drop-kick her from here to Siberia, and send his miserable brother-in-law spiralling the South Pole while he was at it.

He couldn't.

Because Sophia, heaven help him, adored her dear Miss Kate!

'She's such a competent person. So clever. So cheerful. And she takes such good care of the girls. You can't know what a relief it is. Knowing Kate's in charge makes me feel so much better.' Sophia had said all that to him just this morning.

She'd said other equally enthusiastic things about her husband's mistress in the past two weeks. But then Damon hadn't realised what Stephanos was up to.

Now he knew. He'd heard the rumours like everyone else. Except so far, thank God, Sophia. He was going to make sure she never heard them.

And he'd have loved to deal with both Stephanos and his lady love in the way they so richly deserved, except——

'The doctor says I'm doing much better since Kate came,' Sophia had gone on to say. 'She makes all the difference. I don't know what I'd do without Kate.'

So his hands were tied. For the moment at least.

But that didn't mean he was going to tolerate such underhanded goings-on. There was no way he was going to stand by and watch his brother-in-law make a fool of Sophia.

His hands clenched into fists as he contemplated what he'd like to do to Stephanos. Would the competent Miss McKee find her lover quite so attractive with his face rearranged?

But again, he couldn't do that.

Because Sophia would find out.

And now, of all times, the high-strung Sophia needed shielding.

No, he couldn't shift Stephanos's nose for him, and he couldn't blacken his eyes. But he could do a little bit of rearranging.

And Damon intended to start with Kate McKee's expectations!

The phone buzzed. He picked it up, cradling it against his shoulder. 'I thought you'd gone home,' he said to Lilian, his secretary.

'I live here,' Lilian said drily. 'We both do.'

'It seems like it,' Damon admitted. 'What's up?'

'Your mother. On line two.'

'Now?' He glanced at his watch, frowning. 'It's almost two in the morning in Athens.' He sighed. 'All right. Put her through.'

He wondered what disaster had befallen Helena Alexakis this time. His mother was the original clinging vine, a woman who counted on her man to solve everything. And since her husband had died, she never made a move without discussing it with her son. Except, Damon thought grimly, in the case of her search for his perfect bride.

'Damon? Is that you, my son? You are not home? You are still working?'

'Yes, Mama, I'm still working. What's wrong?'

'Nothing. Not one little thing.' He could hear her good cheer even above the transatlantic crackle on the line. 'I'm calling to tell you the good news.'

Damon straightened up, flexing his shoulders, smiling, too, relieved that for once there was no problem. 'Good news, Mama? What's that?'

'I am coming to New York.' A dramatic pause. 'And I am bringing Marina.'

'Your brother wants to meet me?' Kate stopped paring the apple she held in her hand and looked at her employer a bit dubiously.

'This afternoon at three,' Sophia agreed, lounging complacently on the sofa, her knitting untouched in her lap while she watched Kate prepare the twins' lunch.

Kate shook her head. From everything she'd heard about hard-driving, arrogant Damon Alexakis during the three weeks she'd worked for his sister, he didn't seem the sort to waste his precious time on a mother's helper. Even if the mother's helper in question actually owned Kid Kare, Inc. and didn't just work for it.

Unless, she thought with a hint of amusement, he wanted to buy in and start exporting nannies. She supposed, given his penchant for buying and selling, it might be possible. She almost wished it were. Heaven knew it would give credibility to her business's vitality.

'Why would he want to meet me?'

'Damon likes to know everyone involved with the family. It's his way,' Sophia said. 'He feels responsible.'

'Not for me. I'm responsible for myself.'

'Of course. I admire your independence,' Sophia said wistfully. 'I could never be like you. But Damon is a bit old-fashioned, and it's important to humour him. You don't mind, do you?'

'No, of course not.' Kate was aware of the fragility of Sophia's temperament. She had learned quickly not to do or say anything that would make Sophia worry needlessly. She gave the older woman a quick smile. 'I'll be delighted to meet him.'

It would be a chance to tell him a few home truths, she thought. Like what a philandering jerk his brother-in-law was.

If she hadn't known she'd be leaving Sophia in the lurch at a dangerous time, Kate would have left in the middle of the second week, the second she'd escaped from Stephanos's marauding hands and mouth the night he had cornered her in the kitchen. She'd hoped a bit of cold-shoulder treatment would solve the problem. But from the way he was watching her, almost leering whenever Sophia's back was turned, she feared he was biding his time.

If Damon Alexakis was the superman everyone seemed to think he was, maybe he could put a stop to Stephanos's lechery before Kate stopped it herself with a well-placed knee which would cost him some pain, her some embarrassment, and Sophia the woman she needed to keep the twins under control.

Kate wasn't quite sure how she was going to tell Damon Alexakis that, however. She was still mulling it over when the taxi let her off outside the midtown building where Alexakis Enterprises had its offices.

The building was forty storeys — marble and glass. Very sleek and modern-looking, exuding a sort of wealthy energy that reminded Kate all too much of the building four blocks north where her father had his own corporate headquarters.

It made her own tiny office in a converted floor-through brownstone apartment from the mid-seventies seem a store-front venture indeed. She'd certainly been pipe-dreaming when she'd thought he might be interested in it. Damon Alexakis would never be concerned with a small potatoes business like hers!

No, Sophia had to be right. He only wanted to look her over, make sure that Kate McKee wasn't the sort of Irish serving girl whose backward ways and bog-bred brogue might corrupt his precious nieces!

Well, she had no fears of facing him about that.

Lifting her chin and smoothing her hair as best she could, Kate marched into the lift and punched the button for the twentieth floor.

'Mr Alexakis is expecting you,' the secretary, a competent-looking woman in her fifties, told her when Kate gave her name. 'Come with me.'

Turning, she led Kate down a short hall and rapped briskly on the door at the end. 'Ms McKee is here,' she announced, opening it and stepping aside so Kate could enter.

The room was more welcoming than Kate had imagined. The furniture was all streamlined modern teak, but the shelves held more than the requisite books and papers. On them Kate also saw beautifully crafted Greek pottery, olive wood carvings and a set of jade chessmen. Hanging from the ceiling in the corner of the room was a mobile of various fantastic fish, glittering and iridescent, moving gently now as the door opened and closed.

Damon Alexakis didn't seem to notice. He was sitting at his desk, scanning an invoice. He didn't look up until he'd finished it and signed it at the bottom. Then his gazed lifted and Kate found herself staring into a pair of dark brown assessing eyes. He didn't smile.

Kate did. It was the first thing she told all her prospective employees. 'Smile. First impressions are important. And our clients want to know they're entrusting their children to happy people.'

She'd always been sure that smiles swayed people's opinions. She was quite sure hers had no effect on Damon Alexakis.

'Mr Alexakis,' she began determinedly, offering her hand, 'it's a pleasure to meet you.'

He didn't rise, didn't take her hand. He stayed right where he was, his only movement the lifting of one dark brow. 'I can't imagine why.'

The slight hint of a Greek accent she'd been expecting, the cold disbelief in his tone she had not. Kate pulled her hand back and frowned. 'Sophia has spoken of you a great deal.'

'Indeed? And did she tell you I won't tolerate adultery.'

Kate straightened up sharply. 'I beg your pardon?'

He gave a harsh laugh and stood up. She took a step backward. He was far taller than she'd expected. Stephanos was only an inch or two taller than she was. Sophia was a tiny woman.

'Nervous, Ms McKee?' he drawled.

'Should I be?'

'Damned right you should. I know you've pulled the wool over Sophia's eyes. She thinks you're God's gift.' His mouth twisted bitterly. 'The more fool she. But I know different.'

'And what exactly is it that you think you know, Mr Alexakis?'

'All about you. And Stephanos.'

'Stephanos? *And me*?'

She didn't have to guess what he thought any longer. It was all too clear. Be calm, she always told her prospective nannies. Be steady and rational.

Kate saw red. 'You think Stephanos and I —? Let me tell you something about your precious brother-in-law, Mr Alexakis! Stephanos Andropolis is a womanising creep. It's no wonder you can't keep a mother's helper, the way he acts! Every one of my girls had the same complaint.'

It was Damon Alexakis's turn to look astonished. Still his eyes narrowed and he paused before he asked, 'What are you saying, Ms McKee? Are you denying that you and Stephanos —'

'I most certainly am!'

He gave a rude, disbelieving snort. 'You didn't meet him at the Plaza Hotel last Wednesday?'

Oh, hell, Kate thought. She knew her cheeks were reddening. It was the curse of her ivory complexion. 'I was meeting my father,' she said stiffly.

'Your father looks a lot like Stephanos?'

'No, of course not. I had met my father for lunch. It was my day off. He was there with a business associate and —' she didn't want to explain this, didn't want to even think about the foolishness she'd committed last Wednesday '—and as we were leaving, I—I ran into Stephanos.'

'Who just happened to be there, too. A coincidence?' Damon asked in a silky tone.

'I don't know what he was doing there,' Kate said flatly. She had only thanked heaven at the time that he was.

'You must have been very glad to see him,' Damon said. His eyes were watching her intently.

'I was, as a matter of fact,' she said irritably.

'So glad that you tucked your arm in his and kissed him? So glad that you went off with him towards the rooms?'

'I never went to his room! I didn't even know he had a room!'

'Of course you didn't,' Damon said with patent disbelief.

'If you think I'm having an affair with your brother-in-law, you're a fool.'

'You're the one who's the fool, Ms McKee,' Damon said flatly. 'Stephanos won't marry you, if that's what you're hoping for.'

'I don't want to marry Stephanos! I don't even like him! He makes me sick!'

'Protesting a bit much, aren't you?' he asked with deceptive mildness.

Kate sighed. She wanted to tear her hair. Damn Stephanos. Damn her father, whose plans she'd been trying to thwart by pretending to be glad to see Stephanos. And damn Damon Alexakis for putting his own construction on what had been an act of desperation on her part, and certainly not encouragement to Stephanos.

The last thing Kate wanted was an affair.

No, that wasn't quite true. The last thing she wanted was to get married—and that was her father's plan.

She ventured a look at Damon. He was looking at her, his expression harsh and sceptical. She remem-

bered everything she'd ever heard about him—how
clever he was, how smart, how, according to her
father, a man would have to get up damned early in
the morning to put anything over on Damon Alexakis.

She didn't imagine he was going to be satisfied with
anything less than the truth.

Did she want to tell him the truth?

No.

Did she have a choice? Not really. Not when a man
as powerful as Damon Alexakis thought she was out
to ruin his sister's marriage. All it would take would
be a few words from a man like him and Kate's
fledgling business, which she had worked so hard to
develop, would die without a prayer.

Her father, disapproving all the while, had at least
vowed not to act against her business venture.

'I won't stop you, Kate,' he'd said when she'd
announced her plans to open Kid Kare. 'I won't have
to. You'll see how hard it is, and you'll come around.
You'll stop yourself.'

His certainty that she would fail had done more to
encourage her determination than anything. She'd
begun Kid Kare the next week, and had worked now
for three years. At last she was getting a reputation for
placing competent, well-mannered, responsible people
in childcare situations.

She was succeeding in spite of his prediction of
failure. Eugene DeMornay didn't acknowledge it, and
he certainly hadn't ever given his daughter his blessing.
But it was a sure sign of her success, that he was now
taking another tack—he was proposing a marriage
between her and Jeffrey.

There was no way Kate was marrying Jeffrey. Or
anyone else. Not after her marriage to Bryce!

If her father wanted a male successor, he'd have to

adopt one. Kate's future was all tied up with Kid Kare — provided Damon Alexakis left it standing.

'I can explain,' she said quietly now, composing herself as best she could.

'Oh?' Once more he lifted that mocking brow.

'It will take a little time.'

'If it's an entertaining story, I suppose I can make the time,' he said with a hint of irony. He gestured towards the chair facing the desk, inviting her wordlessly to sit down.

Kate did. He sat down opposite her on the other side of the desk. He looked as tough and intimidating sitting down as he had standing up, as if he could squash her entire future with a phone call.

That thought gave her the courage to begin.

'You have, perhaps, heard of Eugene DeMornay?'

She saw a flicker of surprise in Damon's eyes at the start of her story. 'I've met him,' he acknowledged. 'He's a barracuda.'

'Takes one to know one,' Kate muttered. 'He's also my father.'

This time there was no concealing the surprise in his expression. He scowled and leaned forward to look at her ringless hand. 'McKee an assumed name?'

'I'm a widow. My husband died four years ago in an accident.'

He looked momentarily taken aback. 'I'm sorry.'

'I've recovered now.'

'Obviously.'

'By throwing myself into my work,' Kate said firmly through gritted teeth. It wasn't entirely the truth, but she wasn't detailing her disastrous marriage to Bryce for Damon Alexakis. 'After Bryce died, I needed something to keep me busy. I was an early childhood education major in college. I have a graduate degree in psychology. I decided to start Kid Kare because I believe very strongly that with so many families in which both parents work, it is essential for parents to have loving, caring people to entrust with their children.'

'Like you?' His sarcasm was clear.

'Exactly like me,' Kate said. 'And like Tracy Everson, and Stacy Jerome and the three other girls whom I sent to take care of your nieces. But trust is a two-way street, Mr Alexakis. And your brother-in-law violated it in every case.'

He stared at her. 'You're telling me Stephanos was after all of them?'

'That's exactly what I'm telling you.'

He didn't say a word. A line appeared between his brows as he continued staring at her. Kate stared back, determined not to look away.

Finally he shrugged. 'Go on.'

She blinked, then coloured. 'Go on? With what? You want me to tell you what he did?'

A faint smile touched Damon's mouth. 'If you like. Or you could tell me why you were after him.'

'I was not "after him",' Kate said sharply.

He steepled his fingers and looked at her over the tops of them. 'Then suppose you tell me what you were doing.'

Kate sighed. 'I had just finished having lunch with my father and his associate, Jeffrey Hardesty. We were having a slight. . .difference of opinion, and I. . .well, I. . .needed an excuse to get away. I looked up and saw Stephanos. I don't know why he was there. But I went up to him and I——' she stopped for a moment, gathering courage, then plunged on '—I acted more enthusiastic about seeing him than I felt.'

'Linked arms with him? Kissed him? That sort of thing?' The sarcasm was evident in every word.

'I didn't kiss him. He—he kissed me,' she muttered,

looking down at her fingers for a moment before lifting her gaze and staring at him, defying him to dispute it.

'And if I believe that, you're going to sell me the Acropolis, right?'

'Oh, forget it!' Kate got to her feet. 'I don't know why I'm bothering. You've already decided what sort of person I am. And given that, no doubt you'll convince Sophia to fire me. Well, fine. I'll save you the trouble. I quit.' She turned and started for the door.

'Ms McKee!' His voice cracked through the air like a whip. 'Sit down.'

She barely glanced over her shoulder. 'No, thank you.' She reached for the doorknob.

A second later, she was nudged aside and Damon Alexakis had positioned himself between her and the door.

'I said, sit down.' The words were measured and menacing.

Kate didn't budge. 'I'm not one of your employees, Mr Alexakis. I don't have to obey you.' She met his gaze defiantly.

He was standing so close now that she could count the breaths he took, could see the tautness around his mouth and could even notice the way a muscle ticked in his jaw. She wanted to take a step back. She stood her ground. 'We teach children politeness, Mr Alexakis. Did no one teach you?'

She saw his mouth tighten even further. 'Please, Ms McKee,' he said after a long moment. 'Sit down.'

There was no sarcasm in his tone this time, but no friendliness either. He had given an inch, but no more.

'I won't sit here listening to you throw accusations at me.'

'But I should sit here and listen to you throw them at Stephanos?'

'You accused him first.'

A corner of his mouth twisted when he caught her point. 'So I did.'

'Then do my accusations seem entirely unreasonable?'

He shoved a hand through his black hair. 'I don't know. I suppose not,' he said reluctantly. 'But some of those girls were no more than sixteen!'

'They were at least eighteen, all of them. I only place adults. Not that that excuses your brother-in-law,' Kate added quickly.

'Why do you keep sending them, if he's such a lecher?'

'I'm not sending them for him! Your sister needs someone to help with the girls. And——' Kate gave a tiny shrug '—placing a mother's helper in such a prestigious family would be a coup for the agency. The business is only three years old. We need all the recommendations we can get. Besides, it was a matter of pride.'

'No job too dirty?'

Kate flushed. 'Something like that.'

'So you took it on yourself?'

'I thought perhaps he was attracted because the girls were relatively young.'

'And you're so old.'

'I'm twenty-eight.'

'A veritable ancient,' he mocked.

'Old enough to handle your brother-in-law.'

'Apparently not. He doesn't seem to be able to keep his hands off you, according to Alice.'

Alice was the cook. Kate wondered how many other spies Damon had in his network.

'He will. I'll make sure of it. I hadn't intended to be there long anyway. I have a perfect woman for the job, Mrs Partridge. She's nearly sixty. A delightful grandmotherly type. Unfortunately she's finishing up a temporary assignment at the moment and so I was filling in.'

Damon didn't comment on that. He cocked his head. 'Tell me more about this disagreement with your father.'

Kate groaned inwardly, having hoped he'd forgotten about that. 'It wasn't important.'

'Liar.'

Kate bristled. 'What makes you say that?'

'Either you're having an affair with Stephanos or you're using him as a decoy to get away from Daddy. Which is it?'

'He had just suggested that Jeffrey and I get married,' she admitted.

'What did Jeffrey have to say?'

'He didn't. Not then. But I suppose he was willing.' She was crimson, embarrassed as usual at the crassness of her father's tactics.

'And you weren't?'

'No!'

'Not in love with Jeffrey?'

'Certainly not. Besides, I'm not interested in marrying again. I don't want any husband.'

He considered that. She knew what he was concluding—that she had loved Bryce too much, that she was sure she'd never love again and be able to replace him. It was what everyone thought, and Kate was quite willing to let them think it.

'Interesting,' Damon said. He looked at her assessingly for a moment, then his gaze moved to the chair. 'If I move away from the door are you going to bolt again?'

'Are you through accusing me?'

He nodded. 'For the moment.'

Kate, who had begun to relax, stiffened again at his words.

He smiled grimly. 'Sit down, Kate McKee. We have things to talk about.'

'What things?'

He nodded at the chair and moved towards the desk himself. But this time, instead of sitting down behind it, he hitched one hip up on the corner of it and waited until she'd come and sat.

'Things like what you told your father when you hit on—excuse me—when you "approached" Stephanos so, shall we say, enthusiastically.'

'What difference does that make?'

'It makes a difference.'

'I don't see how,' she said stubbornly.

'Tell me.'

'Oh, good grief. You can guess, can't you?' She glared at him irritably.

'I can make a fair stab at it, yes. Something about not possibly being able to marry Jeffrey because Stephanos was your man?' He said it all with just enough mockery in his voice to make her cringe.

'Something like that,' Kate mumbled, mortified to hear it all spelled out. It had been such a spur-of-the-moment thing! And so incredibly stupid. She had been horrified at her father's suggestion, had made desperate excuses, met her father's doubting gaze, then glanced up and spotted Stephanos—the rest had simply happened!

Kate had never lied in her life. And with good reason, she thought now, if every time she did so, she was going to get caught up in a mess like this one!

'I know it was stupid,' she admitted gruffly.

She expected he'd agree with that, but all he asked was, 'Did you tell your father his name?'

'Of course not! Do you think I'm a complete idiot?

I just said, "There he is now," and jumped up and ran over to him. I certainly didn't introduce them!'

'What will happen when Daddy finds out you lied?'

She shifted uncomfortably in her chair. 'I'll cross that bridge when I come to it.'

'How?'

'I don't know yet,' she said crossly, looking away across the room. Beyond the mobile she could see the Empire State Building, the lights beginning to gleam as the sun set. She focused on them, trying to blot out the man leaning on the desk barely eighteen inches from her.

'Perhaps I can help you out.'

She blinked and looked back at him. 'Why should you?'

He shrugged. 'I'm a businessman, Ms McKee. If I can help you and help myself at the same time, I think that's good business.' He looked almost bored as he spoke.

Kate couldn't imagine any sort of dealings the two of them might conduct that would be mutually beneficial. But then he was the business tycoon, not her.

'What did you have in mind?'

'I want you to marry me.'

CHAPTER TWO

'VERY funny.'

Not only was Damon Alexakis powerful, he had a warped sense of humour. Just what I need, Kate thought irritably.

'Who's laughing?'

She looked up at him, startled. He was staring implacably back at her, not a glimmer of laughter in those hard, dark eyes.

'You can't be serious!'

One heavy brow lifted. 'I don't joke about business matters, Ms McKee.'

'Marriage is not a business matter!'

'Sometimes marriage is not a business matter,' he agreed smoothly. 'Sometimes it's a matter of hormones and pregnancy and some ridiculous thing called love. But for thousands of years it's been an economic decision, no more, no less.'

'And that's what you want?'

'That's what I want.'

She shook her head. She felt as if she'd walked through the looking-glass or fallen down a rabbit hole. Certainly she felt as if she'd missed something vital in this conversation. 'It doesn't make sense,' she said finally. 'Why would you want to marry me?'

'I don't want to marry you. I need to marry you.'

'But why?'

He shoved away from the desk, pushed his hands into the pockets of his trousers, and paced around the room, all vestiges of cool detached boredom a thing of the past.

'I do, that's all,' he said after a moment. He didn't look at her, choosing instead to stare out the window into the deepening twilight.

Kate regarded him quizzically, interested in how suddenly agitated he'd become. 'Not fair, Mr Alexakis,' she said after a moment.

He spun on his heel and glared at her. 'What's that supposed to mean?'

She gave him a faint smile. 'I had to tell you my sordid little tale. Let's hear yours.'

He gritted his teeth. 'There's nothing sordid about it.'

'But there is a tale?'

'It's business.'

'And as the person you've approached to take part in this business, however non-sordid as it might be, I have every right to know the particulars.'

He scowled at her. Kate smiled equably back and didn't say a word. He muttered something under his breath, then raked his fingers through his hair, mussing it even more.

'It's my mother,' he blurted out after a moment.

Kate smiled. 'Ah. I see. Your mother and my father.'

'My mother has nothing in common with your father!'

'Maybe not. As you so aptly described him, my father is a barracuda. What's your mother like?'

Damon rubbed the back of his neck, considering. Then his mouth twisted slightly. 'Holding to a sea-world metaphor? A barnacle.'

'Once she attaches herself, she doesn't let go?'

He nodded grimly. 'Ever since my father died, she's focused on me. Consults me about every damned thing from changing the light bulbs to buying and selling stocks.'

'Well, I can see where that might be a bit of a trial,' Kate agreed. 'But I hardly see how getting married will solve it.'

'That's the other part,' he muttered. 'She's determined to see me happy.'

'Married,' Kate translated.

'Right.' He shot her a harried look. 'She's got five daughters left to marry off and that isn't enough. She's determined to find me the perfect wife. She even says it in hallowed tones: 'The Alexakis Bride'. Like the Holy Grail.'

Kate smiled at his tone. 'Well, in the words of one of our former first ladies, "Just Say No".'

'It won't work.'

'It never does,' Kate agreed complacently. 'That's what's wrong with it.'

Damon gave her a narrow look. She gave him an impish grin in return, then sobered, remembering that the proposition he'd made her was no laughing matter.

'Well, I don't see how marrying me will solve your problem. Married is married, however you look at it.'

'No. Married to you is a business arrangement. Married to Marina is——'

'Whoa! Hold on. Who's Marina? This isn't a hypothetical marriage she's trying to arrange, then?'

He grimaced. 'Not any more.'

'She found her? The Alexakis Bride?'

'Apparently.'

'So, who is the lucky lady?'

He glowered at her sarcastic tone. 'Her name is Marina Stavros. She's the daughter of one of my mother's dearest friends.'

'Your version of Jeffrey.'

'If you like,' he said with bad grace.

'You don't, I take it.'

Dark brows drew together. 'Like Marina? Of course

I like Marina. She's young and sweet and beautiful and everything a man could ask for in a wife.'

'Then why don't you marry her?'

'Because, damn it, I don't want a wife! Not now. And when I do, I'll pick her.'

'But if you marry me——'

'You're a business deal. I marry you and you can stay on to help Sophia, as her sister-in-law this time. I guarantee——' he said the word as if it had a hundred-pound weight attached '—that Stephanos won't lay a finger on you. I also guarantee to send plenty of business your way when we're done.'

'We're going to be done?'

'Of course we're going to be done,' he said impatiently. 'You don't think I want to be married to you forever, do you?'

'No, of course not,' Kate said hastily. 'I don't want to be married to you at all,' she pointed out, in case he thought she was enthusiastic about his little plan.

'Not even to save your business?' He gave her a nasty little smile. 'That is what you've been worrying about, isn't it? That I'll do you in?'

Kate's teeth came together with a snap. 'You wouldn't dare.'

'Wouldn't I?'

She had a pretty good idea that he would. And he wouldn't lose any sleep over it either.

'Plus,' he went on, as if their last exchange hadn't even taken place, 'you get proof positive that you were telling the truth to Daddy and can't possibly marry Jeffrey.'

'But I'd still be married to you,' Kate reminded him.

'In name only.'

Her eyes widened. 'Don't you. . .I mean, is there. . . Do you not—um,—*like* women?'

'Damn it! Of course I like women!'

'Oh. I see. You mean you'll be. . .getting it. . .elsewhere.'

'It?' He gave her a sardonic look.

'You know what I mean,' Kate said awkwardly, aware that her colour was deepening again.

'Yes, Ms McKee,' he drawled mockingly. 'I know what you mean.' He sighed and rocked back on his heels. 'And no, I won't be getting "it" anywhere as long as the marriage lasts. I promise you that. I don't condone adultery. I told you that.' He gave her a level look and she remembered what he'd thought about her and Stephanos. 'Well?'

Kate knotted her fingers together, wishing she was dreaming, hoping to wake up. 'This is the most ridiculous thing I've ever heard,' she muttered. 'I can't think of anything crazier.'

'Marrying Jeffrey?' he suggested smoothly.

'I am not going to marry Jeffrey! I have no need of a man to support me. I have a business of my own.'

'For the moment,' he agreed silkily.

Kate's eyes snapped up to meet his. 'Damn you.'

'Damn me all you like,' he said easily. 'But I'm trying to do you a favour. Stop being such an obstructionist, Ms McKee. It's tiresome. Do you want to save your business or not?'

'Of course I do.'

'Do you agree that Sophia needs help?'

'Yes.'

'And do you agree that being able to produce a fiancé on demand will get your father to lay off about Jeffrey?'

'Probably,' she muttered.

'Then where's the problem?'

Kate couldn't answer that. Everything he said made perfect sense in a horrible skewed way.

'But I don't love you,' she protested.

Damon snorted. 'And I sure as hell don't love you. I told you, marriage has nothing to do with love. It's——'

'Business,' Kate filled in for him.

He nodded. 'Ah, you're catching on. Forget love, Ms McKee. You had that once, apparently. So cherish it. I promise I won't usurp his place in your heart. All we'll be doing is acting out the old axiom: you scratch my back and I'll scratch yours.'

She just looked at him. The room was eerily silent.

'For how long?' Kate asked at last.

He gave her a long look, as if he knew she was really considering it at last. 'Not long. A few months.'

'But once you're divorced, won't they——?'

'Marina's family won't accept me if I'm divorced.'

'I see.'

'Will Jeffrey?'

'Accept me? He'd accept me if I was breathing, I think,' Kate said grimly. What mattered to Jeffrey was getting his hooks permanently in DeMornay Enterprises. She was a means to an end, nothing more. And she suspected her father knew it—and didn't care. He liked Jeffrey. That was enough.

'Well, how long, then?' Damon was looking impatient.

'I haven't said I'll even do it.'

'How long?'

'Six months. A year. I don't know.' Kate shifted restlessly. 'Another marriage to someone he didn't approve might make my father think I was hopeless,' she said, voicing the notion as it occurred to her, musing, considering the notion. It was the first comforting thought she'd had in several hours.

Damon looked at her closely. 'He didn't approve of your first marriage?'

'No.' Her eyes met his defiantly.

'All the more reason, then. Sophia will have what she needs. Stephanos's hands will be tied. And you and I will be protected from our respective parents' meddling in our lives.' Damon gave her a confident businessman's smile. 'What have you got to lose?'

'Plenty, I'm sure,' Kate said wryly.

'If it's money you're worried about——'

'Money is not the issue.'

'What then? Not love again?' His tone gave the word a bitter twist.

Kate shrugged helplessly. 'I don't know. I——'

'Look, Ms McKee, you can sit here and dither all night and never be any more certain. The question is, who are you going to let run your life? You or your father?'

'How about you or my father?' Kate suggested.

'I'm not trying to run it. I told you, this is business.' Damon shot back his cuff and took a look at his watch. 'And I have another business deal to make in a phone call to Hawaii in ten minutes. So what's it to be, Ms McKee? What I'm proposing is a one-year marriage. Are you in or not?'

Are you in or not?

Far below in the streets Kate could hear the wail of a siren, the blast of a taxi horn; far above there was the steady thrum of a jet engine. Right in front of her, Damon Alexakis's fingers beat an impatient tattoo on the top of his desk.

Will you marry me or not?

A myriad images collided in her mind: Sophia's exhausted face, the cherubic smiles of Leda and Christina, her five-year-old twins, the smugly smiling face of Jeffrey Hardesty, the tired determination in her father's eyes, the newly stencilled sign in the brownstone's window that said in elegant silver gothic 'KID KARE, INC.'.

Her baby and Sophia's. Those were the images that stayed in her mind. Sophia did need her, there was no doubt about that. And Kate was glad to help out. Perhaps she was even living vicariously. She would never have a child of her own now. KID KARE was her child.

Her business was all she had — she'd been no great success as either a daughter or a wife. If she lost it, she didn't know what she would do.

And Damon could see that she did lose it if he set his mind to it. She hadn't a doubt in the world about that.

Her father wasn't going to take no for an answer any more than Damon's mother would. He was almost seventy. Old enough to retire, he'd been pointing out. If only he had someone in the family he could trust. A reliable, hard-nosed businessman like himself. Someone like Jeffrey, for instance.

Or someone like Damon Alexakis.

The thought brought a smile to Kate's face. Wouldn't Jeffrey's smug smile vanish if he were faced with Damon Alexakis across a boardroom table?

And what would her father think of Damon? He was certainly more of a force to be reckoned with than the smug, bland Jeffrey. In that way at least he was a man cast in Eugene DeMornay's stainless steel mould.

Even when the marriage ended in divorce, her father's opinion of her could hardly be worse than it was already. Besides, he might not even live to see that happen. He had a bad heart. He was always telling her that, too, in an effort to prod her into suitable matrimony.

'You're amused?' Damon's voice cut into her reverie.

'Yes, I am.'

He pushed away from the desk, standing up and

frowning down at her. 'I take it then that you're
declining?'

Kate thought about her father, about Jeffrey, about
Sophia and Stephanos, about babies, both human and
business. She sat up straight and looked at him with
guileless blue eyes. 'On the contrary, Mr Alexakis.
I'm saying yes.'

He couldn't believe he'd done it. He sat in the stillness
of his office and listened to her footsteps recede down
the hallway and thought he needed his head examined.

Had he really just proposed marriage to a woman
he didn't know? A woman he'd wanted to wipe off the
face of the earth less than an hour ago?

Yes, he thought, and his mouth twisted into a grin
as he thought it. He had indeed. And it was perhaps a
further sign of his mental befuddlement that it didn't
seem far-fetched.

What was a wife, anyway, but one more encum-
brance, why not have one who was pert and willowy
and had big blue eyes that snapped when she was
angry? Besides, Kate McKee was at least destined to
be useful, helping out with the twins.

He rubbed his hands together, pleased with himself.
It was a great solution. It would spike his mother's
guns, take care of Sophia's problem, infuriate
Stephanos, and incidentally help out the determined
Ms McKee.

Best of all, in a year, she would be gone.

What more could he ask?

'Damon!' Sophia beamed the moment he appeared in
the doorway of the living-room. 'How lovely! What a
surprise!'

She moved to get up from the couch, but he waved
her back down, crossing the room and kissing her

cheek. He glanced around for any sign of Kate and the children, but Sophia was alone. She was round and smiling, and Damon thought, albeit grudgingly, that she looked better than he'd seen her in several months.

'How are you feeling?'

'Tired. The baby is kicking me day and night. The twins were easier than this one. But I'd certainly be worse if it weren't for Kate.' Sophia's gaze went fondly to the hallway which led to the children's room where Damon supposed she was. 'So, what did you think of her when you met her yesterday? Isn't she a dear?'

'A dear,' he echoed, allowing a hint of approval to creep into his voice. He had to give the impression of being intrigued, smitten almost, without seeming besotted. 'And very attractive as well.'

Sophia's eyes widened. 'Kate? Attractive?' She looked at Damon closely. 'I suppose you're right. She's not striking really. Not tall. No cheekbones to speak of. But there is a sort of warm wholesomeness about her.' She gave her brother a shrewd look. 'Not precisely your type, I wouldn't have said.'

Damon tried to look hurt. 'Am I so predictable, then?'

'So far. You've always gone for the showgirl sort— the love 'em and leave 'em ladies.'

He grinned rakishly. 'The ones who aren't really ladies, you mean.'

Sophia laughed. 'Just so.' She yawned and stretched and set her book aside. 'So, what *are* you doing here, Damon, at five o'clock in the afternoon. Surely you didn't come because of a fascination with Kate.'

'Can't a brother visit his sister without having an ulterior motive?'

'Some brothers can. Not you.'

Damon sighed. 'How devastating to be so transparent. I came to take my nieces for a carriage ride in

Central Park. I promised them, if you'll recall, the last time I was here.'

'At Christmastime.'

'I've been busy.'

'You are here to see Kate, aren't you?' She gave him an assessing look.

'She can come, too.'

'You're not to trifle with my mother's helper, Damon,' Sophia warned. 'I need her.'

Tell that to Stephanos, Damon thought grimly. 'Don't worry, Sophie.' He turned and headed towards the hallway. 'I'll have the kids back by supper.'

'And Kate?'

He grinned. 'Only if I have to.'

'It's not my evening off.'

'Sophie says you can have it.'

'I don't want it!'

Damon tossed a pair of lightweight jackets at his nieces. 'Yes, you do. Stop arguing. How's anybody going to believe you're the least bit eager to see me if you won't agree to dinner after we dump the kiddies?'

'I'm not eager,' Kate protested. She'd been having second thoughts ever since she'd agreed to his preposterous scheme. She'd planned all day long to call him up and tell him she'd changed her mind. But Sophia hadn't given her a moment to breathe.

Now here he was, bursting into the den, commandeering her as if he owned her, barking orders at the twins, herding them along to do his bidding. She stopped in the doorway.

'Move,' Damon said. He nudged Kate through the door, then turned back to his nieces. 'Hurry up, you two.'

'Yes, Uncle Damon. We're coming, Uncle Damon,' they said, scrambling into their jackets and tumbling

after him. The girls were as awestruck as everyone else
in the presence of their uncle. If he'd told them to
jump out of the window, Kate thought, they'd have
asked which one.

'I don't think ——' she began, but Damon cut her
off.

'You don't have to think. Just smile at Sophia and
tell her you'll see her later. There's a good girl.' His
hand was against her back and his fingers were practically pinching her as he steered her through the room.

Sophia watched them curiously, a smile on her face.
'It's so nice of you to keep your promises, Damon,'
she said. 'But then, you always do. Eventually.'

'I do my best.'

'Are you sure you wouldn't rather I stayed and
helped you, Sophia?' Kate asked a little desperately.

'No, no, dear. That's quite all right. I was telling
Damon that the baby has been active this afternoon,
but he seems to have settled down at last. I think I'll
nap a bit until Stephanos comes home.' She gave Kate
a little waggle of her fingers. 'You have a good time.'

'We will.' Damon ushered them all out of the room,
shutting the door firmly behind him.

'This is crazy,' Kate hissed at him as the girls
bounded ahead and pressed the button for the lift.

'Necessary,' Damon corrected.

It was a beautiful afternoon for a carriage ride, Kate
had to admit that when Damon ushered them out of
the taxi near the carriages across from the Plaza Hotel.

The nippy April winds that had plagued the city
earlier in the month were absent this afternoon, leaving almost balmy breezes in their stead. Kate could
see beds of red and yellow tulips beginning to open
and tender shoots of other young plants peeking out
of the warming soil. The buds on the trees in Central
Park had begun bursting into leaf.

The girls, skipping on either side of Damon, were enchanted with the prospect of their outing, and Damon was smiling and indulgent as he let them take his hands. Kate, seeing no way out, followed them, apprehension giving way to bemusement — for the time being at least.

The apprehension reappeared when they were bundled into the carriage and she found Leda and Christina on one bench facing forward, while she and Damon were wedged together on the opposite one. The feel of his hard body next to hers caused a momentary quickening of her heart. She edged away.

Damon slipped his arm around her and pulled her back. 'Cosy, isn't it?'

Kate shot him a fierce look. 'A little too cosy.'

He grinned. 'What's the matter, Ms McKee? Don't you like men?' His taunting rephrasing of her question to him was clearly deliberate.

'Sometimes, Mr Alexakis, I wonder if I do,' Kate said frankly.

He looked startled, but before he could respond Leda pointed to the sky and said excitedly, 'Look, Kate! Runaway balloons!'

Sure enough, more than a dozen helium-filled balloons had somehow been let loose and were floating past the treetops, their bright colours vivid against the cloudless sky.

'And look, there's the zoo where we saw the polar bears and penguins, Kate!' Christina added, bouncing up and down on the seat. 'Have you been to the zoo, Uncle Damon? We're going again next week. Do you want to come?'

'I'm sure your uncle is much too busy,' Kate said.

Damon disagreed. 'Sounds like a good idea at that.'

'You shouldn't make promises you won't keep,' Kate chastised him under her breath.

'What makes you think I won't be keeping it?'

'You're a busy man.'

'Ah, yes. But I'm also intending to be an attentive suitor.'

'We need to talk about that,' Kate began.

He closed the space between them and touched his lips to hers. 'Later,' he promised in loverlike tones.

Both girls giggled.

'Damon!' Kate said, outraged. But one glance at his nieces told her that she wasn't going to get anywhere discussing their agreement with them around. But she vowed to let him know as soon as they were alone that she couldn't go through with it.

At least that was her intention until they dropped the twins off and, instead of letting Kate go in with them, he told Sophia he was taking her to dinner. They went to Baudelaire's.

She didn't know if his choice was made by coincidence or design. But the moment they were seated and Kate opened her mouth to tell him the agreement was off, she noticed that directly across the room her father and Jeffrey were entertaining a group of Japanese businessmen.

Her father seemed equally astonished. When he first realised it was Kate he was looking at across the room, he stopped mid-sentence and stared, then recollected his purpose and continued his conversation.

But throughout the evening Eugene DeMornay's narrow gaze strayed in her direction more often than Kate would have liked, and she found herself determinedly smiling at Damon and keeping the conversation going animatedly. She didn't say a word she'd planned to say to him.

There would be time for that later, she promised herself.

Her father made no move to speak to her or even

acknowledge her during the meal. Kate wasn't surprised. Eugene DeMornay always put business first. Even when she and Damon finished and got up to leave, Kate didn't expect he would do more than stare at Damon with his laser-like gaze.

But when they were within ten feet of the table, Eugene DeMornay rose from his chair.

'Katherine.'

Kate felt Damon's fingers tighten briefly on her arm and was grateful for them there.

Her father stepped into her path and reached for her hand. 'What a surprise! I had no idea you'd be here this evening. You should have said.' He leaned towards her and Kate gave him a light peck on the cheek.

'It was a spur-of-the-moment thing,' Kate said nervously.

'Gentlemen,' Eugene turned to his guests, 'I'd like you to meet my daughter, Katherine and——' He looked from Kate to Damon expectantly.

'Damon Alexakis,' Damon introduced himself before Kate could. 'Her fiancé.'

The two Japanese gentlemen offered polite bows.

Jeffrey's jaw dropped.

Kate's father's mouth opened—and shut. His eyes widened, then narrowed. A muscle ticked in his cheek. His gaze went from Damon to Kate where it remained, harsh and accusing.

If she'd seen the slightest bit of wonder, the slightest bit of fatherly concern she would have denied Damon's assertion. She would have said there had been a mistake, they weren't sure yet, Damon was hoping.

But Eugene DeMornay didn't look fatherly. He looked furious. And if there was concern, it was all for his business and Jeffrey.

Kate pulled her hand away and slipped her fingers

through Damon's. 'You know how busy you are, Daddy. I haven't had a chance to bring Damon by to meet you.'

'I can see I've made a mistake by being so inaccessible.' His gaze went once more to Damon. 'Alexakis,' he acknowledged. 'Won't you two join us?'

'We'd be delighted,' Damon said over Kate's incipient protest. He drew over two chairs from the unoccupied table next to theirs, seating Kate next to him so closely that, every time he moved, his suit coat brushed her arm. Instead of moving away, he moved closer, slipping his arm behind her shoulders.

Eugene watched them narrowly. 'Mr Mori and I were going to have a brandy. But perhaps I should order champagne? To toast your engagement?'

'That would be appropriate,' Damon agreed smoothly. He turned and smiled into Kate's eyes, looking every bit the besotted lover.

Eugene's jaw clenched for a split second, then in a tight voice he summoned the waiter. The two Japanese gentlemen spoke to each other quietly in their own language. Jeffrey didn't say a word. Kate was gratified to notice that there was no smile on his face, smug or otherwise.

She didn't know how much her father knew about Damon. No doubt he'd heard of him. The movers and shakers of the world were always well aware of each other, even if they had never formally met.

As she sat there she could almost see their brains clicking round, adding and subtracting, assessing and defining, deciding exactly in which piegeonhole the other belonged.

She should have been feeling far more guilty than she did. But for once, as far as her dealings with her father went, it was nice to have the upper hand.

The champagne arrived and was poured. Eugene

lifted his glass. 'To my daughter, Katherine,' he said, fixing her with a speculative look. 'A woman of surprises.'

'And passion,' Damon said loud enough for Jeffrey to hear.

Kate choked on her champagne. Her face flamed. She began to cough and her eyes began to water.

Jeffrey's eyes bugged. He sat, transfixed. It was Damon who patted Kate's back, offered her water, and then his handkerchief to dab her streaming eyes. The moment she regained her breath, Kate gave him a speaking look.

He gave her a conspiratorial smile in return, then leaned forward and touched his lips to hers. 'Better now?' he asked softly.

Kate opened her mouth, still stunned by both the kiss and the tone of his voice. No sound came out. Gamely she cleared her throat, then tried again.

'S-some.' But she was never going to be able to pull this off. She wasn't the actor Damon was. 'I th-think perhaps we should go.'

'I do, too, love.' Damon got to his feet and smiled apologetically at her father, then turned to Jeffrey. 'See what I mean?' he said in a low tone. 'She can't wait to get me alone.'

Jeffrey's jaw clenched.

Mortified, Kate stepped on Damon's foot. Enough was enough, damn it.

'Goodnight, Daddy. Nice to meet you,' she said to his guests. 'Jeffrey,' she acknowledged briefly, trying to move away as quickly as she could, but Damon's hand held her fast as he made his farewells, beginning with the businessmen, ending with Kate's father.

'Good to have met you at last, Mr DeMornay.'

Eugene didn't look as if he agreed, but he did manage a frosty smile and a nod. 'Alexakis.' There was a pause, then, 'I'll speak to you tomorrow, Katherine.'

'But how long have you known him?'

'Not long.'

'Where did you meet him?'

'I've been working for his sister.'

'Babysitting?' Eugene DeMornay got a surprising amount of disgust and horror in one word.

'Caring for her five-year-old twins, yes.'

Her father snorted. 'I thought you ran the agency, Kate. Don't tell me things are so bad you have to go out and babysit yourself now!'

'I am doing it as a personal favour,' Kate said, which was as close to the truth as she was going to get. 'Sophia hasn't been well.'

'Hmph. And I suppose Damon Alexakis just happened by one day and fell head over heels?' Her father's scathing tone told Kate exactly how likely he thought that idea.

'Something like that.' If she'd felt a bit guilty after they'd left him last night, today facing his hard words and harsh tone, she felt no guilt at all.

'Nonsense. Pure nonsense. I can't believe a daughter of mine would believe such drivel. You can't possibly think he's in love with you, Katherine.'

'And why shouldn't I?'

'Oh, Kate. Grow up. He wants what you've got. DeMornay's,' he elaborated when she didn't respond.

'He has an empire of his own twice the size of yours. He doesn't need DeMornay's, Daddy.' She said it frankly and was glad to be able to say it.

'Of course he doesn't,' Eugene said irritably. 'But that doesn't mean he wouldn't like it. Men like Damon Alexakis don't take what they need, Katherine. They take what they want. I'd heard he was a clever bastard, but by heavens I didn't think he'd stoop this low.'

At his words, Kate felt the anger surging through her veins. 'Why is it so difficult for you to believe that anyone might want me for myself?'

Her father gave a short half-laugh. 'The way Bryce did?'

His words were like a knife slipped between her ribs. Bryce. Oh, yes, Bryce. Her first love. The man she'd adored. The man she'd run away with, had promised to live happily ever after with.

The man who, when he found out her father wasn't going to give them a penny, had left her flat. She supposed she was lucky that only she knew. Her father had always suspected, of course, but it had happened so quickly, he'd never found out. Bryce's fury, fuelled by drink, had led him to drive too fast. Kate became a widow only hours after she'd become an abandoned wife. She'd kept the knowledge to herself.

She spoke to her father now with as indifferent a voice as she could muster. 'Damon and Bryce are different people.'

'Alexakis is a damn sight smarter, I'll grant you that. But he's still not getting his hands on DeMornay's. I pick my successor, Katherine. Not you.'

'I never intended to pick your successor. I only want to pick my own husband. And I've done so.'

'The more fool you,' Eugene rasped, and hung up.

CHAPTER THREE

'DON'T you think you're being excessively attentive?'
Kate asked Damon the following afternoon. 'This is
the second day in a row you've spirited me away, for
goodness' sake. What's Sophia going to think?'

'Exactly what I want her to think — that I'm mad
about you.'

Kate gave a muffled snort. 'Even Sophia isn't that
gullible.'

'Sophia's a romantic, my dear. That's why she ended
up with a fool like Stephanos.'

Kate shook her head. She was a cynic herself as far
as love was concerned. Who wouldn't be after having
fallen for Bryce? But Damon Alexakis was worse than
she was by far.

She glanced out the window now, frowning as she
noticed that the taxi was heading uptown towards the
Tri-borough Bridge rather than into the heart of the
city. 'Where are we going?'

'Reno.'

'Is that a new restaurant?'

'It's a city. In Nevada.'

Kate's head whipped around and she stared at him.
'*Reno, Nevada*? You're joking.'

'I'm not.'

'Surely you don't expect us to get mar-
ried. . .today?' Kate couldn't imagine why else they'd
be going to Reno, but she hoped she was wrong. She
wasn't.

'I do.' Damon smiled a bit sardonically. 'You see. I
already know my line.'

'But — I thought you meant weeks from now! I don't want — '

'Sophia needs you right away. I want things settled so Stephanos knows right where he stands.'

'But — ' Kate stopped, her mind spinning as she tried to fathom this sudden push towards matrimony. He hadn't even hinted at it last night when he dropped her off. She looked at him suspiciously. 'What happened?'

He shifted uncomfortably. 'What do you mean? Nothing happened. We already agreed on this. I'm only getting the ball rolling.'

'You didn't mention a word about it yesterday. So what happened in the meantime? Is Marina on her way?'

Damon gritted his teeth.

Kate gave him a knowing smile. 'I thought so.'

'They'll be here in a week.'

'So give me an engagement ring.'

Damon shook his head. 'Won't work. A brief engagement is worse than no engagement at all. My mother will know it's a dodge. An engagement ring won't even slow her down. A wedding-ring will. So we're getting married.'

'It's insane,' Kate muttered.

'It's business,' Damon said flatly. 'And don't you forget it.'

Kate was hardly likely to. Damon wasn't acting like any of the other prospective grooms standing idly outside the fake New England wedding chapel that night.

While the others were holding their fiancée's hand, nibbling their ears, sneaking kisses as they waited their turn, Damon was reading the pre-nuptial agreement his lawyer had sent along, stopping now and then to

stick his cellular phone to his ear and check on the
wording of certain clauses.

Kate sat at the far end of the bench and twiddled
her thumbs. So what if everyone was giving them odd
looks? she thought.

This marriage, farce though it was, had more going
for it than her last one had.

Finally Damon said, 'It'll do the way it is. Don't
worry.' He cut off the connection, punched out
another number, and began another conversation, this
one about a crystal shipment that hadn't arrived from
Venice before he left New York.

Kate sighed and sank lower in her seat.

'Mr Alexakis? Miss McKee?' An elderly lady
appeared in the doorway to the chapel and looked
expectantly at the waiting couples.

'It's not going to spoil if it sits there overnight. It's
glass, not eggs,' Damon said into the phone, not
paying the least attention to the summons.

Kate wished she hadn't been either. She wished she
could blot the whole thing out, go home, and wake up
in the morning to find out it was all a bad dream.

'Alexakis,' the woman said more loudly, consulting
her list. 'McKee? Are you still here?'

'Here,' Kate said wearily, getting to her feet and
looking at Damon. The woman's gaze followed her
own, then she shook her head sadly.

'I told you that yesterday, Spiros,' Damon said
impatiently. 'I have to go. Talk to you later.' He rang
off, bounded to his feet, tucked the phone into the
pocket of his suit coat and grabbed Kate's hand. 'Let's
get this over with.'

Kate thought that if there was a prize given to the
woman who married most unpromisingly, she would
have won both times, hands down.

At her first wedding Bryce had been glancing over

his shoulder at every second, as if he expected her father to come striding into the Justice of the Peace's office with a shotgun and blow him away. At her second Damon stood like a mannequin, unmoving and unblinking, as if only the shell of the man was present, but the real Damon Alexakis wasn't there at all.

Probably, Kate thought grimly, he wasn't.

He was probably deep in mental machinations about some business deal that he was in the middle of. Why else would he pause so long when the minister asked him if he took her for his wife, for pity's sake?

Was he thinking they should have signed that pre-nuptial agreement, limiting her access to the Alexakis millions? Was he thinking about the meaning of the vow he was about to make? Was he considering the implications, even at the last moment, of what it meant to take someone for richer and poorer, in sickness and health, promising to love and honour her all the days of his life?

Was he coming to his senses at last?

Kate shot him a quick look.

The minister persisted in his long one, finally clearing his throat.

'I do,' Damon said suddenly. His voice was clipped, his tone brisk. There was no faltering, no hesitancy. It had all been a product of her overactive imagination, Kate told herself.

The minister turned to her. 'Do you, Katherine, take Damon —?'

She could say no. She had a choice. She could put an end to the foolishness here and now. She could act like the adult she considered herself most of the time.

And she could find herself with a bankrupt company, a chortling father, and a smug Jeffrey Hardesty just waiting for her to say yes.

A choice?

Who did she think she was kidding?

She felt Damon's fingers tighten on hers and was suddenly aware that the minister had stopped speaking, that he and Damon were both looking directly at her.

Kate swallowed. 'I do,' she said.

'I hope you weren't expecting a honeymoon,' Damon said, pouring her a glass of celebratory champagne as the jet left the runway on its return trip to New York.

Kate took the glass when he handed it to her. 'Hardly. I wasn't expecting to get married.'

Damon lifted his glass in toast. 'Life is full of surprises.'

Kate gave him a narrow look. 'I bet you aren't as philosophical when they happen to you.'

'I try to anticipate,' Damon agreed. 'To us.' He clinked his glass against hers. Kate lifted her glass to her lips and sipped in silence. It seemed a farce, a toast to foolishness. She had done it, but she couldn't celebrate it.

'Now what?' she said to Damon.

He glanced at his watch. 'We should be back in the city by dawn. I'll drop you off at Sophia's before I go to the office. I'll call a mover and have your things brought to my place in the afternoon. Then I'll be back to pick you up when I get done at the office.'

Kate stared. 'Wait a minute. What do you mean, call the mover? I never agreed to that! I have my own apartment!'

'And you can move back there. After the divorce. For lord's sake, Kate, you can't believe anyone's going to think this is a real marriage if you stay at Sophia's, and keep your things at your apartment.'

'Who cares what they think as long as you don't have to marry Marina?'

Damon's jaw tightened. 'My mother, for one. I need her to think this is a real marriage. She'll raise holy hell if she thinks I've done it to thwart her.'

'And you're afraid of your mother?'

'I'm not afraid of anyone. I respect her, though. And I don't want to hurt her?'

'You don't think marrying someone other than her choice is going to hurt her?'

He rubbed a hand through his hair. 'Maybe it will. Hell, I don't know. But there's a line a man has to draw between letting people run his life and making them happy.'

'And you, of course, never run anyone else's life.'

He ignored her sarcasm. 'I didn't ask you to marry me in order to hurt you.' The look on his face was earnest and intent, surprising Kate in its sincerity.

'I know,' she muttered. 'It's just — I'm just — not used to it yet, I guess.' She gave him a weak smile and a little shrug. 'Sorry. I'm not as good at these machinations as you are.'

He grimaced. 'It's too bad we had to stoop to them. If it wasn't for your father and my mother —— '

'And Stephanos. And Jeffrey. And Marina.'

Damon's mouth twisted. 'Right. Well, it won't last forever. A year and it will be a bad memory.'

'How comforting.'

'I wasn't trying to be comforting,' Damon said flatly. 'I was being realistic.'

'So you were.' Kate leaned back in the seat and shut her eyes, suddenly weary. The adrenalin that had kept her going strong throughout the earlier flight, their thirty-minute taxi ride, twenty-minute wedding and subsequent return to the plane slipped away.

She didn't want to trade remarks with Damon Alexakis any longer. She didn't want to even think about the man who was—heaven help her—her husband. He seemed to feel the same way.

'I'll let you rest,' he told her, getting to his feet. 'I've got some contracts to read over.'

Kate didn't think she'd sleep. But she must have, for the first thing she noticed upon opening her eyes was that the city lay sprawled below them, a blanket of twinkling lights, and far out to the east the first rays of sun were beginning to turn the sky a faint pink.

She shifted and stretched, turned her head and noticed that Damon had returned and was sitting next to her again.

He must have brought back the papers he intended to work on, but they lay untouched in his lap and he, too, had fallen asleep. His face was turned towards hers, his eyes shut, his lips slightly parted.

Kate allowed herself the luxury of studying him closely for the first time. According to the forms they'd filled out, he was thirty-four. Her initial impression was that they'd been hard years. For the first time now she actually found herself thinking he looked younger than his age. His mouth looked gentler, his lips fuller. The silky half-moon lashes that touched his cheeks gave him an innocence totally absent when his cool brown eyes were assessing the world at large. He had shed his suit jacket and loosened the knot of his tie. His collar button was undone, affording her the glimpse of a strong throat. As she watched, his eyelids fluttered and he swallowed.

Kate looked away quickly, not wanting to be caught staring if he opened his eyes. But he only shifted his position as the plane banked. His head now rested against her shoulder. She didn't move away.

'Sell it,' he muttered. His jaw tightened. He scowled in his sleep.

Kate smiled a bit wryly, wondering if he ever got away from Alexakis Enterprises. It didn't look like it.

She certainly didn't know much about this man she'd wed. She wasn't sure she wanted to. He wasn't her type at all. He reminded her altogether too much of her father.

She wondered how much luck they would have convincing his family that he'd fallen madly in love with her and she with him. Perhaps they were more gullible than her father had been.

Damon had done his best with her father, that was certain. It wasn't his fault that Eugene DeMornay hadn't believed for a minute that Damon was serious.

What would the old barracuda, as Damon had called him, say when he found out that she and Damon had actually gone through with it? She stifled a laugh.

'Things looking up, are they?' Damon's voice was husky with sleep. He seemed in no hurry to lift his head as he regarded her through bloodshot eyes.

Startled at the sound of his voice, Kate turned to look at him. The hint of innocence was gone. The mouth was thin again, the jaw hard. But she couldn't quite forget the other, younger man she'd glimpsed when he was asleep.

She shifted so that he had to lift his head. 'Just thinking about what our families are going to say. Sophia, Stephanos. Your mother. Your sisters. My father. Jeffrey.'

Damon's mouth twisted. 'I'm sure it'll be interesting.'

'Married? To Damon?' Sophia stared, then began to giggle. 'Oh, my. Oh, my dear!'

'You're married? to K-Kate?' Stephanos's face went white. He licked his lips nervously and eased his collar away from his neck.

'Married? Damon's *married*? To who?' One of the sisters stood stock-still and stared. Electra, Kate thought. She wasn't sure. It didn't matter. The three they'd found had said more or less the same thing.

'Married? Oh, for heaven's sake, Kate.' For once Jeffrey didn't look smug at all.

'You never learn, do you, Katherine? Well, it's your bed. Lie in it.' Eugene DeMornay shook his head. He walked them to the door of his office, holding Kate back for a moment after Damon had gone ahead. 'If Jeffrey's still here when Alexakis divorces you, we can see if he'll have you then.'

Kate didn't reply. She was too tired.

She and Damon had gone straight from the airport to beard them all, one after another, starting with Sophia and Stephanos at breakfast. They'd moved on to whichever of Damon's sisters he could find, then driven straight to the head office of DeMornay Enterprises. Kate hadn't wanted to, protesting that it was already mid-afternoon and surely it could wait. But Damon had insisted.

In retrospect, Kate supposed she was glad they'd gone. Now, except for telling Damon's mother on Friday, the hard part was over with.

Their families' reactions had hardly been surprising. Still Kate found she was trembling by early evening when Damon took her back to her apartment to get an overnight case.

The moment she opened the door she felt her strength desert her. She'd only been home one night a week since she'd started taking care of the twins, but this was the closest thing to a refuge she had, and now she sank down on the sofa in blessed relief.

Damon stood silently right inside the door, staring down at her, his expression brooding. Kate shut her eyes.

'Don't go to sleep,' Damon said. 'Get what you need and let's go.'

'Can't,' Kate mumbled. She wanted nothing more than to crawl into her bed, pull the covers over her head and not surface again until Christmas. Perhaps not even then.

'We've been through that. You're coming with me. If they call looking for us and we're not there——'

'We could pretend we weren't answering the phone.'

'My housekeeper will.'

'So let's both stay here. I know it's not a penthouse, but it's comfortable,' Kate said quickly. 'Besides, don't you think it will be better to let her tell them we're gone? After all, who would be expecting us to spend the first night we're home chaperoned by a house-keeper? Here we have the place all to ourselves. Much more romantic,' she added wryly.

One of Damon's brows lifted. 'And that's what you want?'

'Of course not. I want to sleep in my own bed.' Kate yawned hugely. 'I'm sorry.' She gave him a wan smile. 'I'm afraid I'm not a very good co-conspirator.'

Damon hesitated, pacing around the small living-room, rubbing a hand through his hair. Finally he sighed. 'Maybe you're right. OK. One night.'

Kate smiled, this time with more enthusiasm. She hauled herself to her feet. 'I'll make up the sofa for you. It won't take a minute.'

Damon stared at her. 'The sofa?'

She stopped and stared at him. 'This is a one-bedroom apartment.'

'I'm supposed to spend my wedding-night on a sofa?'

'You spent your wedding-night on a jet,' she reminded him with some asperity. 'You're the one who wanted to get back as quickly as possible. Besides, this marriage is business, remember?'

Heaven help her, he couldn't be thinking of changing the rules now, could he?

'Right,' Damon muttered. He dropped down on the sofa and grimaced, then began to take off his shoes.

Kate went into the bedroom and sank down on to the bed. She felt as if she'd been awake forever. She kicked off her shoes, then stood up again to shed the wrinkled shirtwaister she'd been wearing for the last thirty-six hours.

Going into the bathroom, she splashed water on her face, ran a brush through her hair, then slipped on a thin cotton nightgown and a pale blue terrycloth robe. Feeling almost human once more, she grabbed clean sheets and a pillow and went back to the living-room.

Damon was lying on the sofa, his tie loose, his collar button open. His eyes had been closed, but when he heard her approach he opened them. The clear male admiration in his gaze made Kate suddenly self-conscious.

'I was grubby. I needed a change.'

'Am I complaining?'

She ignored the appreciation in his voice. Damon Alexakis wasn't interested in her — not that way. Not really. He already had her in the only way that mattered to him: on a marriage licence. She wasn't his type. When it came time to choose the real Alexakis Bride, she was sure the woman would be nothing like her.

'Get up, and I'll make the bed for you.'

He stood, scowling now, his gaze never leaving her. Kate had seen pictures of him in the business weeklies where he looked like that — a sort of dangerous modern-day pirate. Not a man to tangle with.

She turned her back, trying to pretend he was just another overnight guest, like her college roommate Missy or her prep school friend, Antonia. But when he cleared his throat, it was difficult to pretend he was anything less than he was — a strong, virile adult male.

She tried to forget he was also her husband.

No matter what he'd said about how businesslike their arrangement was, she couldn't help but recall how married couples often spent the night.

'Are you hungry? You can check the fridge if you want, but I doubt if there's much here. I've been eating most of my meals at Sophia's.' She knew she was babbling. She couldn't help it.

'I'm not hungry.' His voice was flat.

Kate ventured a sideways glance in his direction. He was staring at the cleavage where her robe gapped. 'Are you th-thirsty?'

'I'm fine.' His voice was brusque. He stepped around her, careful not to touch her, snatched up one of the pillows and shoved it into the pillowcase. 'Let's get on with this.'

They made up the bed together, not speaking. When they finished, Kate nodded towards the bathroom. 'There are fresh towels in the cupboard and new toothbrushes in the medicine cabinet.'

'You have a lot of sleep-over guests, do you?'

'Sometimes I have friends who —— '

'Spare me the details,' he said harshly. 'Just remember: there won't be any "sleep-over" guests while you're married to me.'

Kate stared at him, astonished. How dared he misunderstand her? How dared he assume —— ?

Damon apparently took her stunned silence for guilt. 'I told you: there won't be any women in my life while I'm married to you. I expect the same courtesy in return.' He fixed her with a hard glare. 'In fact, I demand it.'

Kate slapped her hands on her hips. 'Demand what

you damned well please. I don't have to run my life to suit you, Damon Alexakis!'

'Yes, my dear Mrs Alexakis, you do.' He reached for her then, taking her chin between his thumb and forefinger, holding her so that she would be looking straight into his eyes unless she panicked and looked away.

She wouldn't give him the satisfaction.

'As long as you're my wife, the only bed you'll be sharing is mine. Got that?' he asked softly.

Kate jerked her chin out of his grasp. 'I'm not sharing a bed with you. And you can stop jumping to conclusions. I don't sleep around.' Her tone was sullen. But she wasn't going to let him think he'd cowed her into behaving according to his dictates.

He looked at her long and hard. It was a hungry look, a possessive look. It looked like more than business. 'Good. Then we should get along fine.' He brushed past her and headed for the bathroom.

Get along fine? Sure. Right.

Damon was up and gone by the time Kate had awakened the following morning. The sheets and blankets were folded and sitting on the end table when she came into the living-room. On top of them was a note.

I'll pick you up at Sophia's for dinner at seven. Have your bags packed. Damon.

Simple and to the point.

It made Kate grit her teeth, but in a way she was glad. It meant that things were only business after all. She didn't need to worry. She'd been overwrought last night, thinking Damon wanted her. She crossed two days off on her calendar. Only three hundred and sixty-three more.

She took her bags with her to Sophia's where she spent the day deflecting all manner of questions from Sophia, the girls and, even Stephanos, who was clearly worried about how much she might have told his brother-in-law about his pursuit of her.

By seven that evening she was so tired of trying to play the besotted bride and reply to the countless questions that she was almost ready to fling herself into Damon's arms in her eagerness to get out of there.

Damon went one better. He opened the door, spotted her across the room and, ignoring his sister and brother-in-law completely, he strode right over, hauled her straight into his arms and kissed her.

Whatever Kate had been expecting, it wasn't that.

Business, her mind screamed. It's only business.

But her body didn't believe it for a minute! It reacted at once, moulding itself to Damon's, pressing against him, seeking warmth and comfort and the satisfaction of pent-up desires. It was insane, but Kate felt powerless to stop it.

And Damon appeared to want those desires satisfied as well. His lips were hot and hungry. His tongue slipped into her mouth, probing, tasting, inciting urges that made Kate's mind reel and her knees sag.

There was a masculine clearing of throat behind them. 'Don't start anything you can't finish in the presence of five-year-olds,' Stephanos said gruffly.

Kate froze. Damon loosened his grip, stepped back and held her out at arm's length, a bemused smile on his face. 'I think I'd better take you home,' he said to her with a wink. 'My bride missed me,' he said to Stephanos.

Stephanos glared.

Kate's face flamed. She couldn't look at Stephanos or Sophia. She wanted to sink through the floor as Damon towed her out and shut the door behind them.

'Good job,' he said. 'Sophia was impressed.'

'The hell with Sophia,' Kate muttered, wobbling towards the elevator. 'What'd you kiss me like that for?'

'Why did you throw yourself into my arms?'

'I'd spent the day fielding a million stupid questions about our relationship. I was eager for rescue.'

'And that's how you ask for rescue? I'll be looking forward to seeing you when you're really glad to see me.' He winked at her and ushered her into the lift.

'Shut up, Damon.'

He laughed. 'Do you want to go out to dinner or go home?'

'What I want,' Kate said snappishly, 'is to go to my apartment.'

'We'll go to mine.'

His housekeeper, Mrs Vincent, was a motherly sort, at odds with the chrome and polished teak surroundings that pervaded Damon's penthouse flat. She was clearly delighted that Damon had tied the knot, and was all too willing to turn all the decisions over to Kate. Kate liked her at once and tried to listen as Mrs Vincent explained how she normally did things. But the tense days and sleepless night were catching up with her and she kept yawning and apologising.

'Kept you up all night, I'll bet,' Mrs Vincent said with a fond smile in Damon's direction. He was already on the telephone and didn't hear, thank heavens.

'Mmm, well,' Kate mumbled, embarrassed.

'I'm so glad he's married,' Mrs Vincent confided. 'He needs a wife. And so much better to have one he picked himself. I don't hold to that arranged marriage business his mother was up to. All that nonsense about her finding "the Alexakis Bride". Like she was buying some plaster saint. I tell you, a man like that needs a real woman. A strong woman.' She gave Kate a conspiratorial smile. 'Good for you.'

Kate swallowed.

'Now you tell me what you want, I'll do it,' Mrs Vincent said.

Kate smiled and yawned again. 'What I really want is to go to bed.'

Mrs Vincent laughed. 'Ah, young love.'

'I didn't mean——' Kate began hastily, her cheeks burning.

But Damon hung up then and came across the room. 'She's a hot-blooded woman, Mrs Vincent. Now you see why I was so eager to get her to the altar.' He grinned and looped an arm over Kate's shoulders. 'Come, my love. I'll show you to our room.'

'Our room?' Kate spluttered as he steered her down the hallway, '*Our* room?'

He led her into a room at the end of the hall. 'What'd you want me to say, that you'd be sleeping on the couch?'

'Don't be an ass, Damon. I'm not sharing a room with you!'

'Think again.' He shut the door to the spacious master bedroom with floor-to-ceiling windows looking out across Central Park.

It was dusk and amid the trees she spied the thousands of fairy lights that surrounded the Tavern on the Green restaurant and, above them, the tall apartment houses that lined Central Park West.

It was far better to concentrate on that than on the king-size bed which, even in the shadows, was the focal point of the room.

Damon was putting her bags down, opening cupboard doors, pointing out the empty rod and hangers, saying, 'You can use these. And then you can go to bed.'

'I'm not sleeping here.'

'Don't argue. We're never going to make it if you dispute everything I say, Kate.'

'Tough.' She glowered at him, feeling like a stubborn child in the face of his stony determination and not caring in the least.

'I'll leave you to get settled in. I have some more calls to make.'

'Damon, I'm not sleeping——'

'Obviously,' he said mildly, and walked out.

He didn't even listen! He treated her like one of his nieces, not his wife!

Kate flung her handbag at the door he'd just shut. It rebounded with a satisfying thunk. 'I'm not a child,' she told the door furiously.

It opened again. Damon poked his head around the corner. He grinned. 'Then don't act like one.'

Once more he was gone.

Kate glowered after him. She was tempted to take off her shoes and throw them as well. But who knew what he might do if she did? She contented herself with flopping down on the bed and pounding her fists against the mattress instead.

Why on earth had she let herself get into this mess?

She was as tired as she'd claimed. She was also hungry. Her stomach growled even as she lay there. She wished she'd asked for a meal, but she wasn't about to change her mind now. She sat up and drew her knees up to her chest, wrapping her arms around them, thinking about what she should do.

Getting into bed was tempting. Pulling the covers over her head and falling into the blessed oblivion of sleep seemed the better part of valour at the moment. And yet—and yet her lips still remembered the taste of Damon's mouth on hers. Her body still tingled with the imprint of his. And her mind could not quite ignore the possibility that he might come back and slide into the bed beside her.

And then what would happen?

She didn't want to think about it. She'd had enough of men after Bryce. Loving hadn't been at all what she'd expected. She hadn't, she remembered with chagrin, been very good at it. Bryce had been all too willing to point that out.

She could imagine what Damon would say.

Not that she was ever going to give him a chance!

The door opened and Damon came in bearing a tray.

'Don't you believe in knocking?' Kate demanded.

He ignored her, setting the tray in front of her. Kate tried not to look interested at the sight of the thin slices of chicken, fruit and salad on the plate. Her stomach growled, betraying her. 'Thank you,' she said with bad grace.

She dug in, then looked up at Damon still standing there. 'Aren't you having any?'

'I'll eat on the plane.'

'What plane?'

'I just found out I have to fly to Paris tonight. I'll be back on Friday.'

'Paris? Now?'

'I thought you'd be thrilled,' he said drily. 'You get the bed.'

'Well, of course, but you haven't had any more sleep than I have.' And he looked even wearier than she felt.

'I'll live.'

'I'll go home, then,' she said quickly, setting aside the tray and moving to get out of bed. It was too unnerving, staying here, sleeping in Damon's bed.

'The hell you will! We're married, remember.'

'I'll go to Sophia's. I mean, if you're not here, why can't I stay there?'

'Stephanos.'

'He won't ——'

'Damned right he won't. But I'm not letting him even think about it. You come back here, Kate. That's final. I'll be home Friday afternoon, hopefully before my mother arrives. I'll pick you up at Sophia's and we'll go deal with her together.'

He gave her a quick hard kiss and was gone.

Kate stared after him, tasting Damon on her lips and not the food she had hungered for. She lifted her hand and touched them.

Why had he kissed her? No one had been watching.

On Friday, she told herself, there would only be three hundred and fifty-seven days to go.

'I'd stop this. I mean, if you're all here. . .'
'No. . .no, you said. . .'

CHAPTER FOUR

IT WAS Friday. It was in the middle of Sophia's living-room. It was the moment of truth.

There was only one thing Damon hadn't got right: they hadn't had to go anywhere to see his mother. She had arrived at Sophia's, with Marina in tow, only moments before Kate was expecting him.

Now she stood quaking in the family-room, knotting her fingers together, not knowing what to do or say.

'You mean he hasn't *told* her you're married?' Sophia demanded, when Kate insisted on staying there by herself instead of coming in with the twins to see their grandmother.

'Not yet. At least I don't think he has. He's been gone, you know, and. . .and he's had a lot on his mind.'

'More important things than his marriage?' Sophia grumbled. 'I know my brother. He wanted to hit her with a *fait accompli*. That way Marina——' She broke off suddenly and shot Kate a guilty look.

'That's all right. He's mentioned Marina.'

'And that Mama has been expecting him to marry her?'

Kate nodded, unsure whether she should be admitting it, but needing to be as truthful as possible.

'I should have known. To be honest, I'm glad he met you when he did. It's always been such a big thing, this business of finding 'the Alexakis Bride'. It's so much better to marry for love.' She gave Kate a quick hug.

Kate smiled uneasily, feeling guiltier than ever.

'I wish my clever brother had handled things better.

61

I mean, what's he going to do, walk right past Mama and Marina, grab your hand and say, "This is my wife"?'

Kate didn't know what he was going to do. She couldn't imagine how he was going to explain her to Mrs Alexakis. She was waiting with trepidation when suddenly she heard the front doorbell and Sophia went to answer it.

'Ah, Damon,' she heard Sophia say. 'Here you are at last. Mama and Marina have been waiting.'

'Where's Kate?'

A second later he was beside her, grasping her hand, pulling her into the living-room.

'Mama,' he said to the woman sitting on the sofa, 'I'd like you to meet Kate.'

Kate had tried to imagine what Damon's mother looked like, dreaming up varying combinations of all the formidable women she'd ever met. The reality was something less. Helena Alexakis was not really very large at all. She wore her greying black hair in a matronly style. Her dress was more comfortable-looking than of the latest style. Kate found herself thinking that her mother-in-law looked as if she might be friendly.

Or would have been until she heard the next words out of Damon's mouth.

'She has done me the honour of becoming my bride.'

The world stopped.

Damon's mother's smile froze on her face. She looked in the first instant as if she hadn't grasped the word. And Kate wondered if she even spoke English. It didn't matter for the next moment Damon repeated it once more, this time in Greek.

'Your *bride*?' Helena Alexakis said at last. She looked at her son, then at Kate.

Kate swallowed carefully, standing very still, not

even breathing, as if any move would cause the room to explode.

'Your bride,' Helena Alexakis said again, and this time she sounded less shocked than bemused. A tiny quizzical smile played about the corners of her mouth.

She considered Kate slowly and carefully and Kate felt as if the yardstick measuring 'the Alexakis Bride' had been taken out and laid alongside her.

Kate didn't doubt she'd come up short.

She tried to remain calm. It was, after all, nothing she hadn't expected. She'd known. She'd been warned. But as the seconds stretched into minutes, Kate thought again that she'd made a very big mistake.

Helena Alexakis looked like a kind woman, a loving, caring woman. The sort of woman Kate had always wanted for a mother. Not the sort of woman she'd want to dupe.

And then there was the little matter of the gorgeous young woman still seated on the couch beside her mother-in-law. The young woman who apparently fit Helena Alexakis's requirements for 'the Alexakis Bride'.

Marina still looked shocked by Damon's revelation even if his mother no longer did. Her gaze moved from Kate to Damon and back again. Her eyes were wide and bewildered. Kate didn't blame her a bit.

Helena's gaze shifted to Damon and Kate felt minutely relieved, even though an instant later he slipped an arm around her shoulders and drew her closer.

At last after another minute of silence and one more consideration of Kate, Helena looked at her son and said, 'So why are you here?'

Damon frowned. 'Why am I here?'

'You just got married, yes? So why are you in New York dancing attendance on your mother? You should be on your honeymoon.'

Kate gaped. She felt Damon stiffen next to her.

'Don't be silly, Mama. We don't need a honeymoon.'

'Everyone needs a honeymoon, Damon. To be together, to bond your relationship, it is important. Especially important since you must not have known each other long?' One thin brow lifted as she gave them a speculative, knowing look.

Damon ground his teeth. 'Long enough.'

'He did rather — um — sweep me off my feet,' Kate put in lightly.

Her mother-in-law smiled for the first time. She got up off the sofa and put her hand out to Kate, drawing her close, away from Damon, looking at her again, smiling more broadly. 'A sweeper, is he? My Damon? And I always thought he was so calculating. Good.' Once more she looked at Damon. 'You need a honeymoon.'

'Mama, I have a business.'

'You have a bride, Damon.'

'Yes, but — '

'A bride of your own choosing, yes? One that you love, obviously. So show her.'

'Mama, I — '

'You have Stephanos. You have Arete. Alexakis Enterprises isn't one man, Damon. You have hundreds of people to make business while you are gone. What do I always tell you? You are too busy. You work too hard.' Helena shook her head. Her ample bosom shook slightly as well. She gave her son a look of fond exasperation. 'You just got married. Go away.'

'No.'

'Yes.'

They stared at each other, stalemated.

'Even if I could get away, which I can't,' Damon

said at last, 'Kate is helping out here. She's Sophia's nanny.'

Helena's eyes got wide. 'Her nanny?'

Damon's chin jutted. 'Something wrong with that?'

'As long as you love her, Damon, nothing is wrong with it.'

Damon swallowed. Kate expected him to deny it. She was surprised when he said roughly, 'Of course I love her, but I can't take her on a honeymoon. She takes care of the girls!'

'I will.'

'*You*? Mama, you never——'

Helena Alexakis stiffened. 'Damon! Do not argue with your mother.' She paused. 'Have you been married before?'

He shifted uneasily, then slid a finger inside his shirt collar. 'No, of course not,' he muttered.

'Of course not,' she mimicked. 'So you don't argue with experience. In business you listen to the experts, don't you?'

'Yes, but——'

'I am the expert. I know how important it is to have time together. Your father and I——'

'Kate and I are nothing like you and Papa.'

'You work too hard, same as your papa. You swept Kate off her feet same as your papa. You need what your papa and I needed—to be together. Alone. We spent a month on Sifnos. That is too far, of course. Let's see. Where can you two go. . .?'

'We'll take a weekend in the Hamptons if it'll make you happy.'

'A weekend!' His mother wrinkled her nose. 'Nonsense. A marriage takes nourishment, care, tending, Damon. You can't begin to start a marriage in a weekend. Even when you are in love it takes time. Besides,' she added knowledgeably, 'if you only go so far as the Hamptons, you'll be on the phone all the time. I know! Buccaneer's Cay.'

'No, Mama.' Damon said almost as fast as Sophia said,

'What a good idea. You can go down early and make sure everything is ready for Thanksgiving.'

'I have things to do here. Important things.'

'More important than your marriage?' His mother looked at him, scandalised.

'Damn it —'

'Don't swear, Damon. It's a perfect solution. We will all be down for the holiday. In the meantime, you will have a chance to spend time alone together.'

'We don't need time alone together!'

'What Damon means,' Kate said hastily, 'is that we don't want to shut you out. We want you to share our happiness.'

Helena squeezed her hand. 'And so we will, my dear. We always go to Buccaneer's Cay in late November if there isn't time to go home to Greece. Hasn't Damon told you?'

Kate shook her head.

Helena frowned at her son. 'It's a small island in the Bahamas. We have a small family compound there that Aristotle bought years ago. My husband loved island living, said it gave him the proper focus.' Helena smiled a nostalgic smile. 'Please, do say you'll go.' She gave Kate a look of such entreaty that Kate could think of nothing to say at all. She looked at Damon helplessly. She could see a muscle ticking in his temple, could imagine the wheels turning in his brain, looking for an escape route.

Apparently he didn't find one, for a moment later she felt him let out his breath slowly and carefully. 'All right.'

Helena beamed. 'Don't worry, dear. Stephanos and Arete can take care of things here.'

Damon's expression grew even grimmer. He gave his brother-in-law a stony glare which had Stephanos taking a step backwards. 'Stephanos had better,' he said icily. 'Arete isn't working for us any more.'

'*What*?'

'She's gone over to Strahan Brothers.'

'Strahans? Why? What did you do to her? Damon, if you hurt her feelings——' Obviously all thought of Damon's honeymoon was gone. Arete was the one who mattered now.

Damon's teeth snapped together. 'You'll have to talk to her about that, Mama.' Kate felt herself being towed towards the door. 'Come on, Kate. If we're going on honeymoon——' he came down with lead feet on the word '——I've got work to do.'

They were almost out of the room, when he turned back and looked at the girl still standing behind his mother. 'Nice to see you again, Marina. What brings you here?'

'I can't believe you did that!'

Damon couldn't either, but he didn't need some elfin termagant flinging herself around his living-room berating him for his manners. He already knew they were appalling. He put it down to stress. Normally he was the most tactful of men.

'You're lucky she didn't kill you,' Kate raged on, casting longing glances at anything she might throw at him. Damon was glad he didn't have knick-knacks. She had to settle for glowering instead.

'Should I have ignored her?'

'In the circumstances, you probably should have. Good heavens, Damon, the girl was mortified! Have you no compassion? She came all the way from Greece to marry you!'

'I'm already married.'

'That doesn't signify. You should apologise! You should have been a little more sensitive to her feelings!'

'I was trying to be sensitive to yours.'

Kate snorted. 'If you'd ever thought I had any feelings you wouldn't have asked me to marry you.'

He grinned. 'You're probably right.'

'Stop smiling. This isn't funny. I don't know why I agreed to this! It's a disaster! And now a honeymoon, for heaven's sake!' She grabbed a pillow and flung it at him.

Damon caught the pillow. *She* thought it was a disaster, too? He felt curiously nettled hearing it. 'What are you complaining about? My mother's taking care of the girls.'

'I don't simply take care of the girls. I run the agency. Or have you forgotten?'

He had, as a matter of fact. He'd watched Kate taking care of Sophia's girls and had thought what a good mother she'd make. He hadn't been thinking about her as a career woman. 'What do you expect me to do about it?'

'You could have said no.'

'You heard her. Honeymoons are sacrosanct. If we declined, she'd know the marriage wasn't real.'

'We have the certificate.'

'But we could still get an annulment. We haven't consummated it,' he reminded her. His gaze shifted to the bedroom door. 'Unless, perhaps, you want——' He gave her a suggestive leer.

Kate grabbed another pillow and flung it.

He fielded it, too. 'Then I guess we go to the Bahamas and make them think it's real.'

Kate muttered something distinctly unladylike.

Damon grinned, unsure exactly why he was enjoying this. It wasn't as if he wanted to go on a honeymoon with her, for heaven's sake.

Was it?

The thought gave his stomach a curious queasy lurch.

'When?' she asked sullenly after a moment.

He tried to shake off the feeling. 'Huh? Oh, the sooner the better. If my mother thinks Stephanos can handle the business, she's out of her mind. But if I can spend tonight and tomorrow wrapping up what I absolutely can't trust to anyone else, we can go Sunday and be back the following weekend.'

'What about the Thanksgiving business your mother mentioned?'

'We don't have to stay for that.'

'But your mother said——'

'She can only push so far. I'm damned if I'm going to stay around for family bonding time.'

'Family bonding time?' Kate looked puzzled.

He grimaced. 'My father started it when he came to America, dragging everyone out to the island to spend time together. He was busy always. Never home. So once a year he would insist. And the American Thanksgiving was a natural.'

'It sounds nice,' Kate said almost wistfully.

He stared at her. 'Nice?'

'I only meant——' she gave a helpless shrug '—that it's nice when a family want to be together.'

Damon looked at her more closely. Was that yearning he saw on her face? He couldn't imagine it. If she wanted a family, she ought to get married and have one. She never should have married a guy like him. 'Stay if you want,' he said gruffly.

'No.' Kate shook her head quickly. 'That would be

ridiculous. Why should I bond with your family when I'll be out of it in three hundred and fifty-seven days?' She gave Damon a brisk nod, turned and headed towards the bedroom. 'Goodnight.'

She'd sounded—she hoped—considerably more sanguine than she felt. A week in the Bahamas with Damon? Kate wasn't sure it bore thinking about, but as she undressed for bed she couldn't seem to stop.

It's not as if it's a real honeymoon, she reminded herself, as she tugged her shirt over her head. She probably wouldn't even see him. Once they got there, naturally they could go their separate ways. And would.

But something had been happening to her since she'd married Damon, something she'd never expected. She was remembering all the dreams and fantasies about marriage she'd had before she'd wed Bryce.

In those days she'd been an incurable romantic—a starry-eyed child who'd had dreams of her prince coming to carry her off to his castle, far from her uninterested father and his economic empire. And one of those dreams, she recalled now, had been a honeymoon on a beach.

She reached for her bathrobe. That particular fantasy hadn't even been rooted in the far reaches of darkest adolescence. Right after she'd agreed to marry Bryce, she'd read a magazine article about honeymoons in the Bahamas.

She knew these articles were nothing more than travel come-ons. She knew the happy couples were not newlyweds, but really professional models from New York.

Still, she'd seen the photos of them frolicking on pink sand beaches, standing waist-deep in turquoise water, their arms around each other, smiling, kissing.

She'd smiled at the sight of them strolling through the foamy surf at sunset. And she'd dreamed.

Bryce had taken her to Atlantic City where he'd lost seven hundred dollars at the tables and she'd broken out in hives. So much, Kate thought, for dreams.

The door opened suddenly.

Kate jerked around, clutching the robe against her breasts. 'What do you want?'

Damon looked puzzled. 'To go to sleep?'

'*Here*?' She knew it was a yelp of indignation, but she couldn't help it.

He scowled. 'Hell, yes, here. And don't try to send me out to the sofa, either. We've been through that. Mrs Vincent lives in. She knows what goes on. I'm sleeping here.'

They glared at each other. In the five days he'd been gone, Kate had got used to having the bedroom to herself. There was so little of Damon apparent in its very stark furnishings that she had managed to put him out of her mind.

Big mistake.

She edged towards the bathroom and scooted behind the door. Then she gave an airy wave of the hand that wasn't still clutching the robe. 'Fine,' she said, poking her head around the door to look at him. 'Sleep. You can have the floor.'

'The floor! Like hell!'

'We've been through this before, too, Damon, and you're not sleeping with me. This is a marriage of convenience, nothing else. We never agreed to. . . to. . .' She couldn't seem to say the words.

'Make love?' Damon suggested, smiling.

Kate scowled. 'Have sex.'

'We didn't agree not to, either.'

She stared at him, outraged. 'You said "in name only".'

'That doesn't mean it has to be that way.'

'For me it does.'

He cocked his head. 'Why?'

'Because. . .because we aren't in love!' Were all men so obtuse?

Damon seemed unfazed. 'Well, no, but —'

'I don't have sex with men I don't love. And I don't sleep with them, either. As I said, you can sleep on the floor.'

'It's my room,' he reminded her.

'Yes, but I'm sharing it, and if you don't like it, I won't.'

His eyes narrowed. 'Is that a threat?'

Kate licked her lips, then swallowed. 'It's a statement of fact.'

'This marriage is as important to you as it is to me.'

Kate deliberately refused to think about how he could affect the future of her business. 'I can handle Jeffrey if I have to. Can you handle Mama and Marina?'

Damon muttered something rude under his breath. He raked a hand through his hair. He stalked to the cupboard and took out a quilt and flung it on the floor.

'You're all heart,' he growled.

Probably, Kate thought. Getting into this mess certainly proved she didn't have a brain.

Torture took many forms and Damon felt as if he were discovering new and varied ones every day since he'd been married to Kate.

Lying there listening to Kate's soft humming in the bathroom as she got ready for bed, Damon felt as if he'd found yet another. Nothing about this damnable marriage was working the way it was supposed to!

He was supposed to have spent the hours he was in Paris trying to close a deal, not thinking about Kate.

He was supposed to maintain a disinterested distance, not hurry back to her, ready to propose a cosy candle-light dinner strategy session for dealing with his mother, and be disappointed when his mother was already there. He was supposed to ignore her, not use whatever excuse he could come up with to touch her and taste her lips.

And he certainly was supposed to fall asleep without a thought of her, not lie on the floor of his own bedroom wanting to creep into her bed!

What the hell had he done, proposing this marriage anyway? It was supposed to be a business deal — pure and simple. It was turning out to be anything but!

And his mother, blast her, seemed intent on making it worse.

A honeymoon in the Bahamas! She knew how he loved Buccaneer's Cay. She knew it was the one place in the world where he could kick back and relax, where he quit worrying about the business and enjoyed himself. The one spot where there were no tensions and no pressures. Ever.

And his mother wanted him to take Kate?

He closed his eyes and groaned. With no distractions, with only sun and sand and surf, he would have nothing to keep him from getting to know his new wife, and his mother knew it.

Damon didn't *want* to know his new wife.

He already knew far too much.

He knew that her cheeks turned bright red when she got angry and that she had one tiny off-centre dimple in the left one when she laughed. He knew that she looked as fresh as a daisy with the wind in her hair. He knew she could laugh with the exuberance of a seven-year-old.

He knew she could charm the pout off an unhappy child and bring a smile to the face of another with a newly skinned knee. He knew she could stop a fight that had been brewing, could make Sophia nap when no one else could, could keep his brother-in-law in line.

He knew that her lips felt soft and full beneath his, that her curves fitted snugly against the hard lines of his own frame. He'd learned those curves when he'd held her against him this evening as they'd stood in front of his mother.

And now he knew she sang soft snatches of romantic songs while she got ready for bed.

She was driving him insane. And all the while the damned woman sounded as if she didn't have a care in the world!

Probably she didn't, he thought, his fingers tightening on a fistful of crumpled quilt.

She didn't have a multinational corporation to oversee. She didn't have a mother and six sisters determined to drive her crazy. She didn't have a philandering brother-in-law to keep on the straight and narrow.

Mostly, he thought irritably, she didn't have a delightful, delectable wife she wasn't allowed to touch!

Thoughts about her upcoming week in the Bahamas with Damon would have been enough to bedevil Kate throughout the weekend. Helena Alexakis complicated matters further.

'She's invited me to lunch tomorrow,' Kate told Damon on Monday afternoon when he picked her up from Sophia's. 'She and Sophia.'

Damon grimaced. 'So be busy.'

'It's not as simple as that. For one thing, my busyness at midday generally involves the twins, who happen to be going to a birthday party. But even more important, I'm not sure I should beg off.'

Damon looked at her, aghast. 'You want to get the third degree?'

'Not particularly. But I'm afraid it will be worse if I avoid her. I mean, right now she sort of seems to like me.'

This last astonishing fact had been borne in on Kate over the weekend. At the family dinner on Saturday night, Helena had been quite genial, asking Kate about her father, about her schooling, about her plans for Kid Kare. And when Sophia had her mother and Damon and his new wife over for brunch on Sunday, Helena had shooed the twins away so she could once again converse with Kate.

This time they had talked about Kate's first marriage, and, rather than resenting Damon's mother's probing, Kate found herself telling Helena more about it than she'd ever told anyone.

At first, of course, Kate had been wary. But Helena was calm and kind and not given to the snap judgements that Kate had always been used to on the parental front. Anyway, it was difficult to keep up one's guard all the time. Particularly in the face of unexpected acceptance.

Damon grunted. 'I'm glad she likes you, at least.'

'Has she said anything negative to you?' Kate wanted to know.

'She hasn't said anything at all to me. She smiles like the cat in that children's story.'

'The Cheshire cat?'

Damon grimaced. 'That's the one.'

Kate didn't know if it was worry about his mother or something else, but Damon had been increasingly stormy and irritable. At first she thought it was a result of his night on the hard wood floor. But he'd slept on the floor of the bedroom for three nights now without comment, declining her suggestion that they add a futon so it would look like a sofa, but would provide him with a bed.

'Don't bother,' he'd muttered.

'I only want to help,' Kate had replied, miffed by his irritable tone.

'Do you?' Damon had asked sarcastically. 'Do you really?' And without giving her a chance to reply to that, he'd stalked out.

Kate watched him go and wondered about how they'd cope for the next three hundred and fifty-four days.

She was still wondering when she met his mother for lunch.

Helena had reserved them a table in a small French restaurant not far from Damon's office. She was already there, waiting, when Kate arrived, apologising.

'No, you are not late. I am early. I stopped to see Damon on my way downtown. I had hoped we'd have time to talk, but, as always, he is too busy.' She gave Kate a conspiratorial smile. 'It is a good thing you are going on this honeymoon. You can straighten out his priorities.'

The waitress led them to their table in an alcove on the second floor. It was a cosy, intimate setting—the sort that seemed to call for secrets shared and hearts bared. Kate took a mental inventory, making sure all her defences were in place.

Then, once they had ordered, Helena undermined them all.

'I can't tell you how happy I am that at last Damon has found his bride.'

Kate, about to take a sip of her wine, set it down, grateful she wasn't choking on it.

Helena laughed at the expression on her face. 'You are surprised?'

'Well,' Kate hedged, 'he — um — wasn't quite sure how you'd feel about — um — me. I mean, since he hadn't told you and simply foisted me on you.'

'I admit I would have liked to have come to your wedding,' Helena said. 'One doesn't get to see one's only son married every day. But. . .as long as he has found the right woman. . .' Her voice trailed off. She smiled benevolently at Kate, who felt as if she should disclaim all right to being any such thing.

'I'm sorry,' she said in a small voice.

'The wedding, it is a small thing. The marriage, that is what is important,' Helena said. 'Don't be sorry, my dear. Everything is wonderful. Damon has found his bride. I tell you, I was about to give up hope. I was afraid I would have to do it for him.'

'I thought — I mean, he thought — I mean —— ' Unable to say what it was either of them had thought, Kate took a quick, desperate gulp of her wine.

The waitress brought their meals. Helena dug right into her bowl of bouillabaisse.

'I was getting desperate, I don't need to tell you,' Helena went on. 'For years I have been talking to him about what he should look for in a bride. She must be strong-willed, I tell him. She must have integrity and strength of character, and a certain sense of joy. All these things she will need to deal with you, I tell him. And I never know if he listens.' Helena stabbed a shrimp. 'He grunts. He mumbles. He goes to meetings in the middle of what I say. "I know women, Mama," he tells me. "I got sisters." And I tell him, Damon, sisters aren't the same.'

Kate laid her fork down and simply listened.

'I never thought he took it seriously. Every time I brought it up, he would get this look on his face and he would say, "More advice about the Alexakis Bride?" and I would say, "Damon, it's important, the most important decision of your life." And he would ignore me. So I told him last time I came to New York, you can't do it yourself. I will help.' Helena crunched down the shrimp with considerable relish.

Kate sat mesmerised.

'I will find you a bride, I tell him. And you know what he says? He says to me, "Go ahead. I have a business to run".' Helena shook her head and smiled at Kate. 'And all the while he was listening to me. He married you.'

Kate wanted to sink right through the floor.

'I couldn't have done better myself.'

Kate hesitated, then had to ask, 'What about Marina?'

Helena made a tsking sound and shook her head. 'Marina is a lovely girl. Spirited. Charming. She would have made a passable Alexakis Bride — I think. But she is so young, so untried in the trials of life. I told Damon I would find him a bride, and so I brought Marina with me —— ' Helena chuckled ' — more to irritate him than anything else.'

'Then. . .you didn't intend him to marry her?'

Helena sopped up some of the stew with a piece of French bread. 'If he loved her, of course. Mostly I wanted him to sit up and take notice. To think about marriage, about what he wanted in a bride. And all the time I was worrying, he had done much better than think. He had fallen in love!'

Kate closed her eyes and prayed for divine intervention.

'I worried a little when I first met you. Damon is a strong man. A stubborn man.' Helena sighed. 'But now that we have talked, I feel much better. You, too, are strong. You would have to be, to grow up with your father, to resist his will and marry without his permission. You are strong in other ways, too. You

are making your own business. I envy you your independence. It will be good for Damon not to be the
only businessperson,' she said cheerfully. 'You must
keep your hand in after the children.'

'Children?' Kate croaked.

'Surely you want children?' For the first time Helena
looked worried.

'Of course I want children! But ——'

'I was sure you would. Seeing you with Leda and
Christina was enough to tell me you will be a wonderful mother.' Helena beamed. 'I'm sure Damon saw
that, too. I must give my son credit. He has done well
indeed.' She finished her bread, then cocked her head
and looked at Kate. 'Is there something wrong with
your meal, dear? You aren't eating.'

CHAPTER FIVE

'WHAT do you mean, we didn't have to get married?'

Kate finished tossing the salad, glad that it was Mrs Vincent's day off and that she wasn't around to hear this conversation, not that they'd have been having it if she had been, of course.

'Just what I said. You jumped the gun. Marina wasn't a prospective Alexakis Bride.' She gave Damon a bright smile which brought her a glower in return.

'How do you know?'

'Your mother said.'

'*You asked her?*'

'Well, sort of. Not precisely,' Kate added quickly when Damon looked as if he might explode. 'She was discussing all the—er—things she hoped you would find in the woman you married. And then she said she was happy you'd found them in me.' She offered this last a bit hesitantly.

Damon didn't say anything. He leaned against the kitchen counter, eyeing her narrowly.

'She—er—didn't think you were paying attention when she talked about what you needed in a bride. And she's glad you did.'

Damon muttered something under his breath. 'And Marina?' he prompted when she didn't add anything else.

Kate set the salad on the table and took the steaks out of the broiler. 'Marina was—um—sort of a—er—prod, as it were.'

'Prod!'

'To stimulate your thinking.'

The muttering became more furious. Kate was glad it was in Greek. She didn't think she wanted to know what he was saying.

'Sit down,' she said. 'We can eat.'

Damon sat, but he didn't eat. He picked up his knife and stabbed his steak. He watched the juices ooze all over the plate. Then he pulled out the knife and stabbed it again.

'So,' Kate said, 'we can get an annulment if you want.'

Damon's head jerked up. His gaze was as sharp as the knife. 'The hell we will!'

Taken aback, Kate scowled. 'But if you don't actually need to be married to me. . .I mean, I won't hold you to it — I mean, on account of Jeffrey and all.'

She'd given it considerable thought on the way home in the taxi this afternoon, and as tempting as it would be to hold him to his part of the bargain, she decided that it was only fair to let him go.

She could handle Jeffrey and her father, especially now that she had another abortive marriage under her belt, and Damon certainly wouldn't damage her business at this point.

'Jeffrey hell! This has nothing to do with Jeffrey.' Damon was looking at her, outraged. 'Do you honestly think we're going to get an annulment now? Do you have any idea what my mother would think if we did?'

'Oh,' Kate said, considering it.

'Yes, oh,' Damon said with scathing mockery.

'Well, it was really pretty idiotic,' Kate retorted, stung.

'Which makes you as big an idiot as I am.'

Kate muttered under her breath. It wasn't exactly polite of him to mention it, but it didn't surprise her. 'So what do you suggest?'

Damon stabbed the steak one more time. 'I suggest we go have our honeymoon in the Bahamas.'

Be flexible, Kate always told her mother's helpers. Roll with the punches.

Good advice in the face of two-year-olds throwing temper tantrums and capricious society mamas. Not bad when one found oneself confronted with a scowling, grouchy Greek husband, either.

Kate had done her best, despite feeling equal parts guilty and foolish, to face the honeymoon prospect with equanimity. Damon had been alternately brusque, silent and sulky.

Considering that his nights on the floor might be causing some of it, Kate offered to go out and get him a fold-up mattress. He practically bit her head off.

'I was only trying to help,' she protested.

'That's not the kind of help I need,' Damon snarled, and stalked out.

The rest of their encounters hadn't been much better. She hoped that once they got away from work and family, things would improve.

'Damon loves Buccaneer's Cay,' Helena had told her at their fateful lunch. 'It will be the best possible place for you to go.'

But now, as the plane dipped low over the turquoise waters just beyond the Atlantic coast of tiny Buccaneer's Cay, Kate wasn't sure about that.

Certainly Damon didn't look pleased. He'd played the cheerful bridegroom that morning at the airport until his mother and sisters had disappeared, then he'd pulled a sheaf of papers out of his carry-on bag and proceeded to ignore Kate for the rest of the time.

Kate had attempted a couple of conversational gambits, but when they both met with monosyllabic replies she gave up. Be that way, then, she thought, you old grouch.

However bad the situation was, she couldn't help feeling an inkling of excitement, a tremor of eagerness to see this new and wondrous land. She fully intended to enjoy herself. What Damon did was his problem.

The plane banked and came across the island, allowing a clear view of the narrow sand beach and the string of houses that dotted the jungle behind it.

'Which house is it?' Kate asked.

Damon glanced up briefly and pointed. 'There.'

She picked out a two storey, tangerine-coloured stucco building with stone fireplaces, tall shuttered windows, and wide verandas, tucked among the trees. There were two or three smaller buildings nearby. Sheds or caretaker's cottages, no doubt.

'It's lovely,' Kate said.

Damon went back to his papers.

They didn't land on Buccaneer's Cay itself. The airstrip was on a larger island nearby. A taxi and the boat would take them at last to the landing at Buccaneer's Cay.

She had learned that from Helena, too. Damon didn't say a word. Not until they finally crossed the bay and the boat docked at the custom's house.

There they found themselves hailed by a burly black man, and Damon put away his papers and broke into a grin. 'Joe!'

It was the first smile Kate had seen on him all week.

'Hey, mon, good to see you. You down early this year.' Joe shook Damon's hand. 'An' with a pretty lady.'

'I'm on my honeymoon.'

Joe's eyes bugged. Then he clapped Damon on the shoulder and pumped his hand. 'You sure are! A mighty pretty lady!' He laughed, then stopped and gave Kate a friendly, but clearly assessing look. 'The Alexakis Bride!' he said after a moment. 'Yes, sir. Your mother done good.'

'My mother had nothing to do with it.'

Joe looked momentarily taken aback as he led them to the moke. He started to say something, but didn't. 'Ah. Like that, is it?' He winked at Kate. 'You must be a pretty special lady.'

For the thousandth time Kate wished she weren't there under false pretences. She gave him a hopeful smile. 'I try.'

Joe grinned. 'You got him to th'altar. That says it all. You got it made.'

'We'll see about that,' Damon said, but he was smiling, too.

And there was still a hint of that smile hovering on his face as they bounced their way through the jungle towards the house. Kate found herself wishing that smile would disappear.

All week long she'd wished he wouldn't be so crabby and remote. Now she thought it might have been a blessing. He was gorgeous when he smiled!

At last the moke halted at the end of the road behind the huge two storey house Damon had pointed out from the plane. Its tall, narrow windows and broad white porches reminded Kate of something out of a nineteenth-century seafaring novel.

She was charmed. Also relieved. In a place this big she and Damon would have no trouble avoiding each other.

Before she could say anything, down the path towards them bustled a tall, robust woman in a yellow dress.

'Mr Damon! Your mama call last Monday and say you got married! Let me see this lucky lady!'

Damon said to Kate under his breath, 'Her name is Teresa, and she's as quick as they come.'

'I'll keep it in mind.' Kate pasted on a bright smile as Damon stepped out and dragged her out after him into Teresa's embrace.

It was like being hugged by a pillow, warm and sweet-smelling, and Kate felt an irresistible urge to return it.

'Let me look at you, honey,' Teresa said at last, pulling back and holding Kate out at arm's length, beaming at her. Kate's gaze slid guiltily away.

'She shy?' Teresa demanded of Damon. 'You don' need to be shy, honey. Not with me. Why, you're just as pretty as the missus said you is. She's so pleased! I always knew Mr Damon would find hisself a beauty.' She turned an assessing gaze on Damon. 'Had to find one to match him, didn't he?' she said to Kate with a grin.

Kate was surprised to see Damon's cheekbones lined with red.

'You're blind, Teresa,' he said gruffly, reaching for the suitcases, hauling them out of the back of the moke.

Teresa laughed. 'You want to eat first or unpack.'

Damon looked at Kate.

She shrugged.

'We'll unpack,' Damon decided, heading towards the house.

'You ain't sleepin' here;' Teresa said. 'Your mama said to get the cottage ready.'

Damon stopped dead. 'The cottage?' The colour seemed to drain from his face. 'That belongs to Sophia and Stephanos.'

Teresa's teeth gleamed in a broad smile. 'No. It don't. It belongs to married folk. You got a right to it now.' She grinned even more widely. 'You don' want to be rattlin' round in here with me on your honey-moon, boy. You want some privacy. Leastways, that's what your mama said.' She cocked her head. 'She wrong?'

'Of course not,' Damon said irritably. He turned and strode up a narrow tree-lined path without looking back.

Kate stared after him for a split second, nonplussed. Then seeing him disappear around the corner of the house, she followed.

'What cottage?' she asked his back. 'What's going on? Why can't we stay in the main house?'

'Because Mother is manipulating again.' He didn't stop until they reached a small one-storey white house. One of the tiny buildings she'd seen from the air. It was set closer to the ocean than the main house. With its tangerine-coloured shutters and narrow veranda, it looked as if it had been designed and painted as a counterpoint to the main house.

It was darling. It was charming. It was homey. It wasn't big enough.

Kate, with sinking desperation, said so.

'You think I don't know that!' Damon almost shouted at her.

Wincing, Kate opened the door and went in. The living-room-kitchen was bright and airy, painted white and fitted out with a table and chairs as well as a white wicker settee and matching chairs with gaily flowered cushions. Ten steps took her across the room and through the only other door.

It was a bedroom. Equally bright. Equally airy. Just as tiny.

With one double bed.

Kate looked at him narrowly.

Damon said an extremely rude word. 'The cottage wasn't my idea.'

'The marriage was. Honestly, Damon, this gets worse and worse. Didn't you think at all before you proposed this stupid scheme?'

He rubbed a hand through his hair. 'It seemed like a good idea at the time.'

'Do you always make spur-of-the-moment business decisions.'

'Of course not.'

'Well, then. . .?'

He shrugged and leaned against the wall, closing his eyes. 'Put it down to stress.'

Kate thought he did indeed look stressed. If she'd dared she would have reached out and touched his cheek, perhaps brushed that stray lock of hair back off his forehead. She stuffed her hands into the pockets of her skirt.

She looked around the tiny bedroom with its soft white walls and light wicker furniture, its lazily spinning ceiling fan and its flower-quilted bed. She couldn't help thinking what a really lovely place it would be if she were on a real honeymoon.

Deliberately she went back into the other room. 'At least you can sleep in the living-room here,' she said off-handedly.

Damon said a very rude word.

He let Kate have the bedroom.

She told him he was a gentleman.

He could think of another word for it. 'Idiot' sprang to mind. And the longer he lay on the hard wood floor and listened to her humming in the bedroom, imagining her with her long hair loose and free, her face freshly scrubbed, her nightgown barely covering the curves he knew were a part of her, the more certain he was.

Damn! What was he doing here?

Damon didn't like it when things got out of control, and there was no doubt that, as far as his marriage to Kate went, things had. Not that Teresa didn't believe in their wedded bliss. She did. But that was thanks to Kate, not him.

Kate had done everything she should have with Teresa, laughing and smiling over dinner, answering her questions with the right amount of eagerness, even appearing suitably smitten with Damon when it seemed to be required.

It had been his own behaviour that had caused Teresa to lift her brows in wonder. He'd been reluctant to touch Kate when they sat on the sofa side by side. When Teresa had teasingly asked him some silly question about his love-life, he'd almost bitten her head off. And when they were leaving and Kate had casually put her hand on his arm, he'd jumped.

Why? Because he wanted her.

He'd hoped that ignoring her the past week would put a damper on his desire. He'd hoped that she would do something or say something that would turn him off.

She hadn't yet.

He saw the light in the bedroom flick off and heard the bed creak. He remembered the nights last week when he'd lain on the floor of the bedroom and watched her slip into bed. Here he didn't even have the pleasure — or pain — of doing that.

He cursed and rolled over. Something small and dark scuttled across the moonlit floor.

He muttered a word as unprintable as the one he'd used earlier. It was going to be a long night.

Night? Hah. It was going to be a hell of a long week. He tried not to think about the year of marriage that lay ahead of him.

When he did, he told himself that it was purely a

matter of hormones. He hadn't had a woman in a long time. Most of the time it didn't matter. Now it did simply because of the propinquity.

Everywhere he went, there she was.

And he couldn't have her.

Damn it, why hadn't he found a woman who liked casual sex? It would be so much easier to be married to her if she did!

He shut his eyes; he dreamed of Kate.

He dreamed of stripping off her nightgown and learning the line of those curves, discovering the depths of her. He dreamed of making love to her until she was senseless with desire. And then he dreamed of her hands on him — light hands, delicate hands — tempting, teasing as they tripped up his bare calf. His need woke him, made him moan.

And then in that half-awake and half-dreaming state, he realised he could still feel that light touch.

It wasn't Kate.

He yelped, leaping to his feet. A palmetto bug fell to the floor and scurried out of sight under the cupboard. Damon stood, white-faced and shaking, stunned and muttering. He spoke English now without a second thought. He'd used it every day, all day, since he'd been sixteen. But swearing in Greek was far more satisfying.

He muttered one last curse and shuddered, then raked his fingers through his hair and looked longingly at the closed bedroom door. But it didn't take much imagination to conjure up the furore that would result if he invaded that sacred domain.

Muttering, he dragged the sheet over and folded himself onto the short narrow settee. He tucked the edges of the sheet around him, letting none of it touch the floor, and willed himself to sleep again.

This time he dreamed of plate-sized palmetto bugs,

of tarantulas and scorpions, of blue lizards and snakes. He awoke in a cold sweat so often that, at last, he gave up and hauled himself to his feet. There would be no sleep tonight, that was certain.

And no point in sitting there staring at the door that separated him from his wife.

Tossing the sheet on to the settee, Damon strode to the door, then let himself out into the darkness.

The moon had sunk lower and was now behind the trees. He heard soft scuttling sounds in the underbrush, but in reality they posed no menace. Damon didn't even think about them. He stalked straight ahead down the path towards the beach.

The tide was going out and there was almost no surf. The ocean lay like a still sleeping pool. Damon walked without stopping straight across the damp sand and plunged in.

To wash off the touch of the palmetto bug, to cleanse himself of the dreams of tarantulas and snakes, he told himself.

And he did that.

But even when he'd swum for over an hour, even when his lungs were near to bursting and his body longed for rest, even when he finally hauled himself out of the water and dropped down belly-first on to the sand, he still couldn't sleep.

Because it wasn't the memory of the palmetto bug that was keeping him awake. Or the tarantulas and snakes of his nightmares.

It was Kate.

'Yessir,' Teresa said with awful cheer as she spooned scrambled eggs on to their plates that morning at breakfast, 'you do got the look of a man on a honeymoon. Them bloodshot eyes and deep sockets is a dead giveaway.' She gave Damon a broad wink.

'Had a lot of experience, have you?' he asked sourly into his mug of coffee.

Kate nudged him with her elbow. If she had to be polite, there was no reason he shouldn't be.

He raised his eyes to glare at her. He'd been glaring at her all morning, ever since he'd come in at half-past seven, looking as if he'd been dragged backwards under the reef, and she'd asked, 'Oh, did you go for an early swim?'

He'd grunted and stridden past her, heading for the bathroom without speaking. A shower and a shave hadn't improved his disposition much. Kate supposed it was the floor, but she could scarcely offer to provide him with a futon here.

'An' what you going to do today?' Teresa looked at them curiously. 'Or shouldn't I ask?' Another grin.

'I don't know about Kate,' Damon muttered, 'but I need some sleep.'

'Honeymoons be like that,' Teresa said unsympathetically. Kate blushed. Damon ground his teeth.

'The trouble with her is she's known me since I was eight,' Damon grumbled when Teresa went back to the kitchen. 'Thinks she can say anything.'

'She's only teasing,' Kate pointed out.

Damon grunted and bit down on his toast with considerable ferocity.

Teresa's light gibes continued throughout the meal, and Kate could see Damon gradually losing control. All his admonitions to her about making sure Teresa thought they were deeply in love would come to naught by his own mouth if he weren't careful.

'Come on,' she said as soon as they had finished breakfast. 'I'm taking him home,' she explained to Teresa, 'before the wild beast emerges.'

Teresa chuckled. 'You do that. Have your way with him.'

Damon opened his mouth, but Kate didn't wait to see what he was going to say. She grabbed his hand and began hauling him towards the door. 'Cool it,' she muttered. 'Just cool it. We'll go back to the house and you can take a nap.'

'Nap?' Damon sounded outraged.

'Isn't that what you said you wanted?'

'Yes, but —— ' He stopped, as if he'd been going to say something more, then thought better of it.

'It's not a bad idea, actually,' Kate said, warming to it. 'We can share the bed.'

He made a pleased sound. 'Ah.'

'I'll take it at night and you can have it during the day.'

'*What*?' He stumbled over a root and crashed into her.

Kate grinned. 'It's the perfect solution. After all, Teresa is sure to think you need plenty of rest during the day if you're going to keep up your amatory exploits all night.'

'And you don't need it, I suppose?' he demanded irritably.

Laughter bubbled up inside her. 'I'm not supposed to have to work so hard, I guess. Teresa probably thinks I just lie back and think of New York City.'

Damon scowled.

'Don't be a spoilsport,' she chided him, moving on ahead again. 'It's a better solution than you've come up with.'

'I could think of an even better one,' Damon muttered at her back.

She stopped again and glanced back. 'What?'

He looked at her, his gaze hot and hungry, and Kate didn't need to ask again. 'Forget it,' she said.

She wished she could. She was doing her best.

In fact, it would suit her to a 'T' if he wanted to

sleep the day away. They wouldn't have to pretend undying love for each other if he was asleep.

Though she was at pains to deny it, being around him all the time was making her increasingly nervous. He attracted her, and he shouldn't.

She clapped a broad-brimmed straw hat on her head, waggled her fingers in his direction and headed out of the door.

'Stay away from the house,' Damon's voice called after her. 'Teresa will expect you to be here with me,' he added when Kate turned and frowned.

'I'll head towards the beach first, then go to town. Can I get there by following the beach?'

'When you get to the sand, go right. It's about a mile to a path that leads inland past one of the inns. You'll be able to tell—the sand's been swept for the tourists. Follow the path to the water tower. You can see the town from there.' He paused then added, 'Behave.'

Kate looked back at him, startled.

'Everyone will know who you are. Don't say anything we'll regret.'

'I've already said enough that I regret, starting with "I do",' Kate told him.

'Me, too.'

Their gazes locked for a moment in silent battle. Then Damon turned and strode into the bedroom without another word.

So he didn't like their marriage any better than she did. She was annoyed that the thought disturbed her. It shouldn't, she told herself. She should be glad and she certainly shouldn't be surprised.

But damn it, it still hurt.

Because of Bryce, she told herself. It was because she was still smarting over her failure with Bryce. It certainly couldn't have anything to do with Damon himself. That would be the height of folly.

Deliberately she put Damon Alexakis out of her mind and forced herself to concentrate on the island she was about to explore. They had arrived rather late yesterday, so she'd only caught a glimpse of the town as they'd passed through, and after dinner last night there'd been little chance to explore. Still Damon had taken her down to the beach briefly and she was enchanted by what she'd seen so far.

It was every bit the tropical paradise she'd often dreamed of. But if she hoped to lose herself in it, forgetting Damon and her marriage to him, she soon realised that she was out of luck.

Damon was right—everyone knew about her.

'Mornin', Miz Damon,' the plump lady at the basket shop greeted her.

'How you doin' today, Mrs Damon?' said the old man feeding the chickens.

'Hot 'nough, ain't it, Miz Damon?' said the teenage boy working on the outboard motor by the dock.

And when she tried ducking inside a tiny establishment called Rebecca's Pineapple Shop to buy a soda and recover from the smiling, knowing eyes, the proprietor, a jovial young mother whose toddlers were playing underfoot, asked, 'How long you and Mr Damon stayin'?'

Kate gave up trying to pretend it was coincidence that everyone knew her name. 'A week.'

'A week? Only a week?' the woman looked dismayed.

'We have work to get back to,' Kate said apologetically, and was surprised to note that she really felt that way. She liked the islanders' friendliness. She would have liked to get to know them better.

Rebecca finished shelving some cans of vegetables.

She made a tsking sound. 'Mr Damon, he work too much. Always takin' care of everybody else. Don't ever take time for himself.' She shook her head. 'Hey, Silas,' she called out to the men playing dominoes on the porch. 'You hear that? Mrs Damon say they only be stayin' a week!'

Two elderly faces, both with grizzled beards, peered in the screen. One of them gave Kate a sly grin before turning his gaze to meet Rebecca's. 'She a pretty lady. I reckon maybe Mr Damon figure he gonna get the job done in a week!'

'Silas!' Rebecca looked scandalised.

Kate looked at first one then the other, confused, until the man called Silas cackled and explained, 'Only son, ain't he? Son of his own. Stands to reason. . .' He winked at her.

Kate felt the heat rise in her cheeks. She looked about hopefully for another exit, knowing even as she did so that there wasn't one.

'Don't mind Silas,' Rebecca told her. 'He be a dirty ol' man with a one-track mind. But he right. You sure pretty. Family don't be comin' for the holiday this year?'

'Family? Oh, you mean Damon's. I think they are, but——'

'Then you be here.' Rebecca smiled and handed Kate her soda. 'Alexakises always are.'

Kate could hardly say she wasn't going to be an Alexakis for long. She thanked the lady, smiled weakly and went out onto the porch.

'You an' Mr Damon wanta go fishin'?' Silas said as she passed. 'You tell 'im Silas'll take you. Be my pleasure. He not workin' now, is he?'

'He's sleeping.'

Silas chuckled. 'Wore out, is he? Can't say I'm surprised. Always was a hard worker, that un.'

Blushing furiously, Kate bounded down the steps and set off up the street in a hurry. Silas's cheerful laughter echoed after her as she went.

She didn't go in any more shops. She didn't even finish her trek along the street that skirted the harbour. Instead she headed back across the island towards the beach. It had been almost deserted when she'd walked to town earlier. She was relieved to find it was the same now.

She took her time walking back, scuffing through the fine coral sand, composing her thoughts — or trying to — doing her best to come up with a plan of behaviour.

You must act, not simply react, she always told her fledgling nannies. Children can sense when you're losing control.

Kate knew she was losing control. And she was afraid that the whole world — especially Rebecca and Silas — knew it.

She felt guilty for trying to deceive them and at the same time knew that, even if she was, she wasn't deceiving herself.

There was more to this incipient panic she was feeling than simple deception and the resultant guilt it entailed. There was the way she was reacting to Damon.

The awareness. The tension. The desire.

All day — no, all week — she had tried to ignore it, hoping it would go away. She had thought herself immune to such reactions after Bryce. Heaven knew she ought to be!

But she wasn't.

It was foolishness what she was feeling for Damon Alexakis. It could only cause trouble. He wasn't interested in her. And even if he was staying married to her when he no longer had to in order to keep

Marina at bay, he wasn't staying married to her because he loved her! It was simply that he'd look like an idiot if he admitted it was all a sham now.

He certainly wouldn't want to get involved with her.

And for that matter, Kate McKee, she told herself firmly, kicking the sand, you don't want to get involved with him!

Alexakis.

What? She stopped dead, the word echoing in her mind.

Alexakis, the tiny voice repeated insistently. You're not Kate McKee any more. You're Kate Alexakis now. Damon Alexakis's wife.

Kate shut her eyes and shook her head. She didn't want to think about that.

Still, within minutes she would be upon him again. She would have to decide how to act.

Sinking down in the sand, she drew her knees up and wrapped her arms around them and tried to come to terms with things. But it was no use. The afternoon was not made for thinking.

In New York she could have done it. In New York she was remarkably clear-headed and sensible. There she could have shut everything else out of her mind— the horns and sirens, the suffocating heat reflecting off the buildings, the diesel fumes and car exhaust—and sorted out her relationship with Damon easily.

Not here. Here the island breeze teased her hair, like a lover's fingers loosening it from the knot she'd fixed at the back of her head. Here the sun kissed her back and she shut her eyes. She leaned back, lifting her face towards the warmth, imagining how it would be if this really were a honeymoon, if she had really come here with a man who loved her.

She remembered Bryce. *Always* she remembered Bryce.

But somehow here the disaster that had been her marriage seemed remote and ineffectual. It had hurt her once; it had nearly destroyed her. But now its power over her seemed oddly lessened.

Here in this island paradise that, until a few days ago, Kate had never known existed, she felt the pain fading. She closed her eyes and saw, not Bryce's fair good looks and handsome sneering face, but another face — this one darker, not quite so classically handsome — and she remembered the touch of Damon's lips, their hint of promise, of magic, of hope.

She felt tired. So very tired.

She had worked so hard for so long. She hadn't really taken a day off since Bryce had walked out on her. There hadn't been time to. She'd fought to develop her business, to make her contacts, to hold off her father. She put in hours and days and months and, now that she thought about it, years.

And never once had she flagged. Not even for a weekend. The only times she'd left the city had been to see to home situations. There'd never been a lazy Sunday in the Hamptons or a weekend antiquing with friends in Bucks County. There'd never been a Christmas ski trip or a jaunt to Vermont in the autumn to see the leaves. There'd always been work to do. So very much work.

And anyway, it had helped keep the memories of Bryce and her foolishness at bay.

It had been so long since she'd relaxed like this. So long since she'd stretched out on the sand and let the earth and the sun warm her body. So very, very long since she'd felt as settled and comfortable. The sound of the surf soothed her, lulled her, made her smile.

Of course she would have to sort out what to do about Damon Alexakis soon. But first — if only for a few minutes — she had to close her eyes.

CHAPTER SIX

'You stay out much longer, I be servin' you for dinner 'stead of the lobster.'

The words startled Kate out of a sound sleep and she jerked up to see Teresa standing beside her on the beach, shaking her head and smiling down at her.

'You be cooked, Mrs Kate,' she said, her tone a mixture of disapproval and dismay.

Wincing as she touched her now rosy forearm, Kate nodded. 'I fell asleep. What time is it?'

'Dinnertime. Mr Damon didn't know where you were. Them sisters of his.' She shook her head, irritated. 'I thought maybe I take a look.'

'What about Damon's sisters?'

'They been callin' all day. One problem an' another. Can't leave the poor man alone even on his honeymoon. I don' blame you for goin' for a walk, listenin' to all that.'

'Er — yes. I didn't realise it was so late. I only meant to close my eyes.' But it had been two hours at least. And she hadn't stirred. She had dreamed, though, she remembered that much. They had been incredible dreams. Sexy dreams. About Damon.

If it were possible to turn a deeper shade of red she would have done so.

She shoved a hand through dishevelled hair and scrambled to her feet. 'Thanks for waking me, Teresa. Do I have time for a shower?'

'Depends,' Teresa said darkly, 'if that Electra ever get off the phone. You don't got to let him spend all his time with them, you know.'

'I know,' Kate said.

'Ah, good. He finished.' Teresa grinned. 'I serve dinner now. You can shower later. Mr Damon be happy to help you clean up later, I bet.'

Kate didn't want to think about that. If Bryce had found her wanting, Damon definitely would, all dreams to the contrary. There was no point in complicating matters further over a few hormonal urges.

Damon wanted it to be business. So did she.

She hurried up the beach following Teresa's broad back, trying to put her hair into some semblance of order as she went.

Damon was standing on the veranda. He looked hassled and harried and no more rested than when Kate had left. She felt an unreasoned burst of sympathy for him.

Damon looked her up and down, taking in her rumpled, sweaty clothes, sunburnt face and tousled hair. 'What happened to you?'

All sympathy fled. 'I fell asleep on the beach.'

'Stupid thing to do.'

'I didn't do it intentionally.' She waited until Teresa had disappeared into the kitchen and added, 'I got tired of playing the devoted newlywed in town. I was trying to give us some space. And you some sleep, if you'll recall.'

'Sleep? There's a laugh. I didn't even get my head near a pillow. I didn't bloody get a chance!'

Teresa reappeared carrying a bowl of succulent lobster stew and with obvious effort Damon modulated his tone as she dished it out.

'My sisters called,' he grumbled.

'They miss you that much?'

'They miss coming to me for help at every turn.' He shoved a hand through already tousled hair. 'Pandora is stuck in Vegas without a dime. Electra's show closed. Chloe is in Dar es Salaam and needs me to wire her some money to get home. Arete quit at Strahans', came back to our place and promptly got into a fight with Stephanos about who was running things. They both called me. Twice.' He leaned his elbows on the table and rested his head in them, then lifted his bloodshot gaze to meet hers. 'I ought to fire both of them.'

'So, why don't you?'

He looked momentarily startled, then ignoring her, went on, 'The last one was Daphne trying to unload a truckload of chinchillas on me. And you.'

'*What?*'

Damon rubbed a hand across his face. 'Don't ask.' He slid back in his chair and closed his eyes as Teresa left again. 'God, I'm tired.'

'You look like hell.'

'Thank you very much.'

'Always glad to be of help.' If she'd really been his wife in more than name, she'd have been far more sympathetic. She'd have told him he worked far too hard and let his family take far too much advantage of him. But in the circumstances, she had no right to.

In the circumstances, it was easier to be flippant, and safer, too.

Fixing her eyes firmly on her plate, she dug in. It was a savoury, succulent blend of lobster, potatoes and vegetables, and it went a long way towards making things right with the world as far as Kate was concerned.

'It's very good, ' she said.

But a minute or more passed before Damon hauled himself upright and, muttering under his breath, began to eat as well.

They didn't speak again until their plates were clean and Teresa came to clear the table.

'Not much of a honeymoon,' she commented sadly.

Damon's head jerked up at that. He glowered at her. 'What's that supposed to mean?'

'You all day talkin' on the phone, Mrs Damon goin' to town by herself.'

'We don't have to live in each other's pockets, Teresa,' Damon said shortly.

But Teresa just clucked her tongue. 'What'm I gonna tell your mother?'

'My mother?' Damon looked so horrified that Kate almost laughed. 'You don't have to tell my mother anything!'

Teresa stepped back. 'You don't got to yell, Mr Damon. I hear you. I be right here. Course I got to tell her. She askin'.'

Kate saw Damon visibly try to control himself. With considerable effort he softened his tone. 'Our honeymoon and our marriage are our business, Teresa. Not my mother's. I will thank you not to say a word.'

Kate watched with interest as the two stares met, Damon's hard and fierce, Teresa's mild and curious.

Finally the older woman shrugged. 'Not one word, Mr Damon?'

'Not one word.'

''f that's what you want.' Teresa turned almost sadly and started towards the kitchen.

Damon grunted his satisfaction.

As much as in this instance Kate agreed with him, she did wish he'd be a little less high-handed with Teresa.

'It was a lovely meal, Teresa. Thank you,' Kate called after her, determined to be polite even if her husband wasn't.

Teresa turned and beamed. 'My pleasure. You have a good night, now. I be seein' you at breakfast. You take extra good care of Mr Grouchy here.' She shot a quick look at Damon, noted his fierce expression, giggled and vanished into the kitchen.

'God, I don't know what's got into that woman,' he complained, shoving his chair back and heading for the door. 'She never used to be so cheeky.'

'She's pleased for us.'

Damon snorted. 'She has a damned funny way of showing it.'

'She thinks we're madly in love and she's enchanted.'

'The more fool she,' Damon muttered and strode towards the cottage without looking back.

Kate hurried to catch up. 'Dibs on the shower.'

He glanced back briefly, his expression distasteful. 'You could use one.'

'How gallant of you to say so.'

He gave her a twisted smile. 'Always glad to be of help.' His echo of her earlier words mocked her as she hurried past.

Damn it, she groused as she undressed, why did it have to be like this? Why did they have to continually snipe at each other? Why couldn't they get along?

Kate couldn't ever remember a man who could provoke her the way Damon could. Nor a man who attracted her quite so much either.

She didn't want to think about that.

Deliberately she turned on the water as hard as it would go, stepped under the shower and welcomed a cleansing rush of water beating down on her naked body.

She didn't know how long she stayed there.

Long enough, she hoped, to get herself firmly under control, long enough to tamp down all interest in Damon Alexakis, long enough to recite the list of every nanny she had ever placed, every family she had ever served, every goal she had set for herself.

She hoped, too, as she finished drying off and slipping into her nightgown, that it was long enough for Damon to have settled down in the living-room and fallen asleep. She didn't want to have to face him again tonight.

He was asleep all right. On her bed.

Scowling, Kate crept towards the bed and peered down at him.

Damon was sprawled across it, face down, one arm outflung, the other tucked under his head. The khaki shorts and T-shirt he had been wearing lay in a heap on the floor. He was clad now in only a pair of light blue boxer shorts.

Kate stood quite still taking in the prospect of his smooth tanned back, the curve of his firmly muscled buttocks, the length of his hair-roughened legs. She'd always thought the Greek god business so much hot air. Now she wasn't so sure.

She closed her eyes and took a deep, steadying breath, then licked parched lips.

'Damon,' she said firmly. 'Get up.'

He didn't stir.

'Damon!' Her tone was louder and more irritable this time. She opened her eyes as she did so.

Still he didn't move.

Kate reached down and tugged on one of his feet. He groaned and pulled up his knee.

'Damon! Get up. It's time to go to bed.'

He made a muffled sound. ''m in bed.'

'It's my bed. My turn.'

'Share,' he mumbled into the sheet.

'No, I'm not going to share.' That way lay disaster. 'You're going to leave. Now.' Once more she reached for his foot and gave it a jerk.

A hand reached out and grasped hers, yanking her down on to the bed beside him.

'Oooff! Damon! Damn you!' She struggled against a surprisingly strong grip. 'Let go! Get up and get out of here. Now!'

'No. Too damn tired. Here——' he shoved over slightly '—your space.' His eyes fluttered shut again; his breathing deepened.

Kate wrenched her wrist out of his grasp and scrambled off the bed. She felt like punching him, like kicking him. Hard. She contented herself with smacking him once on the rear end.

He rolled on to his back and regarded her scowlingly from beneath hooded lids.

Kate stepped back hastily. 'You agreed. I took your word as a gentleman.'

'Your mistake.' A slight smile flickered across his mouth. 'You don't need to stand there with that look of outraged virtue on your face. I'm hardly any threat to you tonight. I can't keep my eyelids up, much less anything else.'

'Don't be crude.'

'I'm not being crude. I'm being accurate.' And he rolled over once more and started to snore.

Kate, hands on hips, glowered at him.

So, fine, he wasn't a gentleman. He was right about that. She should have known that from the first. A gentleman would never have proposed such a marriage!

Well, she certainly wasn't going to sleep in the same bed with him, then. How did she know he wasn't lying this time, too?

She should go straight up to the main house and sleep there. That would teach him. And it would certainly give Teresa something to call home about!

But even as she thought it, she knew she wouldn't. And not only for Damon's sake either. On her own behalf, she didn't want to disillusion Helena. She liked her new mother-in-law. She regretted that she was only going to have her a year. But as long as she did have her, Kate didn't want to see the worry and sadness she knew would appear on Damon's mother's face.

The more fool she, she thought grimly, echoing Damon's words.

Cursing both him and herself, she yanked the afghan off the back of the wicker chair and stalked into the living-room, shut out the lights and curled on the settee.

Half an hour of twisting this way and that convinced her she'd never get a moment's sleep if she stayed there. Grumbling, she placed the cushions on the wood floor and stretched out on them.

There, she thought, lying down, that was better.

Outside she could hear frogs croaking and insects chirping above the soft sound of the surf. Inside she could hear the bed creak as Damon rolled over. Her jaw tightened.

She turned on to her side, tucked the afghan around her, and willed herself to sleep. The moonlight bathed the room in a soft silvery glow. It was peaceful, she told herself. Soothing. She could sleep here. She knew she could. There was nothing to fear with Damon in the other room ——

Except that dark shape scuttling across the floor towards her.

'Aargh!'

Kate leapt to her feet and scrambled to the chair, standing on it, her knees shaking, teeth chattering. 'God!' It was pure prayer, a desperate pleading for salvation. 'What the ——' She unscrewed her tightly shut eyes and ventured a peek. It looked like the cockroach from hell. Used to the rather small, mundane New York City variety and hating them, she didn't even want to think about one the size of her fist.

Still trembling, Kate licked her lips. Another one appeared from beneath the cupboard.

She suppressed a squeak of horror, sinking on to the chair and wrapping her arms around her knees, clenching her teeth together to stop them from making noise. Her heart felt as if it were doing a fast-stepping dance in her chest. She took deep, even breaths, hoping it would slow down.

And all the while she gazed with morbid fascination as the two bugs trundled about the room, one of them moving towards the cushion she had just abandoned. She shuddered.

There was no way, *no way*, she was sleeping down there again tonight. Or ever.

Slowly, carefully, she relaxed her grip on her calves and stood up, still in the chair, still watching them unblinkingly as if one might suddenly decide to fly right at her.

Could they fly? It didn't bear thinking about.

She took a mighty leap and almost flew herself into the bedroom where she bounded into the bed next to Damon. He grunted as the bed jostled.

'I'm not sleeping out there! There are *bugs* out there!'

'Mmm.'

'You sleep out there!'

'No.' One arm reached out and slid around her shoulders, pulling her down firmly next to him.

'But——'

'Be quiet, Kate. Just be quiet and go to sleep.'

She tried wriggling out of his grasp, but he had her pinned beneath one strong arm and one hair-roughened leg.

''s me or the bugs, Kate,' he said sleepily. 'Take your pick.'

Some choice.

For what seemed like hours Kate lay, stiff as a board, as far towards her edge of the bed as possible while Damon made a soft whuffling sound, curled on his side and breathed more deeply.

At first she watched him expectantly, with as much trepidation as if he'd been one of those monster black bugs about to attack her. But time wore on and Damon didn't move.

Gradually she relaxed, felt the tension slip from her shoulders and her spine, felt her legs slacken and her fists unclench. But she didn't sleep. Couldn't.

She was too wide awake. Too aware.

Slowly, carefully, she turned on to her side so she could watch this man to whom she was married.

She remembered studying Damon briefly as he'd slept on the aeroplane, but that hadn't seemed nearly as intimate as this did. Then his features had softened slightly, his eyes had been closed, his collar button opened and his tie askew, but he'd still seemed remote and formidable in his starched white shirt and navy wool suit.

But as she lay beside him in bed, she found that he was formidable in an entirely different way now. It wasn't the hard-edged, decisive businessman that she felt in awe of this time, it was the supremely fit, well-muscled male.

And yet for all his masculine potential, she found herself feeling oddly protective of him.

Damon looked even more exhausted now than he had on the night flight back from Vegas. The lines of fatigue on his face seemed more pronounced, the hollows of his eyes more deeply shadowed. And Kate

found herself wanting to edge closer to him and put
her arms around him, letting him rest his head against
the softness of her breasts.

Oh, yes, right, and then what? she asked herself,
irritated at her own foolishness. Would you really want
what would happen next?

For there was no doubt in her mind that comforting
would not be what would take place. He would want
to make love.

Kate remembered the last time she had been in bed
with a man, remembered the fiasco that had been her
marriage — her *first* marriage, she corrected herself.

She had been eager and willing to make love with
Bryce. At least, at first she had.

Of course she knew she was inexperienced; she
hadn't thought it would matter. They loved each other,
didn't they? So if things were awkward at first, it
wouldn't matter. The expertise would come.

But Bryce didn't have the time or the patience for
that.

He wanted his satisfaction and he wanted it now.
Even that very first night he had reached for her rather
impatiently and had taken as much satisfaction as he
could get with her — 'not a lot,' he'd told her scornfully
the day he'd left — then rolled away and fallen into a
heavy slumber.

And Kate had lain awake at his side on their
wedding-night feeling lonelier and less fulfilled than
ever.

It hadn't got any better.

She cringed now at the memory of it. Worse, she
recalled, she seemed to have been powerless to change
it.

With Bryce the closeness she'd craved had always
eluded her. They'd had sex, but they'd never had true
intimacy, nothing like the soft words, gentle touches

and implicit understanding that went beyond the body to touch the heart.

They hadn't had love.

Not really.

And in this marriage there was no love either.

For all that she was attracted to Damon, for all that she wanted to reach out to him, there was no use. No use pretending. Damon might awaken, he might reach for her, he might even consummate their marriage.

But he, too, would be simply assuaging a physical need.

And he would doubtless find her as lacking as Bryce apparently had. He would slake his need, use her the same way Bryce had, and he, too, would see the lack in her.

Kate couldn't even bear to think about it.

She'd loved once. She'd tried. She'd failed.

She didn't want—couldn't take—more of the same with Damon.

He awoke late. Restless and rested at the same time. The sun streamed in the window halfway up in the sky. Damon groaned. He could imagine what Teresa would say about that.

He could imagine what Kate would say too, for he realised that he was still lying in the bed. *Her* bed.

He remembered toppling on it last night, remembered listening to her turn on the shower, remembered telling himself that he'd move in a minute.

And then he remembered. . . What?

What did he remember? Some vague discussion with Kate. . .something about its being her bed, something about his being a gentleman. . .or not.

He groaned again.

Obviously he hadn't been.

And then? And then. . .

She'd left. And come back.

He rolled on to his back and rubbed his fists into his eyes, then pressed on them, trying to recapture the memory. Or had it been a dream?

He supposed it could have been a dream. He'd had enough of them lately. Lurid, erotic fantasies in which he and Kate had made slow, tantalising love.

This time he remembered — dreamed about? — reaching out in the night and finding her there. He'd been too tired to do more than draw her close and wrap his arms around her, then settle his chin in the curve of her shoulder and breathe in the sweetness of her hair.

He pulled the pillow over his face and folded his arms across it. He ached just thinking about it.

'Is this a new form of meditating or are you suffocating yourself?'

Damon jerked the pillow away from his face to see Kate at the foot of the bed looking down at him. He groped wildly for the sheet and was relieved to find that it covered him. Of course he was clothed — barely — but that didn't mean she wouldn't be able to notice his obvious arousal.

Hastily, still keeping the sheet over him, he sat up. 'How about trying to compose an apology?'

Kate cocked her head.

'I stole your bed.'

Was it his imagination or was she blushing? She took a quick step backwards.

'Yes, you did.' She avoided his gaze, going to open the blinds, then straightening the cloth on the small round table in front of the window.

He watched her, curious now, memories flitting in and out of his mind, teasing him, making him wonder. He traced a pattern in the sheet but his eyes never left her. 'So you slept on the floor?'

'Of course! You don't think I slept with you, do you?' Bright spots of colour stained her normally ivory cheeks.

'A man can hope.'

'Don't be ridiculous.'

'I have these memories, you see.' And he did even as he spoke. It was coming back to him now. 'Something about a bug. . .?'

Kate glared. 'Well, what did you expect me to do? Stay on the floor when there were insects the size of dinner plates waltzing around?'

'Ah.' He leaned back against the headboard and grinned up at her. 'So it wasn't a dream.'

'Some of it was! You were. . .you were. . .*snuggling*. . .up to me! Making noises!'

'Noises?' That wasn't the way he remembered it. 'Maybe I was kissing you.'

Her teeth came together. She lifted her chin and stared at the far corner of the ceiling and didn't reply.

'Was I?'

She stuffed her hands into the pockets of her shorts. 'Maybe you were.'

A corner of his mouth lifted wickedly. 'Couldn't you tell?'

Kate stamped her foot. 'All right, you were.'

'And obviously with great success. Did anyone ever tell you that you're terrific for a man's ego.'

'No one asked you to kiss me.'

'Was it disgusting?' He tried to sound as if it were purely a matter of idle curiosity. It wasn't. He wanted to kiss her again now that they were both awake. He wanted to grab her hand and pull her down on the bed beside him, strip off her shirt and smooth the shorts from her hips. He wanted. . .

Damn it! This was not the way to gain self-control and composure.

'I didn't come to talk about your kissing me,' Kate said stiffly. 'I came to tell you that Silas is up at the house. He wants to know if we want to go fishing.'

'Do we?'

Kate blinked. 'He said to ask you.'

'And I'm asking you. We are husband and wife on our honeymoon. We are spending the day together. Would you like to go fishing?'

She hesitated.

'What's the matter?' he asked.

'No one's ever asked me before.'

'To go fishing?'

'No. Well, that too, I guess. But what I meant was, no one's ever asked me whether I wanted to do something. My father, I mean. Or. . .or Bryce. They always just. . .assumed.'

He stared at her, amazed, and she shrugged help-lessly, then ducked her head, the colour blooming in her cheeks again.

'It's not a big deal,' she said gruffly.

But Damon thought it was. He felt an unaccountable anger towards her father and her husband. What kind of men were they, not to take her wishes into consider-ation? 'Would you like to go fishing, Kate?'

She shot him an oblique glance as if to see if he meant it, and then gave a jerky nod. 'That would be nice.'

'And safer than kissing,' he said, needing to make her smile.

She looked startled, her eyes widening, her mouth making a silent O. Then she smiled, only a little at first, then more broadly as if they were co-conspirators again and not adversaries.

'Much safer,' she said and danced off towards the door. 'I'll tell Silas.'

*   *   *

Fishing. Yes, fishing was safe. Nothing could happen in a boat the size of Silas's. Especially with Silas in it, too, Kate told herself.

They moved from one fishing spot to another while Silas studied the reefs and the weather, which promised late day storms, muttered an occasional monosyllable and then nodded his head when he thought the fishing would be good.

Damon didn't dispute it. At first Kate found that surprising, expecting that as he was an expert in so many areas he would naturally assume he was an expert in this one. Heaven knew her father would have.

But Damon seemed content to let Silas do the leading today, only offering his expertise when it came to teaching her how to bait her hook. She felt all thumbs and more than a little foolish when she tried.

'I can't,' she said at first, pushing it away after she'd fumbled and dropped the piece of langousta Silas had offered her for bait.

· 'Here. Like this,' Damon said, and he was surprisingly patient as he showed her once more how to slip it on to the hook. 'Don't get so frantic. No one's grading you.'

Kate shot him a sceptical look, expecting sarcasm in his words, but he looked quite sincere and when he offered to demonstrate one more time, she nodded her head.

This time she got it, then cast the line overboard as Damon instructed her to. 'Now what?'

'Now we wait.'

If Kate had ever given much thought to fishing before, and she didn't remember having done so, she was fairly sure she would have thought it boring.

It wasn't.

It was soothing, centring. It gave a person time —

time to relax, to muse, to bask. All those things that fast-lane, big-city people like herself and Damon rarely had time for. And the miracle was, it could all be accomplished under the guise of actually doing something!

What a racket, she thought, smiling.

There was a sudden tug on her line and the reel began to spin. 'Oh!'

Damon grinned. 'Looks as if you've got a live one.'

The reel spun madly as she tried desperately to catch the whirling knob. At last she clamped down on it and stopped it. Then she thrust it towards Damon. He shook his head.

'It's your fish. Reel it in.'

It was harder than she'd imagined. This was no guppy on the end of her line, or if it was, they would be writing about it in Guinness. Her arms trembled from the exertion.

'You doin' good. Hang in there,' Silas encouraged her. 'Look there, he be comin'.'

Kate looked where he pointed and saw a silvery flash against the surface of the water, then felt the line jerk and she almost lost all the ground she'd gained. She bit down on her lip and tensed her fingers.

By the time she finally hauled him in, her arms were shaking, and she expected a fifty-pound barracuda to appear on the end of her line.

'A grouper,' Silas said as he netted the huge ugly yellowish fish. 'A baby.'

'A baby?' Kate croaked. 'Baby whale.'

Silas laughed, unhooking it and dropping it into the well. 'Naw. He be four, five pounds maybe at most.'

Kate stared.

'Bigger than mine,' Damon said, and Kate turned to note that while she'd been duelling with her grouper, Damon had landed a fish of his own.

'Yours is prettier,' she told him. It was a slim, shiny fish, much handsomer than hers.

'Thank you very much,' he replied, amusement in his tone. He grinned at her and Kate couldn't help responding in kind.

'Need some help baiting your hook this time?'

She shook her head. 'I'll try it on my own.'

It occurred to Kate then that Damon Alexakis wasn't very much like her father after all. Her father never would have bothered teaching her to bait the hook, nor would he have sat by and tolerated her clumsy attempts to follow his instructions. Neither would he have let her land it herself. He would have taken the whole project out of her hands and done it better.

He always did everything better. Including live other people's lives.

As she baited the hook, with less trouble this time, and cast, she thought about how, according to Teresa, Damon had spent the better part of yesterday dealing with his sisters' various complaints.

Eugene wouldn't have dealt with them.

'You made your bed, lie in it,' he would have told them, just as he'd told Kate when she married Bryce. And as long as she was married to Bryce, he'd never spoken to her. No matter how awful his sisters were, she couldn't imagine Damon turning his back on his family that way.

And that made her like him even more.

She didn't want to like Damon Alexakis. Being attracted to him was difficult enough. If she liked him as well. . .

Kate turned away from him, deliberately concentrating on Silas's strong calloused hands hauling in a hand line. But then Damon said, 'I've got another one,' and moments later he pulled in a shiny iridescent fish with frantic eyes and a gaping mouth.

Kate watched as it wriggled and twitched in the last throes of battle-weary panic fighting the man who'd caught it.

It reminded her of herself.

'I got to pick up some divers been to Doctor's Cay 'bout two o'clock,' Silas said after they'd fished for another couple of hours. 'You want to go home or—' here his grin widened '—you want to go to Rainbow Cove, do a little swimming, an' I pick you up later?'

'I don't have my suit,' Kate said doubtfully.

Silas grinned. 'Don't matter.'

Kate supposed it wouldn't. She could paddle around in her shorts and shirt perfectly well, and since the breeze had dropped she was feeling very hot and sticky.

'Let's go swimming,' Kate said impulsively. 'It would be so refreshing.'

Besides, they'd be gone from the house that much longer, away from the bedroom, out in the open where it was, as Damon had pointed out earlier, 'safer'.

'You tol' her 'bout Rainbow already, huh?' Silas nudged Damon.

'No, I didn't,' he said shortly. 'What about your sunburn, Kate?'

Kate shrugged. 'It's not bad. Please?'

'Such a willing woman.' Silas chuckled. Damon looked decidedly uncomfortable.

'What's it got, sharks?' Kate asked.

'No,' Damon said, and Silas laughed more heartily than ever. He opened the throttle and they surged away, heading north around the top of the mainland.

Rainbow was a secluded horseshoe-shaped cove entered by a narrow inlet. With a pristine pink sand beach tucked into a mangrove jungle, it looked like paradise. Kate was enchanted.

'It's beautiful, like a Garden of Eden.'

'You got that right.' Silas cut the engine and the boat slipped smoothly through the wave-less water towards the shore. 'You enjoy it, now,' he said as he helped her out in the shallow water. He winked at Damon and handed him some towels. 'I reckon I don't have to tell you that. Keep those clothes dry now.'

Then he opened the throttle and churned away.

'What'd he mean, keep our clothes dry?' Kate asked. 'How can you swim and keep your clothes. . .?' Her voice trailed off. Her eyes narrowed. She looked at Damon accusingly.

He scowled at her. 'Don't blame me. I wasn't the one who said, "let's", when he mentioned Rainbow Cove.'

'You didn't say it was the. . .the. . .'

'Skinny-dipping beach? It always has been.'

'How was I supposed to know that? You should have said no.'

'I'm supposed to say we can't go because it's a nude beach?'

'You didn't have to say *because* it's a nude beach. You could have. . .I don't know. . .you could have thought of something.'

'I did. Your sunburn.'

'Well, we don't have to,' she said after a moment.

'It's custom.'

'We'll break it.'

'Silas is a bigger gossip than any woman on this island. You think he won't tell? We're supposed to be newlyweds, damn it. I'd *want* to come here if this was a normal marriage!'

'Well, it's not, is it?' Kate said scathingly.

'No, it sure as hell isn't,' Damon said through gritted teeth.

'So swim if you want,' Kate said. 'I'll sit here until he comes back. Nice and dry, how's that?' She plopped herself down on the towel, brushed away a mosquito, and glared at him. 'I'll pretend I swam.'

'Maybe you can pretend your hair's wet, too.'

Kate picked up a handful of sand and threw it at him. 'Just shut up and swim. I'll close my eyes.'

'Don't do it on my account,' he said as his fingers went to the snap of his shorts.

She should have.

For a moment she did, shutting her eyes against the sight of his hands lowering the zip. But the temptation was too great, and her eyes flicked open again to watch as Damon slid the shorts down his hips and stepped out of them.

He was only the second male she'd seen totally nude. The first, of course, had been Bryce. But it took scant seconds for Kate to realise that Bryce naked was as different from Damon as it was possible for a man to be.

Blond and slim, Bryce had always looked suave and sophisticated in the three-piece suits he favoured. But whenever Kate had seen him undressed he had always seemed diminished somehow, lanky and hesitant, as if the clothes had indeed made the man.

The opposite was true of Damon.

If Damon Alexakis in a suit and tie had seemed to Kate the embodiment of masculine power, he was no less so stark naked. In fact, he was more.

Damon was lean without being lanky, firmly muscled without the least hint of fat. His chest was broad, his hips narrow, and his. . .well, his. . .Kate blushed and looked away, but not without having assertained that it was everything she might have expected.

'Little late to be checking out the merchandise, isn't it?'

'You said you didn't mind!' Kate muttered, her cheeks burning.

He grinned. 'I don't. Want to return the favour?' He stood right in front of her, looking down at her, still smiling and making no move to cover himself.

'No, I do not.'

'Spoilsport.'

'Just go swim.' Kate said to the sand.

'Sure you don't want to come along?'

'I'm fine.'

'Suit yourself, but you'll get awfully hot.'

He failed to mention that she would also get bitten by a million mosquitoes. She slapped one and then another, and another, and another. She jumped up and wrapped the towel around herself, swatting at the dive-bombing insects even as she did so. Damon, swimming away from her out in the middle of the cove, didn't notice.

'Drat!' She smacked her arm, getting two with one blow. But she couldn't even feel much satisfaction; three more took their places. She scowled fiercely, walked towards the trees in hope of some respite. But the insects were, if anything, worse there than they had been on the sand. She walked back towards the water.

Damon was perhaps forty yards out now, not really moving any longer, just floating, looking back at her. She slapped a mosquito on her leg, then another on her arm, then glared at him.

He smiled.

There was no breeze to speak of in the cove, either. Heavy dark clouds hung on the horizon, but they moved so slowly that Kate felt as if everything had stopped. She felt clammy, sticky, sweaty. Rivulets of perspiration ran down her neck, sliding along her spine, sticking between her breasts.

She glanced at her watch. Silas wouldn't be back for at least another two hours.

'Damn it,' she muttered under her breath, then out loud she called, 'Shut your eyes!'

'What?'

'You heard me, Alexakis. Damn it, shut them!'

He grinned. She couldn't tell if he shut them or not, he was too far away.

She wrapped a towel loosely around herself, then fumbled beneath it, unbuttoning her shirt. Then, holding the towel close, she slipped the shirt off. Her bra was sticking to her and she held the towel with her teeth while she wrestled it off. Then she wriggled out of her brief white shorts. She considered leaving her panties on. Silas would never know.

But the shorts she wore turned almost transparent when wet. A pair of wet panties under them would guarantee that the secret would be out.

Fuming, Kate peeled the panties off as well. She lay her clothes in a neat pile, Then with the towel still wrapped around her, she headed for the water.

'I think Silas is going to notice if the towels are wet, too,' Damon said from only twenty feet away.

Kate spun around. 'You're supposed to have your eyes closed.'

'It isn't as if I haven't seen a naked female before. I did grow up with six sisters.'

'And I suppose your sisters were the only ones you ever saw.'

'Well, there were maybe a few others.' He was smiling as he moved towards her.

'I'll bet. Stay where you are.'

Obediently Damon halted. 'I'm not the philanderer you seem to think I am.'

Kate wasn't going to argue with him. But she couldn't imagine Damon had spent much of his adult life as a practising celibate.

She was out past her knees when she knew she would have to get rid of the towel because she couldn't throw it any further. She cursed the gradual drop-off, but she had no choice. Whipping the towel towards the shore, she dived beneath the water in one fluid motion. She banged her nose on the shallow bottom and came up spluttering.

Damon stood a few feet away now, laughing.

'Wretch!' she cried, and flung herself at him, intending to drown him.

It was a major mistake.

CHAPTER SEVEN

'Ooof! Kate! Wai——'

But there was no waiting, no stopping. There was only fury, wild, unbridled frenzy, the product of a week and more of pent-up emotion, anguish, hunger.

Desire.

Of course, Kate didn't recognise that particular emotion at the moment of impact. All she wanted then was to throttle him, to choke his laughter, to wipe the mocking grin off his handsome devil's face.

But as satisfying as it was to knock him down, her own jolt was greater. He took her with him, grabbing her so that they both went under, their heads banging, their legs tangling, their bodies rubbing one against the other, inciting, exciting.

And when, at last, they righted themselves and stood, trembling, still touching, in waist-deep water, he didn't let her go.

'D-Damon.'

'Shh.' He drew her closer until her sea-slick body pressed once more against his, and then he bent his head and kissed her with a hunger that matched her own.

She knew she should be stopping him, pulling back, saying no. She didn't.

She couldn't.

She wanted it—she wanted *him*—too much.

She was wrong. She was foolish. She'd be sorry. She wasn't far enough gone to deny any of the above. And yet still she parted her lips under his and welcomed the touch of his tongue, meeting it with her own.

Perhaps it was because she'd been alone so long. Perhaps it was the pressure of propinquity, the temptation of this island paradise, a conspiracy of God, Greek mothers and mosquitoes. Kate didn't know.

She only knew she could fight no longer.

As his hands roved over her back and slid down to cup her buttocks, her own glided up the length of his arms and laced against the back of his neck. She rocked her hips forward into his. Then she felt herself being lifted and carried towards the shore.

He was as uncontrolled as she, as desperate, as hungry. He lay her down on the hard-packed sand at the water's edge and covered her body with his own, his damp hands stroking her with a fine tremor, his lips learning the line of her jaw, then touching her mouth again.

If there were mosquitoes then, she didn't notice them. If there was sand in her hair, she didn't care. The only thing that mattered was this terrible need that had been building for as long as she could remember.

And the only place to assuage it seemed to be in Damon's arms.

He pulled back for a brief moment to settle himself between her legs and even that fleeting separation found her reaching for him, drawing him down once again.

Damon didn't argue. He came to her, crushing her into the sand, biting down on his lower lip as he reached the centre of her, shuddering as he stopped, held perfectly still, his eyes locking with hers.

It was insanity. Madness.

It was the most beautiful thing on earth.

Love.

Or if it wasn't love, it was the closest thing Kate had

ever known, the closest she'd come to feeling favoured, cherished, beloved in her entire life.

For Damon was nothing like Bryce had been. Bryce had been so perfunctory, so mechanical and sometimes so obviously elsewhere that she'd despaired of reaching him. There was nothing like that about Damon. He was so clearly eager for her that Kate found herself coming to meet him, lifting her hips to draw him further within, arching her back so that her breasts brushed against his chest, digging her fingers into his hard-muscled buttocks, making him lose control.

'Oh, Kate! I can't—I need—' His thrusts became quicker, stronger.

Kate's did, too, because something else was happening, something new, something powerful. She forgot Bryce, forgot the past, forgot everything but Damon. Her own movements became more abandoned, her body more responsive to the delicious friction growing between them. And then as he tensed and his muscles contracted, the same thing happened to her own.

It was as if she was still in the water, being lifted and lifted and lifted by the surge of the ocean's power, and then, at the peak, she felt herself slip over and fall headlong into the rush of the wave. It was liberating, shattering, mind-boggling.

It had never happened before.

Kate shut her eyes and delighted in it, revelling in sensations, in the feelings, in the weight of the body lying on top of her own. Her heart slammed against the wall of her chest. She turned her head and her lips brushed a faintly stubbled cheek.

She drew back and opened her eyes to meet Damon's brown ones. And then the crush of reality weighed more heavily than her husband's body.

She held her breath, waiting for him to roll away, to leave her the way Bryce always had, or—worse—to tell her, as Bryce had, exactly how disappointed he was, how unresponsive she was, how little she met his needs.

But though Damon did move off of her, he didn't leave. Instead he settled himself in the sand alongside her, their bodies still touching, one of his hands stroking lightly down the length of her. She felt his fingers tremble.

'Well,' he said after a moment, giving her a faint grin, 'that was worth waiting for.' And the husky, ragged tone of his voice made her pull back, startled.

'What do you mean?' she said cautiously.

'Do you suppose it was the frustration that did it?' he mused, still smiling. 'Or is it the chemistry between us? I think we ought to find out, don't you.'

And before Kate realised what was happening, it was happening again!

Damon's hands skimmed over her, learning her curves and hollows. His mouth explored her breasts, laving them leisurely, suckling deeply, setting off tremors within her. She arched her back, clutching at him, moaning.

'You like that, do you?' he whispered. 'Me, too.'

But then he pulled back and instinctively Kate reached for him. Then she looked up from beneath heavy lids to see him positioning himself above her once more.

He settled himself between her thighs, urging her legs to part for him. And they did, flexing and lifting so that her heels pressed against the back of his thighs as he slid into her.

'Yes,' Kate murmured, 'oh, yes.' Because this was the way she knew loving was supposed to feel. This was the connectedness she'd always hoped for, that she'd sought with Bryce and never found. 'Oh, my love, yes.'

And then she felt the hot surge of his seed within her, felt her own body contract around him and her mind explode at the climax of her desire. She shut her eyes. Her heart hammered, then gradually slowed. Her muscles relaxed and she began to hear again the soft beat of the rippling waves against their bodies, the cry of the gull overhead, the whisper of the wind through the palms.

Slowly, with considerable trepidation, she opened her eyes. Damon still lay on top of her, but he had braced his torso with his hands alongside her arms, and he was looking down at her, his expression unreadable.

Tentatively Kate smiled.

And Damon smiled back. He levered himself up and off her. 'Amazing.'

And Kate's smile broadened because, yes, it had been.

Damon got to his feet and held out his hand to her. When she took it, he pulled her up beside him. Then, lacing his fingers together with hers, he led her into the water.

It was more than Eden, Kate thought. It was heaven—the warm clear water and the soft blue sky. It didn't even feel as warm now. Or maybe, she acknowledged, that was because the heat of frustration and anger no longer tormented her. She was basking in the glow of fulfilment.

She supposed she ought to be worrying. She'd made love with a man who had never said, 'I love you'. She'd shared her most intimate self with a man who was going to be gone in less than a year.

And yet she couldn't regret it. She tried. She couldn't. It had been too beautiful. Too fulfilling. Too wonderful to second-guess or to wish it had never happened.

She slanted a sidelong glance at this man who was for twelve short months to be her husband, and she couldn't help thinking, yes, this is the way it's supposed to be. This is the point at which two souls connect.

And what if she never came closer than this? What if for the rest of her life she was destined to miss such connections? Wasn't it better to have experienced it once?

Was she a sinner to have enjoyed it? To have found with Damon's help a part of herself that no man, certainly not Bryce, had ever touched?

No, Kate decided, she was not. They were married, for however long or short a time. They had a right to the happiness they could find.

And after?

But Kate knew better than to ask the answer to that. She knew better than to count on happily ever after. She'd done that once to her everlasting regret.

For now it was enough to live in the moment. And to share with Damon that most elemental connection that two human beings can share.

She studied her husband's unyielding profile. Her eyes traced the hard lines of his face, unsoftened now by his dark wavy hair which was plastered wetly to his skull. He was, she thought, even more handsome than usual, more striking, more vitally masculine. Damon Alexakis was the essence of what was truly male.

And for the first time in her life, in Damon's embrace, Kate felt as if she'd touched that essence.

Who'd have believed it?

Damon sat silently in the stern of Silas's boat and studied the woman he'd married less than three weeks ago. Whoever would have thought there was all that passion, all the eagerness buttoned up inside the proper, professional Kate McKee?

Not me, that's for sure, Damon thought now.

And yet. . .

And yet, hadn't she attracted him almost from the first? Hadn't he wanted to touch her ivory skin, kiss her delectable mouth, ruffle that shiny, silky brown hair?

His hormones had known, Damon thought wryly, even if his rational mind hadn't.

And his hormones were pleased. He couldn't help grinning. And when Silas looked at him and muttered about newlyweds, then shook his head, Damon laughed aloud.

Kate turned and caught them both looking at her. Beneath her already sunburned cheeks he saw a hint of deepening colour. But when they continued smiling at her, she began, albeit shyly, to smile, too.

And when she did, he wanted her again.

He'd thought an afternoon's loving would do it. He'd expected that learning her mysteries would quench his desire. In fact, what he'd learned had only whetted his appetite for more.

She'd been so responsive, so abandoned, when he'd touched her. And afterwards she'd seemed almost astonished by it all. Hadn't her husband made her feel like that? Damon wondered.

Then he thought, of course he had. She wouldn't have loved him so much if he'd left her unsatisfied in bed. What Damon had tapped in her was, quite obviously, a well of long-denied yearning.

Maybe she hadn't loved a man since her husband's death. It hadn't taken long for him to realise that she clearly hadn't been interested in Stephanos.

Maybe he was the first to have touched her in four long years. Of course she'd have exploded like match-struck kindling, if she hadn't known intimacy in all that time. Of course she'd have been eager.

He wanted to strike a match to her desire again. And again.

'You look like you done got the catch of the century,' Teresa said when she saw them coming up the walk. He had his arm around Kate, had done since they'd left the village, and she hadn't pulled away. 'You be smilin' big.' Teresa smiled even bigger in demonstration. 'Or maybe,' she said, cocking her head, 'you got other things make you happy.'

'Maybe,' Damon agreed.

Kate stepped on his foot and nudged him in the ribs. He grinned at her, but he didn't let go. 'Silas is bringing the fish up when he cleans them,' he told Teresa, 'We got a box fish.'

Teresa nodded, pleased. 'That be almost cause for those smiles. I'll stuff it for dinner.'

'We'll be here around seven,' Damon said, leading Kate towards the cottage.

This morning he'd hated the cottage. Had spent the first part of their time fishing, trying to contrive a means to stay out of it for as long as possible. It had seemed like the cage containing all his frustrations.

Now he wanted to lock the two of them in and throw away the key. He wanted all the privacy the honeymoon cottage would allow.

He knew that getting to make love to Kate was more than he'd bargained for. He could scarcely believe his good luck. It was turning into a far better honeymoon than he'd had any right to expect. She could make the year they had to spend together a hell of a lot more pleasant than he'd anticipated it being.

'You can have the shower first,' she said to him as he opened the door.

'You don't think we might share?'

If he'd thought her face turned red before, it was nothing compared to the colour it turned now.

'I don't—I mean, I've never—' She stopped and turned away, pressing her palms to her cheeks in dismay.

Charmed, Damon turned and drew her into his arms. 'You've never been that wanton, huh?' he said, smiling.

She shook her head against his chest. He was unaccountably pleased: at least she hadn't been there before with Bryce.

'Scared?'

She lifted her eyes and shot him a quick glance before ducking her head again. 'Don't be silly,' she said gruffly.

'Come on,' he said, tugging her with him towards the bath, 'let's give it a try.'

She didn't protest. She allowed him to lead her into the bathroom, and she leaned against the door while Damon turned on the shower and adjusted the temperature of the water and the angle of the spray. He flicked a bit of water at her. 'Warm enough?'

She nodded. She didn't say a word. He pulled his T-shirt over his head, then turned to her.

'Waiting for me to do it?' he asked softly.

She swallowed. 'N-not really.' She started to lift her own shirt, but he put out his hands and stilled hers.

'I want to.'

Slowly, carefully, he slid his hands under the hem of her shirt and skimmed it upwards. His thumbs brushed against her silky midriff, then skated lightly across her nipples. Gathering the shirt as he went, he tugged it over her head, then dropped it at their feet.

Kate didn't move. Damon lay his hands on her arms, slid them down and then up, stroking her warm flesh. She trembled under his touch.

'Cold?'

'N-no. Burning,' she admitted.

So was he. 'You can touch me, too, you know.'

For a moment Damon didn't think she would. She looked at him, her eyes wide and slightly wary as she hesitated. Then she licked her lips quickly and brought her hands up and lay them against his chest.

Her touch made him tremble. He swallowed, holding quite still as her fingers traced lightly on his chest, then lifted to touch his shoulders and skim down the length of his arms. Her fingers laced with his. Then she leaned forward and touched her lips to his chest, laving first one tiny hard nipple, then the other.

Damon let out an explosive breath.

'Don't you like that?'

'Hell, yes, I like it! Too much. I'm going to ——' He shook his head desperately.

She smiled. It was a wanton smile, a teasing smile, a very definite 'come hither' smile. And Damon had no inclination to resist. He loosed his fingers from hers, reaching out to undo the fastening of her shorts and pull down the zip. They fell to the floor, pooling at her feet.

Kate stepped away from them. She started kissing him again, her lips feathering across his chest and lightly brushing his shoulders, while her palms flattened against his abdomen. Then they stroked downwards and hooked inside the waistband of his shorts.

Damon held his breath as the backs of her fingers caressed his taut belly, then tugged his shorts down past his hips. He kicked them off and drew Kate with him into the shower.

Her skin felt soft and slick and wet as he wrapped his arms around her and nuzzled against her neck. She made a tiny, hungry, whimpering sound that sent a fierce shaft of desire surging through him. He could have taken her then in scant seconds. Deliberately he did not.

He was no randy teenager in the mood for a quick fix. He was a man grown, a man willing and able to appreciate the finer things in life. And making love with a woman as warm and responsive as Kate was definitely one of them.

He stepped back, reached for the soap and, taking deep, calming breaths, tried to concentrate strictly on the satiny texture of her flesh as he smoothed the soap over her shoulders and down her back. Closing his eyes, he let his fingers stir up a lather, then slide forward to wash her small, but perfect breasts. They were faintly pink from being bared to the sun, and his fingers trembled as he moved the soap in gentle circles on them.

Kate trembled, too. She stood very still, but he could feel the tremors running through her. And he smiled to see her lean into the stroke of his hands. He slid the soap lower, still circling as he moved to her abdomen. Bending his head, he kissed each of her breasts in turn.

She reached out and gripped his shoulders with surprising force, her nails digging into his back. He left a trail of hot kisses down her belly until he reached the top of the soft triangle of dark hair at the apex of her thighs. His hands continued stroking down her legs. First the left, then the right, down the front of her thighs, then up the back. Around to the front again and down. He let the soap fall to the floor of the shower.

Then slowly his hands slid between her knees and he let his fingers move upwards, brushing lightly, stroking gently. Kate shifted, widening her stance. Damon smiled, pleased.

He rested his forehead against her abdomen, watching as he slowly let his fingers creep further up the tanned length of her legs until they reached the soft petals of flesh that hid her secrets from him. And then he touched her and felt her fingers let go of his shoulders only to clench frantically in his hair.

'Damon!'

He lifted his face and smiled up at her, his fingers stroking her all the while, finding her wet and welcoming, trembling themselves at her readiness to receive him. Her legs quivered and her hips surged against his hands.

'Damon! What are you doing to me!'

'Giving you pleasure.'

'Yes, but you——'

'Don't worry. I'll get mine,' he promised. It was pleasure enough watching her, seeing a Kate he'd only just discovered—a wild, passionate Kate who burst into flames at his touch.

She was close to doing so now. He could see it in her face, could feel it in the movements of her body, in the eager thrust of her hips against his hand. Her fingers twisted in his hair, tugging it, pulling him up.

And he came up willingly, lifting her as he did so. She wrapped her legs around his hips as he pressed her against the wall and slid into her welcoming warmth.

As much as he would have liked to prolong it, he couldn't. The feel of her body around his overwhelmed him, and he moved with an eagerness that matched hers. He was only relieved that he brought her satisfaction before succumbing to his own.

'H-heavens,' Kate mumbled as he let her body slide down his until her feet touched the floor again. 'Good grief. I've never——' She glanced up at him, then looked away, apparently embarrassed. She bent over and snagged the bar of soap.

Damon kissed the nape of her neck, then leaned

against the wall of the shower, his legs still trembling. 'Me neither,' he said.

Kate shot him a quick look. 'Really?'

'Really,' he answered mockingly.

She blushed. 'You liked it?' she asked almost hesitantly.

Damon stared. 'What do you think?' He wrapped her in his arms and gave her a wet, soapy hug. 'So much that if I didn't think it would kill me, I'd do it again right now.'

Kate beamed.

She couldn't believe she was acting this way. She was like some wanton woman who couldn't keep her hands off a man. Not just any man. Damon Alexakis.

And of course, she couldn't discuss the way she felt with anyone. They'd stare at her as if she'd lost her mind. Why shouldn't she want him? they'd ask. Why shouldn't she *have* him? After all, he was her husband.

'In name only,' she said aloud now in the still darkness of night.

Really? she replied. Who was she trying to kid?

They'd made love again that evening after dinner, hardly able to wait, barely enjoying the box fish and conch salad Teresa had prepared. They were too eager for the taste of each other. And though she knew she ought to be trying to control her desire, nothing in Kate seemed to want to rein it in.

It was too new, too astonishing. She was like a child with a new toy—an amazing, unanticipated toy. And she couldn't get enough of it.

Of him.

She was, to her everlasting chagrin, wanton and embarrassed by her wantonness at the same time.

It was her insatiable need to be close to Damon that had forced her from the bed in the middle of the night.

She awoke to find herself snuggling against his back, wrapping her arms around him, touching him in places that would have shocked her less than twenty-four hours before.

She knew that she could awaken him, rouse him, make the world spin for both of them again. And at the same time she didn't dare. She didn't want to want him this badly. She didn't want to give in to the temptation to make love with him once more.

It was too marvellous, too exciting, too passionate.

It scared her. *She* scared herself. What had become of the steady, reliable, no-nonsense woman she'd been for the past twenty-odd years, especially for the past four? Of course she'd dreamed of finding such an all-consuming love, but she'd expected to find it with Bryce, with a man she loved.

'At least,' she told her reflection in the mirror, 'you found it with the man you married.'

For a year.

'A lot can happen in a year,' she went on determinedly.

And you think he's going to fall in love with you?

Did she?

She pressed her palms against her cheeks, staring at her reflection, as her mind delicately probed the notion of Damon Alexakis loving her.

Twenty-four hours ago she'd have laughed at the idea. Now she wasn't sure. She only knew that in the space of a day they had connected on a very basic level, on a level she'd never come close to with another man, even Bryce.

Damon had pleasured her, just as he'd said he was pleasured. But he'd done more than that. He'd taught her things about herself that she'd never even suspected. He'd shared himself in a way that Bryce never had. He'd made her aware of her potential as a woman.

She shut out the light in the bathroom and crept quietly back to the bed. In the silver moonlight Damon lay sprawled, the sheet draped loosely over his hips. His dark hair was mussed and spiky, his cheeks and jaw shadowed with a day's worth of beard. Kate eased herself down on the bed beside him, feasting her eyes, remembering the way his hands had moved over her, recalling the tension in his face as he had loved her, and the fierce possession when he'd made her his own.

She'd left the bed so she wouldn't be tempted to touch him. It was no use. She stroked a lock of hair off his forehead, smiling at his restless response, at the way his hand groped, seeking hers.

His eyes opened. 'Kate?'

'I'm sorry. I was restless. I didn't mean to disturb you.'

He smiled, a lazy, slumbrous smile. 'Didn't you?' And he drew her down into his arms once more, his hands tracing her curves, exploring her hollows, making her shiver and begin again to burn.

'I'm not sure a week is long enough,' he said against her lips.

'What do you mean? Long enough for what?'

'A honeymoon. I think we ought to stick around, really convince my mother.' He smiled into her eyes. His hands were melting her. 'What do you say?'

'Yes.'

CHAPTER EIGHT

IT TURNED into a beautiful honeymoon.

They had a beautiful island, gorgeous weather, a private cottage, and the occasional smiling approval of Teresa.

They'd had all that from the first, of course. But then all it had done was frustrate them, highlighting exactly what they were missing: each other.

When they came together at last, the equation became complete.

Teresa obviously noticed. As she was cleaning up after supper the following day, she gave them a big grin. 'You two lookin' better. I think maybe this marriage be gonna work.'

'You've given it your stamp of approval, have you?' Damon said to her, but he was looking at Kate.

'Hard not to, lookin' at the two of you. You lookin' like the cat that ate the hen, and the hen lookin' like she enjoyed every minute.'

Damon laughed and Kate blushed furiously.

'Your mama goin' to be so pleased,' Teresa went on. 'She can't hardly wait to come, she that happy you're going to stay on for the holiday.'

He had told Teresa they would be staying on over the holiday when they'd come for breakfast that morning, and she had obviously wasted no time in passing the word on to the rest of the family.

'Your mama say Mr Stephanos and Mrs Sophia stay in the big house. You get to keep the cottage.'

Damon smiled at her, but spared a wicked one for Kate as well. 'You'd better believe it.'

Teresa chuckled at the renewed flush on Kate's face.

'You don't have to be quite so blatant,' she muttered once Teresa had departed.

Damon's gaze was one of guileless innocence. 'About what?' Then he laughed and rubbed his ankle where she kicked him. 'You're beautiful when you blush,' he told her.

Kate made a face. 'Thanks very much.'

'I mean it, Kate.' His expression sobered.

Kate swallowed at the heat she saw in his eyes. 'You've been celibate too long,' she said gruffly. 'You'd think anyone was appealing who satisfied you.'

'Is that what you think?'

'This is a marriage of convenience, isn't it? And I'm ever so convenient.' She shot him a defiant look.

Damon didn't reply. He pushed back the chair and stood up. Kate's gaze followed him warily. He looked taller and more powerful than ever this morning. He held out his hand to her. She hesitated. Then, when he kept holding it out, waiting, she put her own in it. His fingers closed around hers and he pulled her to her feet.

More convenience? she wondered, but she didn't dare ask. There was something dangerous in his expression, something she didn't completely understand, and wasn't sure she wanted to.

But what else could it be? she asked herself. And really, she wasn't objecting. Making love with Damon under whatever circumstances was amazing.

She was surprised when they got back to the cottage that he didn't haul her into the bedroom. He said only, 'Get your suit and let's go for a swim.'

After they'd changed, they went down to the beach. Damon was quiet, and Kate, still unsure of his mood, but aware that something had changed, kept her mouth shut as well.

She wondered if she had hurt his feelings somehow, implying that any woman would have done. But she didn't see how that could have hurt him.

It was more likely to hurt her, which was, if she was honest, why she'd said it. She didn't want to let herself believe it was as wonderful for Damon as it was for her. If she did, she might start hoping. . .

And that would be disaster.

Damon walked down the beach without speaking until they reached a tall sculpture made of the flotsam and jetsam that had washed up on the pink sand.

Kate hadn't walked this way before and until they'd come close she hadn't even realised what the sculpture was made of. Now she stood looking at it, awed at the vision that had created beauty out of scrap. Damon seemed in no hurry to move on, and she ventured to ask. 'Who made it?'

'Whoever came by. It was started before we first came here. Even if it gets washed away in a storm, someone starts it again.'

'It's beautiful.'

'You think so?'

Kate glanced at him, surprised. 'Yes. Don't you?'

He nodded. 'But it doesn't appeal to everyone. Not enough structure.'

'Its spontaneity is what makes it beautiful, and its ability to take whatever comes to hand and make it work.'

Damon didn't say anything, and Kate wondered if she'd made another mistake. Then he took his towel from around his neck and asked, 'Do you want to swim?'

'Here?'

'There's a good reef out there.' He pointed, then shrugged. 'But if you'd rather not. . .'

'It's fine,' Kate said quickly. 'I'm getting hot.'

A corner of his mouth quirked. 'Are you?'

She felt her cheeks begin to warm. 'Not that kind of hot,' she said quickly.

'More's the pity,' Damon drawled. He dropped his towel and walked towards the water. When he reached the edge, he turned around. 'Come on, then.'

Whatever had been bothering him seemed to fade as they waded into the water and began to swim. He helped her fit on a snorkel and fins, then fitted on his own and led her out to swim over the reef. It was even more beautiful than the sculpture, and Kate told him so.

'I thought you might like it.' He smiled at her. She smiled back, and suddenly the day seemed bright again.

He didn't let her stay out too long. 'Too much sun at midday,' he told her. And she went with him willingly back to the cottage.

This time he did lead her into the bedroom. And after another shower together, they shared the bed for a nap and an afternoon of quiet loving.

Damon Alexakis quietly attentive was as awesome as Damon fiery and passionate had been. There were so many sides to him, so much to find out that she didn't know, that Kate lay awake watching him sleep, marvelling at the man she was married to, trying to decide what it was about him that fascinated her so.

What she decided was that there was no one thing. There wasn't simply the smooth, polished charm that she'd been taken in by with Bryce. Damon had charm, of course. He had charm in spades. But besides the charm, he had strength, passion, gentleness, humour, determination, vulnerability. More things than she could count.

If she'd guessed there was all this to the man who'd

proposed to her those few short weeks ago, would she have dared to say yes?

'It's a miracle,' Sophia said.

'It is,' Electra echoed.

'The eighth wonder of the modern world,' Pandora affirmed. 'I'd never have believed it if I hadn't seen it.'

'What are you talking about?' Kate asked her sisters-in-law. They were all sitting under beach umbrellas, sipping long, cool drinks while Damon taught his nieces how to swim in the shallow water before them.

'That,' Sophia said, nodding towards her brother and her daughters. Damon was crouching low in the water, Christina hanging on his shoulders while he helped Leda keep her legs straight as she kicked.

'That's it! You're getting it! Good job,' he praised.

'He tried to drown me,' Electra recalled.

Kate laughed. 'You're kidding.'

'I am not!'

'Maybe you deserved it,' Kate said with a small grin, remembering how trying Damon sometimes found his sisters.

Electra looked offended, then chagrined. 'Maybe,' she allowed.

'You were sort of a pain,' Chloe chipped in. 'But I think it's a miracle anyway.'

'Actually,' Sophia said, 'it's Kate.'

Kate glanced at her, startled. 'You mean, it's because of me that Damon is paying attention to the girls? Nonsense. He took them out before we were married.'

'He took them out when he was courting you. Before that I think he came to their birthday parties with gifts picked by the corporate buyer at F.A.O. Schwarz. He certainly never taught them how to swim. Nor did he read them bedtime stories.'

'Well, perhaps that was my fault,' Kate allowed. 'I was reading to them last night and he. . .dropped by.'

'He's in love,' said Chloe.

'Deep.' Pandora.

'And he wants to be a daddy.' Electra.

'Amazing,' Sophia said, shaking her head yet again.

Kate wanted to protest. She didn't dare. What was she going to say? That her husband wasn't in love with her, certainly not deeply so. And he didn't want children at all from her. He only wanted sex.

She wished she could dig a hole and bury herself. Instead she jumped to her feet. 'I need a swim,' she said and strode quickly down the beach and plunged into the water, heading out past Damon and the girls without even stoppng, though Leda shouted,

'Hey, Auntie Kate, lookit me swim!' and Christina said,

'Can I come with you, Auntie Kate?' and Damon said,

'Where are you going?'

She didn't answer, just plunged beneath the incoming wave and stroked straight ahead. She needed coolness, she needed space, she needed time to think.

Damon's head popped up next to hers. 'What's going on?'

'I thought you were teaching the girls to swim.'

'I took a break. They don't have long attention-spans.' He winked. 'You taught me that.'

She had, damn it. She'd said it only last night that a short book was better than a long one with them. She'd wanted to get back to the cottage with Damon and make love. She knew he remembered, that he was thinking about it now.

'Well, I'm sure they can use a little more than you've given them,' Kate said, turning and swimming away.

Damon followed her. 'They'll get their turn. Is

something bothering you? Are my sisters hassling you?'

'What do you care?' Kate said sourly.

He reached out and caught her arm, stopping her easily. She scrabbled for a toehold on the ocean floor, but it was too deep, and she started to sink.

'Damon!'

He hauled her against him, keeping her head above water. 'There. Got you. Relax.'

'How'm I supposed to relax like this?' She was plastered against him, could feel the slip of his thigh between her legs and the hard press of his chest against her breasts.

'You did a pretty good job of it last night,' he said into her ear, then kissed it, nibbling lightly on the lobe. A shiver ran through her.

'Damon! Stop it! They're watching!'

'So?' He kissed her again, this time trailing light kisses along her jaw, then taking her mouth with even more thoroughness. She gripped his shoulders and tried to pull away. He held her fast. An unbroken wave surged past them, lifting them together, rubbing their bodies one against the other, and Kate could feel the evidence of his desire. She shut her eyes, remembering how he had looked last night, naked and aroused.

'What did they say, Kate?'

'W-who?' She shook her head, trying to think straight. It wasn't easy. 'Oh, you mean your sisters? Th-they're amazed. They think you're in love with me.' She gave a weak half-laugh. 'You've really got them convinced.'

'Have I?' There was a note of strain in Damon's voice.

'Yes.' She gave him a shove and was delighted to

find that he let her go. 'You really have,' she added tightly.

'And you don't like that?'

She tried to shrug it off. 'It's what we'd hoped for, certainly. And. . .we do have most of the year left so I suppose they have to think something.'

'I suppose they do,' Damon said quietly after a moment. He was treading water now, staying next to her, but not touching her. Kate felt better, more in control.

'So,' she said lightly, 'I guess it's all right. For the time being.'

'Of course.' He paused. 'And after, Kate?'

'After?'

'After Thanksgiving. When we're home again. What do you want them to think?'

She managed as carefree a smile as she could. 'Oh, I don't care. I guess we can see what happens, can't we?' She allowed her gaze to meet his only for the briefest of moments. She was afraid he might see that their marriage was beginning to matter to her — that *he* was beginning to matter.

But she wasn't sure how to feel when he gave her a small, lopsided smile. 'I guess we can.'

What the hell had he expected from her? A declaration of undying love?

Yeah, right, Alexakis. Damon had been arguing with himself all the way down the beach, running as if the hounds of hell were after him. 'Working out' he'd told his mother. 'Going for a quick jog,' he'd told Stephanos. *Trying to make some sense out of the mess he'd been making of his life*.

Probably, he thought as his feet pounded along the hard-packed sand, he shouldn't have suggested staying for Thanksgiving week. Lord knew why he had.

Well, actually he knew, too. He'd done it because he hadn't wanted to go back. He and Kate had connected that day at Rainbow. They'd had the most marvellous sex he'd ever experienced in his life.

He'd only guessed that sex like that existed. Probably he'd listened to his sisters long enough to have some sort of imprint on the back of his mind that convinced him there could be more to sex than the simple physical satisfaction that he got from playing a good hard game of racquet ball or having a quickie with his most recent girlfriend.

But he hadn't really known for sure — until Kate.

And then he'd thought it was a fluke. A once-in-a-million type thing. Except now it had happened eight times out of eight, and he was looking for chances to make it happen again.

And there was more.

He liked her.

He liked to talk with her. She was witty and well-read. She listened to him, then offered her own views. And she wasn't hesitant about disagreeing with him if she felt he was wrong.

'Don't you know you're not supposed to argue with your husband?' he'd teased her last night after the family supper and she'd taken exception to his view on a recent book they'd both read.

'Don't you know you love it when I do?' she'd countered. And they'd both stopped dead, flushing deeply, when they'd realised the truth of what she said.

'And now one of you had better haul the other off to the cottage and show each other just how much,' Pandora drawled, and all the sisters giggled, while the nieces looked confused and Stephanos looked at Damon and Kate intently.

Helena's knitting needles clicked complacently as

she smiled at her son and new daughter-in-law. 'I told you so,' she'd said.

Damon's feet pounded harder now, trying to blot the memory out of his head.

Why?

Why did he care?

It was what he wanted, wasn't it? To make his mother think he'd fallen in love? To make sure he had the freedom to pick his own bride in his own time?

Hell, how long ago had Kate pointed out to him that that reason was no longer valid?

God, he was confused!

He stumbled and crashed down on to the sand, his heart hammering like an anvil in his chest, his ears pounding, the blood roaring in his veins. And all he could think was that the last time his heart had hammered and his ears had pounded and his blood had roared, he'd been making love with Kate.

'Where were you?'

'Out.'

'What were you doing?'

'Thinking.'

'About. . .us?'

'What else?'

She was sitting in the bed, a lacy white cotton nightgown barely covering her breasts, her glossy dark hair freshly washed and curling damply against her head. She looked cool and self-possessed and absolutely delectable.

He groaned.

'What's wrong?'

He gave her a wry look. 'Pulled a muscle.' He hooked his thumbs in the waistband of his shorts and peeled them down, kicking them off and moving towards the bathroom as he did so.

He went in and shut the door, then flipped the shower on to cold. For a moment he stood braced with his hands on the white marble countertop and hung his head, breathing hard, fighting his desire. He had to be able to control it if he was ever going to control what he felt about her. He had to be able to walk past her and not want her, had to be able to look at her and see a business associate, not a woman he wanted.

The door opened.

He looked around. 'What do you want?'

His tone was rough enough to make her hesitate. Then she gave him a hopeful smile. 'I thought I'd help.'

She was already moving past him, sticking her hand under the tap, shuddering at the icy spray. She turned it down and turned on the hot, adjusting the temperature, putting the plug into the bottom of the tub.

'What the hell are you doing?'

'Running you a bath.'

'I want a shower.' A cold one, he thought desperately.

But Kate ignored him, opening the taps full force so that warm vapour from the water soon fogged the mirror and began to fill the room. Then she turned to him and waited.

'I'll wash your back.'

'Swell,' he grumbled. But he got into the tub and sank down into the water, wishing that it didn't feel so good, wishing that she'd just go away.

'You'll enjoy it,' she promised.

'That's what I'm afraid of,' he muttered.

Kate cocked her head. 'Why?' Her blue eyes were wide and curious.

Damon's jaw tightened. 'Never mind.'

'Are you afraid you're falling for me?' Did she sound as if she hoped he was? Like hell. She didn't give a damn as long as she got her passion, her climaxes, all the sex she'd missed since her hot-blooded husband had died.

He snorted and was surprised to see a flicker of hurt in her eyes. Did she care?

He didn't know what to say. He handed her a washcloth. 'Since you're here, maybe you should make yourself useful,' he said gruffly.

The hurt, if that was indeed what it had been, vanished. She took the cloth. 'Whatever you say.'

He shouldn't have encouraged her, though God knew she needed no encouragement. She was all too happy to run her hands over him, to soap his shoulders and his back, to let the washcloth drift slowly back and forth across his chest, then move lower still.

'Kate,' he muttered through clenched teeth.

'Mm hm?' She was sitting beside the tub on the floor, smiling at him, her gaze slumbrous and enticing as she moved the washcloth over him.

'You're going to get it if you keep that up.'

Her smile widened as she touched him. 'I'm not keeping it up Damon. You are.'

He surged up out of the water, reaching for her at the same time.

'Damon!' She scrambled out of his way, then grabbed a towel and came back towards him. 'You should have let me finish washing you.'

He lifted a brow. 'Was that what you were doing?'

She blushed. It made her look young and innocent. But she wasn't, damn it. He knew that. 'Did you do it to Bryce?' he demanded before he could help himself.

She flinched, then looked away. 'This has nothing to do with Bryce!'

The hell it didn't. Everything he did with her in bed had to do with Bryce. It was like having a ghost there with them. He scowled and grabbed the towel from her, drying himself off.

'It doesn't, Damon,' she insisted. 'Really.'

He wiped his face, looking at her over the top of the towel. She was looking at him with a sort of urgent sincerity that made him begin to believe her. 'It doesn't?'

'No.' She turned away then somewhat hastily and went out of the bathroom, shutting the door behind her.

Didn't it? Damon asked himself, staring at the door between them. Didn't it?

Then did it have to do with him?

And if it did?

He felt a combination of panic and confusion. He felt lost and hopeful. He finished drying off, then toweled his hair as well, before opening the door.

The light was off, but in the glow from the bathroom light he could see that she was in bed, lying on her side, facing away from him. He shut off the light and crossed the room to stand next to the bed on the side away from her. For a long moment he debated going into the living-room and trying another night on the settee.

He couldn't.

He pulled back the sheet and slipped into bed beside her. Touched her arm. 'Kate?'

She didn't move, but he heard her swallow.

With his hand he stroked her bare flesh and felt again the quickening of his desire. He edged closer. 'Kate? Come to me. Please.' He turned her, unresisting in his arms and drew her close, kissed her cheeks, her shoulders, her lips. 'I want you.'

And Kate stifled her worries and her fears and her better judgement because, heaven help her, she wanted him, too.

* * *

She wanted him.

Oh, yes. And that would have been bad enough, but there was more. She began to realise it when they were back in New York, back to his work and hers, to the pursuit of their daily lives.

She loved him.

She wasn't sure exactly when it began, when the uninterest turned to interest, when the interest turned to liking, when the liking turned to love. She only began to realise gradually that it had.

Her feelings had begun, she supposed, even before they left — that last night on the island, when she and Damon and all his family had been in the big house. Pandora had been playing the piano and Daphne the guitar. They'd been singing — everything from Greek folk tunes to Lennon and McCartney favourites — and when she'd returned from the kitchen with a cup of tea for Damon's mother, he had reached out and snagged her hand, pulling her down into his lap, where he held her close in his arms.

And Kate had let him. She'd come willingly, and she'd realised as she did so that she wasn't doing it to show his family that she loved him, she wasn't doing it out of some need to perpetuate a fiction, she was doing it because it was where she wanted to be.

Just as she wanted to be a part of the Alexakis tribe. That had become increasingly apparent to her, too. They were the family she'd never had — the laughing, squabbling siblings she'd longed for, the fussing mother she'd missed, the husband who made her feel warm and cherished and beloved.

Maybe he was only doing it because he was acting. She couldn't tell any more. Sometimes she thought so. Sometimes she thought he was beginning to care for her as much as she was learning to care for him.

And every night now when she crossed the days off

the calendar, she did it with less conviction, with more anguish, and she knew she no longer looked forward to the end of their year together.

She wasn't sure how Damon felt. He didn't bury himself in his work the minute they got back to New York. He came home early some nights, picking her up at Sophia's to take her out to dinner. Now and then he suggested taking the girls with them to give Sophia and Stephanos a break. And those nights were wonderful, too. They gave Kate an even greater sense of what Damon would be like as a father. He would be great.

Most nights, however, he brought her straight home. Sometimes he encouraged Mrs Vincent to take the evening off and he helped Kate cook dinner. Afterwards, as they did the washing-up, he asked her how her day went, listened to her problems, shared some of his own, then he took her to bed and loved her with a passion and a thoroughness that Kate had at first been unable to believe existed, and now knew she couldn't live without.

Thanksgiving became a wonderful memory. Christmas was right around the corner. They were, in spite of their beginning, in spite of their intent, making a marriage together.

And as the holiday approached, Kate smiled every day. She blossomed under Damon's watchful eye.

Most of all, she hoped.

CHAPTER NINE

'ARE you sure you'll be all right if I go to East Hampton tomorrow for the weekend?' Kate asked her sister-in-law, who was sitting placidly on the sofa next to the window overlooking Central Park. She wanted Sophia to say no.

Sophia gave an airy wave. 'Of course. *I'll* be fine. Mama is surprisingly helpful, really. Damon isn't going to be happy, though.'

Kate hoped she was right. Damon didn't know about her proposed trip to East Hampton. He'd still been at a late-night board meeting when it had come up, and when he had got home there had been far more interesting things to occupy them!

Anyway, she'd hoped that a quick glance through her files would find her the replacement nanny she needed and she wouldn't have to go at all.

No such luck. And the Barlowes, early and valued clients, deserved a perfect stand-in for their beloved Charlotte who'd broken her leg on a skiing holiday. No, the only thing for it was to go out there and see to things herself, then find the right woman to fill in.

Unless Damon said no. She hoped that he would object. She hoped he would tell her in no uncertain terms that she wasn't going anywhere five days before Christmas, that she belonged at home with him.

But for the time being, 'It's my job,' she reminded Sophia.

'I don't understand why you persist in doing it. Good heavens, it isn't as if Damon can't afford to support you!'

153

'I need to do it. For me.' Which was as close as she dared come to explaining that there might be a time when Damon would no longer be supporting her.

Their marriage was working out far better than she'd ever dared hope, but so far she'd never ventured a word about extending it, making it permanent, and Damon hadn't either. She had fallen in love, but she didn't know that he had. He liked her, he liked the sex they shared. Beyond that. . .Kate hoped. She dreamed. She was afraid to ask.

Maybe when she told him she had to leave, he would say something. Maybe he would give her some hint about how he felt.

'You're going to miss the Christmas party!' Sophia remembered suddenly. She looked at Kate, stricken.

Kate had already realised that. The Alexakis Enterprises Christmas party had been the topic of much conversation recently. Though Greeks traditionally celebrated Christmas at the feast of Epiphany in January, the Alexakises had, ever since Aristotle had begun the main US branch many years ago, taken this opportunity to share the joys of the season with all the people with whom they did business. Kate remembered Damon saying his father had never met a holiday he hadn't had a use for. She smiled.

But, as much as it had begun as a purely business event, it had grown to become a family occasion, too. And this year was to be the first they'd all attended in five years.

Recently one sister or another had been missing each year. Once Damon's mother hadn't been able to come. Three years ago Damon himself had had an unavoidable conflict and had been unable to make it. But even though they might not always get there, they always tried.

It had to do with being there for one another, being a part of the family. Sophia had explained it to her. So had Helena. And Pandora. And Daphne.

That was perhaps why, Kate thought, her proposed trip to East Hampton might prompt him to share some indication of how he felt. Would he care if she missed the party? Did he really want her to be part of his family? Or was she no more than a playmate who happened to be his wife?

'Damon won't let you miss it,' Sophia said positively now.

Kate gave a little shrug and tried not to let Sophia see how she felt.

'You'll see,' Sophia promised.

Kate didn't because, ultimately, she didn't see Damon.

He called when she had gone to take the girls skating at Wollman Rink.

'He said he's flying to Montreal,' Sophia told her disgustedly when she and the girls returned. 'Some crisis or other. It was Stephanos's account actually, but Damon didn't think Stephanos should go right now. Because of the baby being almost due,' she added apologetically.

'I understand,' Kate said. She did. And she shouldn't be disappointed. She wasn't a child, after all. She was an adult. She should know by now she had to make her own decisions. And anyway, Damon wasn't letting their marriage stop him going places. 'Did he say when he'd be back?'

Sophia shook her head. 'Like everything else, it depends.'

Kate managed a wan smile, knowing how true that was. There were a thousand vagaries connected with exports and imports. Weather. Shipping schedules.

Trade agreements. It wasn't surprising, and it was, of course, the right thing for Damon to do.

She had better do the same.

'You'll stay here tonight, then, won't you? Mama will be alone with the girls while Stephanos and I go to a play. She'd love to have you, and there's no sense in going home if Damon's not there.'

No, there wasn't. It would be lonely as anything rattling around the big apartment alone. But Kate didn't really want to stay at Sophia's either. With Helena alone this evening, there would be lots of conversation, lots of dissembling, lots of worry that she might say the wrong thing. Kate still felt guilty about deceiving her mother-in-law.

'I think,' she told Sophia, 'that I'll head on out to East Hampton.'

He went to the party straight from the airport. So what if he wasn't wearing the dinner-jacket still hanging in the closet in the apartment? Who cared that his trouser cuffs were wet from the new snow? What difference did it make if he didn't stop to shave? Why worry about what all the dealers and company reps thought?

None of it mattered—as long as he could be with Kate.

Damon wasn't quite sure when he'd begun to realise that. Maybe it had begun to crystallise when he'd found out that Stephanos had fouled up yet another account and the only way to settle it was to go to Montreal and take charge. He hadn't wanted to go.

It was a first.

Ordinarily, troubleshooting was what Damon liked most. He sometimes thought he relished his brother-in-law's screw-ups because they gave him a chance to do what he did best: rush to the rescue and save the day.

This time he'd wanted to send Stephanos.

He couldn't.

Sophia was due the first week in January, slightly less than three weeks away. Damon didn't necessarily imagine that she would go into labour the moment Stephanos left the country, but his sister was high-strung, the baby was active, and Sophia had already had several occasions of false labour pains.

He considered sending Arete, then rejected it. Tension between Arete and Stephanos was already high. Each of them continually vied to be considered Damon's second-in-command. It would only make things worse if he allowed his sister to step into Stephanos's territory.

So if they weren't going to lose the account, Damon would have to go himself.

And that was when he'd thought of taking Kate along.

Would she go? He'd thought she might. She didn't seem to be able to get enough of him. And he damn sure couldn't get enough of her, he'd thought, smiling as he'd dialled Sophia's number.

But Kate had been out with the girls. They wouldn't be back until right before supper, Sophia told him.

Hell, he'd thought. Damn. So much for snatching her away and taking her with him.

'Tell her I have to go to Montreal,' Damon had said.

He'd tried to call her later when he'd got to Montreal. She wasn't home. Neither was Mrs Vincent these days. He and Kate had given her weekends off and she usually went to visit her daughter in Philadelphia.

He'd called back to Sophia's, but only his mother was there. She didn't know where Kate was.

He tried again for the rest of the evening between

meetings with Monsieur Belliard. The only voice he heard was his own on the answering machine.

It had been past midnight when he got back to his hotel room. He'd tried one last time, got nothing and dialled Sophia again.

Stephanos had answered. 'What's wrong?'

'Where's Kate?'

'Damned if I know,' Stephanos had grumbled sleepily.

'Ask Sophia.'

'She's sleeping.'

'Wake her up.'

'Not on your life! She gets little enough sleep these days with that baby, and I'm ——'

'Wake her up!'

Stephanos did. He came back a few moments later. 'Kate's in East Hampton. Business, Sophia says. Now go to sleep.' He hung up.

So did Damon. He didn't sleep.

He lay awake missing her, thinking about the way she curled so comfortably into his body, about the silky smoothness of her skin, the soft luxuriance of her hair, the little moans and gasps of pleasure she made when he loved her.

It was the first night he'd spent without her since he'd come back from Paris. It was the first time he'd slept alone since they'd made theirs a real marriage.

Was it a real marriage, then?

The question caught him by surprise.

Did he want it to be? Did he want to love and honour and cherish Kate for the rest of his life? Did he want to take the vows he'd made as a business proposition and turn them into a lifetime commitment?

Did she?

He was on the phone to Sophia at the crack of dawn.

'Where in East Hampton is she?'

'I haven't a clue,' Sophia said sleepily. 'Don't fret. You ran out on her first.'

'I didn't run out on her!' Damon almost shouted.

'Whatever. Can I go back to sleep now? I need my rest, Damon. You'll understand better when you have children.'

Something else he hadn't thought about. He swallowed. 'Yeah. I've got one long meeting this afternoon with Belliard, then I'll be home. Tell her.'

It hadn't been his most successful rescue attempt, but he'd managed to do a fairly creditable job. It was over, that was what counted. He shook hands with Belliard, caught a taxi, cursed the snowstorm blanketing the east, bullied his way through the Christmas crowds at the airport. First class tickets, usually no problem to come by, were at a premium due to the holiday. Economy had long since been sold out.

'We're doing the best we can, Mr Alexakis,' the counter attendant assured him. 'The snow is slowing us down and everyone wants to get home for Christmas.'

Not the way he did, Damon had thought, and was sure that God was on his side when an hour later there was a vacant seat. He made it to LaGuardia, caught another taxi. This one slipped and slid its way through the snow directly to the posh East Side hotel where the party was already in progress.

He didn't stop until he set foot inside the festively decorated room. And then his eyes searched the premises for Kate.

Arete appeared out of nowhere and took his arm, drawing him with her as she spoke. 'You might've shaved, and why didn't you change? Well, at least you're back. Just in time to charm Mrs Fredericks, too.' She steered him towards the wife of one of their main shipping contractors.

'Where's Kate?' Damon demanded.

Arete shrugged. 'How should I know?'

'Have you seen her?'

'No. But I haven't looked.' She turned him forcibly and shoved him in the direction of Martha Fredericks. 'Charm,' she commanded.

He did his best, all the while scanning the crowd for the sight of his wife. He thought he saw her once near Sophia. But then the woman turned his way and he saw that he was wrong.

'. . .hear you got married recently,' Martha Fredericks was saying. 'Love to meet her. Like to get a glimpse of the woman who brought you down.'

Had she, Damon wondered, brought him down? Was that what had happened to him? He still couldn't find her. Mrs Fredericks rabbited on. He smiled vaguely, spotted Pandora and another woman coming their way and reached out to grab them. He'd been charming. It was their turn.

'Tell Mrs Fredericks about your trip to Italy,' he commanded his sister.

Pandora, who had been smiling, looked as if she was about to burst into tears, and Damon suddenly remembered why she'd gone to Italy, with whom, and that the skunk had dumped her when her money ran out.

'Sorry,' he muttered. 'I mean, tell her about the Knicks game you went to.'

Pandora didn't look particularly mollified, but she shrugged. 'Sure. And you can get Eleni a glass of champagne. You remember Eleni, don't you?'

The woman with her, she meant. And yes, now that he looked at this Eleni, he did remember her vaguely. A tall, striking young woman with thick dark hair and lustrous brown eyes. A beauty, certainly. He remembered her as something less.

'You were a — uh — school friend of Pan's?'

Eleni smiled. 'I was. She used to bring me home sometimes for holidays. You know my father, Nikos Vassilakis.'

'Of course. How is he?'

He led Eleni over to the table and snagged two glasses of champagne, not really listening as she talked about her father, his business, his hopes for the future. He still hadn't found Kate.

Hadn't she come back yet?

Finally he dumped Eleni on Electra and asked once again for his wife. 'Ask Sophia,' Electra advised.

His sister was holding court on an elegant white silk sofa that Arete had arranged for her. Stephanos was, thankfully, hovering over her, making sure she was comfortable, making sure she was protected from jostling and cigarette smoke, being the sort of husband he should have been all along.

'Where's Kate? Isn't she back?' Damon asked his sister.

Sophia gave him a sympathetic look and shook her head. 'I'm sorry.'

Damon was, too. He sagged down on to the sofa next to her. Why had he hurried? Why had he busted himself to get here? What difference did it make?

None, obviously, as far as Kate was concerned.

Kate opened the door quietly, unsure what to expect, knowing what she wanted to find but fearful just the same. She'd spent the entire day yesterday with the Barlowes, had got a feel for their children, and had realised that the best possible interim replacement would be Ellie Partridge, the sixtyish lady she had in mind for Sophia after the baby was born. Her own replacement.

Ellie had, bless her heart, been willing to come. In fact, at Kate's urging, she'd caught a late train out from Manhattan and had arrived last night. But by the time Kate had introduced her to the family, it was too late to head back to the city herself.

Early this morning, however, Ned Barlowe had got up and taken her to the station. She'd fidgeted and fussed, her mind totally consumed by Damon, day-dreaming about him all the way home.

She wasn't sure he'd even got back yet. But in the best of all possible worlds, he would be waiting for her when she came in. He would open sleepy eyes and smile at her, reach for her and pull her into bed with him, making love to her with the passion she relished. And she would love him. Then he would tell her that he'd missed her, that he loved her, that he wanted their marriage to last forever.

And that would be as good as or even better than his not wanting her to go to East Hampton in the first place.

She hung her coat in the cupboard, slipped off her shoes and padded down the hall towards the bedroom. Her pace quickened when she heard water running in the master bathroom. She reached the door, then slowed, wondering what his reaction would be.

The door to the bathroom was slightly ajar and she could see Damon's back as he stood facing the mirror. He wore a pair of dark wool trousers, but nothing else, and as Kate watched him shave she could see the muscles flex in his back. She felt a quickening inside her, a need to touch him, to run her hands over that smooth bronzed skin. She moved forward, wanting to go to him and put her arms around him.

He either heard her or caught a glimpse of her in

the mirror for quite suddenly, he turned, the razor still in his hand, one side of his face still lathered.

'You got back,' she said and smiled, walking towards him. 'When?'

'Last night.' His tone was even. He didn't smile. He didn't act loverlike at all.

Kate stopped. 'Oh,' she said brightly. 'Then. . .you got to the party after all?'

'I was the host,' he reminded her shortly.

'But you had to go to Montreal. I thought Sophia and Stephanos. . .' But what did it matter, really, who was the host? He had been there and she hadn't. 'I-I'm sorry. I wanted to be there. But I had this crisis come up. The Barlowes——'

'Don't worry about it.' He turned and went back to shaving, concentrating on his reflection, ignoring her.

Kate watched him, dismayed. She felt shut out, frantic. She swallowed and bit her lip. 'I missed you,' she offered after a moment.

Damon made a non-commital sound and kept on shaving. 'You had work to do,' he said after a moment, excusing her. And it didn't sound as if he cared at all.

Kate felt her throat tighten. She stepped back into the bedroom. 'Shall I—shall I fix us some breakfast?'

He shook his head. 'I've eaten. I have to get to the office.'

'It's Sunday.'

'I have work to do.'

And, fifteen minutes later, he left. He didn't even come into the kitchen to say goodbye. She heard the door shut and, by the time she ran to open it the lift door was sliding shut and he was gone.

Kate closed the door and slowly dragged herself back to the kitchen. Last night's storms had disappeared, leaving a cloudless blue sky. Bright winter light still shone in the wide glass, but it seemed to Kate as if a cloud had blotted the sun.

After breakfast she went to Sophia's. She didn't want to be alone and, even though she knew that going to Sophia's would get her more deeply involved with the family, she told herself that Sophia would appreciate help with the girls.

Sophia was, in fact, delighted. 'They're driving me crazy,' she admitted. 'They're getting so excited about the holiday. They were allowed to attend the first half-hour of the party last night. It was supposed to mollify them. I think it was a mistake.'

'If I'd been there I could have kept them away,' Kate said.

'No, if you'd been there, Damon would have monopolised you.' Sophia smiled.

Kate doubted that. He hadn't seemed to care at all. She wondered if he'd even noticed she was gone. 'Would you like me to take the girls to the park for a while?'

'Would you? Just for an hour or so.' Sophia yawned. 'The baby didn't give me any rest last night.'

Sophia retired to her bedroom while Kate bundled the girls into their jackets and mittens. The door to the study opened as they were leaving. Stephanos smiled at them.

'You're back,' he said to Kate, and he seemed more pleased to see her than Damon had.

'Kate's going to take us skating again, Papa,' Leda told him. 'Can you come, too?'

'Please, Papa,' begged Christina.

'Girls, your father has plenty of work to do,' Kate said quickly, but Stephanos shrugged.

'Why not?'

Kate opened her mouth to protest, then realised she couldn't. Not in front of the girls. Stephanos seemed to know what she'd been going to say, though, for he gave her a brief smile.

'Don't worry,' he told her, 'I've learned my lesson.'

'What lesson, Papa?' Christina demanded.

Stephanos shrugged into his jacket and opened the door for them. 'It's not important, little one,' he said gently. 'Let's go.'

The girls were delighted to have their father along. And as they walked to the park, Kate felt less self-conscious and apprehensive in his presence as well. Stephanos had come a long way from the lecherous man who'd sought a nanny and something more. Damon had been right: he'd never made a move on her again. In fact, over the past couple of months Kate had seen him grow increasingly more doting when it came to Sophia. And now his interest seemed to extend to the girls as well.

He helped them lace up their skates, then stood back and watched, a proud father expression on his face, as they let go of his hands and skated away. 'Amazing,' he said after a moment. 'One minute they're babies, the next they're off to school. I missed a lot of it.'

Kate didn't say anything, just stood watching the girls. Privately she agreed, but she didn't imagine he wanted to hear it.

'I owe it to you, waking me up,' he said. 'You and Damon.'

Then she did look at him. 'What?'

He had the grace to look embarrassed. 'Watching you two fall in love made me take another look at Sophia. At what I'd had with her — and was in danger of losing.'

Kate could feel her own cheeks warm. She looked away, not wanting Stephanos to see the guilt on her face.

'I'm not saying this to embarrass you,' he told her. 'I'm trying to say thanks.'

'You're welcome,' she mumbled.

'When I married Sophia, I was in love with her. Desperately in love. I'd have done anything for her. Including going to work in her family business, which was what she wanted. Including always coming in second to Damon.'

Kate shot him an oblique glance, interested in what he was saying, edging closer, still however, keeping most of her visible attention on the girls.

'I don't like admitting it, but it began to get on my nerves. Everything I did, everything I tried, it seemed as if the whole family thought Damon could have done better. I got mad. And——' he raked a hand through his hair '—I started staying away. Going out on my own. Finding my own friends. What the hell? I thought. What do they care? I figured I was a disappointment to Sophia.'

'She never said that to me,' Kate told him quickly. 'I think she loves you very much.'

'I do, too,' Stephanos admitted. 'But it took you to make me see it.' He dug his toe in the newly fallen snow. 'I thought Damon was only marrying you to make sure I kept my hands off. I thought, good, serves him right, getting in a marriage like that, him so bound and determined to do everything right. And then I saw that he really loved you.'

Kate blinked. 'You did? When?'

'Everywhere. Right from the first. The way he looked at you. How attentive he was. How he didn't let you out of his sight on the island.'

Sex, Kate told herself. It was because he valued her physically. But somewhere deep inside she felt a shaft of hope.

'And if you'd seen him last night when you weren't there.'

'What happened last night?'

'He came rushing in late straight from the plane from Montreal. He didn't even change. And he wanted to know where you were.'

'And that shows how much he loves me?' Kate knew she might be betraying her doubts to Stephanos, but she couldn't help it. She needed to know what he knew.

'If he didn't, he'd have been drooling all over Eleni.'

'Who's Eleni?'

'A friend of Pan's. Gorgeous woman. Her father was a colleague of Mr Alexakis. Eleni's got a business of her own now — something in textiles — but Pan says she'd give it up in a minute if the right man came along.'

'Damon?'

Stephanos scowled at her. 'Of course not. He's married to you. Oops, there goes Leda, right on her nose!' And Stephanos took off across the ice rink to rescue his daughter.

Damon loved her.

Kate wished she could believe it. With all her heart and all her soul, she wished that the man she loved loved her.

Sometimes, like in the middle of the night when he turned to her in passion or in the middle of Christmas afternoon when he walked behind her chair and brushed a hand across her hair, she could almost believe he did.

Or maybe then she was just better able to fool herself. For certainly other times he seemed preoccupied, distracted, as if he really wasn't a part of her world at all.

Still, Kate was loath to believe otherwise as long as she had a chance.

And she thought she did, until the day that Nestor Stephanos Adropolis made his appearance in the world.

It was the day after New Year's. Sophia had awakened before dawn with a faint backache. She hadn't wanted to bother anyone, she told the family later, so she'd waited until the vague ache had escalated into contractions five minutes apart. Then she woke her husband.

'You have to come now! Now!' Stephanos was frantic when Kate picked up the bedside phone.

'I'll be right there.'

'Tell him to relax,' Damon said loud enough for his brother-in-law to hear.

'I'll tell him that when you're having your first,' Stephanos said roughly to Kate. 'Get over here now.'

'We will,' Kate promised in her best soothing voice and hung up. 'Come on. It's time.'

Sophia, for all that she began her labour quickly, got most of the way there, then slowed down. Kate, at home with the girls, waited by the phone for what seemed like hours until, at last, the call came at five that evening.

'It's a boy,' Stephanos told her, and he sounded exhausted enough to have given birth himself.

'Congratulations,' Kate said. 'How's Sophia?'

'Tired. Fine, but tired. We both are. We'd thought about having you bring the girls up tonight to see him, but I think it would be better if you wait until tomorrow.'

'Of course,' Kate agreed, though she was eager to see the baby herself.

'Damon will bring you the Polaroids.'

'He was there?'

'Waiting in the hall the whole time. You didn't imagine he'd let the next generation arrive without him, did you?' Stephanos teased.

'No,' Kate said. 'Of course not.'

Stephanos was right, of course. The baby would matter a lot to Damon. As much as he might grumble about his mother and his sisters and their problems, he was always right there to solve them or at least to lend moral support. Kate had often thought about what a good father he would be. She tried to imagine a child they might have, then stopped. It was far too tempting.

Damon came bearing Polaroids and Chinese take-away. The girls were so excited to see photos of their new brother that they only picked at the sweet and sour pork. It took Damon's most determined stern-father look to get them to settle down and eat.

'You won't be able to go see him tomorrow,' he told his nieces, 'if you don't eat a good dinner and get plenty of sleep tonight.'

The girls calmed down enough to eat. After an hour of television and three bedtime stories, they allowed the light to go out. Eventually they even slept, leaving Damon and Kate alone together.

For days it seemed they'd done nothing much more than pass in hallways and chat inconsequentially over meals. There'd been nights of passion, of course, but the closeness Kate had sensed building between them seemed to be eluding them now.

She told herself that it would pass. She knew Damon had a lot on his mind with the problems in Montreal, and she knew more work than ever was falling on his shoulders, especially since Stephanos was preoccupied with his wife and new arrival.

But ever since her conversation at the ice rink with her brother-in-law, Kate had told herself that it would work out, that she had reason to hope.

Damon loved her.

Now she came back into the living-room to find Damon concentrating on a magazine. 'He's lovely, isn't he?' she asked, carrying the pictures as she came back from checking on the girls.

Damon glanced up briefly. 'Wrinkled and red, actually.' His dismissive tone surprised her.

She laughed. 'All babies are. They improve.'

Damon shrugged. 'Good thing.' He went back to his magazine as if it were far more interesting than she was.

Deliberately Kate sat down on the sofa next to him, edging close, hoping he would put his arm around her and draw her into an embrace, hoping that Nestor's birth would spark a paternal instinct in Damon, would make him want sons of his own—with her.

He stiffened slightly, then stood up and rubbed a hand against the back of his neck, leaving her alone on the couch. 'I've got work to do,' he muttered. 'All those hours at the hospital. . .'

He didn't even look at her, just crossed the room and grabbed his briefcase which was still by the front door. 'I'll use Stephanos's study.'

When Stephanos came home about ten he was still there. Kate listened to her brother-in-law, bubbling and eager to talk about his new son. She smiled, praised, said all the right things. Then she went to bed in the guest-room where she and Damon had agreed to spend the night.

Damon was still working.

It was past midnight when he came in, but she hadn't slept; she'd thought. And she was still thinking as she watched him strip off his clothes in the dark and slip into bed beside her.

'Damon?' she touched his arm.

He tensed for an instant, then turned to her, took

her into his arms and kissed her. It was a hungry kiss. Almost, Kate would have said, a desperate kiss.

And then he loved her, shattered her. . .and then he slept.

She saw Nestor Stephanos the next afternoon. He was wrinkly and red and very, very beautiful. Simply seeing him made her ache with maternal longings. She sat beside Sophia's bed and held him in her arms and cooed down at him, marvelling at the way his dark eyes tried to focus on her, at the way his tiny hand gripped her finger so fiercely. She looked over at Sophia and smiled.

'He's gorgeous!'

Kate looked up to see Helena, Pandora and a dark-haired woman she didn't know standing in the door-way. Behind them, looking at her, was Damon. He ushered them in as Helena looked at the unknown woman with grandmotherly disdain.

'Of course he is, Eleni,' she said. 'How could you possibly think otherwise?'

The dark-haired woman, obviously the Eleni that Stephanos had mentioned, laughed and crossed the room to stand by Kate and smile down at her and the baby. 'May I?'

Reluctantly Kate gave him up, watching as the other woman cuddled the baby close. 'Isn't he precious?' Eleni asked. 'Don't you wish you had one of your own, Damon?' She slanted a glance at her friend's brother.

And Kate, looking at Damon, saw an expression on his face that she'd never seen before: a wistfulness, a hunger that sent a shaft of yearning right through her.

And then he looked at her and something happened. The wistfulness faded, the hunger died. His expression closed. He shrugged.

She couldn't lie to herself any longer. She couldn't pretend that their marriage would ever be more than the sham Damon had offered her at the first.

No matter what she'd begun to hope, they had a marriage of convenience, nothing else.

The passion, the sex, the joy they'd taken in each other's bodies was physical release and nothing more. Of course he'd taken her when she'd been willing. He was a man, wasn't he? Men were quite willing to share sex without love.

And, despite what Stephanos had claimed, he didn't love her.

If he did, he wouldn't withdraw from her. He would talk to her, share with her, confide in her. He wouldn't brush her off and walk away.

He wouldn't pretend uninterest in children when it was clear he wanted some of his own.

What was even more clear was that he didn't want them with her.

Did he want them with Eleni?

Kate didn't know. Maybe. Maybe not. Certainly he'd looked enchanted at the sight of Eleni holding the baby.

But it really didn't matter whether it was Eleni or some other woman that he some day fell in love with. It only mattered that he didn't love her.

It was cowardly, and she knew it, but she couldn't live the lie any longer. She waited three days, until the Barlowes' nanny Charlotte was back on her feet and able to cope. Then she called Mrs Partridge back from East Hampton and settled her in with Sophia, the twins and a far less red and wrinkled Nestor. It was nothing more or less than what she'd intended to do all along, she told them — and herself.

She kissed the baby and hugged the girls. She smiled. She waved.

'You're not leaving forever,' Sophia said. 'You're only going home to Damon.'

Kate smiled again as she backed out of the door and blinked back the tears. She did go home to Damon's, but only long enough to leave him a note.

Then she packed her bags and left.

CHAPTER TEN

SHE was gone.

He couldn't believe it. No, that wasn't true. He believed it; he just didn't want to.

The pain was terrifying. The hollowness he felt went almost beyond bearing. And even telling himself that he'd expected it didn't help at all.

Because, no matter how much he'd got the feeling since she'd come back from East Hampton that he was losing her, he'd told himself she wouldn't really go.

And when he'd come into Sophia's hospital room and had seen Kate sitting in the chair, holding the baby in her arms, he'd felt they might really have a chance. She'd looked so beautiful, so content. And when Eleni had taken the baby from her, she'd seemed bereft.

And he'd imagined giving her a child of her own. *Their* own. A child who would cement the bonds that had begun to form between them, a child who would give them an excuse for prolonging their marriage, for making it a forever proposition.

Even when he'd looked at Eleni holding his nephew, in his mind's eye he'd still seen Kate, had envisaged her cuddling their own child like that, then looking up at him as if he'd made her universe complete.

And then she was gone.

No warning. No discussion. Nothing but a terse little note.

I think we've done this long enough. I can't lie any longer. Regards, Kate.

Regards. *Regards*! As if they were no more than acquaintances, fleeting ones at that.

Maybe we are, Damon thought wearily. She'd been gone a week. He hadn't heard a word. She didn't love him. That was obvious. He had been enough for her in bed, taking the place of dear departed Bryce while the lights were low. But in the long run he'd never had a chance. When she'd seen the baby, when she'd realised what she was missing, the physical relationship she'd had with Damon had paled. She hadn't been able to lie about what she really wanted. And a family with Damon wasn't it.

He poured himself another drink — one of the many too many he'd had since she'd left. Then he flung himself down on the sofa and stared through blurred eyes at the ceiling.

In his hand he held a small calendar he'd found in the drawer of the bedside table. Kate's calendar. With the days marked off one by one since the day she'd married him.

How long would she have kept marking? The question was rhetorical. He knew the answer without asking — until at last she was free of him.

His throat ached and tightened; his head throbbed.

He was supposed to go to a meeting at three with Belliard. The old man had flown down from Montreal to finalise the deal. Damon didn't care. He should have been at the office hours ago. He'd never missed a day in sixteen years. Until now.

Now he'd missed a week. Four days, really, but even when he'd gone to work, he hadn't been there.

'What's the matter with you?' Arete had demanded more times than he could count. 'You aren't listening to a thing I've said.'

'What do you mean, you don't know where the

Belliard file is,' Stephanos asked him. 'You're the one who had it.'

'Damon, are you sick?'

'Damon, is there something wrong with Kate?'

'Damon, you can't go on like this.'

It had taken four days and considerable harassment from Stephanos and Sophia for him to even admit what was wrong.

'What do you mean, she's left you?' Sophia demanded, horrified. 'What did you do to her, Damon?'

Damon couldn't answer that. He'd simply sat in their parlour, staring at the scotch in his hands and shaken his head.

Sophia quickly changed her tack. 'She'll be back,' she prophesied. 'She's probably just having some post-honeymoon jitters.'

'Post-honeymoon jitters? Never heard of them.' Stephanos had said.

Sophia shot him a hard glare. 'Not surprising.'

'No,' Damon had said in a low voice. He drained the scotch and heaved himself to his feet. 'It's not that.'

He headed towards the door. 'Damon?' Sophia's voice stopped him. 'Is there anything we can do?'

He shook his head. 'I did it all myself.'

Kate had known it would be difficult. She hadn't expected to get over him just like that. But they hadn't been married very long. They hadn't even married for love. Surely those circumstances should dull the pain a bit?

The day she left Damon, she left the city, too. She didn't imagine he'd come after her, but if he had, she didn't know if she'd have had the strength to say no to him. So she fled, took herself off to New England.

Cape Cod in January seemed an appropriate place to go. A place as cold and bleak as her heart. Deserted, windswept miles of bare sand beach and chilly Atlantic surf were supposed to make her forget.

They reminded her of the Bahamas instead.

They reminded her of days in the sun, days of warmth, days in Damon's arms.

She lasted a week. Barely. Then she went home.

Only that didn't work either because her apartment, she discovered very quickly, wasn't home any more. Home was where Damon was.

As soon as she'd unpacked her bags, bought herself some groceries and spent a sleepless night remembering what it was like to share a bed with the man she loved, she took herself off to work.

Work had saved her from the pain of Bryce's defection and death.

It didn't save her from her love of Damon.

For three days she buried herself in interviews, home checks, the business of matchmaking families and nannies to help them. Nothing on earth helped her.

'You really ought to get some rest,' Greta, her office helper, told her late Thursday afternoon. 'That was supposed to be a vacation you took, but you look worse now than when you left.'

'I have a cold,' Kate lied.

'Then you should go home and drink orange juice and go to bed.'

But Kate shook her head. 'I have work to do.'

Greta reached over and plucked the file out of her hand. 'Then you'd better let me help you. You're putting the Barlowes under the Ms.'

She didn't fall apart while Greta was there. She waited until Greta caught the bus at five o'clock, then she stopped trying to pretend. Her occasional sniffles turned into honest sobs. She felt her heart rend.

There was a knock on the door.

Kate wiped her eyes, blew her nose, cleared her throat. 'We're closed. Come back tomorrow,' she said and her voice wobbled precariously.

'Kate? Is that you? Open up!'

She bolted up, wiping at her eyes even more furiously, hesitating, wondering if she should deny it, then going to the door. 'Stephanos?'

She opened it, still unsure. But, yes, it was. He looked frantic.

'Thank God!' He strode in, grabbing her by the arm.

'What's wrong? Is something wrong with Sophia? With the baby? Didn't Mrs Partridge — ?'

'Sophia's fine. The baby's fine. Mrs Partridge is a blessed saint.'

'Then what?'

He glowered at her. 'It's Damon.'

Kate's heart lurched. 'Damon? What's wrong with Damon?'

'You tell me.' Stephanos dropped his hold on her arm, but he didn't stop looking at her.

She shook her head, perplexed.

'He doesn't eat. He doesn't sleep. He doesn't shave. He doesn't work. Imagine, if you can, Damon not working! He does, however, drink. He drinks too damned much! And he looks like hell. And why? Because you left him, that's why!'

'I — ' Kate faltered, stunned.

'Why, Kate? Why did you leave him?'

She wet suddenly parched lips. 'Damon knows,' she said tonelessly after a moment. She looked away out the window into the darkness, unable to face her brother-in-law.

'That's what he said,' Stephanos admitted. 'But it doesn't make sense. You love each other!'

Kate didn't say anything. She couldn't deny it — not the part about her loving him.

And the other part? Wishful thinking, she told herself.

'You know, Kate,' Stephanos said carefully, 'marriages are tricky. They aren't long, smooth runs to perfect bliss. Seeing the hash I was about to make of mine should have showed you that. But you two had something real — the same as Sophia and I did.'

'We didn't!' Kate protested.

Stephanos just looked at her. 'Then why were you crying?' He nodded at the tissue still wadded in her hand. 'Why is Damon drinking himself sick?' He gave her a gentle smile. 'Take another look, Kate. Risk it. Go home. It worked for me.'

It wasn't the same.

She hadn't been playing around. And, despite what he'd said about fidelity during their brief marriage, she doubted that Damon would have cared if she had been.

At least that was what she tried to tell herself after Stephanos left her in the quiet of her office.

It didn't work.

Damon had proposed fidelity. He would have cared. He'd been honest about that.

But he'd never said he loved her.

And she'd never said she loved him.

She could — and did — argue both sides of the issue back and forth. And when she finished, she was no closer to resolution that when she'd begun.

She needed to talk to Damon to do that.

Could she?

Did she dare?

Wouldn't she be in danger of making an even bigger fool of herself than she had over Bryce?

She locked up the office and let herself out the main door onto the street. A brisk winter wind knifed through her, chilling her to the bone. She hurried to the corner and flagged a cab, eager to get home where it was warm.

But even in her apartment, she shivered. She forced down a bowl of soup, but it didn't thaw the cold.

Damon wasn't working. Damon wasn't eating. Damon wasn't sleeping.

Was he, she wondered, also cold?

She didn't know if she dared to hope. She suspected she might only be making her life worse. But in one way at least, she was her father's daughter: she was willing to take a risk.

She put her coat back on, knotted a scarf around her neck, and went back out into the cold.

There were no lights on in Damon's apartment that she could see from the street. Probably he was gone. Probably Stephanos had exaggerated. Probably she'd come in vain.

But she was here now. So she rode up in the lift, padded along the carpeted hallway, and let herself in.

The apartment was dark. Deserted. Damon must have given Mrs Vincent the night off. Kate stood just inside the door and wondered what to do now.

Actually she knew what she should do: leave. Damon wasn't here. Stephanos had been wrong.

She swallowed, turned, started to open the door to go out, then paused, drawn back by a need to touch one last time the place that had brought her closest to her heart's desire.

When she'd left him, she'd been in a hurry. Cold, but still desperate, needing only to get away.

And now—now she needed, if only in the silence of an empty apartment—to say goodbye.

She loosened the scarf, unbuttoned her coat, and slipped off her shoes, leaving them by the door. Then, with only the lights from the other buildings beyond the windows to guide her, she moved into the living-room. She walked slowly, trailing her hand along the back of the sofa, remembering when she and Damon had curled there together. She touched the bookcases, recalling titles she wished she'd read.

She moved on to the kitchen. There was a pile of dirty dishes in the sink. No sign at all that Mrs Vincent had been around. Had Damon fired her? It didn't seem likely. Still, from the look of things, for quite a while now he'd been on his own.

Kate picked up a coffee-mug from the counter, cupping it with her palms. She touched her lips to the rim where not long ago Damon's lips had been. Hastily she set the mug back down.

She paused at the door to the master bedroom. In the darkness she could see that the spread on the bed looked slightly rumpled. Otherwise the room lay untouched.

Slowly Kate entered. She walked around the bed, seeing in her memory the two of them lying there. Her throat tightened. Her eyes stung. Mindlessly she reached down and picked up a pillow, Damon's pillow, hugging it against her, pressing her face in the cool cotton, breathing in the scent of him.

Oh, God, it hurt!

She rubbed her face against it, furiously scrubbing away her tears and stalked out into the hall again.

'Who's there?'

The voice was hoarse. Ragged. Damon's.

Kate stopped dead.

She heard noises now, coming from the back bedroom. Then a silhouette appeared in the darkened doorway. A hand fumbled for the light switch then flicked it on.

'Damn it, Stephanos! Leave me alone. I—*you!*'

Kate's astonishment was just as great. Stephanos was right after all. Damon hadn't been shaving. Or eating, if the gauntness of his frame proved anything. Or sleeping, as the dark circles under his eyes pointed out.

'Damon,' she said quietly.

'What in hell do you want?' He glared at her through bloodshot eyes. He wore only a pair of undershorts and he braced himself by holding on to the doorjamb. He looked as if he might fall over.

'I—have you been sick?'

'I'm fine. I asked you a question. What're you doing here?'

'Stephanos said——'

Damon said something in Greek about Stephanos. Kate didn't need a translator to know it wasn't complimentary. Then, right before her eyes, what little colour there was in his face seemed to wash right away. He turned and bolted for the bathroom. She could hear him being sick.

She wanted to go to him. She didn't dare. If she had any sense, she told herself, she'd leave. Damon certainly hadn't been happy to see her.

Still she stayed right where she was, waited outside the door while she heard the toilet flush, the tap turn on and, minutes later, off again. She took a step back only when the door opened once more.

Damon, still ashen and with damp dishevelled hair, stared at her. 'You're still here?'

'You are sick,' Kate said. 'You should be in bed.'

'I'll go to bed.' Damon's voice was a mixture of

weariness and irritation. 'Just get out of here.' He turned and headed back towards the small bedroom.

Kate followed him. 'Why aren't you sleeping in our ——?' She stopped. *Our room*, she'd been going to say. She couldn't.

Damon shot her a malevolent look. 'Because I don't want to, all right?' He sagged onto the crumpled bedclothes and sat staring at his fingers which were laced together between his knees. He looked worse than she'd ever seen him. Defeated almost.

She had halted in the doorway. Now she ventured further in, only stopping when he lifted his eyes and scowled at her. 'Why don't you want to, Damon?'

His dark eyes glittered. 'What do you want, a pound of flesh? Christ, what did I ever do to you?' He jerked his head towards the door. 'Get out of here, Kate. Leave me alone.'

'You can't be left alone. You're sick. You need someone to take care of you.'

'Not you.'

The words slapped her across the face. She stepped back. 'All right,' she said. 'Not me. But what about your mother or one of your sisters?'

Damon snorted. 'No, thanks.'

'Eleni, then,' Kate snapped, goaded.

'Who?'

'*Who*?' She couldn't believe he'd said that. But he was looking at her, perplexed. 'Pandora's friend. The one who came to see the baby with her. You remember.'

He nodded, then rubbed a hand across his face. 'Why would I want her?'

'Maybe you wouldn't, I don't know,' Kate said, exasperated. 'But she's perfect for you. Lovely, talented, charming, maternal. Not to mention Greek.'

'So I should want her?' He still looked confused.

Then his gaze dropped and he bent his head so that once more he was staring at his hands. 'No.'

No? Kate, watching him, felt equally confused. Was Stephanos right then?

He had been about Damon's drinking, about his lack of sleep and food, about Damon's not working, about his looking like hell.

Was he right about him loving her, too?

Her fingers clenched. Her heart gave a tiny leap.

Damon glanced up at her, his lips thinning when he saw her still standing there. 'You don't have to hang around. I don't know what Stephanos told you, but ——'

'He told me that you love me.'

It was as if the world had suddenly gone still. Damon didn't move, didn't even breathe.

Neither did Kate. She waited. She prayed. She hoped.

At last Damon sighed, shut his eyes and fell back against the pillows. She saw his throat work. Then he opened his eyes and looked at her wryly.

'Does it say something about divine retribution, do you suppose, that I would marry you to keep him on the straight and narrow and he should be the one with the last laugh?'

'He wasn't laughing,' Kate said quietly. 'No one was laughing, because he also reminded me that I love you.'

Damon stared at her. He didn't speak. He levered himself halfway up so he was propped on his elbows as he searched her face. 'You love Bryce,' he corrected her hoarsely.

Kate pressed her lips together. 'Once I did,' she admitted. 'When I married him. He didn't love me.'

'But ——'

'He wanted what I had, the family fortune, exactly

what my father had predicted. And when Daddy cut me off, Bryce left me.'

'He died,' Damon protested.

'As he was leaving me.'

He shoved himself up off the bed and crossed the room, pulling her into his arms, holding her close. 'Oh, hell, Kate. I'm sorry. So damn sorry.'

Kate pressed against him, loving the warm strength of his arms around her. She rested her head against his shoulder. 'Thank you for caring.'

'I thought — I mean, all the time, when we made love —' He shook his head slightly as if he were dazed.

'You thought I was pretending you were Bryce?' She was astonished at his nod. 'Never. I never — it was never like that with Bryce.'

'It wasn't?' His voice was hoarse, his tone disbelieving.

She smiled. 'Not at all. It was barely tolerable. I. . .really didn't like it much. I thought I was frigid. So did Bryce,' she admitted shakily.

Damon snorted and hugged her tightly. 'Hardly frigid.'

She looked up at him, adoring him. 'Then I owe it all to you.'

'Why didn't you say?'

'Because it would have been changing the rules. We weren't supposed to care, remember?'

He pulled back and looked down into her eyes. His own were dark and still held a hint of desperation. 'I remember. It was hell. I wanted more. I thought you didn't. And when you took off for East Hampton, that confirmed it. It seemed that what mattered to you was your work.'

'I thought it was all I was going to have left.'

'No,' Damon said. 'Oh, no.' He kissed her then. It

was a deep kiss, a hungry kiss. 'Oh, God, Kate. I've missed you. I almost died when I came home and found your note. What did you mean, then, about not being able to live the lie any longer? I thought you meant the lie that was our marriage.'

She touched his lips with her own. 'I meant the lie that I didn't care when I did. For a while after we got back from the islands, I thought we might make it. And then. . .then it seemed to start falling apart. You went to Montreal, I went to the Hamptons, and things began slipping away. You got more distant. And Stephanos told me about Eleni.'

'What about her?'

'Just that everyone thought she would have been a good wife for you, except you were married to me.'

'Damn Stephanos,' Damon muttered.

'It wasn't his fault. He was right.'

'No one is a better wife for me than you,' Damon said fiercely. 'You're everything I ever wanted in a wife.'

'And you didn't even know it when you married me,' Kate teased gently.

He smiled. 'I didn't know *you* when I married you. But it didn't take long. You got under my skin. You became a part of me. I love you, Kate. When you left I thought I'd die.'

'I almost did,' Kate said, and it wasn't a lie. The essence of her being was so tied to Damon that she'd barely been able to survive without him.

'I found your calendar—the one where you were marking off the days. . .'

Kate nodded shakily. 'At first it was because I just wanted to get through them, like a kid waiting for summer vacation. And then——' she ducked her head '—then I didn't want it to end.' She buried her head against the strong wall of his chest. 'I love you, Damon,' she murmured.

She felt his lips touching her hair, her ear, her cheek. 'I love you, too,' he whispered and found her lips with his.

'Thank God for Stephanos,' she murmured after a long, long moment.

Damon rested his forehead against the top of her head. 'I guess we do owe him, don't we?' he said a little grimly.

'Yes. You ought to give him a holiday.'

Damon shook his head. 'On the contrary, I think the way to repay him is to give him more work. He's carried the whole business for the past week and a half and right now he's off closing the deal with Belliard. I think I'll have to make him CEO after all.'

She looked up at him. 'But what about you? Won't you miss it?'

'I won't have time to miss it. The company presidency is a bit more than a figurehead title.' He grinned at her, then gave her a wink. 'Besides, I have other plans.'

Kate cocked her head, smiling at him, loving him with all her heart. 'Oh, yes? Such as?'

He drew her against him and touched his lips to hers. 'Such as showing you over and over and over again how happy I am that you're my wife.'

MILLS & BOON®

*M*akes
any time
special

Enjoy a romantic novel from
***Mills & Boon*®**

Presents...™ *Enchanted*™ *Temptation*®

Historical Romance™ *Medical Romance*™

MILLS & BOON®

Makes any time special™

Bestselling themed romances brought back to you by popular demand

Each month By Request brings you three full-length novels in one beautiful volume featuring the best of the best.

So if you missed a favourite Romance the first time around, here is your chance to relive the magic from some of our most popular authors.

Look out for
After Hours **in October 1999**
featuring Jessica Steele,
Catherine George and Helen Brooks

Our hottest

TEMPTATION

authors bring you…

Blaze

**Three sizzling love stories available in
one volume in September 1999.**

Midnight Heat
JoAnn Ross

A Lark in the Dark
Heather MacAllister

Night Fire
Elda Minger